MOONWALKER

Moonwalker

By

Charlie Lauth

The Kid Publishing 2020

For John McGovern

"1, 2, 3, 4..."

Quick Acknowledgments

I can't believe I am publishing my first book! Excited beyond belief. But just like with any endeavor in life, there are wonderful people that have helped get me to this amazing point. I'd like to take a moment to thank them.

Teena, Sammi and Ally: you guys are simply the ginchiest. Thank you for all the love and support – especially on those days when I thought it was crazy to even attempt something like writing a book.

My proofreaders and reviewers: tons of thanks to the following people who took the time out to read my book and offer suggestions and corrections. You all rock! Daksh Dhamsania, the Barnes Family (esp. Ryan and Jason), Al Smith, the East Middle School Book Club, and my dear friend Stacey Bancone.

Colleagues and Cheerleaders: I'd like to thank some other wonderful people in my life that have taken the time to cheer me on and offer me some guidance: Paulo Quaglio, Melissa Rosa, Joe Herringshaw, Tammy Lynn Hettrick of Battershell, Hilary Loyd, Chelsea Cronk and the rest of the Vestal ENL crew, Terry Padavona and her husband and fabulous author Dan Padavona.

Special thanks: I'd like to thank artist and book cover designer Andy Brown for coming up with the killer design. You da man.

Last but not least: You, the reader! Thanks for taking the time to read Moonwalker. I hope you enjoy it and have a howling good time.

Moonwalker Table of Contents

1. 1st Quarter.................................... 11
2. 2nd Quarter.................................... 82
3. 3rd Quarter.................................... 143
4. 4th Quarter.................................... 213
5. Overtime....................................... 297
6. Once in a Blue Moon................. 386
7. Epilogue....................................... 460

1st Quarter

"Ah, pray no mistake,
We are not shy;
We're very wide awake, The Moon and I."

Sir William Schwenck Gilbert

Chapter 1

April 3rd, 2011

Jack Wilson was sneaking out of the house at night...again. The cascading sounds of thunder from an evening storm was just what he needed to cover his exit from his bedroom - a quick dash out the window and a short descent down the wooden trellis, all hidden by the thick, rainy darkness.

Perfect.

If Jack's mom ever suspected that he was creeping out of the house at night, he would be grounded until he was a parent himself, but Jack knew that he could not get caught, especially on a night like this. He was on an important mission.

He carefully climbed the old, wooden fence that separated his yard from the dirt alley that ran behind the row of houses on his street. He threw both his legs over the top and landed hard on the wet ground. It sprang back up at him in splashy defense, muddying his sneakers and pants. Dirty clothes and detergent had become his constant companions the past year. All of this late-night sneaking out of the house had been taking its toll on his wardrobe.

A flash of lightning tore through the night sky. He looked

upward and his eyes blazed alive with the electricity of the stormy night. Although he couldn't see it now through a blanket of rain clouds, he knew the moon was full and ready to make an appearance within the hour when the weather cleared. Jack hadn't missed a single full moon all year. It was not in his nature to do so.

Out of the corner of his eye, he thought he saw a small figure lean back into the shadows between two garbage bins in the alley. It was one of THEM. He was sure of it. Jack turned quickly in the opposite direction and started walking. His feet sloshed through deep puddles as the rain poured down his hair, face and clothes. He could feel his senses becoming sharper – his eyes and ears tingling with clarity. He took another step and then halted his movement abruptly. Behind him, down the alley a bit, he heard the stumble of footsteps as the person following him clumsily tried to stop without being heard. Jack smiled to himself. There's nothing like keeping your opponents on their toes, testing them for weakness, and then using their own shortcomings against them - just like he learned playing lacrosse at school.

He glanced over his shoulder but didn't see his foe, although he could still feel his presence. Jack realized it was time to make his move and get where he had to go. He quickly sprinted down the rest of the alley and came to the twelve-foot fence next to the public park. He could feel animal-adrenaline coursing throughout his body as he scaled his way up the fence quickly. He straddled it at the top and felt the wildness of the night calling to him from all directions. For a brief moment, a hazy hint of moonlight peeked through a small patch of thinning clouds and Jack threw back his head and howled in unscripted agony and ecstasy.

It was almost time.

He scrambled down the other side of the fence and tore his way northwards through the park. He had to shake the person following him and get to his destination fast. When the light of the full moon was fully cast, things would change. Jack knew about these changes all too well. He knew about them because Jack Wilson was a Moonwalker. A werewolf.

Chapter 2

April 4th, 2011

"Jack! Get up, honey. It's time for school."

Jack rubbed at his eyes. "Ugh...school," he muttered wearily to himself. He tried to sit up but fell clumsily back onto the mattress. As much as the night of a full moon caused Jack a heap of trouble, the day after was no picnic either. He was usually physically exhausted and mentally discombobulated. This morning, his legs, arms - even his eyebrows - ached.

"Jack, are you up yet?" called his mother at the foot of the stairs leading to the second floor.

"Up? Um, yeah, Mom...I'm up," he replied groggily. "Be down in a minute."

Jack pulled back the blankets, rolled over onto his stomach and slowly swung his legs over the side of the bed. He was still in his clothes from the night before and they were dirtied up pretty well. What had been a relatively new pair of jeans yesterday were now officially "used" - streaked and caked with dry mud and grass stains. Not only that, his t-shirt was stretched out as if the Moon and Earth had used it in some celestial game of tug-of-war. He dragged himself over to the mirror behind his bedroom door. He gazed at the reflection. It never ceased to amaze him how different he looked each morning after a full moon. At least this time his long brown hair wasn't filled with twigs and other assorted bits of nature.

"Jack, breakfast is on the table getting cold. You're going to be late for school and I'm going to be late for work!" she said impatiently.

"Okay, I'm coming, Mom; I swear."

Energy started flowing back into his body and he took off all of his dirty clothes and stuffed them into his laundry bag. He found some clean ones folded on the chair next to his bed and put them on quickly. He slipped on his sneakers, opened the hallway door and darted into the bathroom to wash the night off his face. Surprisingly, it only took a few minutes and he made his way downstairs to the kitchen.

On the kitchen table was a warm stack of pancakes and bacon. His absolute favorite.

"There you are," said his mother with annoyed but loving surprise as she walked into the kitchen from the laundry room. "What is it about you getting up for school that is so difficult? I mean, most of the time, you get up without a problem, but every so often...," she trailed off, reaching for her cup of coffee on the counter. She took a sip and resumed her conversation. "Are you getting enough sleep?"

Jack sat down at the table and grabbed for the syrup hungrily. "I think I'm going through some sort of growth spurt, Mom. You know us young kids need sleep to stay healthy." He tried to smile but it was cut in half by a robust yawn.

His mother came over and grabbed his face and looked into his eyes with concern. "Maybe your plate is too full." Jack glanced down at his pancakes. "Not that plate, goofy," his mother chuckled. "With all your classes and lacrosse on top of that, maybe you're just doing too much and need a break. You can only burn the candle at both ends for so long."

Jack looked back into his mother's eyes. She was so perceptive and there was so much that he would love to tell her, but he just couldn't. It would never make sense.

"Maybe, Mom," was all he could muster. "Oh, man...look at the time!" he said searching for distraction. He crammed down a pancake, threw back some juice, kissed his mom goodbye and forced his aching body to run out the door. Before she could say anything, he came back in, grabbed his backpack, lacrosse bag, skateboard, kissed his mom again and was even able to grab a piece of bacon with two free fingers before rushing back out.

"That boy..." his mother said to herself with a slightly worried smile.

Chapter 3

April 4th, 2011

The wheels of the skateboard clacked against the cracks in the sidewalk as Jack swerved into the schoolyard. He came to a quick stop and kicked the skateboard up into his hands. His eyes scanned the front of a large building. Barnaby Hills Middle School: "Home of the Champions". Well, at least that's what the banner said hanging over the entrance. This place was home to eight-hundred students and just about half a dozen of them were werewolves. Now that was something you'd never see written on the sign.

"Hey, Jack!" yelled someone from behind. "Wait up!"

Jack turned around and caught sight of his friend Chris running over to him.

"What's up, Chris?"

"Nuthin' much. Hey, did you hear that storm last night? It must have spooked the animals in the woods near my house 'cause I thought I heard some crazy noises outside. Maybe it was the wind or I was dreaming. I don't know, but when I looked out my window in the morning, my yard was a mess."

Jack's mind switched quickly to an internal conversation. *Crazy noises? I'll tell you about crazy, Chris. Crazy is me shedding my human skin and growing fur on a moon-filled night. Crazy is me slinking around the community on all fours. Crazy is me coming to your house to protect you from some bad, bad creatures. Now that is crazy!*

But all he could say was, "Nah, I slept through it. Didn't even know it rained."

Jack and Chris chatted a bit more until they heard the first bell ring. They started walking quickly toward school when they heard a loud commotion coming from behind them, but they already knew what it was: Billy and his boys were here.

Billy Jenkins was captain of the lacrosse team, popular among the "cool kids" and a notorious bully to just about everyone else. If that wasn't enough, during a full moon, he was the pack leader of the werewolf clan at Barnaby Hills Middle School. His day-to-day existence pretty much mirrored his phantasmagorical existence, just minus the fur and fangs. The commotion that he caused coming into the schoolyard took place fairly often. He and his buddies would come tearing into the yard on their dirt bikes wearing their lacrosse jackets, trying to scare the daylights out of anyone in their path. As far as they were concerned, the school was theirs and everyone else should just grin and bear it - or else. Billy didn't like opposition and there were few students (even teachers for that matter) that wanted to bother with him and his boys.

Except Jack.

Jack and Chris continued walking towards the school. The roar of the engines grew louder as Billy and his gang made their way through the schoolyard, students jumping and dodging for cover. Just as the clamor behind Jack rose to its zenith in his ears, he turned abruptly and Billy slammed on his brakes, skidding to a stop not a foot away. The rest of his buddies followed suit right behind him to form an arrowhead of hostility directly pointing at Jack. They all turned off their bikes in unison.

Both boys just looked at each other as if locked in some private duel. Jack stared directly at Billy without wavering and took in everything about his face - especially his eyes, small and brown with fiery specks of orange close to the pupil that gave him an intimidating look.

Billy got off his bike, put the kickstand down, walked towards Jack and broke the eerie quiet.

"Long time no see, Jack," he said with a snarl of a smile. His buddies behind him chuckled at the inside joke.

"If only that were the case, Billy," Jack replied.

"Oh, yeah," Billy snickered, "Now I remember. We did, um, "meet up" recently. Funny how easily one forgets things like that. But then again, Jack, you are quite forgettable."

"I wish I could say the same about you, but I still have your stench on me from the last time, and no matter how much I bathe, it just won't come off," Jack responded.

The boys behind Billy laid down a low chorus of angry groans but stopped immediately when he raised his hand. Billy inched closer until their noses were almost touching.

"You may have won last night, Jackie, but the game is still on and you are out-numbered, out-witted, and soon to be out of luck."

"And you, Billy, are out of your mind and will be out of commission if I have my way."

The boys were almost on top of one another. Chris grabbed Jack's arm and pulled him back.

"C'mon, Jack. Let's get to class."

Billy took a step back, spit on the ground and slowly grinned.

"That's right, Jackie. You'd better get to class. Hey, Chris," he said, directing his attention away from Jack, "why don't you start hangin' out with us for a change? Jackie-boy may not always be around, if you know what I mean. Don't worry; we don't bite."

With that, Billy and his boys erupted into a fit of laughter and mounted their bikes. "See you ladies at practice," Billy called out. Billy and the gang revved up their engines and peeled-out on either side of Jack and Chris, leaving them in a low cloud of white, smoke.

Jack stared at the pack as they rode away through the haze. "C'mon, Chris. You're right. Let's get to class."

Chapter 4

April 3rd, 2011

The ground moved beneath him like he was on a grass treadmill. It was soft and wet from the thunderstorm but Jack's steps were tight and sure-footed. His upper body was positioned low to the ground as he made his way over the grass and between the dripping trees. It was difficult to see as a blanket of mist had come to rest over the park, but Jack knew the way. His senses were keen and sharp and he felt like he could be running this path blindfolded. Just a few more minutes and the moon would be out from behind the clouds and Jack would be transformed into a snarling, hairy mass of sharp teeth and sinewy muscle. His whole body was on alert for the change, especially his arms and fingers that burned with the strange anticipation of running on all fours. As grotesque as the process was, he almost wished the change would take place right now since he would be able to make better time as a full-fledged Moonwalker.

He heard the faint sounds of running and panting. He knew he was doing a good job of outpacing the person that followed him from the alley, but now there were others - at least two more - flanking him on both sides but using the trees and fog to keep themselves out of sight. If they were going to attack him, they wouldn't be able to do much; Jack was a formidable opponent, boy or wolf, but they were definitely going to try and trip him up and slow him down. Billy knew how to use his minions well.

Jack stopped in his tracks just like he did in the alley to gauge where Billy's boys were. But unlike the alley, the footsteps didn't stop in response. They grew faster and louder. Jack couldn't see but he knew things were not good. He dropped to his knees just in time as two boys ripped through the fog and dove into one another above him. The force of their collision caused them to fall to the ground in stupefied pain. Judging by the angle that they hit each other, these guys were head-hunting: hitting an opponent above the shoulders to stop them cold. They were desperate to stop Jack from getting any farther and were willing to go for broke even if they couldn't see very well in the fog. Even when he was off the playing field, Billy couldn't help but encourage his lacrosse buddies to use illegal body checks. Typical. Jack used their misfortune to his advantage and took off into the fog leaving the two boys alone. As he was putting some distance between himself and the boys on the ground, he heard the third boy following him blindly trip over the other two. There was a collective moan of agony and rage. Jack smiled to himself and quickened his pace. He had to get to his destination. His hands were almost touching the ground now. The moon would soon be out.

Chapter 5

April 4th, 2011

The school halls were noisy and bustling with students talking to friends and making their way to their lockers and homerooms. Jack and Chris weaved their way through and around students like they were playing a game of lacrosse. They quickly made it up to the second floor across from the cafeteria. As wonderful 8th grade luck would have it, their lockers were right next to each other this year. They each grabbed at their locks quickly, racing each other to see who would be the first to get their locker open.

"Done!" yelled Chris, throwing his hands up triumphantly.

"Aw, you stink," countered Jack just as his lock clicked open.

Chris reached into his locker and gathered up the things he needed for Math class and closed his locker door.

"Hey Jack..."

"What up, dude?" mumbled Jack, his head still in his locker searching for a pen.

"What was Billy talking about before when he said, 'You may have won last night?"

Jack stopped what he was doing for a split second and wished that he could just cram himself into the locker and close the door to avoid the question. He mustered up some courage and addressed Chris as nonchalantly as he could.

"Ah, you know Billy. He's nuts. He's always saying strange things to get a rise out of people."

"Yeah, he's nuts alright, but it seemed like you guys actually met up last night. Did you?"

Jack thought for a moment about what happened the previous

night, the memory growing faint and distant but still lingering within mental reach.

He forced his mind to swerve back to the present.

"Billy must be talking about lacrosse practice the other day. He can't keep the days of the week straight let alone the time of day," Jack said reaching back into his locker, hoping to avoid further questioning. "Aha! There's my pen."

"Yeah, I guess you're right."

"I always am," laughed Jack. "Enough talk. C'mon...I'll race you to homeroom."

With the challenge of a race before him, Chris pushed Jack back against his locker in a playful way, spun around and took off down the hall. Jack kicked his locker shut and followed suit. As they dodged small groups of students littering the hallway, Jack started thinking about something bothersome that Billy had said in the schoolyard this morning: *Jackie-boy may not always be around.* The ferocity of Jack's encounter with Billy and his boys last night made it difficult for the words to stop swirling about in his brain. He wished he could tell someone about everything, but who would believe him? Jack almost didn't believe all of this himself.

Chapter 6

March 1, 2010

Jack and his mother had moved to Barnaby Hills, a large but rural town in upstate New York. Up until then, they had been living out their lives comfortably in the suburbs of San Francisco. They were especially close. Jack's dad died when he was a baby and his mom tried to make sure that she was as attentive as two parents. Because of this, they shared a strong "you and me against the world" kind of philosophy. They looked out for one another and were both very protective.

One day, his mom came home and told him that she got an unexpected promotion at work and it meant transferring to a different office in another state. Jack didn't want to leave but he knew that there was nothing that could really be done about it; good jobs didn't grow on trees. So he and his mom said goodbye to their west coast life and set off for a new, east coast existence. Life in Barnaby Hills was going to be different, for sure, but Jack was a pretty flexible kid who knew how to make friends quickly. As long as he could skateboard, everything else would fall into place. And just how different could it be anyway?

They arrived on a Friday and after a whirlwind of unpacking, Jack started 7th grade that Monday. With his backpack slung over one shoulder, his feet planted firmly on his skateboard and a few friendly butterflies dancing around his stomach, Jack headed off for his first day at Barnaby Hills Middle School. When he got there, he looked around and skated over to the main stairwell that led up to the front doors. He stopped at the bottom and glanced up at the big banner that said "Home of the Champions!" hanging over the entrance.

"Don't let the sign fool you," a voice quipped behind Jack. "Not everyone here is a champion, only a select few."

Jack turned around and found a small group of boys standing a few feet away. They were all smiling weirdly like they had just shared a funny story between them. There was one boy in the middle who was standing slightly ahead of the others but he wasn't smiling as much as smirking.

"Welcome to Barnaby Hills, new kid," said the lead boy. "I'm Billy Jenkins. What's your name?"

"Jack Wilson."

"Skateboardin' Jack," said Billy in a strange, drawn-out tone as he looked around to his friends for support. They all chuckled on cue.

"What's your poison, Jack?"

"What do you mean?"

"What's your poison? What do you like to do? It isn't just skateboardin', is it? There's more to life than just that."

"Oh yeah, what do you know about life?" Jack asked skeptically.

Billy leaned in a bit closer. "I know lots of things, Jack. Things you wouldn't believe in a million years. Maybe I'll share some of my knowledge with you one of these days - or nights - if the moon is right."

The boys behind Billy started laughing aloud, interspersing their laughter with weird howls.

Jack looked around for a TV camera. This had to be some crazy prank that they pulled on new kids. These guys were just too nutty to be real. But there wasn't any camera to be seen, just kids walking to class and keeping a wide berth of Billy and his boys.

"I tell you what, Skateboardin' Jack...come on down for lacrosse tryouts this Saturday. Let's see if you can drink some of our poison." And with that, Billy leaned in menacingly to see if Jack would recoil or flinch in fear, but Jack stood his ground firmly.

The others laughed and turned to leave, but Billy held onto his position for a second, as if waiting for a different response. Then he backed down the stairs slowly, turning only when he realized that Jack was not intimidated. It would seem that Jack had tougher skin than expected. Billy didn't like that too much.

Chapter 7

April 3rd, 2011

Jack was nearing the line of trees that signaled the end of the park and the beginning of the west side housing development of Barnaby Hills. The night fog was clearing and the rain had slowed to a trickle. He could see First Avenue and a handful of cars parked along the curb. He stopped running and crouched down beside a large oak. He rested for a moment and looked back into the park to see if Billy's boys had caught up. Nothing. He squatted low resting his back against the tree. He was breathing hard and was filled with nervous energy. He only had a little more to go before he reached his destination: Chris' house. For some reason, Billy and his boys had developed a keen interest in Chris recently. Such an interest was sure to have nothing but dire, life-altering consequences. Jack knew that very well. As soon as he became aware of their interest, he made it his mission to guard and protect his friend. He wasn't going to let what happened to him happen to Chris.

Drops of rain water fell from wet leaves above Jack and landed on the ground with a popping sound, as if someone were playing with plastic package wrap that contained all those little air bubbles. It could be heard taking place under all the trees nearby, too. Jack snickered as he imagined nature taking a break from life to pop some plastic. The moment, however, came to an end quickly as he was suddenly seized by a tremendous sensation of heat emanating from the core of his body. He grabbed at his stomach and fell down on the wet grass, rolling side to side on his back. The pain was excruciating. He managed to look upward,

beyond the wet branches and leaves of the oak tree, and dimly saw what his body already knew was there: a clearly visible full moon.

Chapter 8

April 4th, 2011

The rest of the school day went off without a hitch. Math, Science, Social Studies...the daily grind as usual. Jack now sat in his last period class watching the clock tick out the final moments of Language Arts.

"And we know that the last line of the poem contains a *simile* because...let's call on someone who hasn't shared yet today. Hmm, how about...Jack..."

Jack continued looking at the clock, transfixed and unaware that his name was being called.

"Jack! Hello. Anybody home? Earth to Jack Wilson. Yoohoo...Jaaack!"

The boy sitting next to Jack gave him a gentle push.

"What? Oh, oh, sorry Mr. Weber...what's the question?" Jack asked, shaking off his momentary stupor.

"How do we know the last line of the poem contains a simile?"

"Because there is a comparison being made using 'like' or 'as'?"

"Correct. Thanks for coming back to the world of the living, Jack."

The class laughed and Jack chuckled right along with them. Language Arts was one of his favorite classes.

The bell rang and students got up to leave.

"Don't forget that your homework assignment for tonight is to continue to work on your own poem, and make sure you spice it up a bit with metaphors and similes. Be creative like an artist; dip your brush into the rainbow of inspiration and paint your world."

An audible groan could be heard as students made their way out the door. Jack gathered up his books and started out, too.

"Hey, Jack. Are you okay?" asked Mr. Weber, gathering papers together at his desk. "You got a little spacey there for a bit. What's up?"

"Oh, everything is fine, Mr. Weber. Just a little tired. Stayed up too late last night. That's all."

"Well, staying up late on a school night isn't a good idea, especially when you have lacrosse practice the next day, too. You didn't forget about that, did you?"

Mr. Weber was also the coach of the lacrosse team. He was firm yet fair both in and out of the class and was respected by all of his students and players, even Billy and his boys.

"Nah, I forget about lots of things, but not lacrosse."

Mr. Weber shook his head and smiled. "Good to hear. Why don't you make your way to the locker room and get ready. I'll meet you on the field in fifteen minutes."

"Sounds good," replied Jack.

"Jack," added Mr. Weber, "is there any particular reason why you stayed up late last night? Homework? Maybe some girl trouble? Anything that I can help you with?"

Jack looked at his teacher's concerned face for a second and then threw out a half-hearted smile and said, "Nothing that I can't handle on my own, but thanks, Mr. Weber."

"Okay, but remember that I'm here for you if you need it."

"Thanks. I'll keep that in mind."

Chapter 9

April 4th, 2011

By the time Jack got to the locker room to put on his lacrosse gear, most of the other players had made it out onto the field already. Chris had his foot up on a bench lacing his cleats.

"Hey, dude. You're running late. Get suited up. I'll wait for you," he said, tying the last knot.

"Thanks. I kind of spaced out in Mr. Weber's class and he wanted to talk to me afterward."

"Everything okay?"

"Yeah, yeah..." Jack lied. "Everything is fine."

"Speaking of fine," Chris segued with an impish smile while lowering his voice. "Have you seen Sarah Bartley lately? She is really F-I-N-E."

Jack smiled to himself. He knew exactly what was coming next.

"You know, I don't think I would enjoy lacrosse as much as I do if she wasn't one of the cheerleaders for the team."

Jack looked at Chris with sarcastic surprise. "Really, Chris? I did not know that. I mean, you've only told me that exact same thing about a hundred times."

Chris turned pinkish-red for a fleeting second. "Okay, okay...maybe I have told you once or twice or a thousand times, but it's true. She is so cool and pretty and totally awesome."

"So..." continued Jack.

"So nothing. She barely knows I exist."

"Well," said Jack smirking, "you actually have to say something to somebody for them to know that you exist."

"It's not as easy as you think," protested Chris. "She likes to hang out with Billy's crowd. I'm not like them. I'm just a...you know, regular guy. Why would she even want to hang out with me?"

Jack lifted his head from putting on his cleats and stared intently at his friend. "I need you to seriously listen to me, Chris, okay? I've known you for a little over a year now, but you have become my best friend - ever since the first day of lacrosse tryouts last year. You are a great guy. I know it and other people know it, even if you don't. Stop putting yourself down, man. You have more going for yourself than ninety-nine percent of the guys in this school. And Sarah would really dig you if you got off your butt and tried to talk with her. Give it a shot."

Chris looked down at the bench and picked up his lacrosse stick and twirled it around and around in his hands nervously.

"Maybe," he said quietly, more to himself than Jack.

They talked a little more about the subject as Jack got ready. When he was finished, he let out a long breath. "Alright, enough talk about girls. Let's play some lacrosse. Last one out on the field is a ball dog." And with that, he pushed Chris backwards and ran for the door that led to the field. Chris rebounded off a locker laughing and tore right after him yelling, "I'll show you who the ball dog is!"

Chapter 10

April 3rd, 2011

Jack clutched at his throat as if he were suffocating on the moonbeams themselves. His chest was tightly locked - no breath going in or out. He could not speak or scream; he could not utter a sound. And that was the strangest thing of all: he was undergoing the most intense, most painful changes imaginable, yet there was no evidence of it escaping from his mouth. But what was happening to his body spoke volumes. He writhed and thrashed on the wet ground like a fish with a hook through its soul. Thick, coarse fur pushed its way through his skin as the bones underneath crunched, mashed and refashioned themselves into something that was distinctly not human. His muscle tissue spasmed and undulated as it wound its way over a new skeletal mass. His hairy hands pawed at his face, trying to push back the canine snout that was erupting outward. Sharp teeth pushed their way through his jawbone and he gnashed and bit wildly at the taunting change. The being that was Jack Wilson was ceasing to exist as anyone knew him. But just as quickly as it all began, it stopped.

Silence.

The moonlight did little to reveal what now lay still and huddled on the wet, shimmering grass. Anyone walking nearby would have thought it to be a discarded bag of garbage or pile of dirt. No movement. No indication of life.

And then, "the first breath" rushed through the mouth and lungs of the creature - the breath of new life. Its eyes opened to a fine, thin slit and the white of its eyes crept out from the shadows of its face. Slowly its chest rose and fell with each new breath, gaining momentum as its body drank up great quantities of oxygen, feeding the transformed tissues. In a frenzied burst of speed and energy, the creature jumped to its feet and spread its arms and fingers wide to soak in the rays of moonlight. It lifted its head skyward and let out a hair-raising howl of birth and relief. Jack Wilson the human was no more - a full-fledged Moonwalker stood in his place.

Chapter 11

April 4th, 2011

Chris finally caught up to Jack on the lacrosse field and gave him a playful punch to the arm to get him back for the push in the locker room. Most of the lacrosse team were out on the field already throwing and catching balls. Billy and some of his buddies were busy chatting up a couple of cheerleaders on the sidelines.

Chris nudged Jack with his stick and pointed to Sarah Bartley who was laughing with some friends a few feet away from Billy.

"Easy boy," Jack joked.

"Yeah, yeah, yeah..." Chris managed to laugh as he continued gazing at Sarah.

As if privy to their conversation, Billy turned around and cast a knowing glance at Jack and Chris and walked over to Sarah and put his hand on her shoulder and whispered something in her ear.

Chris gave an audible sigh and turned to join a group of players tossing around a ball, but Jack continued staring at Billy as he held fast to Sarah's shoulder. Billy turned again as if reading Jack's mind and stared back cunningly, his face glowing with some form of triumph.

"Alright gentlemen," boomed a voice coming onto the field, "time to get to business. Let's go!" Mr. Weber had arrived and was striding purposefully to the midfield. All the players stopped whatever it was that they were doing and headed out to meet him, equipment in hand.

Mr. Weber continued when all the players were circled around him. "Okay, it's the fourth practice of the season and we are going to make it a good one, seeing how the first few were lacking in what I affectionately call 'Oomph'." The team chuckled.

"Some of you were on the team last year and probably think you are kings of the lacrosse universe. But as good as you might think you are, it seems to me that you are spending more time on the couch playing video games than practicing. That is going to stop right here, right now. Some running drills will get those hearts pumping, and when I say pumping, I mean P-U-M-P-I-N-G! Now ditch your sticks on the sidelines and let's do some full-field running. Let's move it!"

Players turned away from Mr. Weber and started jogging over to the side of the field to drop off their equipment. Jack was the last to put his equipment down and was about to run back out to the field when a warm voice called his name.

"Hi Jack."

It was Sarah Bartley.

"Oh, hi, Sarah," Jack responded somewhat surprised.

"I just wanted to wish you luck this season. I think you guys are going to do really well."

"Yeah, thanks."

Jack was confused. It wasn't like this was the first time he was speaking with Sarah. He would occasionally see her at lunch or passing in the halls and say hello, but this was the first time she ever approached him to start up a conversation.

"We've come up with some new cheers to get you guys psyched for the season. I hope you like them."

"I'll keep my ears open for them," Jack said. "Um, I better get out on the field for practice before Mr. Weber makes me run extra laps."

"Okay. Well, have a good practice," Sarah replied with a big smile.

Jack turned to meet his teammates and saw Billy standing next to Chris, both of them looking straight at Jack. Billy put his hand on Chris' shoulder and whispered something, just like he did with Sarah a few moments before - a smile stretching from ear to ear on his face.

Chapter 12

March 6, 2010

Jack and Chris had met at fall lacrosse tryouts last year, and by the end of the grueling day, had become fast friends. It seemed like every 7th and 8th grade boy from the middle school was there to try out. Mr. Weber and his assistant coach spent the better part of the whole day narrowing the field of possible players to fifteen students who would be on the team. It was a day of physically demanding drills: running, cradling, scooping, throwing, catching, passing, shooting, blocking, stealing...intense stuff. Jack had first heard about lacrosse tryouts during that bizarre encounter with Billy and his boys on his first day of school. He really had no desire to cross paths with Billy again, but he was curious about the sport.

As the day wore on, it was already easy to see which boys would have a good shot at making the team. Later in the afternoon, Mr. Weber called everyone to center field for a meeting.

"Gather round, troops!" yelled Mr. Weber. Students, who were filled with energy and excitement in the morning, now hobbled over exhausted and physically spent in the waning hours of the day. "You have all been trying your best out there today and need to give yourselves a round of applause." A weak but proud response of claps and high-fives ensued. "But we have one final drill before a decision can be made about who is on the team and who will become supporters of the team. And let me tell you, supporting the team is no less important. This last drill involves a poke check - using your stick to poke at your opponent's hand to dislodge the ball. Let's get a couple of people to demonstrate how this works."

Mr. Weber's eyes scanned the boys.

"Billy, come here."

Billy smiled wide when his name was called. A couple of his buddies slapped him on the back as he made his way over to the center of the crowd. Mr. Weber had been the moderator of 6th grade intramural sports last year and had a chance to see Billy and his friends play against other students in the school. He encouraged them to try out for the 7th and 8th grade modified team.

"Billy is on defense. He'll be the one trying to poke the ball out of the hands of his opponent. We need someone else, too." Again, Mr. Weber scanned the crowd. His eyes fell on the new kid. "How about you...Jack, right? Pick up a ball and come on over here." Jack quickly scooped up a ball and made his way to Billy and Mr. Weber as all the other boys watched in anticipation.

"Jack is on offense and is trying to make his way closer to the goal. Alright, gear up and let's see how this goes down."

Jack and Billy donned their helmets and stood about five feet apart from one another. Billy smiled and stared intently at Jack, but there was nothing friendly about it. Jack met Billy's gaze with his own. Mr. Weber blew his whistle and Jack started running at Billy. He faked to the left and went to the right. Billy sidestepped with him and poked his stick forcefully at Jack's bottom hand. Jack adjusted his grip and moved quickly in the opposite direction. Billy went with him and positioned his body between Jack and the goal while trying again to poke the ball out of Jack's control. This repetitive dance continued for a few more moments until Jack turned as if he were going to go in the opposite direction but instead did a quick double step and bolted forward. Billy tried to reposition himself but tripped over his own feet and fell to one knee. Jack was starting to blow past him on the left when Billy raised his stick high and slashed down harshly at the back of Jack's legs. Seeing the stick rising up in the corner of his eye, Jack quickened his step and Billy's slash hit the ground just behind Jack's left foot.

Mr. Weber blew his whistle loudly. "That slashing motion, boys," he said in a stern tone looking directly at Billy, "is an illegal move. And it will not be tolerated on this team." As he said this, he turned toward the rest of the group and made eye contact with as many of the boys as he could to stress the importance of his words. "Not tolerated at all!" He took a deep breath and exhaled. "Alright, everyone pair up and let's see how well you can do this. Billy, I want to talk with you, NOW!"

Billy got up from the ground trudged over to Mr. Weber. As he passed Jack, he paused for a second and spit on the ground. Jack now knew what Billy meant when he said "Let's see if you can drink some of our poison."

Chapter 13

April 4th, 2011

Jack ran back out onto the field for laps.

"Hey, you ready to eat my dust?" he joked as he caught up to Chris and the rest of the team as they began to jog.

Chris was silent and brooding.

"What's up, Chris? Are you okay?" The sound of Chris' feet on the grass as he ran was the only sound that came from him.

Jack thought back to a few minutes ago and put all the puzzle pieces together in his mind.

"What did Billy say to you?" Jack asked. "I saw him talking to you."

Chris turned slowly and met his friend's gaze. "I saw you and Sarah talking on the sidelines. Billy came over to me and said that he heard you liked Sarah." He paused awkwardly and then asked, "Is it true, Jack? Do you like Sarah?"

Jack turned around at that exact moment and took a look at Billy and his buddies running behind everybody. Billy was already looking and grinning at Jack in expectation.

Jack turned back to his friend to undo the damage.

"No. I don't like Sarah. I mean, she's a nice girl and all but I don't like her in 'that way.' You know better than to listen to Billy, Chris. He's just trying to make you jealous and get you to be mad at me."

Chris' shoulders seemed to loosen up a little.

"She came up to me and started talking about cheering for the team. I didn't go up to her, honest. If anything, Billy put her up to it to drive a wedge between us."

A whistle blew from the sidelines and Mr. Weber called everyone back to pick up their gear for practice. Jack and Chris came to a stop. Chris bent down and put his hands on his knees to catch his breath. He tilted his head upwards, a small bead of sweat dripping down his forehead.

"Why would Billy want to mess with our friendship?" he asked, panting slightly.

Jack looked down at his friend and lied. "I have no idea."

Chapter 14

April 3rd, 2011

Jack stood strong under the glow of the moon and brought both arms up high above his head as if to reach out and pluck it from the night sky. He howled in anguish. The moon was both friend and foe and he wanted to embrace it and destroy it in one fell swoop. The overwhelming sense of pure freedom that engulfed him was something that human beings never fully experience. It was ancestral, like taking a giant leap backwards through time and evolution. He felt at one with his surroundings. But the full moon was also a source of frustration; a cruel master holding him on a leash in a netherworld that was neither human nor animal. There was no satisfaction to be found in this existence. Howling at the moon was a Moonwalker's only recourse to soothe the internal pain. Well, not the only recourse, but definitely the least violent and dangerous to others.

After a few moments he grew silent. The pain of the transformation was fading away. Instinct immediately kicked in and he attuned his ears to the sounds of the night. Against the pitter patter of falling raindrops, he distinctly heard large paws running on wet ground. It was Billy's boys now also transformed into werewolves. He could smell them as well as hear them and that meant they were getting closer. Releasing his obsession with the moon from his thoughts, his mind and body zeroed in on his sole purpose: protect Chris. A feeling of defensive urgency tore loose through his gut and he turned away from the park and ran for the streets of the West side of town. On all four limbs now, he could make incredible time. His arms worked in conjunction with his legs as he darted through the wet grass and around the trees with incredible dexterity and speed. He came upon the fence that separated the park from Franklin Street. He jumped high and clawed himself to the top quickly, pausing a second to look back for signs of the other three. Like his other senses, his vision was amazingly acute. He scanned the horizon of the park but didn't detect any movement. He jumped from the top of the fence and landed with a muted thump on the pavement below. Before him stood Franklin Street, lined with strong oaks on the park side and a row of houses on the other. The fastest way to Chris' was to cut across the house yards rather than run the length of streets. He took off in the direction of the nearest house and leapt over the car parked in the driveway. Getting to Chris' house was child's play; saving Chris was something entirely different.

Chapter 15

April 4th, 2011

With an exhausting practice finished, the team slumped back to the locker room to change and go home. Mr. Weber wasn't kidding about getting everyone into shape and today's practice proved his resolve. Most of the boys were too tired to even talk with one another as they put on their street clothes and packed up their lacrosse equipment. Jack was especially tired. Living on the edge of two lives was more than enough to drain anyone dry of energy. He sat in front of his locker, head down with his arms resting on his knees, and tried to muster up some strength to get changed.

"Aren't you finished yet?" Chris asked walking over with all his stuff packed and ready to go.

"Didn't your mom ever tell you not to pester people when they're having some alone time?" Jack responded with a weak smile.

"Hey, leave my mom out of this. Just because she can beat you in a race right now is no reason to get touchy. Speaking of my mom, she is making her world famous meatloaf tonight and I want to get home and get me some. You in?"

Jack grabbed his towel and wiped some sweat and dirt off his face. "Nah, you go ahead. It's gonna take me a bit more time to get dressed. Thanks for the invite, though."

"More for me!" Chris quipped. "Okay, dude. I'll see you tomorrow. And I'm sorry about what happened before. I was just acting stupid. Jealousy doesn't make for a good friend, huh?"

"It's all in the past. You're still my best bud. See you tomorrow."

The two boys gave each other a quick fist bump and Chris

headed out. A few others left a minute or so later and the locker room was empty and quiet. Jack brought the towel back up to his face and placed it over his eyes to block out the light from the fluorescent bulbs that glared overhead.

"Penny for your thoughts, Skateboardin' Jack."

Jack slowly pulled the towel away from his face and looked towards his right. There leaned Billy against the corner locker about four feet away, a mischievous smile stretching ear to ear.

Jack turned back to his locker. "Just a penny, Billy? I knew you were a punk, but cheap, too? Just when you think you know someone..." he trailed off.

"Oh, you have it all wrong, Jackie-boy. I only offer a penny because that's all your thoughts are worth. There was a time when I thought they were worth more...a time when I thought YOU worth more, but that time has come and gone, and a new day is dawning - or should I say, a new moon rising."

Jack stood up from the bench, slammed his locker shut and faced Billy. "You leave Chris alone," Jack said in a low and menacing tone. "You're not gonna do to Chris what you did to me. Last night should have proved that."

Billy's eyes grew wider and the orange flecks began to glow faintly.

"You know, it is so frustrating to spend so much time on training a puppy only to have it disobey its master. Yep, there's nothing worse than a bad puppy." His eyes narrowed to glowing slits. "You were a bad puppy last night, weren't you Jack? A bad puppy and you need to be put down. I guess we'll just have to settle things up for good during the next full Moon - Chris' arrival and your departure."

Both boys began walking slowly towards each other and

stopped within arm's reach, almost daring one another to make the first move. Fists clenched, they watched and waited, ready to strike.

"Hey, what's going on?" yelled a voice down at the other end of the locker room. It was Mr. Weber. He walked quickly down the corridor between the lockers. Within a few seconds he was standing beside Jack and Billy. "Well, what's going on here?"

"Nuthin'. Nuthin' at all Mr. W," said Billy, breaking into another one of his wide smiles. "Jack and I were just talking about things."

"Is that right, Jack?" asked Mr. Weber looking at Jack.

"I guess so, Mr. Weber." Jack continued glaring at Billy. "Just talking. No problems."

"Yeah, okay. No problems," said Mr. Weber with more than a hint of sarcasm. "What is it with you two? You're teammates, but yet you behave like oil and water when you're off the field. I don't get it. It's been like this since day one. Why can't you get along?"

Billy turned to Jack and sneered. "I don't know, Mr. W. I really don't know. I've tried my best to make him feel like he's a friend. I've tried so hard."

Chapter 16

March 8, 2010

Two days after lacrosse tryouts, Mr. Weber posted the list of boys who made it onto the team in the lobby of the middle school. Students gathered around the list hungrily. Billy and his boys pushed through the crowd to get to the front and check out the situation. His was the top name followed by his buddies. They all shouted their approval and high-fived each other. Billy looked back to the list wondering who else made the team and clenched his teeth when he read the rest. As if on cue, Jack and Chris walked into the lobby of the school. Never one to pass up an opportunity, Billy turned from the list and walked right over to them.

"Congratulations, Skateboardin' Jack," Billy exclaimed with mock sincerity. "You made the team. Not first on the list, mind you, but quite an accomplishment for someone who has never played the game before."

Jack shook his head. "And you just couldn't wait to spoil the surprise for me, could you, Billy?"

"Well, what are friends for?"

"Friends? Let's keep it as teammates for now."

"Your choice," Billy said nonchalantly, "but maybe we can try to make things better between us since we'll be spending so much time together."

Jack laughed. "Will it make you feel better?"

"I think it will make us all feel better, Jack," Billy said, forcing a smile.

Chris looked in the direction of the list. "Did I make it, too?"

"I don't know, sport. I only saw Skateboardin' Jack's name. But feel free to check out the list for yourself," Billy replied, as if verbally swatting away a fly. "Now, Jack, what do you say?"

"I say...I'll think about it."

Billy forced another smile. "A maybe is closer to a yes than a no in my book. Excellent. You think about it and maybe one of these nights we'll get to hang out together and, uh, bark at the moon, so to speak. Cool?"

Jack looked closely at Billy as if to see what he was up to more clearly, but Billy either had the greatest poker face or was being somewhat sincere this time around. Jack could only cautiously reply with one word.

"Cool."

Chapter 17

April 3rd, 2011

Running in sure-footed, animal silence under the watchful gaze of the moon, Jack made his way through the west side yards of Barnaby Hills. He was only a few blocks from Chris' house now and the urge to get there quickly grew with each step. He emerged from a driveway on Washburn Street looking quickly from side to side and then crossed over and entered another yard. He jumped over a high fence and landed on an uneven patch of brick patio. He tried to catch his balance but knocked over a lounge chair in the process. The sound immediately stirred the inhabitants of the yard, a pair of large Dobermans. Jack had smelled the dogs before he entered the yard but his speed and agility usually allowed for a quick entrance and exit into yards with minimal worries. Most animals were too afraid to muster anything more than a whimper in his presence - most animals, that is.

The first dog came at him from underneath the nearby patio table. Its growls, low and menacing at first, turned quickly into a teeth-gnashing snarl. Leaping high, it lunged directly for Jack's neck and face. This caught him by surprise but he was able to throw up his hands at the last moment, grab the dog by the snout and push him forcefully to the side. Not wasting a bit of time, the second dog came running in low from the dark, far right corner. Jack swung his right arm in a wide arc and caught the side of the side of the dog's mouth with a back-handed slap knocking him backwards a few feet. Both dogs recovered quickly and turned to confront the large, hairy intruder again.

This was not the fight that Jack wanted to have; it was an unfortunate distraction. He held no animosity towards the dogs and really did not want to hurt them, but at the same time, they did pose a minor threat if not dealt with correctly.

The dogs attacked from the left and right in unison this time. Jack crouched low in anticipation. The dogs jumped high on either side, jaws wide open, teeth gleaming in the moonlight. Jack thrust both his arms out on either side catching both dogs by their throats. Firmly holding them suspended in the air but being careful to not squeeze too hard, he brought them to the front. The dogs squirmed like fish on hooks to free themselves, but Jack's grip was too strong. He pulled them closer so they could both see his face clearly. A low growl made its way from his lower abdomen and grew with intensity as it climbed up through his chest. It was a dark and menacing sound that caused the very air around them to vibrate. This was something they had never heard before from any animal. They were frightened. The dogs wriggled and writhed to free themselves, all instincts telling them to get away as fast as they could. Jack, sensing their fear and reticence to continue the attack, released both at the same time. They fell to the ground before him and quickly retreated, whimpering as they scurried for safety.

Jack wasted no time. He ran quickly to the far end of the yard and climbed the back wall. The real battle lay elsewhere.

Chapter 18

April 4th, 2011

Jack came home from practice and saw that his mother's car was in the driveway. She was already home from work. Most practice days, he would have made it home before her, but he didn't ride his skateboard today. He walked, skateboard in hand, thinking hard about last night's tussle with Billy and the gang. But what bothered him even more was what happened today at lacrosse practice. Something didn't make sense and he couldn't wrap his brain around it. He walked into the house, his mind distracted.

"Hey, Jack. How was your day?" his mother said in a tired voice, resting on the couch with her feet up.

"Huh? Oh...pretty much the same as every day, Mom. Yep...pretty-much-the-same..." he replied, drawing the last few words out to emphasize the daily redundancy.

"I hear ya. My days are about the same. Come on over and talk to me about it."

Jack dropped his lacrosse bag to the floor and let his body basically fall onto the chair next to the couch.

"So?"

"I don't know where to start," he said leaning forward a little. "It just feels like every day is a struggle."

"This sounds like what I was referring to this morning. Maybe you just have too much going on and need to take a step back from something."

Jack considered her words for a moment. He'd like to take more than a few steps back - a few steps back through time.

"It's not really that, Mom. I can make school and lacrosse work out. It's just that so many new things have happened since we moved here. I don't feel like I've had time to catch my breath."

"His mother cast a sympathetic glance at him. "You miss San Francisco; don't you? That's what it is. It's okay if you do; I miss it, too."

San Francisco was starting to feel like an eternity ago to Jack. A different lifetime ago. A fantasy world of normalcy compared to now.

"Yeah, I miss it, Mom, but it doesn't make sense to think about it too much."

"What do you mean, honey?"

"I mean, we all make choices in life and we have to stick by them, right? We made a choice to come to Barnaby Hills - good or bad - and we have to go with what we got," he said solemnly, talking almost more to himself than his mom.

"I know, but I worry about you, Jack. I also worry if I made the right decision in bringing us here and uprooting you from your home. You do well in school and I know you don't have any trouble making friends, but something is definitely going on with you. I can't put my finger on it, but..."

Jack cut her off before she could finish. "There wasn't much of a decision to be made, Mom. I mean, your job is your job and they asked you to take on a new position. You did what you had to do. Don't worry about me. I'm okay. Really. If you want something to worry about, worry about what we are going to have for dinner because I am starving," he said with a slight smile, trying to diffuse the discussion.

"Okay," she countered, "but I'm not letting this drop. We'll talk after dinner. How about we order some pizza; I'm too bushed to cook."

"Pizza sounds good. Extra cheese, please."

"You got it," she grunted as she picked herself up wearily from the couch and shuffled off to the kitchen to make the phone call.

Jack put down his lacrosse bag and skateboard and went over to the couch and laid down. He raised his hands to his face and rubbed his eyes with his fingertips. What was going on? How did life reach this point? And then his own words resounded in his brain: *We all make choices in life and we have to stick by them, right?* Making the right choices, that was the key to everything, but some choices in life are harder than others, and you never really know what the consequences are going to be - good or bad. It was that uncertainty that kept Jack up at night.

Chapter 19

April 1st, 2010

As crazy luck would have it, Chris also made it onto the lacrosse team. Jack was happy about that. It helped to balance things out a little and take the sting out of playing on the same side with Billy.

The team practiced every day for two weeks before their first big game against Centerville Middle School. Each practice was a grueling mix and match of exercises and drills. Mr. Weber was trying to get them into tip-top shape and determine what positions his boys would take on - goalie, defense, midfield or attack. Many of the boys were hoping to spend their time on the field being attackmen. Attackmen were the unofficial celebrities of the team because they usually scored most of the goals. Jack and Billy possessed the skills of natural attackmen. They each had a special knack for getting around defensive players. It was as if their upper bodies moved independently of their legs, allowing them to fake out the opposition. When combined with their stick and ball handling skills, it made them explosively good. But perhaps the most amazing aspect of how they played was that they actually cooperated with one another on the field. During practice games, they had an almost uncanny connection, knowing when the other would be open for a pass or helping each other move the ball closer to the goal. It was as if all personal animosity was set aside on the field. Even Coach Weber didn't know what to make of it, knowing how they got along so horribly off the field. But whatever animosity they may have demonstrated towards each other when not playing the game, they were a joint force to be reckoned with when they suited up.

Within two weeks' time, the Barnaby Hills lacrosse team was ready for the first game of the season against Centerville. Anticipation and excitement ran high in the locker room as the team got ready. Mr. Weber came in to give them a pre-game pep talk.

"Okay, gentlemen. Here we are - the first game of the season. This is what we've been working for day in and day out for the last two weeks. You are ready. I know it. You know it. And soon, they'll know it. Don't lose your cool today. If you lose your cool, you lose the game. Right?" The boys hooted in agreement. Mr. Weber raised his hand to quiet them. "But let's not forget what is important today: teamwork. We are a team, no matter what the outcome of today's game. Win or lose, we are a team. It's not just us against Centerville today; it's how well we work together that really counts. The team is EVERYTHING. Now, let me hear your voices. WHO'S THE BEST?"

The boys yelled in unison, "Barnaby Hills!"

"Who?" prodded Mr. Weber.

"Barnaby Hills!" they cheered loudly.

"I can't hear you!"

"BARNABY HILLS!"

"WELL, THEN, LET'S GET 'EM!" Mr. Weber shouted back.

A deafening roar of approval erupted and reverberated around the locker room as the Barnaby Hills lacrosse team grabbed their gear and followed Mr. Weber towards the field. The game was on.

Chapter 20

April 3rd, 2011

The rain clouds cleared completely from the sky and the full moon cast a wide spotlight on the town of Barnaby Hills. The wet leaves of the trees glistened in the soft glow of the illumination. The streets were eerily silent and the inhabitants of the town were fast asleep - most of the inhabitants, that is.

Jack crept silently out of a yard onto Batchelder Street and squatted down behind a parked minivan. He took deep, heaving breaths of air into his lungs. Fighting off dogs and running and jumping through yards took some of the wind out of him, but all he needed was a moment of rest to get his energy back. He inched toward the driver's side of the van and took a long, hard look down the street. As a human, his eyesight was excellent; as a Moonwalker, his eyesight was phenomenal. He was able to see greater distances with more clarity and definition - especially in the dark. Chris' house was the last one on Batchelder, less than a quarter of a mile away, but Jack was able to see clearly down the road and determine if any activity was taking place. So far nothing.

Batchelder Street had houses on one side and was bordered by thick woodlands on the other. Jack knew better than to stroll down the road in broad moonlight, so he darted over to the line of trees and was quickly enveloped by their protective darkness. He started making his way quickly towards Chris' house, pausing occasionally for sensory input. He lifted his head high into the air, a strong breeze from the east blowing coarse fur away from his face. Apart from the sounds and smells of small nocturnal creatures living in the woods, going about their nighttime business, Jack could not detect other Moonwalkers in the area. Something wasn't right, but Jack couldn't figure it out. They had to be near. Being werewolves themselves, they could move about with near the same speed and strength that Jack could. What happened to the ones that were following him in the park?

Jack continued on until he was within a short distance of Chris' driveway. The house was set back in the woods a bit which gave Chris and his family more privacy than his neighbors. Tall pine and spruce trees dotted the borders of the property, providing perfect cover for an ambush. Jack paused again to take stock of the situation. There appeared to be nothing out of the ordinary taking place. In fact, Chris' house and the woods around it looked picture perfect. How could this be? Either his senses were on strike, or Billy and his boys had given up. Both notions seemed highly improbable, but he didn't know what else to think. Just to play it safe, he decided to go deeper into the woods and approach the house from the back. He looped around through the thick brush and was nearing the yard when he stopped abruptly. How did his sense of smell not pick up his presence? There, standing in the middle of Chris' backyard, was Billy, fur and fangs glistening in the moonlight, a wide smile on his wolfen face - a sight that Jack had grown to know all too well.

Chapter 21

April 1st, 2010

Barnaby Hills was ordinarily a quiet community. A place where neighbors respected one another's privacy and desire for peace. It was the kind of town where people didn't start mowing their lawns until 9 a.m. on weekends and children finished practicing their musical instruments before 8 pm on weekdays. Peace and tranquility reigned, except, that is, during lacrosse season. It was during this time that the community was transformed into lacrosse-loving lunatics. Young and old could be heard cheering on the school team with an excitement and gusto that most people would reserve for seats at the fifty-yard line at the Super Bowl. There was nothing like a good lacrosse game to get the blood of the town pumping fast. Weekend games at the middle school and high school lacrosse fields brought everyone out. The bleachers and sidelines were packed with eager fans and spectators, especially for the first game of the season.

Jack and his teammates ran out of the locker room to face off against Centerville and were met with wild enthusiasm from the townsfolk. People were standing on their feet, shouting and waving red banners that said, "Go, Barnaby Hills, Go!" There were a fair number of Centerville fans, too, trying to cheer just as loudly for their team, but they were easily drowned out by the home team crowd. On the field, the marching band pumped out an infectious fight song while cheerleaders from both teams were doing their acrobatic best to rev up the crowd even more. It was quite a display of fan fever.

Chris caught up with Jack on the sidelines.

"Dude, this is awesome!" he shouted, trying to be heard over the crowd.

"I know," Jack yelled back. "I never experienced anything like this where I used to live. Skateboarders don't usually have crowds of people on the street cheering them as they grind the curb...unless they fall, of course."

"I hear ya," chuckled Chris. "I used to come to lacrosse games with the family all the time when I was a kid. I loved it. It was always a dream of mine to be out on the field with everyone cheering for me as I broke through the defensive lines and scored. Man, I never, ever thought I would be good enough to make the team. I can't believe I'm here. This is a dream come true. I just hope that I don't mess up."

"Yeah, I hope I don't mess up, either."

Chris looked at Jack with surprise. "What do you mean? You're good - REALLY GOOD. We can't lose with you and Billy in the attack positions. You guys are born players."

"Thanks for pumping up my ego, but I've got a lot to learn about this game. Hey, you're good, too, dude."

"Don't get me wrong; I absolutely love the game, but I'll be lucky to get a few minutes of play today," Chris said with a hint of self-deprecation. "You'll probably play most of the game. I wouldn't figure you to have any worries."

"I'm no different than you. I try not to take anything for granted; that's all. Things can change at the drop of a hat. One day I'm riding my skateboard in San Francisco, and then the next I'm about to play my first game of lacrosse. Life is definitely strange. Don't take it all too seriously," Jack said poking his buddy playfully in the ribs.

Chris looked Jack directly in his eyes, the cheers and marching band music far in the distance of his mind. "It's lacrosse. Playing on the team is a dream come true. There's no way to take it BUT seriously."

"Okay," Jack replied, sensing his friend's earnestness. "How about we take that dream to the max and win this game today."

Chris smiled. "Now you're talking. GO BARNABY HILLS!"

As if on cue, the referee blew his whistle to call the players to the field.

Chapter 22

April 4th, 2011

Jack and his mom eyed the last slice of pizza in the box, both still surprisingly hungry even though they had just polished off a total of seven slices between them.

"I'll thumb-wrestle you for it."

"Okay, but no cheating like the last time, Mom."

"Why, Jack, I haven't the slightest idea what you're talking about," his mother said with a mischievous smile.

"Oh really," he chuckled. "You don't remember the Chinese food fiasco of '09 when we thumb-wrestled for the last egg roll?"

"Nope. Doesn't ring a bell. Now, are we going to *talk* about wrestling for this thing or are we actually going to do it," she said cracking her knuckles.

"Oh, it's on."

The two pizza adversaries locked hands together. Jack counted to three and the battle began. Grasping each other firmly, they wiggled their thumbs back and forth, left and right, trying to jockey for leverage to be the first to pin down the other's thumb.

"You must be getting old, Jack," his mother quipped. "Your thumb just isn't what it used to be. Maybe you should give up now before your thumb gives up on you."

"My thumb's fine, Mom. Never better. But I think I hear some creaking noises coming from yours. Is that some early arthritis I'm hearing? I wouldn't want you to hurt yourself. Why don't you just give up?"

Both combatants stared at each other - brows furrowed, faces determined. They were so alike in many ways. Each fiercely independent and competitive. Ready to give their all - even for a slice of pizza.

"Jack, did I ever tell you about...1, 2...Ugh!" she interrupted herself, almost pinning Jack's thumb down. "Almost got you that time. Anyway, did I ever tell you about me being in the Guinness Book of World Records? Yep. My photo is right there for most thumb-wrestling take-downs within a twenty-four hour period."

"Really?" Jack said with feigned surprise. "Wow, that's some coincidence because I just happen to hold a world record of my own - most thumb-wrestling wins against arthritic moms."

Jack's mom burst out laughing and weakened her grip, allowing Jack enough wiggle room to pin-down her thumb.

"1, 2, 3, THE WINNER!" he shouted jumping to his feet and cheering himself.

His mom, still laughing, watched Jack lovingly as he took a victory lap around the kitchen.

"I'll tell you what, Mom," he said coming down from his win. "I'm a generous soul. You get the pizza cutter and I'll share the last slice with you. How's that?"

"Sounds good. You are a generous soul. After all, you learned from the best, Jackie."

Jack froze for a second - his mother's words echoing in his head.

Chapter 23

April 3rd, 2011

"Time to learn from the best, Jackie," snarled Billy, his voice distorted and gnarled from the transformation from boy into werewolf. "I've been waiting for you."

Jack stepped out from the woods onto a grassy area of the yard, keeping a safe distance. He looked around the yard intently and sniffed the air trying to sense where the rest of Billy's wolf pack were. He didn't see or smell them. There was only a large tool shed to his right and an old, playground set close to the house.

"What's the matter, Jackie? Afraid? There's nothing to be afraid of..." laughed Billy, thick saliva dripping down the sides of his mouth.

"Where are your boys, Billy?" Jack growled. "You don't go to the bathroom by yourself, let alone fight without your pack doing the dirty work."

"I don't have a clue as to what you're talking about. Relax, my little puppy. It's a beautiful moonlit night. Shall we dance?" Billy laughed again and spun around and around with his arms lifted high, hands positioned as if dancing closely and delicately with a partner. Around his neck on a chain hung a crystal vial that lifted off his chest as he twirled. It sparkled and reflected the moonlight like a mirrored dancing ball. It would have been a bizarre sight if a human were doing it, but a werewolf feigning a dance in the moonlight was almost beyond description. It was equally fascinating as it was creepy. Billy was trying to throw Jack off balance, but Jack did not react. Letting

Billy inside your head to play mind games could have dire consequences. Jack being a werewolf was proof of that.

Billy stopped twirling and laughing and took stock of Jack standing there on the verge of the woods - no emotion, no deviation of focus.

"Lighten up, Jackie boy. You are way too serious, especially for a wolf. I should have realized that last year. I blame myself more than I blame you. What the hell was I thinking by inviting you into the pack?"

"Inviting? Is that what you call it, Billy? I don't think I had a choice."

"If I remember correctly, you were given a choice before being "persuaded" to be one of us. We all have the ability to choose, Jack," Billy said with a matter-of-fact tone. "Personally, I made a very bad choice last year - to bring you into the clan. It was a very bad choice, indeed, and one that I regret making. And now I have to fix it. Oh well, say goodbye to the old and say hello to the new - the new wolf, that is." The claws of his right hand gently tapped the vial around his neck as he spoke.

"You leave Chris alone," Jack snarled defensively.

"You leave Chris alone!" Billy mimicked. "I'm sorry, Jack. That's not possible. He's been chosen; it's a done deal. Chris is moving up in the world. His lacrosse game is getting quite good and he is showing himself to be quite the team player - unlike someone else I know. But look at it this way. You had your chance. How many people can say that, huh? You just didn't make the final cut. No hard feelings. And after tonight, you won't feel anything ever again. This is your last dance, Jackie, I hope you enjoy it. I know I will."

With those words barely out of his mouth, Billy clapped

his hands together. From the other side of the tool shed, all five of Billy's pack emerged quickly from the shadows. Jack was surrounded.

Chapter 24

April 1st, 2010

The Barnaby Hills team ran out to meet Centerville in the middle of the field for the National Anthem and to wish each other good luck. Soon after, the referee called for the game to begin. Starting players took their positions while the rest headed to the sidelines. Two midfielders came to the center for the face off. All the noise that dominated the field before was now dissipating as the players and fans awaited the referee to blow the whistle to signal the start of the game - the calm before the storm.

Jack, being one of three attackmen, was positioned down in Centerville's defensive area. He was joined by Billy and a rather large boy named Lucas. Lucas was one of Billy's best friends. He wasn't as quick or agile as Jack or Billy but he could handle a lacrosse stick just as well. His real talent, however, lay in his aggressive style of play. When he had control of the ball, he was like a junkyard dog finally free of the fence. He intimidated defense players to the point that they were reluctant to get too close to him - a veritable locomotive on two legs. On top of that, his loyalty wasn't so much to the team or Mr. Weber as much as it was to Billy. He was as unpredictable as he was dangerous - both on and off the field.

The midfielders crouched low on either side of the centerline, sticks at the ready waiting for the game to begin and to gain control of the ball on the grass between them. The referee lingered a moment and then blew the whistle. The midfielders rolled their sticks forward to capture the ball, shoulders clashing brutally against one another. After a couple of seconds of straining and struggling, the Barnaby Hills midfielder gained possession and ran out with the ball seated firmly in the webbed pocket of his stick. He passed it quickly to another midfielder who was open nearby and that player started advancing to the offensive zone. Jack, Billy and Lucas sprinted to key points, positioning themselves for a pass.

Centerville was playing man to man - a defensive strategy in which each defender was covering one of the Barnaby Hills offensemen. It was a sound strategy except for the fact that no one wanted to cover Lucas, who had positioned himself close to the left side of the Centerville net. Seeing that he was wide open, the Barnaby Hills midfielder shot Lucas a long pass. He caught it easily and was well within reach of taking a shot at the goal, but he didn't. Instead, he cast a quick glance at Billy. Billy was being covered tightly by one of the Centerville defenseman and couldn't take a pass without the possibility of having the ball stolen. He motioned with his hand towards Jack who was coming up left of center. Lucas took Billy's cue and shot a low, fast pass over to Jack. It hit the ground before reaching him but Jack scooped it up deftly without breaking his stride. The defender covering Jack was only a step behind and was trying to poke check the ball out of his possession by reaching around him with his stick. Jack had a decent shot at the goal but was farther away than he would have liked. As if in sync with Jack's mind, Billy broke free from the player covering him and ran a line between Jack and the goal. Jack switched his grip to the left side to avoid interference from the player behind him and shot a pass to Billy waist-high. Billy caught the pass, quickly spun around and fired the ball at the goal. The goalie did his best to stop it but the ball flew past him into the netting. The Barnaby Hills fans jumped out of their seats and cheered in frenzied response. It was as if everyone in the stands had scored the goal themselves. Barnaby Hills was on the scoreboard fast and easy and it was all because of teamwork - Jack and Billy style.

Chapter 25

April 3rd, 2011

Billy's boys circled Jack menacingly. The sound of their throaty, low snarls provided a frightening, almost rhythmic soundtrack to the growing weirdness of the night. They spaced themselves equally in a revolving circle to squash any attempt at escape - their glowing eyes focused solely on Jack and nothing else.

"You were right," Billy interjected with a toothy grin. "Where I go, the pack goes. But a little distraction goes a long way, huh? Now what are you going to do?"

Jack heard Billy talking but kept his eyes on the wolves slowly circling around him. He hunched down and lowered his center of gravity a bit, digging his feet into the soft dirt beneath him. His arms were slightly bent at his sides and he held his hands in front of him as if clutching an invisible lacrosse stick to ward off attack.

"Wondering why your senses failed you, Jackie? Why you didn't smell anyone or anything except your own filth? Don't you pay attention in science class? It's simple: wind direction. You couldn't smell us, but we sure could smell you. And boy do you stink?" Billy laughed loudly, almost barking. The pack joined in on the laughter and stepped forward a little to close the gap between hunters and hunted.

Jack snickered, too, without letting down his guard. "Imagine that, Billy. You actually learned something at school. What are the odds? I guess there is a first time for everything."

"Oh, there are lots of things to be learned at school, Jack,"

Billy said, his smile fading seamlessly into a sneer, "but you'll never get a chance to learn any more. Think of yourself as expelled - officially and permanently. In fact, tonight is the last full moon you'll ever see, and the first one Chris will ever remember. Goodbye, Jackie-boy."

Billy grinned, turned his back quickly and began walking to Chris' house. The pack howled and pounced on Jack.

Chapter 26

April 1st, 2010

The roar of the crowd was near deafening, but Jack couldn't hear any of it. There was only a minute or so left in the game and the score was tied. He was busy making his way towards the Centerville goal with a defenseman trailing right behind. As he neared closer to the goal, Billy came up quickly from the opposite side and crossed his path. Jack flicked his wrist quickly and passed the ball to Billy. Unsure as to what just took place, the defenseman covering Jack slowed down to assess the situation. Jack took advantage of the break in coverage and made a beeline straight to the goal. Billy stopped abruptly and then side-armed him a perfect pass. Now nothing was between Jack and the goalie. With only a few seconds left in the game, Jack darted to the left side of the goal. The Centerville goalie shifted his stance slightly to cover that side of the net and Jack fired a precise shot to the far right side. To Jack, it seemed like the ball was moving in slow motion as it flew towards the goal. The roar of the crowd was but a distant hum and the players on the field seemed to move about as if they were making their way through waist-high water. For a moment, it appeared as if the ball would never reach the goal, as if it would fall straight out of the air onto the ground. But it didn't. The goalie twisted his torso and reached his stick out to deflect its path but he missed. The ball soared securely into the net.

The Barnaby Hills fans jumped out of their seats in unison, as if ten thousand volts of friendly electricity were shocking them into delight. Arms reached high into the sky and voices even higher. The metal bleachers shook from the pounding of feet as children, and even some adults, jumped up and down with wild abandon. A group of middle school students ran onto the field and surrounded the players as they made their way to the sidelines. They scooped up Jack and Billy and hoisted them high for everyone in the stands to see. Chants of "Billy" and "Jack" grew louder and louder. The boys were brought face to face with one another as they sat on the shoulders of their teammates and classmates. With all the hustle and bustle, Jack and Billy paused for a moment and contemplated each other. They worked so well on the field but that was over. What was to happen now? They stared intently at each other, the world around them a muted barrage of indistinct sound. And, for a brief second, Jack saw the orange specks in Billy's eyes glow.

Chapter 27

April 1st, 2010

The Barnaby Hills locker room was alive and wired with excitement. The team was riding high from the win and players laughed, sang and fooled around as if this was the moment to beat all other moments. Billy and Jack had been carried all the way from the field to the locker room like royal warriors - conquering heroes astride human steeds. They were brought to a long bench and they stood atop it as friends and teammates cheered them with wild abandon.

Mr. Weber came striding into the locker room with the assistant coach like a proud papa and jumped up on the bench between Jack and Billy. Everyone in the locker room started cheering and shouting even more. Mr. Weber smiled and let the team enjoy themselves and then raised his hands to get them to settle down.

"Alright, alright," he said as the excitement approached a manageable level. "What can I say except, 'WAY-TO-GO!'"

The locker room erupted again into loud cheers and whistles. Mr. Weber waited a few seconds and then held up his hands to quiet things down.

"Let me tell you what I saw from the sidelines today: teamwork. I saw a group of boys, who only a few short weeks ago, didn't know the meaning of the word "team," and here today showed this community just how a team operates. Every single one of you gave your all for the collective good. A coach couldn't ask for anything better than that. Give yourselves a round of applause!"

The locker room burst into wild cheers and congratulatory high-fives and pats on the back. Mr. Weber put his arms around Jack and Billy's shoulders and looked out into the locker room. Seeing this action, the boys quieted down quickly.

"Special mention must go to these two right here. Not just because they played so well, but more so because of how they worked together to help get the job done. That says a lot about how we do business here." Mr. Weber's voice took on a very serious tone and he looked deeply into the eyes of all his players. "Always remember that we are first and foremost a team. Nothing else matters. Not winning, not losing...nothing. All that matters is the team."

The locker room was silent. All eyes were upon Mr. Weber, his arms still around Jack and Billy. His words almost echoing throughout the room.

He broke the silence. "That's enough from me. Get yourselves washed and dressed and get out of here and have some fun. Rumor has it that a party is waiting for you guys. You deserve it!" With those last thoughts, he grabbed Jack and Billy's hands and raised them high in the air. The room went crazy. Amidst the joyous mayhem, Billy leaned over to cast a smile at Jack. Jack smiled back reflexively, but it just didn't feel right doing so.

Chapter 28

April 3rd, 2011

The wolf pack dove at Jack in unison. Past experience had taught them that trying to take Jack one-on-one was a foolish endeavor. Without thinking, Jack squatted down and then sprang up quickly, just barely jumping up and over Billy's boys as they rammed harshly into one another from all angles. Jack landed off to the side of the pack. He looked towards Chris' house and saw Billy climbing up the side to get to Chris' bedroom window. He only had a moment or so to act before Billy would reach Chris and transform him into a Moonwalker. Leaving the groaning pile of fur behind him, Jack made a beeline for the house. He knew he wouldn't be able to stop Billy in time if he followed the same path to Chris' window, so he veered over to the old playground set and ran up the slide. It moaned and creaked with every footstep and then crumpled to the ground just as he pulled himself onto the main crossbar of the structure. Billy stopped climbing and looked down at the noise behind him. He almost couldn't believe what he was seeing. Jack had bested his boys and was too close for comfort. He turned back to the house with even greater resolve to reach Chris' bedroom and started climbing even faster. Jack darted across the wooden crossbar of the playset and jumped towards Billy in a last ditch attempt to stop him before he entered the house. He clawed the air wildly as he flew. Billy tried to pull his legs up and out of reach but Jack was able to grab one of them. Billy tried to shake him loose but the weight of two wolves was just too much for his arms to bear. They fell to the ground below Chris' window. By this time, the wolf pack had regained its senses and was scrambling towards the house. Jack had landed on top of Billy and looked up just in time to see the boys approaching. He straddled Billy's back, lifted his head off the ground and put his sharp claws directly under his neck.

"Take one more step and your leader is done!" Jack growled at the other wolves.

Billy's boys stopped dead in their tracks. They looked to Billy for guidance but he was still dazed from the fall. A low moan of indecision emanated from all of them as they contemplated what to do next. A light in the house suddenly turned on, forcing the wolf pack's hand; they scattered into the woods behind the house in different directions.

Jack knew he had to get out of there or risk being seen. As much as he detested the idea of helping Billy out of his own mess, he knew that he couldn't be left behind to be discovered, either. He lifted his groggy nemesis off the ground and slung him over his shoulder. He looked towards the moonlit sky and saw that more rain clouds were massing just to the west. Within a few minutes, he would be turning back into his human form, as would the others. He took off as fast as he could with the weight of Billy on his back and entered the woods. He would dump Billy off at a safe distance from Chris' house and then get back home as fast as he could. The night may have been coming to a close for all the Moonwalkers, but Jack's nightmare still persisted.

Chapter 29

April 1st, 2010

The party was in full swing by the time Jack and Chris showed up. Just about everyone in town had been invited to Billy's house by his parents for an impromptu celebration of the Barnaby Hills victory. Jack wasn't going to go but his mother convinced him otherwise.

"Who knows?" she said when Jack expressed his distaste for Billy and his friends. "Something might happen that changes things between you two." Jack doubted it but took her advice anyway.

As they entered the backyard, both boys were pleasantly surprised as friends and neighbors rushed forward to greet them with handshakes, vigorous pats on the back and even a few hair tussles. Jack and Chris didn't know half the people coming up to them, but it was as if they were at a raucous family reunion.

"I could get used to this," Chris said with a big grin on his face.

"Yeah, I hear ya," Jack replied somewhat breathlessly as someone gave him a big bear hug.

As the number of well-wishers started to dwindle around them, a man came forward holding a case of soda in one hand and a gooey yet delicious-looking cheeseburger in the other. "Hey guys, great game today. Can't wait for the next one," he said somewhat clumsily with some bits of burger falling out of his mouth. He finished chewing. "Sorry about that. I'm Billy's dad and our house is your house."

"I'm Jack and this is Chris."

"Chris, nice to meet you. And Jack, no need to introduce yourself. Everyone knows who you are. You've got a bright lacrosse future ahead of you. Hey, make yourselves comfortable. Plenty to eat and drink out here in the yard and I think Billy and the rest of the gang are downstairs in the basement listening to music and having fun. Feel free to join them. Either of you want a soda?" he asked motioning to the case under his arm. Both boys grabbed one from the box. "Have a good time, fellas!" And just as fast as he walked up, he was gone. Jack and Chris cast a glance at each other and started laughing.

"Wow. Seems way too nice to be Billy's dad, huh?"

"Ya think?" Jack replied sarcastically.

"Well, what do you say...head downstairs and join the party?"

"Yeah, sure. But I'm a little hungry. I'm gonna stop over by the grill and grab something to eat. I'll meet you down there."

"You are gonna come down, right Jack?" Chris asked, not exactly sure of the answer.

"Yeah, yeah, yeah, don't worry; I'm not gonna leave you alone in the lion's den."

"Hey, you can't blame a kid for asking. I'll see you in a few," said Chris as he turned towards the house.

Jack looked around and saw the food table in the corner of the yard near a large grill. He made his way over with a few people trying to chat him up on the "great game" as he walked. He tried to pause and be polite but the aroma of yummy food was too big of a draw to keep him still for more than a couple of seconds. The table was everything his nose hinted at, brimming with barbecued chicken, steak and burgers and all the side dishes and fixings to go with them. Jack picked up a plate and started taking samples of everything."

"That's it; dig in, Jack," a familiar voice said behind him. "As Coach Weber said, we deserve it."

Jack turned to meet Billy standing no more than a foot or two away, a big grin on one side of his face.

"I guess we do," Jack agreed cautiously.

Billy stopped staring and looked over to the table. He walked past Jack and grabbed a plate.

"You have skills, Jack. A lot of skills," he said almost enthusiastically as he picked up food and put it on his plate. "I mean...I could tell from practice that you were good, but you never really know how good someone is until you see them in action - in the middle of it all - if you know what I mean?"

"Um, okay..." Jack answered somewhat confused.

"You see," Billy continued, "we're not so different. I've got skills; you've got skills. "That's what sets us apart from all the others. We've got something they don't."

"We didn't win this game by ourselves," Jack said as if to set the narrative straight. "Everyone on this team worked hard and pulled together for the win today."

"Sure, sure..." Billy replied, trying to keep the mood of the conversation light. "I grant you that. Take your friend, Chris. He didn't get to play for more than a couple of minutes but I'm sure he wanted the team to win just as much as you or me. He just doesn't have the skills."

"Yet," Jack inserted quickly.

"Of course," Billy said almost apologetically. "Nothing personal against Chris. But my point is..."

"Hey boys," said Billy's dad running over to the food table. "Sorry to interrupt the personal convo. Billy, when you head back downstairs, would you bring a plate of burgers? We've got to get people eating more food or we'll be eating leftovers for the next month. Thanks. Hey Jack, while you're talking to Billy, make sure you give him some tips to improve his game. And maybe some about how to clean up his room, too." Billy's father winked jokingly, grabbed a burger and was gone just as fast as he came."

"Your dad's a funny guy," Jack said turning back to Billy.

"Yeah, he's a laugh riot. Now to get back to what I was saying. My point is that people like you and me move the team along in the right direction. Whether you want to admit it or not, Jack, you and I make things happen."

"I guess so," Jack admitted with some reluctance.

Billy smiled. "What I'm trying to say is that I want us to stop acting like enemies and be more like friends. I know that I haven't treated you right since you moved to town and I want to make up for that. What do you say?" Billy said, putting out his hand.

Jack's eyes widened in disbelief as he contemplated the outstretched hand before him. He felt off balance, bombarded by thoughts of how and why. What does one actually do when surprised by the improbable?

"C'mon, Jack. I'm trying to make things right. If I can put out my hand in friendship, can't you at least shake it? No strings attached."

Maybe it was a reflex from someone putting out their hand to shake yours; maybe it was what his mother had said earlier about change; maybe it had been a long year and Jack was tired. Whatever the reason, Jack watched his own hand with strange detachment as he put it out and grabbed Billy's.

A wide smile broke out on Billy's face. "Awesome, Jack. This is the start of something amazing. Why don't we head downstairs, get to know one another and have some fun with everyone?"

As Billy directed Jack towards the house, the last rays of sunlight drifted over the horizon. Billy stopped to take a good look.

"An amazing sunset to end an amazing day, right Jack? But the night is gonna be even better. I just know it. Full moon a coming. I just love a full moon. What about you?"

2nd Quarter

"Cold shone the moon, with noise
The night went by.
Trees uttered things of woe:
Bent grass dared not grow."

Richard Arthur Warren Hughes

Chapter 1

April 1, 2010

Music pumping, kids dancing, lights swirling, loud laughter...but none of it seemed to penetrate Jack's consciousness. He was trapped. Trapped and being verbally tortured while a room full of people partied, yet no one had a clue about what was happening to him.

"Think about reality for a minute," droned his tormentor. "What exactly is real? Are we actually standing here talking or are we dreaming about it? How do we know the difference between reality and fantasy? I mean, I see you and I hear you when you talk, but does that mean you are really real? Maybe none of this is real. Maybe none of us are real. Maybe this party isn't really happening. Maybe neither one of us is even here. I mean, no offense, but you could be a piece of partially-digested pizza in my sleeping belly causing me to toss and turn and have strange dreams. Crazy, right? If you ask me, I think people are too concerned about the wrong things. Who cares about what's in space or in the depths of the oceans. The mind is the big 'unknown' as far as I'm concerned. Do you follow what I'm saying?"

Jack's glassy eyes blinked back to life as he realized he was actually supposed to answer this last question.

"Uh, yeah," he muttered.

"I thought you would," said the person standing directly in front of him. "Hey, I need to go to the bathroom. Don't go anywhere. When I get back I want to talk some more about all of this. But before I go, ponder this one: maybe, just maybe, we are all characters in a galactic video game. A video game! Blows your mind, right? Okay, don't go anywhere. I'll be right back. Stay put."

The tormentor scurried away quickly, leaving Jack to look around quickly for a friendly face or a place to hide. He saw Chris waving to him from the far corner of the room where he was playing darts with some of the guys from the lacrosse team. Jack walked over with some haste.

"Hey, who was that kid? I didn't think he would ever stop chewing your ear off," Chris laughed.

"I don't have a clue. He just walked up and started talking to me like we were old friends. Didn't even introduce himself. He said he's coming back. Why me? I'm gonna hang out here with you if you don't mind. Ten more minutes of that and I'd be comatose"

"I don't mind," chuckled Chris, "Friends gotta stick together. Hey, this is some party, huh? There must be like a hundred people in this basement."

Jack looked around and took it all in. "Yeah, Billy doesn't mess around."

"Did you happen to see who is here?"

"Besides, everyone?" Jack joked.

Chris nodded with his head in the direction of a small area with couches that appeared to be the entertainment center of the large basement. Billy was holding court with a bunch of his friends.

Everyone over there was laughing and appeared to be having a great time. It was almost picture perfect.

"Yeah, so what? It's Billy and his friends."

"You're-not-looking-carefully," Chris implored in a sing-song voice.

Jack took another look to satisfy his friend's request. He moved his eyes away from the couch that Billy was on to the couch across from him. He saw some lacrosse players and cheerleaders and then his eyes fell on the object of Chris' curiosity: Sarah Bartley. She was munching on some popcorn and laughing with the others."

"Dude, you are smitten, but you have good taste. Sarah is cute."

"Cute?" responded Chris in disbelief, not breaking his gaze. "Puppies are cute. Kittens are cute. Sarah is out of this world gorgeous!"

"So what's your plan, Romeo? Are you just going to stare at her from across the room or are you going to talk with her, maybe ask her to dance?"

"Don't know. Probably nothing."

"Yeah, that's not such a great plan," laughed Jack.

"Well, it's all that I got right now. And as lame as it is, I'm gonna go with it."

"You do that. I'm gonna go and get something to drink. You want something? Having a major crush is sure to make one thirsty."

Chris stopped looking at Sarah. "Ha, ha. Joke all you want at my expense. But one of these days, Sarah will see me staring and think, 'Who is that kid? He's kind of cute.' And then I'll have the last laugh. Or something like that..."

"I have no doubts, Chris. Fantasy makes for great reality. Something to drink?"

"Nah, I'll probably be heading home in a little while. What about you?"

"Probably." Jack looked around for a place to get something to drink and his eyes caught the annoying boy heading back in their general direction.

"Dude, do what you gotta do. That kid is coming back," Jack said, ducking his head down quickly. "If I don't see you before you go home, I'll catch you in school on Monday. Later." And with that, he snaked his way through the crowd to escape.

"Chicken!" Chris called out, not realizing the person Jack was trying to avoid was now standing next to him.

"Chickens, huh? Which do you believe came first - the chicken or the egg? Doesn't matter really. Let me tell you why you would be wrong on both counts," opined the strange boy.

Chris looked around desperately for Jack. "Oh, he's so gonna get it on Monday..." he mumbled to himself.

Chapter 2

April 4, 2011

"Jack. Jack. Are you okay?" his mother asked.

"Huh? What?"

"I said, are you okay? You looked like you spaced out there for a moment. I thought you were in a pizza coma," she chuckled.

"Uh, oh, yeah. I'm okay, Mom. Just mentally drifted off for a moment - being so tired and all."

"I asked you this morning if you were getting enough sleep. You need to go to bed early tonight. No buts about it."

Jack smiled weakly at his mother. "No argument there. I'll help you clean up and then I'm heading straight upstairs to write my poem for Mr. Weber and go to bed."

"Thank you. After the day I had today, I'll be hitting the sack early, too."

Jack picked up the used paper plates, napkins and paper cups and threw them into the empty pizza box. He got up from the table and started bringing the box to the trash when a thought popped into his mind. He turned pensively to his mother.

"Mom, what was Dad really like?"

"What do you mean?" she asked with some confusion.

Jack finished pushing the pizza box into the trash and came back to the table.

"Well, you know. What was he really like? What kind of a person was he? I know you have told me about him - what a great guy he was and all, but I just want to know more."

"I thought you wanted to go to bed early tonight?" his mother joked.

"Oh come on, Mom. I'm just curious. I'll hit the sack soon; I promise."

"Okay, just a little bit more, Jack. I'm bushed."

"So..." Jack said as he settled back comfortably into his chair.

"So...he was just awesome - smart, handsome, great personality - just like you."

Jack smiled.

"I guess you could say he had a calmness about him, a thoughtful kind of stillness. No matter what was going on, he could think his way through it. Nothing really rattled him too much. He wasn't the type that went looking for trouble, but he also wasn't the type to back down when trouble came around. I remember one time when he and I went out for a wonderful romantic dinner and we were walking back to the car. Some guy came out of nowhere and tried to grab my pocketbook hanging from my shoulder. He almost got it but your father grabbed him and wrestled him down to the floor. He kept him there until the police came, but throughout the whole thing, your dad just kept talking to him, trying to calm him down so neither one of them would get hurt. I don't know. I think most people in that situation would have acted differently. Does this make any sense?"

"Yeah, I think so. I guess I'm kinda like that, too, but sometimes it's hard to keep your head straight and not feel like you are going to just lose it."

"Lacrosse?" his mother said more than she asked.

"Yeah, um, lacrosse," he responded quietly.

"Jack, you know if lacrosse is starting to interfere with your studies and social life, you can always drop it. I'm not going to be upset. I just want you to be happy. Actually, it's not what I want; it should be about what you want. And I have a strong inkling that your father would say the same exact thing if he were here right now. So you have to ask yourself what it is that you want."

"I've asked myself that, Mom. I don't think I have an answer. I don't even know if Dad would be able to help me answer it."

"That's okay," she smiled. "You may not have an answer now, but who knows, maybe tomorrow."

Jack returned a weak smile. "I hope so, Mom. I hope so..."

Chapter 3

April 1, 2010

"Jack, where you goin'?"

Walking up the stairs to leave the party and go home when he heard his name, Jack twisted his body around to see who was calling him.

"Oh, hey, Billy, I was gonna head on out of here. Great party. Please thank your folks for me," Jack said, hoping to quicken his quick exit.

"You can't go home now. I thought we were going to hang out tonight. You know, work on our 'new friendship' and all."

"Yeah, Billy, that sounds awesome but I'm really beat tired. The game really took its toll on me. And I promised my mom I'd wake up early and mow the lawn and do some other stuff around the house. You know what I mean..."

"Nah, actually I don't," Billy laughed. "We have someone who cuts the lawn and a woman who comes twice a week to clean, so I don't have a friggin' clue. But the night is young and so are we. C'mon, dude, you shook my hand. You gotta hang."

Jack wrestled with the idea for a moment in his head. He really didn't want to stay and build a friendship with Billy, but he had to admit he was going out of his way to make amends. At least that was something. And Jack did shake his hand in agreement...

Jack turned from going up the stairs and faced Billy completely. "Okay, but not too long. Tomorrow is gonna be a long day."

"Alright, Jackie-boy! This party is dying out anyway. Everyone is going to be heading home soon, but me and the boys were going to head on over to Howl House and have some fun."

"Howl House?"

"Yeah, it's an old abandoned shack we found tucked away in the woods - a couple of miles or so away from the old W&W timber damn. It's hidden pretty well, though, and no one even remembers that it is there. We turned it into a clubhouse. It's awesome, a little home away from home. We go there once a month and raise a ruckus."

"Sounds great, Billy. Yeah. Very cool," Jack said trying not to sound as if he already regretted it.

"Sweet. Why don't you go hang out on the couch with the crew and I'll put an end to this party so the REAL party can begin."

Billy clapped Jack on the shoulder and darted off into the basement crowd.

"Jack," he said quietly to himself, "how do you do you get yourself into these things?"

Chapter 4

April 5, 2011

The cries for help were getting louder now. They were definitely coming from inside the house, hidden and lurking eerily just beyond the row of nearby trees and shrubs. He ducked behind a thick oak to avoid being seen. Above him, the light of the full moon streamed through a canopy of branches and leaves and illuminated patches of ground. Something was wrong. The moon was out and brilliant, but Jack hadn't transformed into a Moonwalker. None of this made sense. Why was he even here? He remembered hearing the screams and having the overwhelming urge to follow them. They were muted and distant at first but he was able to track them into the woods. As he followed the sounds, the full moon rose over the horizon. Jack braced himself for the change but it didn't happen. This didn't make sense. Not a bit of sense at all.

The cries started up again. They were more intense now. Jack shook off his thoughts and quickly made his way towards the house. He crept up the rotting, wooden steps of the porch. The door was open. Jack walked in cautiously checking all around for evidence of a trap. Nothing. A loud scream came from the hallway to his right. Jack crouched down low and moved in the direction of the sound. At the far end of the hallway, he could see white light poking out from underneath a door. He walked down the left side of the hallway, his body hugging the wall for protection and comfort. He reached the door. On the other side, he could hear the whimpering of a person in pain and low growls. The whimpering stopped and then he heard someone's voice.

"You see. You see, Chris. It is beyond all control. Become one of us. Don't be foolish."

CHRIS WAS IN THERE! Jack grabbed the doorknob and pushed the door open forcefully. He looked around in shock. A body lay on the floor surrounded by Billy's boys in Moonwalker form. Billy and Chris stood closest to the body, but unlike the others, Billy had not transformed into a Moonwalker. Everyone turned their attention to Jack, but no one moved. They appeared startled by his presence. He walked over to what appeared to be a male figure on the floor. Without seeing a face, Jack felt that there was something very familiar about him. He bent down and turned the head of the person so he could see their face. He jumped back up in fear and confusion. The person on the ground was him! How could that be? He raised his numb gaze from the body to Billy. Billy met his eyes and uttered something incredibly weird.

"Welcome, Master. We've done what you asked of us." he said with a demure, almost fearful expression.

Jack thrust himself upward. He frantically looked around; his body was bathed in sweat. He put up his hands reflexively to protect himself, but nothing attacked him. Slowly, slowly, reality began to take hold. He recognized where he was. He was in his bed...in his room. He hadn't been in the woods, at the house. It had been a dream - a nasty dream. But convincing his heart of that was going to take some more time. Jack hung his head down on his chest and took some deep breaths. He sat there a little while longer and pondered what he just experienced. "Welcome, Master." Who was Billy referring to and why was Jack essentially both the victim and victimizer in the nightmare scenario? He laid down on the bed and tried to go back to sleep. "Just a dream," he said to himself. "Just a dream..." But deep down,

Jack knew that dreams were often distorted mirrors of reality.

Chapter 5

April 1, 2010

With the party done, Billy, Jack and the rest of Billy's boys made their way through the woods to Howl House, flashlights helping them to forge a path through the underbrush and around the dense groupings of trees. A gentle headwind added a little chill to the night air, but this was welcome as the boys had been trudging in the forest for about thirty-minutes without stopping. Billy's right-hand, Lucas, led the way, followed by the others with Jack and Billy in the rear. Lucas was all business as he pushed forward through the darkness, but the other boys were laughing and joking around throughout the trip. Billy would occasionally laugh at what the others were doing. The only thought running through Jack's mind was the word WHY. Why was he doing this? Was a "friendship" with Billy really worth tromping through the woods at night? Sure, they played well together on the lacrosse field, but that didn't mean that their lacrosse relationship had to continue off the field. For a relatively strong-minded kid, Jack was feeling quite unsure of himself.

He looked over at Billy. "Hey...as cool as this is and all, I think I'm gonna just call it a night, alright? I'll find my own way home."

Billy stopped and spoke for the first time since they started walking. "Jackie, c'mon. Where's your sense of adventure? Don't go through life like a stick in the mud. Live it like you do on the lacrosse field - fierce, hungry, uncompromising..."

"Yeah, that sounds all well and good," Jack countered with a hint of sarcasm, "but it's late and I hear my bed calling out to me. We'll get a chance to hang out another time. Promise."

Billy whistled. The other boys stopped walking and turned

around.

"You know what, Jack. You're right. It's late. I'm tired. You're tired. We're all tired. Right fellas?"

The boys murmured in agreement.

"If you want to go home. No problem. Go for it. But let me tell you this: we are only about fifteen minutes away from a place that is going to blow you away. Me and the rest of the boys wouldn't mind hitting the sack either, but we are doing this for you...for US. We're all on a team together, but we don't act like a team. I wanted to bring you here so we could kick back and have some good times. You know, maybe start behaving like we are teammates...even friends. Nothing good comes easy. Yeah, we could have left things like they were back at the party, but I wanted you to really experience what we all have together so we could really be on the same page. I know it seems a little strange to walk through the woods near midnight, but it means a lot to us and I know it will mean a lot to you. But, hey, I'm not in control of you. If you want to leave, I understand. But I tell you, just over the next couple of hills is something outta this world cool. Choice is yours. Free will."

Billy stood there waiting for Jack's decision, the glow from his flashlight illuminating his face just enough to punctuate his words with some visual sincerity. Jack was starting to understand how Billy got others to follow him. He was very charismatic and persuasive. When he addressed you, he made you feel like you were the only person in the world who mattered. But Jack also knew the Billy who could bully others, the Billy that could treat people like they were trash. Was it possible for that Billy to turn over a new leaf? Maybe reaching out to Jack was just the beginning, a new start.

Jack looked into Billy's eyes. There was no menacing glare like he had seen so many times before. There was something else.

Something that he had never seen before. Excitement. Billy was excited to share this experience with Jack. That had to stand for something.

"Okay. Just fifteen minutes, right?" Jack questioned, his actions hinging on the answer.

"Just fifteen," Billy responded calmly.

"Ok."

"Alright, Jack! You won't regret it. You won't regret it one bit," Billy smiled widely. "Oh, and just so you know, I had my mom call your mom and tell her you might sleep over tonight, so no worries there."

Jack looked at Billy suspiciously. "And my mom was okay with that?"

"Oh, yeah. My mom told me that she said something like 'Oh, good. Sounds like they are finally getting along.' And we are, right Jackie?"

Jack stood silently.

Billy took control of the quiet. "Hey, Lucas, let's speed things up before our good friend Jack changes his mind," he chuckled, elbowing Jack in the ribs playfully. Lucas started walking again and quickened his pace and the rest of the boys followed him. Jack turned and joined them with Billy walking closely behind. The orange flecks of Billy's eyes began to glow gently in the darkness.

Chapter 6

April 5, 2011

"Hi, Jack!"

Jack was rifling through the books and papers at the bottom of his locker in search of a pen - his usual morning ritual. Hearing his name, he turned around quickly to see who was calling him and banged his head on the locker door in the process.

"Oh, wow, sorry about that," said the sweet voice. He put his hand to the painful part of his temple and slowly lifted himself off his knees. Sarah Bartley stood before him.

"That is totally my fault. I'm so sorry; I shouldn't have snuck up on you like that."

"No, no, that's okay," Jack replied. "I'll be okay. That was pretty stupid of me."

Sarah giggled. "Well, not stupid really, but definitely a little clumsy."

"Is there something that I can do for you, Sarah, you know, that doesn't involve me getting injured?" he laughed, still smarting a little from the pain.

"Actually, I just saw you digging around in your locker and thought I'd just say hello and maybe continue our conversation from yesterday."

"Yesterday? My brain must be bruised from the locker. What conversation was that?"

"At lacrosse practice...you know...I said that we had come up with some new cheers...remember?"

Jack took a moment to shrug off the pain of hitting his head and then yesterday came flooding back into his brain. "Oh yeah. I totally remember now. Sorry. Yeah, yeah...the new cheers. I can't wait to hear them. You guys are so awesome for doing that."

"Well, I was thinking that maybe you wouldn't have to wait until the game to hear them. Maybe we could hang out after school today and I could do one for you."

"Hang out? After school? Today?" Jack stammered.

"Yes, yes and yes," Sarah chuckled.

"Um, that sounds great. I just don't know, Sarah. I mean...I told my mom that I would come home and..."

Jack's mind raced quickly. Sarah Bartley was asking him to hang out after school. SARAH BARTLEY. In any other universe, there would be nothing inherently wrong with that, and, to be honest, he would probably really enjoy hanging with her, but not in this universe. Not when his best friend was so smitten with her. Chris almost melted into a gooey, jealous puddle when she approached him yesterday at practice. "NEVERMIND YESTERDAY!" Jack yelled at himself in his head. Chris was due to stop by his locker any minute now. If he saw Jack talking with Sarah Bartley, it would just usher all the craziness of the previous day right into today. Jack had to think fast and get Sarah away from his locker - pronto.

Jack continued with his excuse. "...and, help her with the...gardening. Yeah, she's a total klutz when it comes to planting and growing things in our garden. She should be arrested for abusing vegetation. So, I really can't meet up this afternoon. Maybe another time, alright?"

"Yeah, okay. Another time would be fine. Maybe I'll see you later and we can work out a time and place."

"That sounds awesome. Um, I gotta find my pen in this stupid locker, so I'll see you later," Jack said trying to speed the conversation to an end.

"Okay. Watch your head this time," she laughed as she started down the hall.

"I will," he replied as he quickly turned to hunker down low in front of his locker before Chris showed up. He rubbed the side of his head that banged against the locker and resumed looking for his pen.

"Does anything ever go right in my life?" he mumbled painfully to himself.

Chapter 7

April 1, 2010

The group of boys finally stopped walking. They aimed their flashlights directly ahead, and out from the shadows loomed their destination - Howl House. It was only about 50 yards away but could easily be missed, as it was tucked away behind a thicket of bushes and closely spaced oak and elm trees. Whoever built it didn't want it to be readily found; that was for sure. Jack was both intrigued and wary at the same time.

As if sensing his curious apprehension, Billy broke the silence. "Something else, huh, Jack?"

Jack continued staring at the old structure without blinking his eyes. "Uh, yeah, I guess you could say that".

"Told you," Billy smiled. "C'mon."

Billy moved to the front and led everyone through the narrow path between thorny sticker bushes. Jack followed but couldn't take his eyes off of the house. One of his sleeves snagged on a thorn and he got pricked multiple times as he tried to free himself.

"Careful there, Jack. Don't get yourself hurt before we even get in the house!" Billy yelled from the front as if he had eyes in the back of his head. "Lucas, help him out!"

Lucas turned and walked back to Jack. He grabbed Jack's arm and pulled it forcefully, ripping his sleeve free of the bush but tearing the shirt and scraping his arm in the process. He then turned forward again and followed the rest of the boys.

Jack aimed his flashlight down to see the damage to his arm and shirt and shook his head. "Hey, thanks, Lucas. Thanks a lot, buddy. What a pal..." he said loudly with some measured annoyance.

No one even turned to acknowledge his words, so Jack continued on and met up with the rest of the boys who were now standing directly in front of the house.

"Here she is," Billy said proudly. "Howl House."

The two story structure was straight out of a haunted house movie. It was old with creaky loose shudders that swayed in and out with the breeze. The steps leading up to the front door were cracked and looked as treacherous as one would expect stairs would look that led up to an abandoned house in the woods. There were broken windows, loose shingles and rotted spindles. The only things missing were the horror-film crew and some unknown actors waiting around for their next scene.

"How did you even find this place? Who owns it?" Jack asked, almost combining the two questions into one.

"Don't know for sure, but it might be part of the W&W Timber Company. It is old, really old. No one in town really knows about it or seems to remember it ever existing. We found it...by accident, so to speak," Billy replied with a barely noticeable grin.

"It looks pretty run down. Someone could get hurt going in there."

"Looks are deceiving, Jack. Howl House is perfectly safe. Perfectly perfect in all its perfection."

"Why do you call it Howl House?"

Billy turned around slowly. "Would you like to find out, Jack? Would you? Cause I would love to show you. Just say, 'Yes,' and we'll all have a howling great time."

The rest of the boys started laughing as if on cue.

Jack looked back and forth between Billy, the house and everyone else. Geez if this wasn't the strangest night of his life. His instincts told him to just turn and leave, but his interest was now piqued. After all of this, how was he NOT going to take the last crazy step? What do you do when the decision to do or not to do something is equally bizarre?

"Well, Jack?" Billy said without the slightest degree of impatience.

Jack looked directly into Billy's eyes. He made his decision. "I'm game. Let's do it."

Chapter 8

April 5, 2011

"Alright. Who's going to be the first victi...I mean "person" to share their poem with the class?"

Mr. Weber's 1st period Language Arts class looked down into their laps almost in unison. Looking directly at the teacher was a sure-fire way to get called on - or at least that is what every student in the last one hundred years was led to believe.

"Hmm, imagine that. No takers. I guess I'll have to call on someone. But who? Hmm...Dana Hutchins."

The rest of the class collectively relaxed their shoulders.

"Dana, who do you want to read their poem first?"

Shoulders immediately re-tightened as most of the students immediately tried to make eye contact with Dana and silently beg her not to pick on them. Mr. Weber chuckled at the nonsense of it all.

"Um, I think...that Jack should go first, Mr. Weber," said Dana - a few sighs of relief easily heard.

"Excellent choice, Dana. Jack? You're up, buddy."

Jack lifted himself reluctantly out of his desk, grabbed his poem and headed to the front of the class. It was way too early in the morning for something like this. Today was an "odd day" at school and it meant that periods and classes were reversed, so Jack had Language Arts first period instead of last period like he did on "even days." It helped to break up the monotony of having the exact same schedule day after day. Most of the kids liked it, including Jack, but he wasn't exactly happy with it right now, having to get up in front of the class the very first period of the day.

"What's the title of your poem?" asked Mr. Weber.

"Um, it's called 'Without You'."

"Great. Let's hear it. Nice and loud for the back row to hear, please."

Jack cleared his throat and scanned the poem for a couple of seconds before he began.

"Without You"

Without you
I'm lost
Like a clown without an audience
Painted for a performance
That will never be
Without you
I'm frightened
As frightened as a balloon
Floating away from the hand
Of a loving child
Without you
I'm lonely
Like the last person
On the last day
Watching the last sunset
Without you
I'm unsure
As unsure as a boy
Writing a poem
For the first time
Without you

Jack looked up from his paper to find all the students in the class staring at him. He stared back, not knowing what else to do, not knowing what to expect. And then came the applause. Every student in class was clapping. He turned to look at Mr. Weber, and he was clapping, too. A tiny smile, almost too tiny for anyone to see, appeared on Jack's face.

The clapping died down allowing Mr. Weber to speak. "Fabulous, Jack. Just fabulous. Your use of repetition and simile really helped to capture the emotion of the piece vividly. Do you mind if I ask who the speaker of the poem was addressing his words and feelings to?"

Jack thought about that for a moment. "Well, when I wrote it, I was kind of thinking of my dad, so I guess the speaker is talking to a father figure, but as I read it more and more, I kinda believe that the speaker is almost talking to himself. I don't know if that makes any sense, but it is just feels right to me."

"That's the beautiful thing about poetry, Jack: it can have different meanings for different people based upon their own experiences. Poetry is a window to the soul for both the writer and the reader. There may be universal experience within the writing but there is also room for individual interpretation. The same holds true for music and art. Thanks for sharing this with us. Great job." Some of Jack's classmates chimed-in with agreement as he made his way back to his seat.

"Okay, Jack was the first," Mr. Weber said turning towards everyone else. "Who's up next? And looking down to avoid my gaze will only make things worse."

Shoulders stiffened.

Chapter 9

April 1, 2010

If Jack thought the outside of Howl House was strange and creepy, the inside certainly did not disappoint in that regard, either. The first thing that struck him when they entered the front door was the heaviness of the air, thick and stale with forgotten age. It smelled like an old carriage house or barn - the animals long gone but their smell remaining. And although all the boys had flashlights, the innate darkness of the space seemed to hold any light in submission, only allowing a small amount of illumination. The front doors opened into what looked like a living room space, minus any furniture. There were stairs to the immediate left leading up to the second floor, but there were huge gaps and missing boards making it obvious that climbing them was not in one's best interest. On the far right appeared to be a narrow hallway, but it was way too dark to discern anything else about it. There seemed to be an unnatural stillness lurking in its shadows, as if some otherworldly entity was waiting patiently to pounce.

After everyone entered, Billy closed the door. "Ah, home away from home. What do you think of the place, Jack?"

"Not really sure what to think, Billy, but I am wondering what the attraction is. Why do you guys even come here?"

"Good question. Let me answer it by asking you a question. Why did you come here?"

"Um, you brought me here," Jack said, surprised at the weirdness of the question.

"Wrong. You're here because you're curious."

"Yeah, okay...but I don't get the point."

Billy started walking around the room, his flashlight casting a harsh glow on and around his face.

"The point is Jack that we all came here for the same exact reason: curiosity. Do you feel the energy in this place? Only certain people are drawn to it. It calls out to those who crave to know more...to want more...to be more. Kind of like lacrosse, Jack. You had never even played the game before you came to Barnaby Hills, but you were curious about it. Curious enough to come to tryouts and make it onto the team. And the way you play makes you a winner. In fact, every one of us here is a winner, Jack. We are the best of the best. I'll be honest; at first I didn't think you had it in you. I thought you were just another one of those "nobodies" that we go to school with. But seeing how you play lacrosse convinced me; you've got the spirit in you."

"Spirit. What spirit?" What are you talking about?"

Billy's eyes grew wide and the tone of his voice changed from pompous and egocentric to reverent. "What do you know about lacrosse, Jack - its origins and history?"

"I think the game was first played by Native Americans hundreds of years ago, right?"

Billy nodded in agreement. "Yes, that's true, but it wasn't just a game, Jack, like it is now. When the Europeans came, they changed it to the watered-down sport we play today. But when it was played by the Native Americans, it was raw, wild and beautiful in its chaos - almost spiritual. Participants would paint their faces and bodies to strike fear in their opponents. Matches could last for days and the possibility of mortal injury was ever-present...often intended. It was because of this that tribal shamans would bestow blessings on players and the sticks that they used prior to games. They would often beseech the spirits of nature to enter the souls of the young men of the tribe. Some of these spirits represented the elements - earth, air, water, fire - others represented animals. Animals, Jack."

All of the boys were completely silent and completely transfixed by Billy's words at this moment. Howl House was no longer a house, but more like a place of worship and Billy was the pastor proselytizing to his flock.

"What animal was revered by many Native American tribes, Jack?"

Jack sighed. "You know, Billy, if I knew there was going to be a quiz tonight, I would have studied for it. C'mon, what's with all the weird questions? You said that we were coming here to see something cool. What's going on?"

Billy smiled. "Don't fret, Jackie. You will see something cool. We're just getting to the good part."

Chapter 10

April 5, 2011

"Lunch time at Barnaby Hills Middle School. More like feeding time at the zoo," Chris joked as he looked around the cafeteria.

"Yeah, it does get kind of crazy," agreed Jack.

"What are you eating today?"

"Your basic roast beef and cheese sandwich with mayo. What about you?"

"Mom's famous meatloaf leftovers."

"Famous, huh? Can I get an autograph - from the meatloaf, I mean."

"Dude, don't joke about the meatloaf, alright? It's the bomb."

"Don't worry; your mom's meatloaf is safe from my lunchtime buffoonery," laughed Jack.

Both boys dug into their bags and pulled out the day's eats. Lunch time at the middle school was usually loud - too many kids in too small of a space - but it was an important time of day. Beyond fueling up with food, some students used it as a place to finish homework or to study for exams. Others reveled in spending time with friends and unwinding from academics for a little while. What was really interesting about it was how students divided themselves up in the space. Human beings are generally creatures of habit and comfort and this really showed itself to be true when everyone made their way into the lunch room and went immediately to familiar tables and friends. It was a rare occasion to see anyone wander away from where they traditionally sat or to spend time with anyone else except their preferred lunch buddies. And that is why everyone within view of Jack and Chris was surprised when Sarah Bartley came over and sat down next to them.

"Hi, Jack."

"Um, hi, um, Sarah," he managed to get out with a mouthful of sandwich.

"Do you mind if I have lunch with you?"

Jack glanced quickly over at Chris who was just staring at Sarah, eyes wide with nervous disbelief.

"Uh, no. Sure. Take a seat."

Sarah sat down and started taking out her lunch.

"Sarah, do you know Chris...from the lacrosse team?" Jack asked, trying to rack his brain for something to say - anything to say.

"Hi, Chris."

Chris stared at Sarah dumbfounded until Jack kicked him under the table until he managed a weak "Hello." Sarah smiled and turned her attention back to Jack.

"Well, Jack?"

"Well what?"

"What we were talking about this morning...getting together after school..."

At first when Sarah came over and sat down, Jack was completely surprised, but now, with her talking about their conversation in the morning, he was completely panicked. Chris was sitting right next to him and now he would know that he and Sarah had been chatting earlier. This was not good, not good at all. He had to reign in this situation fast or Chris would just assume the worst.

"Geez, I guess banging my head on the locker this morning really knocked a couple of screws loose. I don't remember. Did we talk?"

"Earth to Jack! You are so nutty. I said that I wanted to hang out and show you one of the cheers we've been learning. You said that you couldn't because you had to help your mom and I said we should talk about a day when we could get together. Remember???"

"Oh, yeah, I remember. Um, I definitely can't get together today or tomorrow or even the day after. I'm really busy at home, but I bet that...Chris is free! Yeah, I bet he would love to hear one of the cheers. Wouldn't you, Chris?"

These words penetrated Chris' brain loud and clear and he quickly turned his attention from Sarah to Jack.

"What?" he replied in crazed disbelief.

"Wouldn't you like to get together with Sarah...and hear one of the new cheers?"

"I...I...I..." Chris stuttered.

"That's okay," Sarah cut in. "We can talk about it another time. It was rude of me to interrupt you guys when you were hanging out. I'm so weird like that sometimes. I see Donna on the other side of the cafeteria. We can talk at another time. You guys take it easy."

"No problem. Take care, Sarah," Jack said with a relieved smile.

As she walked away from the table, Chris followed her with eyes, but his mouth seemed to be stuck on the same utterance from before.

"I...I...I...can't believe that Sarah Bartley just sat down with us. I'm still shaking. Why didn't you tell me you spoke with her before?"

Jack thought quickly. "I didn't have a chance to tell you. Actually, I was hoping something like this would happen so I could act as a middleman between you and her, to get things rolling between the two of you."

Jack hated lying to his friend, but this was one of those times when a small lie was worth more than a huge blowout. But Jack was still unsure as to how his this would all play out in Chris' mind. Would he accept it or call Jack on it. It all depended on what he remembered about the conversation that just took place.

"Wow, thanks, Jack. I appreciate you trying. Geez. I think I have to go to the bathroom and throw some water on my face. I'll be right back."

"Hey, don't worry about it. Go ahead; take your time."

As Chris walked towards the boy's restroom, Jack stood up a little to look across the cafeteria and find out where Sarah was. Over in the far corner, almost out of sight, Jack saw her talking with Billy. This was bad. Really bad.

Chapter 11

April 1, 2010

Jack took a second to get a handle on what was happening. He was in a creepy, old abandoned house at midnight in the middle of the woods with a group of crazy boys led by a maniac who was quizzing him about lacrosse and Native American history. Okay...

"Well, Jack? What animal did they revere?"

"Um, I don't know. The bison."

Billy made a buzzing sound, like when a contestant gets a question wrong on a gameshow.

"OH, I'm sorry, Jack. That is not the right answer. Would you like to try again?"

Jack fumed. "Alright, enough, Billy. Is this what you brought me out here for? One of your stupid games? And here I thought you were being sincere about wanting to be friends. How could I be so stupid? I swear; if I had known that was your plan I would..."

Billy interrupted Jack. "The wolf. The wolf, Jack. Native American legends going back hundreds and hundreds of years tell of the wolf - its strength, courage and loyalty."

"Okay, great - strength, courage, loyalty - I get it. What's the point?" Jack asked impatiently.

"Some native legends from around this area tell of epic lacrosse matches when the moon was full and players being so overcome with the spirit of the wolf that they transformed, literally, into wolves. These individuals were known as Moonwalkers. They were fierce and hungry, and the matches raged on through the moonlit night with wild, natural abandon. Lacrosse the way it was meant to be!"

Billy's eyes were almost on fire now as he spoke.

"Can you imagine that, Jack...playing lacrosse under a glorious full moon, filled with the spirit of the wolf...to be a Moonwalker?" In unison, Billy and the rest of the boys started howling and yelping, their yells reverberating through the darkness of the house, breathing strange, new life into its stagnant walls.

Jack looked around at each of the boys bellowing before him. When the noise died down, a smile broke out on his face.

"Okay, I get it now. Good one, guys. Let's initiate the new kid and try to scare the pants off of him. Clever. Where is the camera? Is this going to be on YouTube within the hour? Nice. I'll give you guys some credit. Walking in the woods at night was creepy enough, but bringing me to this house and telling the Moonwalker story...near genius. Howl House? They should have one of these at Disney."

Billy looked sternly at Jack. "Don't disrespect Howl House, Jack. It lies on sacred ground. The very ground where transformations have taken place for uncounted years. Howl House is but one structure of many that has occupied this space over time. Show respect for that which you don't yet understand."

Jack's face took on a more serious tone and he nodded his head slightly in agreement, but within a matter of seconds began laughing loudly from his gut.

"You guys are too much! This is awesome. How long did it take to plan this out? Please, no more. It can't get any better than this."

As Jack laughed, Lucas looked at his watch. "Billy, it's almost time."

Billy smiled and started laughing lightly with Jack. "You liked this, Jack? That's good. But believe me, it gets much better than this. Much better..."

Chapter 12

April 7, 2011

Before he knew it, it was Friday afternoon. Jack was slowly skateboarding home from school and mulling over all the events that transpired recently. Although the early part of this week was rough, Thursday and Friday had turned out to be good days. Even yesterday's lacrosse practice seemed to go off without a hitch. Billy and his boys kept to themselves and Sarah was involved with the other cheerleaders. It was as if nothing had happened. Jack knew better, of course, and kept his eyes and ears open, but there weren't any problems to contend with. He didn't know how long this little ceasefire would last, but with the moon waning and almost another month until it was full again, Jack had to use this time wisely to figure things out.

It was obvious for a while now that Billy had designs on Chris and was willing to do anything to get to him - even destroy Jack. The ambush in Chris' backyard was certainly just a preview of what was to come. It would seem that Billy had gotten Sarah involved in this mess, too. She was most likely an unknowing pawn, but her involvement could have dire consequences if Jack wasn't careful. Another person in this that definitely didn't have a clue was Chris. He was oblivious to all the deceptions taking place. Billy was undoubtedly trying to take advantage of his naiveté, especially when it came to the manipulation of Sarah, but Chris was a bright kid and Jack didn't know how much longer this house of cards would stand before coming down. Time would tell but Jack couldn't wait around while the clock was ticking. He had to think things through and a leisurely ride home on his skateboard to clear his head was just what the doctor ordered.

"JACK!"

The distant voice made its way into Jack's busy brain and he turned around to see who was calling.

"JACK, WAIT UP!"

It was Chris, running down the block. It took a moment but he finally came to a panting stop next to his friend.

"I've been calling out to you for a couple blocks..."

"Oh, sorry, dude. I'm in the zone. Got a lot on the brain and was in my own world. What's up?"

"What are you doing tonight?"

"Nothing really. Maybe jump on the computer, play some games, eat some junk and catch up on sleep. You know, the perfect night."

Chris laughed. "Sounds like a regular vacation. How about coming to the movies with me instead?"

"The movies? I don't know."

"Come on. That new horror movie is out and it looks awesome."

Jack smiled. "Horror, huh? Nah..."

"What's the matter - afraid?"

"More than you know."

"I'll protect you from the big, bad monsters, Jack. Come on. Please..."

Jack didn't know whether to laugh or cry from the irony of it all. He looked at Chris' desperate but friendly face and knew there was only one answer to give.

"Okay. I guess I'll go..." he said with a comically overemphasized sigh.

"Yes! You're the best, Jack. The movie starts at 7:20. What time do you want to meet up?"

"I'll meet you in front of the movie theater at 7. Sound good?"

"Yeah, dude. That is perfect. Just enough time to buy the tickets and get some popcorn. Alright, I gotta run home and get some things done before the movies. I'll catch you at 7."

"You got it."

The boys parted company and Jack started up on his skateboard again. Maybe a horror movie would take his mind off the horror in his own life right now. Maybe...

Chapter 13

April 1, 2010

"I don't know about the rest of you, but I've had as much fun as I can stand for one night. Thanks for the laughs," Jack said trying to keep a straight face. "Time to go home."

"But Jack, we still have one more thing to show you. And this, "Billy assured, "is the cherry on the top of everything."

Jack widened his eyes with faux surprise. "Something better than what I've experienced so far? That's hard to believe."

Billy chuckled. "You're a good sport, Jack. I'll admit, I didn't think much of you at first and really had my doubts about bringing you here, but a little convincing goes a long way. I can see that you've got the right stuff - talent, curiosity, biting sarcasm... You're gonna fit right in."

"Convincing? Who did the convincing?"

For a half a second, the grin on Billy's face receded. "Me, of course. A little self-talk, that's all," Billy quickly changed the subject. "So, are you ready for the showcase of the evening, Jack?"

"You know what? The sooner we get this over with, the sooner I get to go home. Yeah, what you got? Bring it on."

"Great attitude, Jack." Billy turned back to the rest of his gang. "You hear that boys? Jack is ready, willing and able. Let's do this! Lucas take the lead. Flashlights off."

All the boys let out a howl, turned off their lights and followed Lucas into the dark hallway on the right. Billy nodded for Jack to follow.

Jack looked towards the hallway. "Why aren't we using our flashlights? It's as dark as night down there."

"Don't worry, Jack. We know our way around here with our eyes closed. When we are in Howl House, we use all our senses, not just the ones that human logic dictates."

"What are you talking about?"

"You'll see. This is like no other place you've ever experienced. I guarantee that when we are done tonight, you will not be the same person who walked in. Just keep an open mind. Can you do that?"

"If I didn't have an open mind, I wouldn't be here, but that doesn't mean I want to trip and break my neck in a dark hallway."

"There's nothing to fear down that hallway, Jack. Just follow the others and you'll be fine. And besides, I'll be right behind you all the way."

"Is that supposed to make me feel better?" Jack asked cynically.

Billy responded in kind. "Does a wolf howl at the full moon?"

Jack shook his head and turned to follow the group as they started to disappear into the passageway. Just as he was about to take his first step into the darkness, he had the urgent feeling to leave, to not say a word and just walk away from the whole thing. But he wasn't going to let Billy and his boys get the best of him and spread stories around Barnaby Hills about "Chicken Jack" and how he was spooked by a walk in the woods at night. Nope. That wasn't going to happen. Jack could take care of himself. He could play Billy's game and not come out on the losing end. But as he looked down into the dark hallway that had completely enveloped all the other guys, he wondered if this was all worth it.

As if privy to his thoughts, Jack heard Billy say behind him, "Keep an open mind."

Jack took a deep breath, turned off his flashlight and slowly pushed himself into the blackness.

Chapter 14

April 7, 2011

Jack arrived at the movie theater ten minutes early. His mom had offered to drop him off, but he chose to walk and get some more alone time with his thoughts. As he rounded the corner, he saw a few people milling about underneath the movie marquee. Chris wasn't there yet, so he sat down on the hood of a nearby parked car to wait. A couple of classmates passed by and wished him luck on Sunday's lacrosse game. With all that had been going on recently, Jack hadn't spent too much time thinking about the first game of the season. Physically, he was in great shape and ready for whatever the Centerville team could throw at him, but mentally, his mind just wasn't focused on the game and he felt unbalanced, which is pretty much how he felt all year long - not a great feeling, by any means. But as unsure as Jack may have been feeling personally, he knew the team was ready. Billy and the rest of his gang were good to go, no surprises there, The other boys on the team, not part of Billy's crew, were okay - not the best players but not the worst, either. They could be counted on to jump into a game and hold it steady while some of the better players got some needed rest on the sidelines. The biggest surprise, however, had to be Chris. Sure, he had made the team last year and did the best he could, but there wasn't really anything special to his style of play. That wasn't the case anymore. Based on how he was performing at practice, this could be the year that Chris became the breakout star of the lacrosse team. His feet and hands seemed like they were on fire. He was moving himself and the ball down the field with a purpose and dexterity that wasn't evident last year. It was great to see him up his game and play with such determination. And that was probably why

Billy was after him. He was proving himself a valuable asset to the team, which in turn made him valuable to Billy. The whole thing was almost too insane to fathom.

"Dude!"

Jack turned around to see Chris running across the street.

"Did you get here early?"

"Yeah," smiled Jack. "Even when I try to be late, I can't do it."

"You psyched for the movie?"

"I'm psyched for hangin' out with you. The movie? Not so much."

Chris laughed. "Just you wait. It's gonna scare the pants off you. You'll go home tonight and lay wide awake under the covers thinking that every sound you hear is the Beast coming to get you."

"Great. Just what I want," Jack smirked.

"C'mon let's go get the tickets and some snacks before it gets too busy."

The boys walked into the lobby of the theater. There were long lines for both tickets and refreshments.

"Geez. Everyone in town must be going to see this movie tonight," Chris lamented. "How about I get in line for tickets and you get in line for snacks? That will save us a bunch of time and hopefully we won't get stuck sitting in the front row looking straight up at the screen."

"Sounds good."

Jack and Chris split up and got on their respective lines. Jack looked to see how many people were ahead of him. He almost wished that they had just waited on each line together. It was a bummer to wait on a line without anyone to talk to. Just as that thought arose in his mind, he felt a tap on his right shoulder.

"HI, Jack."

Jack turned and his eyes widened with surprise.

"Oh, uh, hi, Sarah."

"Are you here alone?"

"No, I'm, um, with Chris. He's getting tickets."

"Oh, okay. I didn't know you liked horror movies."

Jack took a quick look around for Chris. "Well, I really don't, but Chris asked me to come. Uh, what about you...who are you here with?"

"Some of the usual gang from school. You want to sit with us in the theater?"

"Oh, that sounds great, but I came with Chris, so I should just go find him."

"I see him right now."

"You do. Where?" Jack said nervously.

"He's over by the video games talking to Billy. Look."

Jack turned his head all the way to the left and saw Chris and Billy talking and looking over directly at him and Sarah.

"Oh yeah, I almost forgot," Sarah said while Jack was still turned towards his best friend and his worst enemy. "Thanks so much for that nice note you left in my locker about how much you really appreciate me being on the cheerleading squad. That was so sweet of you."

Catching some of what Sarah was saying, Jack started to turn back to her to ask what she was talking about when she leaned in and gave him a kiss on his cheek.

"Maybe we can hang out for a little while after the movie..." she said with a big smile as she backed away slowly. "Okay?"

"Uh...yeah," he responded robotically as his mind had a heated conversation with itself.

"What just happened?"

"I'm not sure."

"Was that a kiss - A KISS FROM SARAH BARTLEY?"

"It was definitely a kiss."

"OMG! CHRIS! DID CHRIS SEE IT? PLEASE TELL ME HE DIDN'T SEE IT!"

Jack cast a nervous glance around the lobby hoping against all hope that Chris did not just witness what took place. It happened so fast. If Chris saw the kiss, it would be hard to explain away. And why did she kiss him in the first place - something about a note in her locker? He didn't write any note. This had Billy's name all over it.

Jack continued looking for Chris. He didn't see him. Maybe he went to the bathroom or something and didn't see anything - a long shot, but a possibility. That's when he felt a stiff finger poke his back from behind.

"What was that?" asked the distressed voice.

Chris.

"Why was Sarah kissing you?

Jack turned to face his friend. "Dude, I'm just as surprised by that as you are. It came out of nowhere."

"Out of nowhere? Out of NOWHERE? How clueless do you think I am?

"Clueless? Chris, what are you talking about?"

"Every time I see you lately, Sarah's there. You tell me that it's nothing or you're trying to put in a good word for me. Well, isn't it obvious? You like her, Jack. And here all along, I've been sharing my feelings about her with you and I guess you just don't care. Why didn't you just tell me that you liked her instead of all this sneaking around? I thought you were my friend. I feel like such an idiot."

"I am your friend, Chris. There's no sneaking around. I don't like Sarah. I swear." Chris looked at Jack intensely, as if trying to read his mind to discern fact from fiction. He shook his head in disgust.

"Nope. I don't buy it. No more. Billy's right. You are trying to play me for a fool. I'm no one's fool, Jack. No more lies. I'm done." Chris turned away, heading to the exit doors of the movie theater.

"Chris! CHRIS! C'mon, man. This isn't what you think it is! Billy's behind this whole thing. He's playing you!"

As Jack watched his friend walk out of the theater, he turned and saw Billy. His friends were next to him and they were all pointing at Jack and laughing, but Billy just stood there staring, a slight smile on his face. Jack could almost hear his voice in his head. "Chris isn't the only one being played, Jackie-boy."

Chapter 15

April 1, 2010

Jack cautiously took his first steps into the hallway. It was so dark, he could barely see the boy just ahead of him. He held out his hands in front of his body, just in case he walked into someone...or something. More disturbing than the darkness was the dank smell that enveloped him - an odor akin to wet dog fur and rotting vegetables. The smell hung thickly about the air and Jack felt like he was tasting it more so than breathing it. And, to add just the right amount of old style Halloween creepiness to the whole thing, each step into the darkness was punctuated by almost supernatural groans from the old wooden floorboards. Jack wondered how the floor was strong enough to hold up the line of boys walking on it right now. Maybe it wasn't. Would they all find themselves crashing through the floor into the basement? And WHAT exactly would be in the basement of this place - rats, snakes, zombies? The horrific possibilities were endless and Jack's mind was willing to entertain them all.

"That's just what they want you to be, Jack: scared," he said to himself. *"Don't let them get to you. This is all part of their plan to make you out as a chicken so that Billy can walk around like a proud rooster. That's not gonna happen. You can take anything they dish out and give it right back to them. Just get through this stupidity and beat them at their own game. No problem."*

"Still with us, Jackie-boy?" Billy whispered from behind.

"Don't worry about me, Billy," Jack replied coolly.

"Oh, I'm not worried. I'm excited."

Jack snickered. "You must not get out very much."

"Good one, Jack. I like your sense of humor. Hold onto it.

You're going to need it."

Before Jack could respond, the line of boys came to a halt.

"We're here," Billy declared.

Ahead of them a door knob could be heard twisting slowly, grinding against age and rust. A loud click reverberated down the hall and Lucas began to push the door open. Jack strained his eyes in the darkness to see what was happening, but still couldn't see a thing. A new odor swept over his senses - a fragrant one, nothing at all like the foul scent of the hallway. This smell was warm, sweet and strangely inviting. He heard the boys start to walk into the now open room, but for some reason, he didn't follow them.

Billy urged Jack on. "What are you waiting for? You know you want to see what's in there. Don't you? You said so yourself. Don't back out now, Jackie-boy. Only fools wait for fate. Do what your inner spirit desires and reap the rewards."

Billy's voice took on a hypnotizing tone and Jack heard the words as if they were emanating from his own thoughts. Of course he was going in, wasn't he? He didn't have any second thoughts. He was going to follow the others. But if he was so sure, why wasn't he moving? The intoxicating, pleasant smell emanating from the room ahead seemed to be calling out directly to him.

"C'mon, Jack," Billy implored. "Be the man you want to be. The man you need to be. The man your father would have wanted you to be..."

"What? My father? What do you mean?" Jack managed to ask with some hesitation, his attention divided between his dream-like curiosity for what lay ahead and Billy's almost intuitive, mesmerizing words.

"We all see it, Jack. The daily struggle. Wanting to be the man of the family while trapped in a boy's body. I promise you what you find ahead will make you more than any man could ever be. Prove it to yourself. To your mother. TO YOUR FATHER. Take the next step, Jack. Take the next step and be one of us. Your true spirit is waiting to be unleashed."

Yes. Billy was right. It was hard. So hard. Not having his father around. Trying to be there for his mother. But also trying to be more than his age would allow him to be. It made sense. Lots of sense. But how did Billy know all of this and what could possibly be in that room that was going to make him feel better? He was so confused, but the room beckoned to him with possibility and promise. Could that be true? Once more, as if waiting patiently to respond to Jack's inner thoughts, Billy was there with a response.

"All will be answered. Just move forward. I cannot take you by the hand. You must enter of your own free will. But trust me; you will not be disappointed."

"All will be answered." Billy's words resounded in his brain. The soft, sweet scent was overwhelmingly compelling.

"All will be answered..."

With reality suspended for the moment, Jack abandoned the last bits of reason and inhibition holding him back and stepped forward into the room.

Chapter 16

April 8, 2011

Looking for Chris on the Saturday before the opening lacrosse game of the season was definitely NOT how Jack wanted to spend the day, but it had to be done. After Chris left the movie theater in a huff the night before, Jack ran out after him and tried to talk with him as he strode purposely home, but he had to give up trying halfway through because nothing he said had any effect on his friend - no acknowledgement at all. But this was exactly what he was afraid of happening when he realized Chris was on Billy's radar. Now he felt like they were nothing but marionettes in Billy's personal puppet show. Billy was not only the puppet master in this strange play, he was the writer, director and rapt audience.

Jack made his way up Batchelder Street on his skateboard. When he arrived at Chris' house, he kicked up his board into his hands and walked up to the front door and rang the bell. After a few moments, the door opened and Chris' mom appeared, a wide smile on her face.

"Hi, Mrs. Stiles. Is Chris home?"

"Oh, hello, Jack. I think he is upstairs in his room. Let me go tell him you're here. Just hold on a second."

"Thanks."

Jack turned and surveyed the area as he waited. Across the street were the woods that he traversed earlier in the week when he came to protect Chris from Billy and the gang. What had happened between then and now? How could he go from being Chris' protector to being his rival within the span of a few days? The world as he knew it had upended itself and he wasn't sure when it exactly took place.

As Jack's mind was delving into the situation, Chris' mother returned to the door.

"Jack, Chris says that he doesn't want to speak with you," she said with a confused expression. "Did something happen with you guys? I asked him what was up but he wouldn't tell me. This isn't like him."

Jack let out a sigh. "It's all a big misunderstanding, Mrs. Stiles. If Chris would just talk with me, I know I can straighten everything out."

"Well, he was pretty adamant about not talking with you. I'm sorry. Maybe if he has a little time to process what took place, he'll be more apt to work things out with you. Maybe even in time for the game tomorrow. I would hate for you guys to play the first game of the season not getting along."

Jack let out an audible sigh. "I appreciate your help. I'll give him some more time. Thanks, Mrs. Stiles."

"No problem. Good luck with the game tomorrow, Jack."

Chris' mom closed the door over and Jack stood on the front steps and contemplated what was said. Sure, they say time heals all wounds, but this wound was new and would only get bigger and bloodier. He needed to suture it up pronto but couldn't wait until tomorrow to patch things up. He needed to speak with Chris now. But how?

Chapter 17

April 1, 2010

The room was dark, but not quite as dark as the hallway. Jack could see his hands in front of him and the silhouettes of the other boys. There was a muted, almost alabaster glow that was coming from somewhere farther in the room that allowed slight distinctions to be made, but just barely. There was a shuffling of feet as the boys ahead of him started moving again. Jack followed. The wooden floor beneath began to feel as if it were sloping downward, as if they were now walking on a ramp. It was a strange, disconcerting feeling like walking on the gangplank of a wooden ship. As they continued, the wood beneath gave way to a dirt path. The white glow was becoming steadily brighter and Jack could tell the ceiling and walls around them no longer belonged to the house. They were made of dirt and rock. At some point in the journey, they must have traversed into the soil itself. They were now in an underground cave. Suddenly, the line began to split in front of him. Some boys moved to the left and some to the right. As they did, the light source became clearly visible for the first time. Before them was a hole in the ground - a foot in diameter - emanating a soft, white, liquid luminescence. It was the source of the sweet-smelling scent that Jack had experienced when the door to the room was first opened. Here it was in front of him and the odor was incredibly tantalizing. Billy's boys moved to the left and right to gather around the hole.

Billy came from behind Jack and stood next to him on his right side.

Jack looked around at the faces of the boys. They were all transfixed by the glowing liquid that lay before them. It cast a warm light that shimmered softly in the darkness of the underground cavern and the smell was so tempting - the smell of warm milk and cookies. It was intoxicating and all Jack wanted to do was to cup his hands and drink from it. It took just about every ounce of his will not to. He averted his eyes. Maybe if he didn't look at it, he would feel less tempted to act on his impulse. He looked over to his right. Billy was staring at him intently.

"Are you ready, Jack? Billy whispered with a wide grin on his face.

"Ready for what?

"For the best part of the night...for your life to change."

Chapter 18

April 8, 2011

"Chris! Chris!" Jack called up to the window, trying not to raise his voice too loudly to disturb Chris' parents.

After speaking with Chris' mom, Jack had walked around to the backyard of the house. If his friend wouldn't come to him, he would go to his friend.

"C'mon, Chris. Come to the window. We need to talk, dude."

Nothing.

Jack looked around the yard for some pebbles to throw at the window. He walked over to the playground set and started picking up some small, scattered stones. A foot or two away lay the broken slide that had fallen under Jack's weight earlier in the week when he had chased after Billy. It felt strange to see the slide laying on the ground rather than attached to a playset. It made Jack think of Chris but also the poem that he had just written for class, "Without You". His mind mulled over a new verse:

Without you I'm broken
Like a playground slide
Fallen to the ground
Waiting for someone to fix what should never need fixing

Why was he creating poetry at a time like this? Jack was pretty sure that Mr. Weber would say writing poetry at a time of crisis was exactly what he should be doing, but he shook his head a bit as if to ward away further thought on the subject. He picked up a few more rocks and turned toward the window. Chris was standing there, looking straight at him, steel-eyed, through the glass.

"Hey, Chris, we've got to talk. Would you come down for a little bit so we can straighten this all out?"

Chris continued to stare down from his bedroom. His face was expressionless and Jack couldn't detect any movement at all.

Jack continued. "I know you're upset and you think I've done something wrong, but I really haven't. I'm just as confused as you. If you would only give me a chance and listen to what I have to say, you'll see what I mean. Please?"

For a brief moment, it looked like Chris' gaze had wavered, as if he were contemplating his friend's words. He reached out to the window and pulled down the shade, shutting out any further conversation.

Jack was about to say something else, but just shook his head instead, grabbed his skateboard and walked around to the front of the house. He slowly rode down the long driveway letting gravity pull him towards the street rather than use his own power.

This was worse than Jack had expected. Chris was totally shutting him out. In contrast to what Mrs. Stiles said, this was not going to get better before the game tomorrow. Not by a long shot.

Chapter 19

April 1, 2010

"Brothers, we come here tonight to initiate a new member into our clan. He has shown himself to be a worthy warrior of ancestral lacrosse. His skill reflects the skill of the ancients, and now their spirit will be reflected in his spirit. He has chosen to reap the rewards of being one with the Earth and Moon, one with humanity and nature. Let the ancestors who join us tonight witness the strength of their legacy in him. Let the entanglements of our Earthly souls fall to the ground as we celebrate the rebirth of our new friend and brother..."

Billy's voice resounded throughout the underground cavern, his face lit up by the white hue of the liquid at their feet. All eyes were upon him, even Jack's. Whatever was taking place, albeit strange, was powerful and electric. The air was alive and forceful. Billy was tapping into something, something unseen yet resonating all around them.

"Jack, do you come here of your own free will?" Billy asked, lowering his voice to a measured, serious tone.

"Um, yeah, but I still don't know what is..."

Billy interrupted him.

"Let it be written in verbal lore that our brother comes to the clan of his own will."

All of the boys grabbed each other's hands and thrust them into the air, letting out a yelp, as if in agreement. When they lowered their arms, Billy began to untie something that was hanging around his neck. He unknotted a worn leather strap and pulled it up and out from under his shirt. It appeared to be a crystal vial of some sort. He knelt down by the glistening pool of white liquid, pulled off the top of the container and dipped it in, filling it to the top. He got back up and faced Jack.

"Jack, this is the transformational liquid of our forefathers - the Moonwalkers. Those who were brave enough to embrace the spirit of the wolf and the true warrior spirit of the ancient game of lacrosse. No one knows how the liquid came to be except for the shamans of old. Where we stand now is venerated ground. The elixir I hold in my hand is their legacy and has been guarded for generations and generations. It holds the key to unlocking humanity from bondage and releasing the natural animal instincts that reside within all of us but is only attainable by a few. You, Jack, are one of those few, one of the worthy. I call on you now, in the company of your brothers and the ancient spirits, to embrace your destiny and partake in the transformation from human to Moonwalker."

Billy held the vial out to Jack. The glowing elixir beckoned through the rustic glass. He felt himself being drawn mentally and physically into it as if he were becoming one with the substance. It was scary but exhilarating at the same time.

"Drink, Jack," Billy said.

Jack continued to stare intensely at the vial. "I don't know. This is all strange and confusing. I don't know what is happening here."

"What is happening," Billy responded, "is that you are on the verge of becoming something great but are chained to your own fears. Break free of that chain, Jack. Fulfill your destiny. All the answers to your questions are right here in this vial. Drink."

"I...just...need some more time to..."

"Drink, Jack. Trust me."

Jack forced his eyes away from the vial and he looked at Billy's face. His gaze was piercing and hot, reaching deep into Jack's psyche, mentally pushing him to partake in the liquid.

Jack reached out slowly, his hand trembling with confused anticipation. His fingers brushed against the vial. He had the momentary urge to pull his hand back, to forget all of this craziness and make a run for the woods, but he didn't. He grabbed the vial carefully yet firmly from Billy's hand and brought it closer. It was both warm and cool to the touch, as if physically embodying the same confusion and disparity that Jack was feeling at that exact moment. But beyond the glass, the liquid beckoned to him.

"Drink," Billy said softly. "All will be answered."

Jack slowly lifted the vial to his mouth, paused for a moment, and drank.

Chapter 20

April 9, 2011

The first game of a new lacrosse season. That could only mean the town of Barnaby Hills was knee-deep in lacrosse madness. There was still more than an hour to go before the start of the game but people had been arriving steadily to get the best seats possible. After all, Barnaby Hills was playing their yearly first-game rivals, Centerville, and the match was sure to be a good one - possibly a great one.

Jack was the first member of the team to arrive at the locker room. He liked to get to games earlier than anybody else; it gave him a chance to mentally prepare in solitude before the room filled with players and the usual pre-game noise. He also wanted to try and talk with Chris before the start of the game. Showing up at his friend's house the day before didn't quite work out as planned, so Jack figured the next best option was talking with him before the game - hopefully before Billy or anyone else showed up. But as the minutes passed, more and more people showed up. Every time someone new came into the locker room, Jack quickly craned his head to see if it was Chris, but it wasn't. Chris usually liked to get to games early, too, but not today. Jack figured that Chris was doing his best to avoid him at this point. He might not even show up until just before game time. Maybe they would have a chance to speak on the sidelines during the game. Maybe...

As he mulled things over in his brain, Jack heard a group of boys make their way into the locker room, laughing and joking loudly.

"So Chris yells out, '*How clueless do you think I am?*' right in the middle of the theater lobby and I swear I almost lost it. You are the man, Chris. Too funny."

Chris smiled as Billy gave him a friendly push.

"Don't mess with Chris, boys; you'll get your head handed to you." Billy laughed loudly.

At that moment, the group saw Jack sitting down by his locker looking over at them. Everybody stopped laughing, avoided his stare and started splitting up to go to their respective lockers. Only Chris and Billy remained. Chris lowered his gaze to the floor but Billy stared directly back at Jack with his almost ever-present grin. He whispered something into Chris' ear and then slowly turned to go to his locker.

Chris walked slowly towards Jack. Their lockers were close, so there was no way that they could avoid each other. It seemed like an eternity for Chris to finally reach his locker and open it.

Jack regarded his friend. He wasn't happy that Billy and Chris walked into the locker room making fun of him, but he knew he had to keep in mind that Chris was being manipulated by Billy. It wasn't his fault. Billy could be extremely persuasive. Jack knew that all too well.

"So, seen any good movies lately?" Jack said hoping to get any response at all from his friend.

"Is that supposed to be funny?" Chris asked in a serious tone, taking his equipment out of his locker.

"Well, I thought it was funny...until just about two seconds ago. Hey, listen, Chris. I'm sorry about the other night. You were right, not about me liking Sarah, but about me sneaking around and hiding things. Yeah, I had spoken to Sarah a couple of times during the week, and yeah, I didn't tell you about it, but that was because I didn't want you to flip out. I guess things didn't work out like I planned, huh?"

Chris began putting on his lacrosse gear without even acknowledging Jack's words or presence.

Jack continued in the uncomfortable silence. "Chris, you have to believe me; I have no interest in Sarah. In fact, nothing would make me happier than to see her with you. But Billy is turning this into something that it isn't. Billy just wants to..."

Chris slammed his locker shut and turned heatedly to Jack.

"Billy just wants to what? Huh, Jack? Why don't you leave Billy out of this! This is between me and you. If anything, Billy has been the only honest one throughout the whole thing. Everything he told me about you and Sarah is true. I've seen it all unfold with my own eyes."

Jack looked at him in disbelief. "You don't believe any of that. Do you?"

Chris turned his whole body to face Jack and leaned in closer.

"You stay out of my way, Jack. You won't be holding me down anymore. Not in lacrosse, not with Sarah, not with Billy and all the guys... We are teammates and nothing more. I've got new friends now and they don't hide things behind my back or tell me lies. In fact, Billy tells me that he can talk with Sarah and straighten her out about you. He said he would even put in a good word for me. That's what a REAL friend does. So don't sit near me today or try and talk with me again. Today is my day to shine on the field and I don't need you spoiling anything for me. Okay, Jackie boy?"

Chris' face was very close to Jack's now. He was breathing hard and his face was red with little beads of sweat dripping down his forehead. Jack looked intensely but not angrily at his friend. Somewhere under all that rage was his buddy, the Chris he knew as his best friend. But right now, all he could see in his friend's face was Billy - pure Billy.

Chapter 21

April 1, 2010

Jack lowered the vial from his lips. He stood absolutely still, looking down at the floor with his hands by his sides, waiting....waiting...

Nothing happened.

After a few more seconds, he slowly raised his head and looked around the cave at all the boys. They stared back at him silent and motionless - no smiles, no smirks, no emotion. Jack opened his mouth to say something when all of a sudden, his hands started shaking. He dropped the container to the ground. He lifted his hands and looked them over incredulously as if they were foreign objects being viewed for the first time. Just when it seemed that the shaking was about to subside, he brought both of his hands to his stomach and he held his abdomen tightly. Something was horribly wrong. He immediately cast a frightened glance at Billy and managed to sputter out, "What is happening to me?"

Billy smiled.

Jack began moving his hands from his lower abdomen up to his chest as if tracking the discomfort he was feeling. This continued up to his neck and he began to sputter and make throaty noises like a cat on the verge of throwing up a hairball. His mouth was closed but his cheeks began to balloon out, filling up with whatever his body was rejecting. He put his hands to his lips to try and stop it from coming out, but he couldn't contain it any longer. He lurched forward, opened his mouth and a huge stream of laughter poured forth from deep within.

Uncontrollable laughter.

The guffaws were so intense that Jack fell to his knees and put both his hands on the ground to steady himself. His howls filled the cavern and echoed all around.

Billy and the rest just watched in silence as Jack rocked back and forth on his knees, his whole body heaving up and down with each outburst.

As his laughter finally began to die down, Jack began struggling to catch his breath and get up off his knees. Billy reached down as if to help him but grabbed the vial instead.

"Ha-ha, Jack. Thought you pulled one over on us, huh?" he smiled as he tied the crystal container around his neck.

Jack tried to speak between breathing and chuckling. "Well...you know...I thought the situation called for some...laughter...hey...I'll admit that the whole thing was kind of...hypnotic and all...the backstory...cave under the house...the liquid...which tastes pretty good...by-the-way...and I was definitely falling for all of it...for a while there....you should become a psychiatrist or hypnotist or something...Billy...you put on a good show...so convincing...props to you..."

"But I guess not convincing enough," Billy said nonchalantly.

Jack rubbed some spit and elixir residue off his bottom lip. "Nah, I guess not. Sorry."

Standing next to Billy, Lucas looked down quickly at his watch and whispered to Billy, "It's time."

Jack continued talking as he bent down and started brushing dirt off his pants where his knees had hit the floor of the cave. "Don't get me wrong, Billy. I appreciate all the effort it must have taken for you to put this together. I totally see why these guys follow you the way they do. You are a riot..."

"Sorry to cut you off, Jackie-boy," Billy interrupted, "but you may want to stop what you're doing right now and take a look around you."

"Just one more second as I get this last bit of dirt and I'll be right with you. Don't tell me that you have something else to show me. How can you top all of this?"

Jack finished wiping off the dirt and stood up to see Billy put his finger to his mouth.

"Shh...wait for it."

That is when Jack and all the others clutched at their throats for real.

3rd Quarter

"Oh, yes, the Wolf is bad, it's true;
But how with-out him could we do?
If there were not a wolf, what good
Would be the tale of Riding Hood?"

Oliver Herford

Chapter 1

April 9, 2011

"BARNABY HILLS!" screamed the crowd in unison as the team's cheerleaders whipped them into a frenzy, physically recreating the letters of the school's name.

"SAY IT AGAIN! WHAT DOES THAT SPELL?"

"BARNABY HILLS!"

The "call and response cheer" was new this season - most likely one of the cheers that Sarah wanted to show Jack the other day - but he didn't even get a chance to hear it being performed at the first game. He was standing right on the sidelines with the rest of the team watching it, but his eyes and mind were focused on other things. The cheers, the crowd, the very game itself were far removed from his attention. Everything that happened within the last week had moved at lightning speed and he was having a hard time catching up. He felt dizzy and disoriented.

"Jack."

He knew that Billy wanted Chris to become part of the wolf pack, but he was blindsided by just how far he would go to make that a reality.

"Jack!"

But as bad as the past week had been, he knew that the next few weeks would be even harder still. He would have to rethink everything, figure out what he was doing right and wrong and then rethink it all over again.

"JACK!"

"Huh, what?" said Jack finally hearing his name.

It was Mr. Weber. "Jack. C'mon. Where are you, buddy? Time to play. Go take your position."

Jack looked around. The rest of the starting players were on the field already. "Sorry, coach," Jack said as he quickly put on his helmet and rushed out.

"Keep your head in the game, Jack!" Mr. Weber yelled behind him.

Jack joined the rest of his team and took up one of the attack positions. Billy looked over at him and joked loud enough for him to hear. "Penny for your thoughts." Lucas started chuckling.

It was tough but Jack chose to ignore them and brought his attention midfield for the face-off.

"Head in the game, Jack," he said, trying to compose himself. *"Head in the game."*

A moment later, the referee blew the whistle and the game began in earnest with both midfielders pushing against one another to wrangle first control of the ball. Being the first to gain possession of the ball really set the tone for the opening game of the season - for the teams and the fans. The Barnaby Hills side of the field was sure to go absolutely nuts if they gained possession first.

Jack hunkered down in his stance and strengthened his center of gravity. If the ball came his way, he wanted to make sure he was ready. A Centerville defender was nearby, but a quick pivot and push off on his left foot would allow him to shake off his opponent, scramble up the nearest sideline and get him deeper into the zone. From there he could pass the ball back to one of the midfielders or over to Billy or Lucas. If he had the room, he could even make his way towards the goal and take the first shot at the net. Although it was tempting in a game to keep the ball to oneself and try to score the most points, it didn't make the most sense. Lacrosse was a very physical game with little down time on the field. Players were in constant motion and by the time the first quarter was over, many were already exhausted and in desperate need of water and a quick rest. A good coach knew how to read his players and swap them out as needed during a game to stop them from physically over-exerting themselves. If a midfielder or attack player tried to hog the ball too much and gain themselves some glory, they would certainly tire quickly and not be playing at their best. Acting like a selfish superstar in lacrosse was counterproductive to everyone. The best way to win and advance in the standings was to play as a well-oiled team. Mr. Weber knew this, as did all the players. As he would often say (with audible but good-natured groans from the team), "There is no 'i' in lacrosse." And even though things were bad between Jack and Billy (and now Chris), they would never stop being a team on the field. Or so Jack thought...

Chapter 2

April 1, 2010

The pain was finally subsiding. Jack lay absolutely still on the floor, barely able to process where he was or what had happened. He was acutely aware of one thing, however; he needed to breathe. RIGHT NOW! It was a burning urge to fill his lungs like he had never done so before. But something was wrong, almost out of place. It felt as though a tremendous, invisible boulder was pushing on his chest, preventing him from taking air into his body. He opened his eyes, but everything above him was hazy and indistinct. He tried to roll his body to the side, to use his arms and legs to get up, to catch the breath that was desperately eluding him.

And then it came.

A rush of sweet, sweet air coursed its way through his mouth and down through his windpipe, filling his lungs with unimaginable relief. His chest heaved up and down with each gigantic breath. The weight was lifted and his entire body awakened immediately as every cell of his being was bathed and nourished in fresh oxygen. He instinctively pushed himself off of the ground and stood upright, arms spread widely as if basking in the glow of newly found strength and vigor. Without a hint of expectation or forethought, he thrust his head upward and burst into a strange, uncontrolled scream. But what came out of his mouth wasn't his voice. It was the howl of an animal, both a natural and unnatural sound to his ears - coming from within him but at the same time not belonging to him. And to make matters worse, his was not the only howl echoing all around within the cavern. He lowered his eyes and slowly looked around in the dim light of the cave. Reality was coming rapidly into focus now and what he saw was too unreal and horrific for words. What had been a group of middle school boys milling about only moments before was now a pack of creatures - wolves in clothing, to be exact - standing on their hind legs and howling with all their might at the cave ceiling.

A nightmare. He was asleep and this was a nightmare. Time to wake up NOW. He rubbed desperately at his eyes to banish the image from his sight and felt coarse hair on his eyelids, not the usual soft skin of his hands. He opened his eyes and saw two large paws covered in thick brown fur with long claws protruding from the ends of what should have been his fingers. His first impulse was to shake them off of his hands. He tried to do so wildly but they wouldn't budge. They were his and were attached to his arms. HIS ARMS! THEY WERE COVERED IN FUR, TOO! WHAT HAPPENED TO HIS ARMS?

Sheer and utter panic set in. Dizzy and feeling as if he were going to pass out, Jack fell down upon one knee and steadied himself with his hands (PAWS!) on the ground. His mind and thoughts were speeding along like an out of control freight train on rusted tracks. If he could just wake up, everything would be alright. Everything would be back to normal...

Two sneakers walked into his field of view and planted themselves directly in front of him.

"Get up, Jack," said a gruff voice. "Time to embrace the new you."

Jack's eyes started to scan upwards from the person's feet to their legs. He stopped there for a moment. He didn't want to get up but knew he had to. As much as he wanted this to be a dream, he could tell it wasn't. He had to find out what this all was and that meant facing it head on. He got up off his knee and raised his head completely. Standing in front of him was a wolf, smiling. Hanging around its neck was the crystal vial.

"Cool, huh?" the smiling wolf said.

"Billy?" croaked Jack in a voice that sounded like a pit bull going through puberty.

"The one and only. But if I had a mirror up to your face right now, Jackie, you'd find it hard to tell the difference between the two of us."

"What just happened? How did it happen? Why are we..."

Billy cut him off. "Plenty of time for questions later. Take a minute for yourself. Look all around and let it soak in. But just a minute. Clouds are due to roll in later and put an end to your "birthday party." We only have a little time tonight."

Jack swallowed some saliva to clear his throat. "Time for what?"

Billy's eyes glowed bright orange as a toothy, malevolent smile drew itself across his furry face. "For lacrosse, of course. The way it was meant to be played, Jackie-boy. The way it was meant to be played."

Chapter 3

April 9, 2011

"Jack, what's happening out there? It's like you're moving in slow motion. What's going on?"

Jack, still trying to catch his breath, looked quizzically at Mr. Weber. Couldn't he see what was going on with his own eyes? Not only was he not moving in slow motion, he was busting his butt to help win the game - problem was that his teammates weren't on the same page.

"Coach, I'm doing everything I can; I swear. No one is passing me the ball."

"They're not passing you the ball because you're not open. You've lost your zip today. No speed, no pivot power. This is totally not like you."

Jack's eyes opened wide in amazement. "Coach, I'm tellin' you; Billy and Lucas are playing the game without me. Even some of the middies have been holding back on shooting me the ball when I'm open. I'll prove it to you."

"No need. You're on the bench. Take a rest and we'll see what you can do later." He looked down the row of players. "Chris, get ready; you're in for Jack."

"But coach..."

"Bench...NOW!"

Jack did as he was told and grabbed a seat, all the while shaking his head in disagreement. He turned his gaze and caught sight of Chris gathering up his gear to join the game. Chris looked over at the same time and cut Jack a quick smirk as if to say "*My turn now, Jackie.*"

The referee signaled for both teams to come to the field for the second quarter. Billy and his boys crowded around Chris and patted him on the helmet and shoulders in congratulations as they made their way out. Billy turned around quickly and smiled. Anyone in the stands who caught the grin would have thought nothing about it - a middle school kid happy to play lacrosse. But Jack knew it meant so much more. This was Billy acknowledging that he was winning. That he could manipulate the play of a game to reach his own warped objectives. That he could ostracize Jack from the team and from the coach and fill his absence with his new lacrosse protégé - Chris. This was Billy letting Jack know that his days were numbered and that the next full moon would solidify all his plans for Chris...and him.

Jack's stomach started churning from the anxiety of it all. He got up from the bench and walked over to Coach Weber.

"Jack, I don't want to hear any more about..."

Jack cut him off. "Not that, Coach. My gut doesn't feel too good. You could be right. Maybe I'm not playing well because I'm not feeling great or something. I'm gonna head over to the locker room. I don't want to get sick here in front of everybody. Is that okay?"

"Oh, okay, Jack. That sounds like a smart move. In fact, why don't you pack up your gear and head on home. No use sticking around here if you aren't feeling well. Go on. We'll be okay without you today. Billy and Chris will help to make sure of that."

Jack looked out on the field just as the referee whistled for the start of the second quarter.

"Yep, don't I know it," he said under his breath.

Chapter 4

April 1, 2010

Jack followed Billy and the gang as they made their way out of the cave. He barely had any time to process what was taking place, but the immediate reality was crystal clear: he was a wolf. A wolf that was running on two legs, wearing clothes and sneakers, no less. He guessed he was more like a wolf/human hybrid - a werewolf. What Billy had called a Moonwalker. But how? The liquid in the vial? How could that be? So many insane questions to ask, and the answers were sure to be even more insane. But he couldn't even ask any questions right now. After his "transformation," Billy said that they were going to play lacrosse. He just turned and left and everyone followed without a word, without a sound. Jack had no choice but to join them. Crazy.

As he trailed behind everyone, he was amazed at the dexterity he had as he navigated his way through the dark. Before he was transformed, he had found making his way through the dim passageways of Howl House to be quite difficult. Now, he could see the other Moonwalkers in front of him as if the path was lit up from an undetected source of light, as if he were wearing night vision goggles. But this ability he now possessed was coming from him, not from an outward source. His eyes and his eyes alone were making it happen. In fact, all of his senses felt heightened and pumped to an extreme. He could literally taste the air, distinguish a handful of different odors, feel the earthy vibrations resonating around him, and hear everything with crystal clarity. It was incredible and overwhelming at the same time. If this was all a dream, it was certainly one for the record books. It was so mind-boggling that he didn't realize they had all arrived in the large living room of the house.

All the boys formed a semicircle around Billy who had opened a panel on one of the walls. He reached in and began to pass around out what appeared to be lacrosse sticks, but they were different from what the team normally used. These were made from wood not aluminum or lightweight carbon fiber. They were heavier and more solid. The head of the stick that had a pocket to scoop, catch, and throw the ball was broader and triangulated with interspersed leather straps to form the netting. These sticks were not made in a factory. They weren't mass-produced or perfected in any way. Some were slightly bent while others appeared to be made from different types of wood. They were of simple construction yet felt sturdy and powerful when grasped tightly in the hands. They obviously had been crafted individually and were very, very old.

"You are about to experience something incredible, Jack. Something that only a lucky few have ever experienced."

Billy's voice was gruff and guttural, as if he had been chewing on the tree bark that the sticks were made from.

"Lacrosse is an ancient game of skill and power. As a Moonwalker, you now have the power. The skill is yours to prove. Are you ready to join us, your Moonwalker brothers, and play the game of lacrosse the way it was meant to be played?"

Jack regarded Billy in the moonlight that filtered into the room through the dirty, cracked windows. This was too surreal to take in. He still wasn't sure what had taken place and why he now stood in a room full of werewolves gearing up to play a game of lacrosse in the moonlight of the forest, but the call of the outside

was too great, too overpowering to ignore. His reply was strangely simple.

"I'm here. I'm a wolf. Let's do this."

And with that, the entire group of Moonwalkers howled loudly in unison and exited the house in a fury of excitement, the full moon guiding them straight to a nearby clearing.

Chapter 5

April 9, 2011

"Jack, is that you?"

His mother called out from upstairs.

"Yeah, Mom. It's me."

"The game's over? That was quick. Did you win?"

Jack closed the door hesitantly behind him. For a second he thought about turning around and leaving. It wasn't because he didn't want to see or talk to his mom. He just wasn't prepared to answer any questions. His mind had been too preoccupied on the way home from the game to factor anything else in.

"Win? Um, not sure. I left early."

"Left early?" He could now hear his mother coming down the stairs.

"Um, yeah. I wasn't feeling too good. Stomach pains."

Jack's mom rounded the corner from the stairs into the living room. "Stomach pains?" she asked with concern as she walked over to him. "Like sick to your stomach kind of pain or something worse?" Her hand was now on his forehead probing for fever. If there was one thing that mothers could do well, it was distinguish a fever from the regular mass of heat that emanated from the bodies of their kids. The word "mom" is in therMOMeter for a reason.

"It's nothing bad, just a little upset stomach. Don't worry; it's not my appendix, stomach flu or that monster from *Alien* about to rip through my gut."

His mother chuckled. "You don't feel warm. That's good. Why don't you put down your lacrosse gear and lay on the couch for a bit. I'll get you something cool to drink - maybe some ginger ale. That helps upset stomachs. But I want you to sip it slowly." She started off for the kitchen but stopped and turned back towards Jack. "Oh, and by-the-way, if that alien did show its ugly head, it wouldn't stand two seconds against me."

Jack smiled. The first smile that he had all day.

"No doubt, Mom, no doubt."

"Okay, get yourself over to the couch, put your feet up and I'll be back in a jiff with the ginger ale."

"Thanks."

Jack put his lacrosse bag in the corner of the room and ambled over to the couch, plopping himself down as if the worry on his mind was literally weighted. He sank into the soft cushion. It felt good, so good that he wanted to continue sinking, all the way into the soft warmth and not come back up, at least not until all was right with the world. Was there ever a time when *all was right with the world*? Before last year, maybe? Back in San Francisco? He couldn't remember. But he doubted that there was ever a time in history when the world wasn't messed up in some fashion. This just happened to be his moment in time. His moment in the eternal struggle between good and evil. But man vs. wolf? Who had a road map to get him through this? Oh, not only was the world not right, it was spinning way out of control. Sinking and disappearing into the couch cushion was starting to look better and better.

His mother walked into the room carrying a glass of soda.

"Why don't you sit up and drink some of this. It will make you feel better."

Jack scooted himself up into a seated position. He took the glass from her and took a small sip. "Thanks, Mom."

His mother sat down next to him. "So," she said looking directly and lovingly into his eyes, "why don't you tell me what is really going on."

Jack's stomach began to grumble in discomfort for real.

Chapter 6

April 1, 2010

Jack went flying backwards a full twelve feet. He landed on his back and skidded on the damp grass, coming to a stop at the base of a towering Oak tree. It felt like he had just been slammed by a truck.

"What the..." he managed to sputter aloud as he pushed with his elbows to lift himself somewhat off the ground.

"Get up, Jack!" he heard someone yell. He looked around trying to find the source. His eyes fell upon a figure a few yards to his left. It was Billy. "Get up, Jack! No time to slack off."

Jack pushed off the ground with his arms and legs and staggered to a standing position. He was immediately hit from behind. His head snapped back as the rest of his body fell forward. He landed with a resounding thump on the ground and felt the air come out of his chest like it was sucked out by a vacuum. In its place was pain. The kind of pain that says, "Don't move until there's no more pain." He tried to draw a deep breath of air and realized that a clod of grass was stuck in his mouth. He spit it out and swallowed some air into his lungs. He took a minute to normalize his breathing and then wiped away the remnants of grass and dirt face around his mouth with the back of his hand. He stopped when he realized the coarse fur felt worse against his mouth than the grass.

"Don't you love it, Jack? The best game ever played the way it is supposed to be played."

Jack lifted himself to his knees. "What game are we exactly playing, Billy? Lacrosse?" he asked, spitting out a few more blades of grass. "I haven't even had possession of the ball once but I've been checked and hit illegally half a dozen times. This ain't no game of lacrosse that I know of. This is a beat-down."

"Jackie, Jackie, Jackie...you didn't think that you would just join us without a little initiation, did you? If you are going to be part of the team, you have to be ready for anything. You aren't playing with the puppies anymore. You're running with the big dogs."

Big dogs was right, and it seemed like Jack was their chosen play toy for the night. But that wasn't going to be the case for much longer, not if he could help it. No way, no how.

"Come on, Jack; get up! Don't go straight from a wolf to a scaredy-cat." Billy laughed gruffly at his own joke, his orange eyes glowing menacingly in the moonlit meadow. "Show us what you got."

Jack pushed off the ground with his hands and got into what appeared to be a weak standing position. Exhausted and rocking back and forth like he was ready to throw in the towel, he staggered forward a few feet. It was then that he heard running steps on the grass behind him. He pretended not to notice and just before receiving a full on body tackle from one Billy's boys, he dropped down to a firm squatting position. As the confused attacker sailed just above him, Jack thrust his arms up and caught him as if snatching a missile out of the air. He held him in this position and then pressed him upward using the power from his legs until he was fully standing. Jack held the boy in this position and slowly turned around in a clockwise circle so all the other wolves could see him and his catch. The boy looked like a large trophy fish being hoisted in the air by a skilled fisherman, struggling and squirming to break free but woefully unable to do so. All movement in the meadow stopped to watch the spectacle.

Jack continued turning slowly until his eyes fell upon Billy. Their gazes zeroed in and locked tightly upon one another. Billy tried not to flinch or give away his thoughts, but he was worried, really worried. Who was toying with whom now? Jack was strong physically and mentally and would not be easy to tame. This was going to be problematic and would not go over well when it came time to discussing it with HIM.

Billy quickly tried to take control of the situation.

"Jack, put him down. Initiation time is over. You passed."

"Passed? Wow, that's great! I can't wait to tell my mom what a great student I am. Stick your initiation, Billy. Playtime is over. You want your boy back? You tell me how to undo everything that has happened tonight and I'll give you your boy back. If not, I'll slam him down over my knee and be done with him."

The boy struggled more upon hearing all of this but still could not break free. Jack meant serious business.

Billy held out his hands in a calming gesture. "Easy, Jack. What do you mean 'undo everything'? There's nothing to be undone. You are one of us now. Better than you were before. A free spirit in the natural world, unchained from human weakness. You are a Moonwalker. There's no undoing what has taken place."

Jack stood and stared indignantly at Billy for a moment, almost refusing to let his words sink in. "Nice try, Billy. Either you mastered the art of mass hypnosis or have invented the greatest Halloween elixir of all time. I don't really care which. Just tell me how to fix all of this and we will all go on our merry way tonight."

"There's nothing to be fixed, Jack. You are a Moonwalker for the rest of your life. When the full moon shines, you will transform. You've been given a gift. You may not realize it now, but you'll thank me for it later."

Jack waited. Trying to let his thoughts catch up with reality. When they did, the gravity of the situation was too much to bear. Jack threw the boy he was holding to the grass beside him and screamed and howled to the sky with all his might. The boy that was struggling seconds ago to get free from Jack's grip now struggled desperately to get away again, clawing at the grass and dirt in utter panic. Jack's bellow was so loud that some of the other boys nearby held their hairy hands to their wolfen ears. Billy's weight shifted onto his heels but he stilled himself from stepping backwards and showing any fear. Billy realized something else: this was wrong. He didn't want to bring Jack into the fold in the first place, but HE said he knew what was best, that Jack was to become one of them. There was nothing that Billy could do but carry out HIS wishes - or else - but this just didn't feel right. Not like this.

Jack's anguish crashed in upon him and he fell silent and sobbing with his head bowed into his chest.

Billy tried to take control of the situation once more.

"Time will change your mind, Jack. You'll see. It was rough for all of us at first, but then we realized how great it is...the power of it all."

Silence. Jack stood motionless as if he heard nothing.

"Billy," Lucas said, pointing to the sky a few miles away where storm clouds were gathering.

"Listen up," Billy said, turning his attention back to Jack. "Clouds are coming and they vanquish the effects of the full

moon. We will leave you to yourself, but know that you will get home faster in wolf form than human. Use your new self to your advantage. Remember, you are one of us now. ONE OF US. Just give in to what you are and all will be better, so much better. Believe me. Don't fight it, Jack. This is bigger than all of us. If you fight it, there are consequences."

Billy turned to the rest of the clan. "Leave! Now!"

All the wolves darted into the forest leaving Jack and Billy alone.

Jack lifted his head slowly and looked over to Billy. No orange flecks of light sparked in his eyes. Billy backed up a few steps, turned, and ran into the forest.

Chapter 7

April 10, 2011

It felt good to be on the skateboard again. Really good. After a weekend of utter craziness and confusion, there was something soothing about being on the board and the sound of the wheels rolling on concrete - a white noise that blocked out everything else going on around in the world. And there was a lot going on in Jack's world. There were so many fires to put out but no water in sight. But right now, as he zigged and zagged his way to school on Monday morning, things felt okay, and that was probably because he had unburdened himself a bit talking to his mom. After coming home early from the game on Sunday, she wanted to talk find out what was going on. She wasn't the type of person that bought into excuses and would know if Jack wasn't telling the whole truth about things, so Jack told her EVERYTHING. Well, everything except turning into a Moonwalker once a month and having to battle for his very existence. But otherwise, things came flowing out of him like he was a faucet.

He told her about coming to Barnaby Hills and the first weird meeting Billy and his friends. He talked about the trials and tribulations of being part of the team and playing with people who off the field were his enemies. And mostly he talked about how Billy was trying to put a wedge between his friendship with Chris - and pretty much succeeding. It felt like he spoke for hours, but the story came out so quickly and that their whole conversation lasted for about 45 minutes. She was wonderfully sympathetic, knowing exactly when to listen and when to give her opinion, and, more importantly, when to give some needed hugs (something that up until that moment, eight grade Jack believed himself too old to want).

Her advice was simple: be true to yourself and truth will prevail.

No getting on the phone with the principal. No calling Chris' mom to straighten things out. No marching over to Billy's house and having this out once and for all. As much as she would go out of her way to protect him with her life, she also knew that she had to let him work out problems on his own. So she basically told him to be himself and stick up for what he knew was right and, ultimately, the right things would happen. Of course, she cautioned at the end of their conversation that Jack wasn't to start anything physical with anyone, but, if Billy or his buddies tried to hurt him, he had the right to defend himself and even "kick some butt" if needed. Jack managed a smile when she said that. After their talk, Jack helped her out with the garden and even caught a nap before dinner. The morning's events weren't forgotten completely, but he sure felt better after letting her know what was going on - as much as he could.

And now as he made his way to school on his skateboard, he still felt pretty good and his worries seemed to lose their power in the beautiful hum and clack of the wheels. Sure, there would be a lot of talk today at school about yesterday's game and Jack leaving early and whatnot, but this moment right now was the first relatively peaceful moment he had in quite some time, and he was just going to take his time getting to school and make it last.

As Jack rounded the next corner, however, he came to an abrupt stop. There lined up on the side of the road sitting on their dirt bikes were Billy and his boys. Right next to Billy, on a brand spankin' new machine was Chris, grinning from ear to ear.

"Well looka-what-we-got-here, boys," Billy almost sang. "Skateboardin' Jack. Top of the morning to you, Jackie. On your way to school? Enjoying the morning ride? Well, so are we. Ain't that right, Chris?"

Chris nodded his head in agreement.

Billy continued. "Don't know what you heard about the game after you ran away yesterday, but we did pretty well. We beat Centerville...with the help of our new star player, Mr. Stiles." He patted Chris on the shoulder and Chris' smile got even wider.

Jack spoke calmly, almost pleasantly. No one was going to harsh his buzz this morning.

"Great."

"It was great, Jack. Too bad you went home with your baby belly-ache and missed it. Chris did so well that I was able to get him his own dirt bike. You know, so he could ride around town like the winner he is."

"Must be nice to have a rich dad." Jack looked at the bike Chris was sitting on. "Nice ride, Chris. Have fun with it."

Forgetting what had taken place over the last couple of days for a moment, Chris dropped his newfound smug persona and replied appreciatively, "Thanks."

Billy's eyes flashed orange for half a second and he brought the back of his hand against Chris' chest to stop him from engaging further.

"Oh, don't you mean it must be nice to have a dad, Jack?"

Everything became quiet. All the boys looked around awkwardly at each other and especially at Jack and Billy. The quiet was interrupted by Lucas who started laughing.

"Good one, Billy."

"Quiet, Lucas." he said still staring at Jack. Billy then changed the subject quickly. "Don't you worry, Jack. He'll have fun with it. Lots of fun. More fun than you'll have on your little baby skateboard. Vroom, vroom."

The rest of the gang chuckled, hoping to relieve the tension.

Jack looked around at all of them while biting his lip. After a moment, he finally spoke. "Well, it's been nice visiting with you guys. I still have half a dozen blocks to go before I get to school. Take it easy." And with that, Jack pushed off on his skateboard and started down the road.

Billy's boys all looked around at each other confused, as if the air had been let out of their good time. Shouldn't they be going after him?

Lucas, who was on the other side of Billy whispered in his ear.

Billy shook his head. "No, not now," he replied, as if talking to himself. "We're gonna leave Skateboardin' Jack alone today. We'll let it sink into his brain that there's some new talent in town. Come on boys."

And with that, the bikes roared to life and followed Billy down the street.

Chapter 8

April 1, 2010

He stood alone in the field, quiet and still, not wanting to move a muscle in fear of something bad happening. The wind began to blow through the trees. A spring storm was near, yet Jack could not move from this spot. His whole life had just been upended. Everything he knew to be real had just turned into fiction. Just a few hours before, he had been an average middle school student who enjoyed skateboarding and playing lacrosse. Now he was a monster. A monster. And it wasn't a dream. It was real. As real as the wind rustling through the leaves of the trees. As real as the grass below his feet. As real as the full moon that shone down upon him from the night sky.

The moon.

The moon was his master now. He would be forever controlled by it, forever a slave to it. How? How did this happen? The events of the night kept crashing down upon him like giant waves, one after the other. His brain felt as if it were being pummeled. He raised his hands to his head and pulled at the wiry fur that now bordered his face. No matter how hard he tried, he couldn't pull it off. It wasn't a mask. This was him. Jack was a Moonwalker.

He looked around the field. He was completely alone. Billy and the others had picked up the lacrosse sticks and left. What did they expect tonight? Did they believe that Jack would turn into a werewolf and all would be right in the world?

"Oh, by the way, Jack, you are now a werewolf. No backsies."

How ridiculous it all was. Taking him to Howl House, offering him the liquid, bringing him here to the field for a beat down...how could that be perceived as a good thing in any realm of being. Jack could still hear Billy's last words clearly in his head, "Just give in to what you are and all will be better, so much better. Believe me. Don't fight it, Jack. This is bigger than all of us. If you fight it, there are consequences."

Consequences? Wasn't he suffering from the consequences right now? The consequences of not listening to himself and not trusting his instincts? That was for certain but that wasn't what Billy was talking about. He was referring to something else, something that put fear into his voice as he spoke - something that was "bigger than all of us." How did Billy and the rest find out about Howl House? How did they know that drinking the liquid would turn them into Moonwalkers? Where did they learn about the history behind the house and the legend of the Native American Indians? So many questions in need of answers.

He had to focus on something or he would lose himself to all the craziness. He couldn't let that happen. He remembered something else that Billy said, "Clouds are coming...they vanquish the effects of the full moon...you will get home faster in wolf form than human...use your new self to your advantage." Jack looked up. The clouds were almost upon the moon now and Jack was pretty far from home.

"Oh man, I've got school tomorrow," he thought to himself. He then took stock of what a bizarre thought that was given the current circumstances. A wolf worried about going to school. It was almost comical.

His thoughts came back to getting home. He had never

been in this part of the woods before, but strangely enough, he felt he knew what direction to go to get back to his house. It wasn't anything visual that he knew or remembered. It was the scent. He could actually smell which way to go. It was as if there was an invisible odor line for him to follow that would take him all the way back. His human side was having a hard time processing this, but he innately knew that his instincts were correct.

He took one last look at the Moon. He could almost feel celestial puppet strings streaming down from the sky tied to his body. But the Moon also gave him power and strength that he had never felt before. It was a duality of existence that he didn't have time to ponder right now. He brought his head back, closed his eyes and howled. His voice echoed in the field and through the forest. When he was done, he did what wolves do best. He ran. He ran as fast as he could.

Chapter 9

April 10, 2011

Well, he was right. The rumor mill was already running on overdrive by the time Jack got to school. More than a few of his classmates came up to him and expressed their concern about him having to leave the big game the day before. Questions like "Is it true someone from Centerville snuck into your house and poisoned your cereal?" to "How come you're back in school so soon after your appendix ruptured?" were asked by kids eagerly wanting to get the big scoop. It was amazing how things could get so blown out of proportion so quickly. Jack glanced up at the Barnaby Hills banner that said "Home of the Champions!" and almost laughed out loud when the thought of replacing it with "Home of the Busybodies!" crossed his mind. Actually, he didn't mind people coming up to him. It was pretty cool that they cared enough to say anything at all. It made him less lonely given what was going on. Jack happily answered all questions to put to him in the same fashion: *Sorry, no poison cereal, burst appendix, broken leg, death in the family, million dollar lottery or alien abduction took me out the game yesterday. Just your average stomach ache. But thanks for thinking about me.*

By the third period, the gossip started to die down. By lunchtime, everything was back to normal.

Jack made his way to the cafeteria and sat in his usual spot. He opened up his lunch box and eyed a pastrami sandwich on rye that his mother must have made for him this morning. It even had the spicy mustard that he really liked - smeared on both sides of the bread. He smiled and took a huge bite. She certainly knew how to make him feel better.

Across the room, Jack noticed Billy and his buddies were holding court. Lots of kids were stopping by as they entered the cafeteria, congratulating them on the win against Centerville. Billy sat there like a pig in slop, eating up every minute of it. Sitting right next to Billy was Chris, but Jack wasn't sure if he was as enthralled by all the attention as much as Billy was. Being the center of attention is easy to wish for but sometimes harder to deal with in reality. Wasn't Chris getting what he wanted the most right now: to be a star of the lacrosse team? Jack couldn't tell for certain, but Chris appeared a little dazed and confused by it all. Billy turned his head and caught Jack looking over at them. He put his arm around Chris in response and gave him an awkward jostle as if to say, "Yep, this is my boy. MINE, Jackie. Keep your distance." Billy tried to stare Jack down but was interrupted by another well-wisher. Jack smirked and turned his attention back to his sandwich. Nothing was going to get between him and it again for the remainder of lunch. He opened his mouth and took another huge bite and felt a tap on his shoulder. He turned to tell whoever it was that it was only a stomach ache but almost choked on his pastrami when he saw who it was: Sarah Bartley.

Chapter 10

April 2, 2010

It was well after midnight by the time Jack got home from Howl House, and he was utterly exhausted. About three fourths of the way back, clouds fully covered the moon and Jack found himself turning back into an average 7th grader again. Just as when he transformed into a Moonwalker, the change back into human form wasn't any picnic in the park, either. It was like being slammed by an invisible semi-truck. He fell to the ground mid run and writhed in agony as his bones and muscles refashioned themselves into their natural state. When it was done, he slowly got to his feet and wondered if changing back and forth was going to get any easier over time. Up until then, Math homework was the thing in life that caused him the greatest pain. It didn't seem so bad in comparison now. When he felt a bit better, he started running again, the thought of getting home his only comfort.

Standing outside his house, hands on knees trying to catch his breath, Jack realized there was an even greater problem: how to get inside without waking his mother.

Earlier at the party, Billy's mom had called up Jack's and told her that the boys would be having a sleepover. If that were true, how could Jack ring the doorbell after midnight, clothes dirty, out of breath, and act as if he were coming home from the movies? What would he say?

"Oh, hi, Mom. Billy and his gang just turned me into a werewolf and we were playing a rough game of lacrosse in the moonlight. Btw, I'll be turning into one of these things once a month so you better get used to me coming home late, dirty and maybe even a little hairy if the full moon is still peeking out. Thanks, Mom!"

Jack was so tired, he couldn't even manage a smile from the crazy thought. He turned his attention back to the problem at hand. His mother always locked the doors before she went to bed, so he would have to get in another way. He checked the first floor windows next to the front door. Locked. He went around to the backyard, checking windows along the way. Everything was locked tight. He looked up to the second floor. His bedroom window was right there. Luckily, his mother's bedroom faced towards the front, so maybe she wouldn't hear anything as he scrambled up the ivy-covered trellis that was mounted against the house. But the real problem was whether the trellis would be able to hold his weight. He didn't have a clue but he also didn't have much of a choice. He didn't have to climb very far, but he had to climb carefully. The trellis was old, he was exhausted, and, even if he did make it to the second floor, there was no guarantee that his bedroom window was open. If it wasn't, then he would have to try and make it down without falling or having the whole thing crash down upon him. If that happened, he'd surely wake up his mom and most of his neighbors. Nothing about this looked promising, but he took a deep breath and started to climb. The wood began to lightly creak and groan right from the start. Jack considered jumping off and taking his chances sleeping in the backyard, but thoughts of his warm bed won out and he continued on. The noises didn't stop but the trellis itself appeared to be pretty sturdy. This was good news. Now that he was a Moonwalker, he would need to get in and out of the house without his mother finding out. Climbing in and out of his window just might be the answer to that issue.

Before he knew it, Jack was right under his window. He reached up to the pane of glass and applied some light upward pressure. It didn't move. His heart sank. He turned his head and surveyed the backyard wondering where he could bunk down for the rest of the night. The thought of being curled up underneath the picnic table literally sent a chill through his body. He turned back to the window, steadied himself on the trellis and reached up with both hands to try pushing on the window once more. At first it seemed like it wouldn't budge but then it did. Jack got so excited that he nearly lost his balance and was about to fall. He grabbed the window ledge quickly. He gave himself a moment to recover and then pushed the window up higher and crawled into his bedroom, making sure not to knock anything over as he made it over to his bed. He set his alarm for a half hour after his mother would be leaving the house to go to work. She thought he was sleeping over at Billy's so she would just head downstairs without trying to wake him up for school. After she was gone, he would wake up, take a shower and then head over to school as quickly as he could. He didn't like the thought of sneaking around and being dishonest, but right now, there was nothing that he could do about it.

He laid down in his bed and closed his eyes. Maybe when he woke up, everything would be just as it was before...the night being nothing more than a bad dream. He knew that wasn't true but he allowed the thought to linger in his brain and eventually guide him to sleep. *Sometimes in order to survive, we have to be dishonest to ourselves, too, was* his last thought before conking out.

Chapter 11

April 10, 2011

"Are you okay, Jack?"

Jack coughed to clear his throat of sandwich. He held up one finger to Sarah to let her know that he needed a second to compose himself. He took a swig of chocolate milk and tried to will his respiratory system to calm down from almost becoming his digestive system. When he felt the worst had passed, he started to speak.

"Sorry, Sarah. That was a close one. I'm okay."

"Try chewing your food before you try to swallow it," she chuckled.

"Thanks for the tip. What's up?"

"I just wanted to see if you were okay. I mean you left the lacrosse game so quickly yesterday. Is your stomach any better, apart from you not knowing how to swallow correctly?" She started laughing again.

"Ha-ha, very funny. But, yes, I do feel a lot better. Thank you."

"Good. So about those new cheers you never got to see at the game. How about this afternoon?"

"This afternoon?"

"How about we hang out together and I can show you the new cheers we have been working on?"

Not again. Jack was tired of playing Billy's games. Obviously he wanted Chris to see Jack and Sarah together again to cement the idea that Jack wasn't really a good friend and that Chris was better off without him. The more distance he put between Jack and Chris, the easier it would be to do what he wanted. And he kept using Sarah as a tool to achieve his desires. Jack was sick of being a pawn in Billy's evil chess game. Something had to be done.

"Listen, Sarah. You can stop all of this now and tell Billy that I'm not interested in this garbage anymore. I know he has been using you to get Chris to hate me and it's not going to work anymore. He's the one who put that note in your locker. Not me. So you can just go back over to him and tell him I'm on to everything and it's not going to work."

Sarah's eyes widened in surprise. "What are you talking about?"

Jack sighed. "You know what I mean. You trying to get me to hang out and all. It's Billy's way of getting Chris jealous. I know you're a nice person, but you can stop pretending to like me just because Billy tells you to."

"Is that what you think?" Sarah asked incredulously. "That I like you because Billy is telling me to? To make Chris jealous? I don't know who you think I am, Jack Wilson, but no one tells me what to do. Not Billy, not his friends, no one. If I like someone, it's because I like them. Period. Where did you even get this stuff about making Chis jealous? And Chris likes me? I mean, he's a nice guy, but I'm not interested. Wow. Just wow."

Sarah was angry and students were starting to look over at the two of them. Jack didn't expect this to happen. Actually, he didn't know what to expect. His emotions got the best of his reason and he didn't think the whole thing through before speaking. All this time, he thought Sarah was being manipulated by Billy. Was he wrong? *Does she really like me?* Jack couldn't wait for his brain to answer its own question. He wanted to calm the situation down quickly or Billy really would take advantage of it.

"Sarah, I'm so sorry. I wasn't thinking and I blurted something out that shouldn't have been said."

Sarah folded her arms and looked at him with contempt, but at least she wasn't yelling. That was a good sign for now.

He continued. "I'd really like to talk about this with you. There is so much going on and I think I got a good chunk of it wrong. Could we meet later on and talk about it? Just for a few minutes. Again, I'm so sorry."

Sarah looked into Jack's eyes intently. For a minute, he felt like she was searching his very soul. Whatever she was looking for, it seemed like she found it because her eyebrows unraveled out of the angry knot they were in and her body language eased up considerably.

"Okay," she said.

"Great. How about right on the front steps after last period?"

"See you then," she said again as she turned around slowly to leave.

Jack looked around. Everyone seemed to be going back to their own cafeteria business. He looked down at the remainder of his sandwich. He wasn't hungry anymore.

Chapter 12

April 2, 2010

Jack woke up when he heard the alarm clock, but it was his mother's, not his. He fought the urge to go right back to sleep. He was so tired from what took place the night before and could use some more rest but he didn't want to take the chance of being found if she came into his room for some reason After all, he was supposed to be sleeping over at Billy's...his new "best friend." He quietly got up, arms and legs aching, and went over to his closet and got inside. He could hang out there for a while until she left for work then jump in the shower and head out to school.

All went according to plan and by the time he showered off the grit and grime of the night, ate breakfast and skateboarded to school, he had only missed Homeroom. Had he missed any of his other classes, the school would have called his mother and nothing good would have come of that.

The day was filled with friends and classmates congratulating Jack on yesterday's big win. That was great, not because it made him feel good or special, but more so because it stopped Jack from obsessively rethinking the events that happened last night. Whenever his mind started to wander, a teacher or classmate would say something nice or pat him on the back and he would have to come back to the present. Nothing about yesterday made any more sense to him, but at least being at school and around others helped him achieve a feeling of normalcy.

At lunchtime, Jack walked into the cafeteria and saw Chris sitting at their usual place.

"The conquering hero!" Chris joked. "Dude, this place is on fire today. Even I'm getting compliments and I didn't do squat."

"What are you talking about Chris? You're part of the team. You deserve just as much praise as anyone else."

"I don't believe that, but coming from you, I'll take it. So how much longer did you stay at the party?"

Jack looked away from Chris and down at his lunch. "Uh, not too much longer than you, I guess. You know, with school the next day and all..."

"Did you hear that Mr. Weber is giving us a day off from lacrosse practice today for kicking butt yesterday?"

"Yeah, someone told me this morning. I don't have Mr. Weber until later but I'm sure he'll say something then."

"He is so happy about the win that he's having a party in every class. I'm so full from chocolate. I don't think I can eat my lunch today."

Jack didn't hear the last thing that Chris said because at that very moment, across the cafeteria, Billy and his boys walked in. Billy's eyes zeroed in on Jack as soon as he entered and both boys remained locked in a staring match that almost defied the time and space of where they were. A silent conversation took place.

You're one of us now, Jackie.

I'll never be one of you.

Why do you fight the gift you have been given?

Gift? More like a curse.

Give it some time. You'll see during the next full moon.

See what?

The power. The incredible power. We can do anything we want.

I don't want your power. I want my life back.

You were just given a life, Jack. Embrace it. This is the new you.

Not if I can help it.

There's nothing you can do, Jack. Nothing. In time, you'll see and come to accept it.

Never.

Jackie, Jackie, Jackie...never say never.

"Jack, Jack, Jack...did you hear me?"

"Oh, yeah, sorry, Chris. What did you say?"

"Dude, the game must have taken a lot out of you. You were in La La Land."

"Yeah, no doubt. Super tired."

"Here. Have my lunch. I think you need it more than me," Chris laughed.

Jack smiled. "Thanks, buddy. I need all the help I can get."

Chapter 13

April 10, 2011

Jack waved to Sarah when he saw her walking out of the school. He had spent most of the afternoon going over what he wanted to say to her, but now, he couldn't remember anything he had prepared. He definitely could see why Chris was so crazy about her. She was kind of awesome - smart, pretty, great personality.... *Jack, what are you doing?* his conscience yelled at him. *Chris likes her. You shouldn't be thinking anything about her.* Jack was about to answer back when reality stopped him.

"You definitely look like someone with something on their mind, Jack."

Jack, turned abruptly away from his thoughts and smiled at Sarah. "Yeah, sometimes I get wrapped up in things mentally - a little too wrapped up. Sorry."

"No sorry needed. The world needs thinkers, but judging by what you said in the cafeteria, I think you have been thinking through some things and coming to weird conclusions. Can you tell me what that was all about before?"

Jack rubbed the back of his neck and took a deep breath.

"Okay, but I need to know something."

"What?"

"I need to know if everything we talk about will stay between me and you?"

"Who else would it be between?"

"Well, I know that you hang out with Billy and his friends sometimes and...and I just need to know what we talk about it is between me and you and no one else. Is that okay?"

"Yes. No worries. Just between me and you."

She wasn't lying. Maybe it was some lingering sixth-sense from being a Moonwalker, but Jack could tell that she was totally telling the truth.

"Thank you. Would it be okay with you if we walked around as we talk? I just don't think I can stand still. Maybe around the block or so."

"Sure."

And so they walked and talked, and just like he did with his mother the day before, Jack unpacked his soul and told her everything about his relationship with Billy and Chris and lacrosse. She listened to every bit of it. Not a yawn or hint of boredom during the whole spiel. This unburdening of the heart thing was so new to Jack but it felt pretty good. He even started telling her about his relationship with his mother and not having his dad around. And she talked, too. About her friends and her parents' divorce and her stepfather and how she was afraid he would be something out of scary fairytale but was actually a really nice guy. They walked and talked for over two hours in what felt like the blink of an eye.

Sarah glanced down at her watch. "OMG, it's almost dinner time," she said. She looked around and laughed. "I know we didn't plan it like this but I only live a couple of minutes away from here."

"I'll walk you home. Sound good?"

"Yeah. So, back to what we were talking about before. Now that you know I'm not a hypnotized spy working for Billy against you, what are you going to do?"

Jack thought for a moment. Sometimes it was hard to talk about events that stemmed from being a werewolf without accidentally giving away that he was a werewolf, but, good or bad, he was getting better at it.

"Well, Chris is my friend and I will do anything I can to make sure that our friendship survives all of this. Billy just wants to use him and I can't let that happen. But he has, without your knowing it, been using you to drive a wedge between me and Chris. I know the truth now, but Chris doesn't."

"So I'll go and say something to Chris so he knows what's going on," Sarah said earnestly.

"I don't think that is the best thing to do right now. That would just anger him more if he knew that we were talking about him. It would just solidify in his mind everything that Billy has been saying all along."

"But the truth is I don't like Chris in that way and he needs to know that."

"I agree. But I'm going to ask you to hold off for a while until I think of a way for Chris to realize that Billy has been playing him all along. If I can do that, it won't matter anymore about what Billy has been saying to Chris about me liking you and getting him all jealous."

A small grin appeared on Sarah's face. "Is there any truth in that?"

"Truth?" Jack's heart skipped a beat.

Sarah stopped walking. "Here's my house." She looked around. "I don't see any spies around. I won't give them anything to report, just in case, but know this, Jack Wilson. I like you and I think you like me."

Jack's face turned radish red.

"So, we will leave it there for now, until this is all figured out, okay? See you in school, Jack." And with that, Sarah Bartley walked up to her front door, turned, smiled and went inside.

Jack, what are you doing? his conscience screamed.

Shut up, he replied.

Chapter 14

May 1, 2010

He crouched down low against a tree. They were nearby; he could smell them as if they were standing right in front of him, but he knew they were still a bit of a distance away. He left the house much earlier than he needed to tonight. It wasn't that he was afraid he would make too much noise and wake up his mother. He had been practicing climbing out of his window and up and down the trellis for the last couple of weeks, making sure he could do it as quietly as possible. That wasn't the issue. He was nervous because this was only the second time he would be turning into a Moonwalker and he wanted to make sure he could get as far away from home as possible before undergoing the transformation.

It worked out exactly as he had planned. He was well into the woods when the full moon shone down and stopped Jack in his tracks. This time around, the change from boy to wolf was no less painful, but at least he knew what to expect. When it was finished, he moved on.

He knew they were coming to the open field near Howl House. Billy had told him that much, but nothing more. And that frustrated Jack the most. He wanted answers - answers to the burning questions he had since that night one month ago. Questions about the liquid in the cave and how they found it. He had tried to find out more at lacrosse practice, but Billy wouldn't say much - usually just something like, "Easy, Jackie-boy. No worries. All will be answered when the time comes."

That wasn't good enough for Jack, but confronting Billy

wasn't going to get him anywhere. Billy would only give something if he was getting something in return, and Jack knew the very thing Billy wanted: loyalty. Billy surrounded himself with people that fed his ego and would do almost anything for him. So, if being a team player was what he wanted, being a team player was what he was going to get. Jack would become Billy's best friend, although the very thought of it made his stomach queasy. Playing Billy's game seemed like the only way. So, essentially, Jack was going to swallow his pride and become one of the boys and try to get what he could out of it all. He didn't know if it was dangerous or just stupid, but he knew he had to do it. His train of thought was interrupted by a raspy voice.

"Jackie, I know you're here. Come join your brothers," Billy called loudly from the other side of the open field.

Jack emerged and walked over to the pack. The moon was behind him shining down unhindered by the trees. His hulking shadow was splayed out before him as he walked. Nothing about it was distinct on the nighttime grass but it served as an ominous reminder of what Jack now was and why he had to betray his own sense of right and wrong and befriend Billy. He stopped looking down and walked the remainder of the way staring straight ahead at the wolf pack. He took some deep breaths and readied his resolve.

"Punctual. I like that," Billy smiled.

Jack grinned back. "Well, this is the place to be, right?"

"Yes, indeed, Jackie. Yes, indeed. But to be honest, I didn't think that you were going to show up. The last time we met like this, you seemed somewhat ungrateful about your gift."

"That was then. This is now. Let's just say that after a month of thinking things over, I'm willing to be more open-

minded about the possibilities."

Billy's shoulders relaxed a bit. "That a boy, Jackie! Great news." He looked around at the group. "See boys. Turns out Jackie is a wolf in sheep's clothing after all." Everyone started to laugh and chuckle, even Jack.

"So what's on the plate tonight?" Jack asked feigning great interest.

"We play the game of our forefathers."

"Great. Can't wait. What about afterwards? The Moon will be out all night."

"One thing at a time, my eager puppy. Being a Moonwalker is not a destination; it's a journey. There's plenty to learn and lots of time to do it. Tonight we play. Beyond that, all will be revealed when the time is right. But enough talk. To Howl House for lacrosse sticks!"

The boys howled in approval and Jack joined in, but all the while he just kept thinking about the long haul ahead of him. How long would he be able to keep up this charade in both human and wolf form? Billy was right about this being a journey, but Jack wasn't sure if he had enough stamina to make the full trip. One thing was certain, he would have to take all of this one full moon at a time.

Chapter 15

April 12, 2011

Three days after the game against Centerville, Mr. Weber stood before the team ready to run them through another practice. All the boys were still pumped from their big win over the weekend and there was a lot of playful banter going around as they waited for practice to begin. Jack stood off to the side waiting for Mr. Weber to begin.

"Alright. Settle down, settle down," Mr. Weber ordered. "You won the first game of the season and that's admirable, but one winning game does not a winning season make. There are more challenges ahead and if your focus is on what is behind you rather than what is in front of you, you can kiss being regional champs goodbye right now. You got me?"

The team reluctantly quieted down and a few of the members shrugged and answered back with a weak "Yes."

"I don't think you did. Let's try that once more. YOU GOT ME?"

Mr. Weber's voice and tone was like a blast of arctic air; the chill made the team straighten up and answer back with a resounding, "YES!"

"That's more like it. Before we get into some serious drills today, let's just review the good and bad about last weekend's game. Good thing number 1: Let's make some noise for Mr. Chris Stiles for a nice first game showing - way to go, Chris."

The team yelped it up a bit and gave Chris some friendly slaps on the back. Jack smiled and clapped in support. Chris looked over to the side to see how Jack was reacting, but was interrupted when Billy grabbed him in a headlock and started shouting, "This boy right here, ladies. This boy right here."

Mr. Weber laughed and then continued. "Bad thing number 1: Jack's stomach bug." The team started booing and hissing in mock annoyance. "Now, Jack did the right thing. He saw that his play was being negatively affected by how he was feeling and he took himself out of the game - probably sparing you guys a dose of that sickness had he stuck around. So kudos to Jack for a smart decision, but it is the duty of every member of this team to alert me right away if you are not feeling up to playing a game. And if you are sick, don't blame your poor play on your teammates. Be a man; step up and take responsibility for your actions. Do you get me?" Mr. Weber cast a sideways glance over at Jack.

"Yes, Coach!" yelled out everyone, including Jack.

"Alright then. As for good and bad things 2 thru 10,000, let's put them on the back-burner and get to practicing. Ten laps around the field, sticks in hand NOW!"

Having just been dressed down, no one grumbled this time. They went right to work.

"Jack, come over here and see me for a minute," Mr. Weber yelled. Jack turned from the group and trotted over.

"Yes, Coach."

"Jack, I hope you aren't upset that I singled you out in my speech."

Jack looked at Mr. Weber nonchalantly. "No, not at all." But the truth was that he was very upset, but he wasn't going to say anything about it. It should have been very obvious to anyone watching Sunday's game that Billy and some of his boys weren't treating Jack as a teammate. They had deliberately kept the ball from him and kept him in isolation. But Mr. Weber appeared to be blind about the whole thing. Was Billy now influencing him? It certainly was plausible seeing how he had turned Chris against him. But Jack knew it was pointless to bring this all up with Mr. Weber - at least at this very moment.

"Good, good. You are one of the best players on the team, Jack, but even the best players have their bad moments. If we all work together, this team can do great things. Agreed?"

"No doubt, Coach."

"Fabulous. Take a page out of Chris' book and up your game. Talk about responsive play! That kid is right on track to receiving the MVP award at the close of the season. You won that last year, right, Jack? You don't want Chris to steal it right out from under you, do you?"

"Um, no, no, I don't want that, Mr. Weber." Jack said, now feeling a little uncomfortable.

"Then you know what you have to do. Now, get out there and join your team. They are depending on you."

"Okay, sure thing. Um, thanks."

Jack turned and ran out on the field to join the boys on their second lap. That was definitely one of the more bizarre conversations he had ever had with Mr. Weber. There was no doubt in his mind that Billy had something to do with all of this. Things were getting deep and dark.

Chapter 16

June, 2010 - March, 2011

Full moon, Moonwalker, lacrosse, home. Full moon, Moonwalker, lacrosse, home. Month in, month out. Summer, winter, and now spring. Nothing changed. Every single full moon brought yet another game of werewolves playing lacrosse in the forest and then returning home. Jack's tried his best to be a compliant werewolf. He never missed a game. He played his heart out (even in the snow). He howled and laughed and cavorted about in the open field like the "good puppy" that Billy wanted. But still there were no answers to questions. He was no closer to knowing why he was a Moonwalker than he did the very first night he became one.

At school, it was no better. The false friendship that Jack thought would grow in the light of day never materialized. Billy remained distant and aloof - popular with his crowd, but not willing to let Jack in. Apart from the lacrosse season practices and games, Billy barely recognized Jack's existence in school. He wasn't unfriendly, but he wasn't friendly, either. It was as if he were afraid to get too close to Jack for some reason. Afraid that if he let Jack in, he would be exposed and vulnerable - unprotected. So he kept Jack out of his inner circle of friends and left it at that. As much as Jack didn't want to become good friends with Billy, he knew that not being invited into the circle of friends would hurt his chances of getting answers. Months and months of this began to frustrate him more and more, and then, on the first full moon in March, Jack's frustration grew to the point of no return.

Lucas ran straight towards Jack, his lacrosse stick held with the ball in the netting to the right of his body. He snarled sharply as he quickly cut farther to the right. Jack anticipated and

maneuvered his feet and body in kind to block his path. Lucas shifted control of the ball to his left hand and feigned cutting in that direction and then quickened his steps to the right and blew past Jack.

"Jack, what are you doing? You are playing like a kitty-cat tonight!" Billy screamed from the center of the field.

Jack stopped moving and just let his arms and head hang for a moment.

"What are you doing now?" Billy yelled again.

Jack took a deep breath and turned abruptly to Billy. "Get off my case!"

All game-play ceased.

"What did you say?" Billy asked in a low, gnarl of a tone.

Jack looked around and saw that all the boys were watching him.

"I said get off my case."

Billy stood silent for a moment and then let out a laugh that eased some of the growing tension.

"Jackie-boy's had his fill of lacrosse for the night. No problem. It can happen to the best of us. Not that you've reached that point, yet, Jack."

Jack started walking slowly in Billy's direction. "What point is that exactly, Billy? Huh? What are we doing out here full moon after full moon? Playing lacrosse? More like wasting time. We turn into monsters and play a never ending game with sticks and a ball. I've been doing it for nearly a year now and I still don't know why. And when I ask questions, you say, 'All will be revealed when the time is right.' What does that even mean? I say the right time is NOW!"

Billy cocked his head slightly to the side and started

shaking it up and down as if to acknowledge Jack's words, but it was soon apparent to all that acknowledgment was only a stepping stone to disgust.

"So YOU say the time is now, huh, Jack? Well guess what? I don't care what you say. I knew you would never become one of us. I knew that no time or training would make you come around. But no one listened to me, did they?"

"What are you talking about?"

"YOU WANT ANSWERS?" Billy screamed. "YOU DON'T DESERVE ANSWERS! What you need is to be replaced. And I have an idea about who will fit the bill: Chris Stiles. He's getting better at the game and there's no way he will ever be a problem. Yep, Chris will do nicely." Billy looked around at the rest of the group for their expected and silent approval.

A red rage swept across Jack's eyes. He didn't even think; he just reacted. He ran straight at Billy and tackled him, his shoulder ramming fiercely into his gut. Billy flew backwards and landed on his back with his arms and legs thrown out to the sides. Jack readied himself to jump on top of his fallen adversary when he felt a hand grab his shoulder and pull him back. He turned to find Lucas pulling him back with one hand and reaching out with his other to grab his throat. Jack deflected Lucas' hand and pushed it off to the side and then fiercely palmed his snout. Lucas yelped in pain, while striking out wildly with his legs. Jack was able to avoid the blows but saw out of the corner of his eye that the others were now running to join in the fight. Jack scrambled over to the side of the field close to the woods to create some distance. Some of the boys went after him while some tried to help Billy and Lucas. Billy yelled for them to leave him alone and join the others. The odds stacked against him, Jack decided to run

for cover into the forest. He quickly sank into the darkness. Rather than take a chance with Jack picking off people one by one, Billy called his boys back. Jack ran from the area with haste but heard Billy's voice loud and clear yelling out to him.

"You'll pay for your treachery, Jackie-boy. Chris will take your place. Skateboardin' Jack will be nothing but a bad dream when we are done with you. Do you hear me? Say goodbye!"

A part of him wanted to turn around and finish all of this once and for all, but Jack continued running. The desire to get home was greater than anything else. He may not have gotten answers, but at least now he had a purpose.

Chapter 17

April 12, 2011

"Walk me home?"

Jack had barely exited the locker room when he heard the growingly familiar voice behind him and off to the left.

Jack turned. Sarah Bartley was leaning against a wall. "You know Billy and Chris will be walking out of the locker room at any moment now."

Sarah smiled. "And you know I don't care."

Jack returned the smile. "Yes, I'm starting to realize that, but..."

She interrupted. "So why should you?"

Logical and beautiful. Jack was so in trouble.

"I don't think I can give you a good answer to that question right now other than Chris is my friend and I don't want to see him get hurt."

Sarah mulled that over for a few seconds. "Good answer. I don't want to see that happen, either. Okay, you are off the hook - today - Jack, but the next time I ask the question about walking me home, I expect a 'yes' and a stop off for some ice cream before we reach the destination. Agreed?"

Jack laughed. "Agreed."

"Good. Now let me see if I can catch up to Dana across the field and walk home with her. Not my first choice but I guess she'll have to do," she said kiddingly. "Bye for now, Jack."

He watched her as she jogged away, the Sun laying low in the distance, making everything it touched almost golden, especially her. Yep, he was so in trouble.

"See. I told you, Chris. He can't keep his eyes off of her."

The annoyingly familiar voice was directly behind him. Jack turned and immediately locked his gaze with Billy's. Chris was by his side, a sour expression creeping steadily over his face.

"Some friend, huh, Chris?"

For a moment, Jack was ready to pounce on Billy and give him the beating that he well deserved for so long. But he stopped himself. What good would that do? It would be playing right into Billy's game. Then he could say to Chris, "Look! He betrayed you and attacked me. He's a piece of garbage. Good riddance to bad rubbish." That would definitely be the last straw for Chris and any chance of repairing their friendship would be lost. No. Jack would have to try something different. Something direct.

"What do you know about friendship, Billy? You buy most of your 'friends' with your dad's money. And anyone who you can't buy, you treat like dirt. You wouldn't even be talking to Chris if you weren't trying to use him in some way."

"Nice try, Jack, but Chris knows good friendship when he sees it."

"That's the first honest thing you've ever said, Billy. Chris does know good friendship when he sees it. That's why we were such good friends. But you got it into his mind that I wasn't his friend and that I was trying to take Sarah away from him."

Jack turned to Chris now, taking an all or nothing approach to get his friend back.

"Chris, I'm sorry that all of this has happened. I was never trying to take Sarah away from you. But the truth is you never had Sarah. She's not yours. You have a crush on her and it's just not mutual. Billy took advantage of how you felt and convinced you that I was making a move on her just to break up our friendship. I never ever made a move on Sarah. I was rooting for you all along. What I had no clue about is that Sarah has a crush on me. But Billy figured that out and piled it on to all the other lies he was telling you, making all of us just pawns in his sick game. I'm not playing it anymore. I'm still your friend, Chris. I know that I may not be your favorite person right now, but please realize why that is. You're my friend and I even hope you win MVP this year. I only ask that you think this all through. But that's enough from me because I'm not going to stand here and argue with Billy Jenkins about what the definition of 'good friendship' is or isn't. I've got better things to do. Take care, Chris."

Jack adjusted his lacrosse bag on his shoulder, dropped his skateboard on the pavement and rolled away from the two boys.

Unsettled by what just happened but not wanting to give up the last word, Billy took a few steps forward and yelled at Jack. "Traitor! Coward! You stay away from Chris! You're nuthin', Jackie-boy. NOTHING! YOU HEAR ME?"

Billy turned back to Chris, angry saliva dripping off his chin. "Can you believe that guy? What a lunatic. At least we know the truth. Right, Chris?

Chris' eyes followed Jack as he made his way out of the school yard.

Billy tried to pull his attention back. "I'm sure you have plenty to say to him, too, right? Well, don't worry. Soon you'll be able to say everything want and more. All of us will."

Chris didn't respond.

"Come on, dude. Let's get out of here and get away from his stink. It's all over the place."

Billy gave Chris a playful punch to the arm.

"C'mon. You with me?"

Chris, cleared his throat a little. "Um, yeah, Billy. I'm with you. Let's get out of here."

"Right on."

The two boys began cutting across the field to get to their bikes, but Billy turned around to take a last look at Jack, his eyes glowing fiery orange.

Chapter 18

April 12, 2011

"Mom? You home?"

"I'm upstairs, Jack. Be down in a minute."

"Okay."

Jack dropped his lacrosse bag and skateboard near the front door and made a beeline straight for the kitchen. He opened up the fridge and grabbed a pitcher of water. He poured himself a large glass and gulped it all down. He started filling up a second when his mother came into the room.

"There you are. How was lacrosse practice today?'

"Interesting."

She sat down at the table and motioned for Jack to do the same. "Do tell."

He put the pitcher of water in the fridge and took a seat.

"Well, I basically told Billy off and hit Chris up with some harsh truth."

"I can pretty well guess what you might have said to Billy, but what do you mean you told Chris some 'harsh truth?'"

Jack took a deep breath. "I had to let him know what Billy was up to...how he has been playing us all."

"Rough stuff. How did it go?"

"I'm not completely sure, but at least I'm standing on solid ground now. I even addressed the issue with Sarah Bartley."

"Oh, she is the girl that Chris likes, right?"

"Yeah...well, about that..."

Jack's mom raised her right eyebrow and curled her lip a little. "Continue."

Jack took an even deeper breath. "It seems that, although Chris likes Sarah, it is not a mutual kind of thing. She doesn't hate Chris; she just doesn't see him in that kind of way, but..."

"But..."

"But she does see me in that kind of way."

"And..."

"And...I'm starting to see her in that kind of way, too."

"And did you kind of tell Chris about all of this?

"Kind of."

"And how did Chris take this news?"

"To be honest, I'm not sure. I told him that Sarah likes me but I didn't tell him that I like her back because I wasn't sure how I was feeling about her and the whole thing. But the more I think about it, the more I find myself thinking about her, so, I guess I like her, too - WHICH IS NOT WHAT I PLANNED! I swear."

Jack's mom looked at him and he looked at her, both wondering where to go next.

"First, wonderful son of mine, I'm glad you stuck up not only for yourself, but also for your friendship with Chris. It's not easy being caught between a rock and a hard place, and you just proved that you're not willing to be stuck where you don't want to be. Second, 8th grade romances are wonderful things..."

Jack interjected. "Romance? I didn't say anything about a roma..."

"My turn to interrupt. Okay, not romance. 8th grade 'crushes' are wonderful things." Jack still rolled his eyes. "So many swirling first-time emotions that make you crazy-happy one second and crazy-crazy the next. Just take it all in stride. When it comes to who we fall for and why we fall for them, there's no logic, just chemistry. I'm glad you were honest with Chris, or as honest as you could be at the time. It's all okay. It's okay if he likes her, but she doesn't like him because she likes you and you like her. Trust me. This is all part of the learning process - has been for thousands of years."

Jack nodded his head and chuckled. "You would think after thousands of years we would have it all straightened out by now, right?"

"If it were all easy, it wouldn't all be worth it."

"You're pretty smart, Mom."

"The smartest."

They both started laughing.

"Now that you've set me straight on love, do you have any advice on what to eat for dinner because that is what I'm worried about now?"

"Oh, that's simple. All you have to do is pick up a phone and dial Chinese take-out. So simple even a lacrosse player could do it."

"Oh, that was a low blow."

"Well, you know how it is: you have to take the good with the bad. One minute you're getting great advice and the next you're getting ranked out by your awesome mom."

"Awesome? How about so-so?

"So-so?" she grabbed at her heart. "Now that is a low-blow. Go grab the phone, you comedian."

"Okay, but first things first." Jack got up and walked around the table and gave his mom the biggest hug.

Chapter 19

April 13, 2011

He saw a man walking towards him wearing a tie-dyed shirt that was almost glowing with all the different hues of yellow, orange and red bursting from a peace sign in the center. He was walking with a girl who had a clown nose on. Everything else about her was relatively commonplace...except for the clown nose. The two of them walked into a store with a window that was crammed with beads and lava lamps and assorted jewelry. The odor of burning incense wafted out the door and seemed to beckon passersby to investigate what was inside. It was strange, but he knew this place. He actually knew it pretty well. He was walking in Haight-Ashbury in San Francisco. It was where he lived with his mother. The sights, the smells, the people...such a delicious stew of life. He was back in Haight-Ashbury!

Across the street he saw the place that made his favorite pizza. OMG! He had to have a slice.

"Mom, can we get some pizza?

He looked up at her. She was holding his hand and they were walking in Haight-Ashbury, but he was small, very small. He was a child.

She looked down at him lovingly. She grasped his hand a little more tightly and said, "Not right now, honey. We have to meet your father."

Father? DAD? They were going to meet his Dad? He had never met his father before. Oh, this was the greatest day of days. Back in San Francisco and about to meet his father. His joy could not be confined. He jumped in the air but didn't come back down. He kept rising and rising slowly like a helium balloon. His mother's hand was the string that kept him tethered to the ground.

"Mommy! Don't let go!" he implored sensing he was in danger.

"Don't worry, honey. Mommy has you."

She pulled on his arm gently and he floated back down. His feet touched the concrete and he knew all was well. They continued walking.

"Oh, there's your father now!" his mother said happily.

Standing on the corner was a man dressed in a button down shirt and jeans. He smiled and waved and started walking over to them. This was his Dad. He had the same color brown hair and brown eyes, just like in the photos. It was him; it was really him.

"Sorry I'm late," he said with an air of casual grace. "You know how busy work can get."

"I know," his Mom answered back with a sigh and a smile.

"Dad? Dad? It's me, Jack. It's so nice to meet you!"

His Dad looked around confused.

"Dad! I'm down here. It's Jack. Your son. Pick me up and give me a hug."

His father looked down with a warm grin. He bent down and grabbed Jack under his arms and started raising him up, but when they were face to face, his father stopped smiling and began to hold Jack at arm's length away from his body.

"Dad, what's wrong? It's me, Jack. Why aren't you smiling anymore?"

An expression of both fear and disgust overcame over his father and he said, "No, you are not my son. You are not Jack.

You're not human. You're a wolf," and he dropped Jack from his grasp.

As he fell, he saw his mother reaching out to save him, the fear in her eyes was as haunting as her voice screaming and echoing, "Jaaaaaaaaack!"

"Jack! Jack! Get up! It's time for school!"

Jack's eyes opened with a snap. He was panting and his heart was racing like he had been playing a game of lacrosse. He lay absolutely still, not sure what was going on.

"Jack, do you hear me?"

Reality slowly started to set in. He was in his bed and his mother was trying to get him up for school. He struggled to answer. "Uh, yeah, uh...I hear you, Mom. Be down in a little bit. Okay?"

"Okay, but please don't be late!"

Jack rubbed his face and tried to calm himself down. He moved his fingers to his eyes. When he took them away, he realized his fingertips were wet with tears. He just had a dream in which he met his father for the first time and was then rejected by him. Could anything be worse?

Chapter 20

April 14, 2011

Friday night lacrosse. Barnaby Hills Middle School was playing Franklin Township and expectations for an intense game were high. Franklin almost won the championship last year and their fans had been waiting eagerly for another chance at the trophy. There was a long line at the concession stand with hungry parents, teens and kids hoping to grab a bite before the start of the game. The Sun was starting to drop down over the horizon and the stadium lights were coming to life. The evening was warm for the time of year and a festive atmosphere prevailed. It seemed to be felt by everyone - everyone except Chris Stiles, that is. He stood at his locker, looking blankly into it as if it didn't even exist, as if he didn't exist. There was noise and movement all around him but he just stared ahead as if waiting for a bus to come and take him away. He wanted nothing more than to be away from everything right now.

Two nights ago, after the confrontation between Jack and Billy at lacrosse practice, Billy and Chris met up with Lucas and some of the other players on the team in Billy's basement. The encounter with Jack didn't play out to Billy's satisfaction and he wasn't happy.

"I'm done with talking. That kid is a menace - especially to the lacrosse team, our team. Did you see him the last game? Blaming his poor skills on a stomach ache?" Billy grabbed his belly and started mimicking Jack. "Oh, my stomach hurts. My stomach hurts. Oh, look at me everybody. I can't play well because my stomach hurts. I'm such a wimp. Feel sorry for me. Oh, coach, I can't play anymore. I have to go home and have my Mommy take care of me. Oh, poor me."

The group laughed at Billy's impersonation, but not Chris.

"But maybe his stomach did hurt?" Chris countered.

Billy shot a sharp glance at Chris. "Don't fall for his lies, Chris. I know you guys were friends, but look at what he has done. He took your girl away from you. You shared your private secret with him and he took advantage of the whole situation."

"I guess..."

"No, there are no guesses here, Chris. He admitted it today! And he has the nerve to call that friendship. You know what real friendship is? What you see right here in this room. Jack is home alone with his Mommy and we are here together. Friends. Brothers even."

The group shook their heads in agreement.

Billy continued on his tirade. "Jack is a nuisance but he is especially dangerous to the good of the team. We might have lost against Centerville if it weren't for you stepping up and taking Jack's place, Chris. Don't forget the awesome power and skills that reside within you. Jack has been keeping you down. Stopping you from achieving greatness. We can't let that happen anymore."

Lucas reacted immediately. "How are we going to stop him, Billy?"

"Good question, Lucas. I'm glad you asked. We have to show Jack who the real boss is. Us."

The other boys began asking how.

Billy looked around at everyone in the basement, a slight smile on his face. "We are going to make sure that Jackie-boy doesn't mess up any more games for us. We are going to take him down in the next game.

"Take him down?" Chris said, his eyes wide with confusion.

"That's right, Chris. Take him down. Jack is going to have an 'accident' at the next game that will force him to the sidelines for the rest of the season."

The group nodded.

"Wait a minute, guys. You want to hurt, Jack? You can't do that," Chris implored.

"Oh, don't worry, Chris. We aren't going to do anything. You are," Billy winked.

"What?"

"Yep, you are going to take him down. Think about it, Chris. Who has been hurt the most by Jack? You, my friend. Who better than to teach him a lesson and save the day for the team than you?"

Lucas joined in. "Billy is right, Chris. It's gotta be you. You've got to teach him a lesson. Not just for you, but for the team."

A mixed chorus of claps and cheers came from the rest of the boys.

Chris' heart was beating fast. "I don't know, guys. This doesn't seem right."

"Was it right when he stole your girlfriend, Chris? Was it right when he said he was your friend and then stabbed you in the back? Was it right when he kept you from rising up the ranks of the team? No, it wasn't right, but what is right is us stopping him."

"I don't think I can do this guys."

"Sure you can. You have to. You want to be part of the team, right Chris? Being part of the team means protecting the team. This team needs protection. We are family, right guys?" Billy implored.

Everyone jumped up on their feet and shouted in agreement.

When the gang quieted down, Billy spoke softly, looking deeply at Chris. "We're counting on you. We are your family now. Orders are orders. But even a family won't leave a member hanging to dry in the wind. When you're one of us, you are never alone. Lucas, you'll help Chris out, right?"

"You got it, Billy. I'll come up with a plan and even help make sure it goes down without any problems." He put his hand out to Chris. "Me and you, Chris."

Chris could barely concentrate. So much being said and planned and he was so scared, but maybe Billy had a point. He wasn't sure what the point was, but Billy was so convincing that Jack was to blame for all the recent things that took place. He had to be. Chris slowly put his hand out to shake Lucas' hand, but it didn't feel like it was his energy alone that was making it happen. It felt like his hand was being guided by some unknown force, a force that he was afraid of.

A grin a mile wide appeared on Billy's face.

Chapter 21

April 14, 2011

"3, 2, 1...HALFTIME!"

The people in the bleachers on both sides of the field cheered. This was a fabulous Friday night showdown between two great teams. The first two quarters did not disappoint and the fans found themselves standing more than sitting, and they were loving every minute of it. Some stayed where they were while many made their way down to the concession stand. Energy for the next two quarters was definitely going to be needed in the form of soft drinks and ice cream.

The Barnaby Hills team ran back to the sidelines, grabbing and slurping down water and sports drinks to quench their thirst. They high-fived and slapped each other on the back. With the score tied right now, they needed to give each other all the encouragement they could muster. Franklin Township was a worthy adversary and they knew it. Ten minutes of rest until the 3rd quarter would end quickly and then they would be back in the fray and playing hard all the way until the end.

Jack put his helmet and stick down and made his way over to the locker room to go to the bathroom. Things were going well tonight. Unlike the last game, the team seemed to be working well together. The tension that had been building up over the week just wasn't there. Instead of excluding him from the action, Billy and the boys were passing him the ball like they used to. Chris wasn't talking or looking at him, but he didn't feel any animosity exuding off of him. Maybe what happened a couple of days ago had a big impact on him. Whatever the case, things felt pretty good, and that was a big relief.

On his way back to the field, Jack saw Sarah on line at the

concession stand. She waved and he came over to her.

"Hey, I didn't know that cheerleaders were allowed to get ice cream during half time. Coach Weber would make me run ten laps if he saw me doing that."

Sarah laughed. "Well luckily Coach Weber isn't in charge of the cheerleading squad, now is he?"

"Lucky you," Jack chuckled.

"You guys are playing an awesome game out there. We don't even have to try and whip the crowd into a frenzy. They are doing it all by themselves. It is so great to see you guys really working so well together."

"I know. Right? We really are playing like a well-oiled machine tonight."

"Totally."

The line started moving.

"You better get back to the team before the Coach wonders where you are. What are you doing after the game?"

"Hmm, that's a good question. There are so many things I can choose from but I think the biggest thing was going home and getting some sleep. That's the kind of exciting life I live."

"You are one party animal, Jack Wilson. I've a got a better idea. How about that walk home that never happened?"

"If my memory is correct, that 'walk home' was supposed to include a stop for some ice cream, but here you are about to have some and I'll wind up hearing you talk about how good YOUR ice cream was but I won't have any."

"I'll tell you what," Sarah said smartly. "I will make the ultimate sacrifice and get out of this line right now and wait until the game is over so both of us can have ice cream together. What do you say about that?"

"I say it's a deal."

They both put out their hands and shook on it, trying to be very serious for as long as they could before erupting into laughter.

"I'll be right here waiting for you after the game - win or lose," Sarah said.

"Awesome."

Sarah walked away and headed over to the rest of the cheerleading squad. Jack turned slowly to get back to the bench and saw someone standing there staring at him. It was Chris and he looked like the saddest kid on the planet.

Chapter 22

April 14, 2011

"Huddle up, guys!"

Coach Weber got down on one knee and brought the players close together in a circle to give a final pep talk before the last quarter of the game.

"I don't usually congratulate the team before winning a game, but I am seeing some stellar play out there on the field. Everyone has really worked hard tonight. I'm proud of you and you should be proud of yourselves."

The boys showed each other some team spirit by slapping each other's helmets.

"But, we still have another quarter to go and Franklin is not going to give up without a fight. Defense, continue what you are doing and make sure you're driving that ball up away from our goal. Middies, don't take any chances with far shots. We don't want to give the goalie ample time to react. Attackers, short throws and close play to their net but with speed and accuracy. Jack, Lucas and Chris you guys are going to start us out up there for this quarter. We can win this boys, but it is going to take teamwork. Right?"

The team bellowed in the affirmative.

"Well alright, let's take this game home, boys."

The players let out a loud whoop, broke from the circle and headed onto the field. Everyone took their positions waiting for the face-off. As soon the referee's whistle blew, the middies for Franklin and Barnaby Hills both tried to clamp down on the ball and gain possession. It looked like they were two bulls in a battle with their horns locked tight. The Barnaby Hills center middie rolled off to the left with the ball cradled in the net of his stick. The fans on both sides of the field went wild and screams of "GREAT JOB!" and "GET HIM!" clashed with each other as if the voices themselves were playing the game.

Jack ran for an open spot, trying to shake the defender that was closest to him. It looked like he would get a pass from the middie with possession when a Franklin player jabbed the ball out from his stick, scooped it up and hurled it down towards the Barnaby goal. This was pretty much how the game had been going all night long - a constant exchange of possession and non-stop passes and throws. The goalies for each team would certainly be lauded for their skills after tonight. The score was low and the saves were high. Jack, Chris and Lucas moved away from the Franklin net to better grab the ball if passed up. They could see that the action around Barnaby's goal was heavy. Franklin was putting their all into wanting a win and they were spot on with shots at the goal, but the Barnaby Hills goalie was on fire, blocking and catching shots as if his hands and stick knew exactly where the ball was heading. As Jack watched, a Franklin player stumbled as he took a shot on net and it went wide and out of bounds. As the ball was being retrieved and play about to resume, Jack cast a glance over at Chris who was standing a few yards away. Almost sensing that Jack was looking his way, Chris turned his head and looked directly into Jack's eyes. He took out his mouth guard.

"I'm sorry," Chris said in a low but audible tone.

Jack raised his eyebrows in confusion. Chris was apologizing? If anyone should apologize, it should be Billy, but Jack knew that would never happen. Jack motioned to take out his mouth guard to respond when Lucas yelled from the other side of the field that the ball was coming back down. Jack turned back to the action and saw that a middie on Lucas' side had possession of the ball and was making his way up. Jack turned to his left and started running to get closer to the goal and he saw Chris follow his trajectory. Jack yelled over his shoulder at Chris.

"Go up the middle, Chris! Up the middle!"

Chris continued following Jack as if he didn't hear him. Jack was nearing the net and Lucas now had possession of the ball. He saw Jack was open for a pass and threw it to him, but instead of throwing it in front of Jack and much closer to the goal, he threw it slightly behind him, forcing Jack to turn around a bit with his arms and stick facing to the rear. The throw was fast and Jack reached out to catch it before it went out of bounds when another stick came crashing down on his left wrist, directly between his forearm guard and glove. The pain was instantaneous. Jack immediately stopped running and dropped his stick as if it were the source of his agony. He instinctively reached out with his right hand to cradle his left and automatically drew both into his abdomen for protection. Although in a tremendous amount of pain, he realized that all the happy noise from the fans in the bleachers had stopped and was replaced by shouts of "Oh, no!" and choral moans of sympathy. Jack looked up from his cradled wrist and saw his coach and a medic running from the sidelines in his direction yelling for players to get out of the way. The very next second, he looked off to his right and saw Chris standing just a few feet away. His stick was laying on the ground, too. Jack wanted to see his face. He wanted to see his eyes like he had just seen them only a few moments before. But Chris was looking down at the ground as if his head were permanently fixed in that direction. Just before anyone else was close enough to help him or in listening distance, Jack heard Chris speak. It was faint but clear.

"Sorry, Jack."

4th Quarter

"Don't tell me the moon is shining;
show me the glint of light on broken glass."

Anton Chekhov

Chapter 1

April 14, 2011

"Lacrosse? You won't be playing lacrosse any time soon, Jack. You have a hairline fracture of your radius. You'll be in a wrist splint for about six weeks. There won't be any lacrosse playing during that time. Sorry, bud. But on the bright side, the injury could have been much worse. You're very lucky. I'm going to get a splint right now. Be right back."

The E.R. doctor left the examining room.

"Well, you heard him. No lacrosse. The season will be over before the six weeks is up."

Jack's mom put her arm around his shoulder, careful to not disturb his injury.

"That doesn't mean that you can't root for the team from the sideline, right? Or maybe Mr. Weber can use your talents for other purposes. You may not be able to play but you can still be involved."

"I don't know. Maybe."

"We have to be positive here," she said with conviction. "The doctor is right. It could have been much, much worse given what I was told."

"I think what would have been worse is if you had been in the stands and saw me get hurt. I don't think I would ever be able to live down my mother running onto the field screaming, 'MY BABY! MY BABY!'" Jack said smiling, trying to make himself feel better.

"Ha-ha, very funny. Go ahead; make fun of the mom that doesn't like violent sports, but seriously, I think you're lucky that you only have a hairline fracture."

Jack knew that to be true. Had it been Lucas or Billy that did what Chris did, the injury probably would have required surgery to repair. As much as Jack was angry at Chris for taking a cheap shot, he knew that Chris probably held back on the power of the blow. And there was no way that Chris planned that hit by himself. Billy's fingerprints were on every aspect of it.

"I guess so, Mom."

The doctor came back into the room. "Okay. One wrist splint ready to go. But before I put it on, I've been told by one of the nurses that there is a beautiful young girl in the waiting room that is eager to see how the patient is. I think Sarah is her name."

A slight grin appeared on Jack's face.

"Is that a smile I see?" his mother said, trying to coax out some more happiness.

"Mom," Jack replied somewhat embarrassed.

"Will I actually get to meet Sarah? And here it only took a broken arm for it to happen."

Jack chuckled. "Mom, don't make me laugh. It makes my arm hurt."

"Oh, I'm sorry, honey."

He laughed. "Just kidding."

Jack's mother shook her head and turned to the doctor. "Do you have any kids, doctor? If you don't, you can have this one; he's potty trained."

"No thank you. I have a toddler at home and she is all the joy and trouble I need. But I can put this on right now and then we'll take care of the paperwork to get you guys out of here."

"When you're done, can Sarah come back and visit?" Jack asked hopefully.

"Yep, right after this is done."

The doctor carefully placed Jack's arm and hand into the wrist splint and tightened it gently with the Velcro straps that would help immobilize the injury. He also placed his arm in a sling to give it more stability.

"You can take off the sling and splint when you take a shower but I want you to keep both of them on during daily activities. At night you can take off the sling, but do yourself a favor and try not to roll over on your arm in your sleep. That won't feel good. Mom, you are quality control here. Make sure he follows everything I just said - for at least six weeks. Make an appointment with your doctor for a follow up visit at the end of that time. If he does experience any pain, don't hesitate to call your doctor or bring him back here. Sound good?"

Both Jack and his Mom shook their heads in agreement.

"I'll get you guys signed out, and in the meantime, I'll send your friend back. You were a good patient, Jack, but please don't make this a habit."

Jack grinned. "Don't worry, doctor. I'll try and stay out of harm's way."

The doctor left and shortly after, Sarah walked slowly into the room, as if not sure what to expect.

"Hey, Jack."

"Hi, Sarah."

They both stared at each other in a warmly awkward fashion.

"Hmm-hmm," said the third person in the room.

"Oh, sorry. Sarah, this is my Mom."

"Hello, Mrs. Wilson."

"Hello, Sarah. It's very nice to meet you. I wish it were under different circumstances, though."

"Yeah, I didn't exactly picture meeting Jack's mom for the first time in a hospital. At your house would have been nice."

Jack's mother smiled. "Well, with Jack on the injured list for a while, we would love to have you come over and have dinner with us. How does that sound?"

"I'd like that a lot."

"Good. I'm going to hit the bathroom before we leave. That will give you guys a little bit of time to talk. Okay?" Mrs. Wilson said with a little side wink to Jack.

"Thanks, Mom."

As his mother left the room, Sarah walked closer to the bed.

"You in much pain?"

"A little. They gave me something about 20 minutes ago and it is starting to work. So what happened back at school after they took me to the hospital?"

"The ref called for a timeout to talk with both coaches and Chris."

"And?"

"Well, from what I heard, Chris told them that he thought the pass was meant for him but it was just out of reach, so he swung down hard with his stick as a last ditch attempt to catch it. I guess that was good enough explanation because they started the game right back up. We won, if that is any consolation."

Jack rubbed the wrist sprint gently with his good hand. "So he was reaching out for the ball, huh?" he said with more than a hint of sarcasm.

"Jack, you're not thinking that Chris and Billy..."

Jack interrupted Sarah's thought. "That's exactly what I'm thinking."

Sarah bit her lip and shook her head gently. "Yeah, after everything that has been going on, you're probably right. But Coach Weber has to be told about this, right?"

Jack looked past Sarah, his eyes falling on a crack in the wall outside his room. If he thought long and hard enough, maybe he could shrink himself down and crawl into that crack for ten or twenty years. But Sarah's voice brought him back.

"What are we gonna do, Jack? This can't go on any longer."

"I know. I know. Something has to happen. I just don't know what that is going to be. I just don't know..."

Chapter 2

April 14, 2011

The ice cream parlor was packed with parents, students and, of course, lacrosse players. Every seat and every space was filled as many in the town joined in the after-game festivities of another win by the Barnaby Hills team. Billy and the gang were sitting pretty in the middle of it all with ice cream cones looking like edibly delicious trophies. As patrons made their way up to the counter to place their order, they stopped by and congratulated the players on an amazing game. Most of the well-wishers asked if there was any word about Jack and his arm, but no one had any information as to the extent of his injury. Chris Stiles sat silently in the group, but winced a little whenever Jack's name was brought up. Jack should have been there with them right now, but he wasn't - and it was all his fault.

"Speech! Speech!" the crowd began to chant after the last spoonfuls of ice cream had been devoured. The boys at the table urged Billy to address the calls. He acted like he didn't want to say anything but then quickly stood up on his chair and smiled broadly at the surrounding group.

"Wow. Thank you all for your support tonight. We couldn't have done it without all of you being there and cheering us on. I wish you could all feel what we feel right now. We are just blown away by it all. Franklin Township played a great game tonight, but I guess it just wasn't good enough. I know that sounds like bragging but how can we not brag with fans like you sticking by us. Thank you. Enjoy your ice cream."

Billy started to get down from his chair and people began to clap and whistle, but a few started yelling about Jack and how he was doing. Realizing that he couldn't ignore the calls, he reluctantly got back up on his chair.

"We don't know much about Jack right now, but some of us were going to go over to the hospital and find out as soon as this is over." Billy cast a glance down at Lucas and raised his eyebrow. Lucas stifled a laugh. Billy continued with mock sincerity. "What happened tonight was a horrible accident. Jack is a great player but it looks like he got in the way as his teammate was trying to get possession of the ball. It stinks but sometimes things like this happen. I think I speak for all the guys when I wish Jack the best and hope he can join us on the field real soon. But that's enough from me. You guys are great. Go Barnaby Hills!"

The crowd cheered. Shortly after many began to make their way out of the store, calling out to the team as they exited and wishing them a final congratulations. Chris remained silent with his head bowed down as if unaware that anything else was going on around him. When the place had emptied out considerably, Billy grabbed Chris by the shoulder and tried to shake him out of his stupor.

"Chris, what are you doing, dude? Give it a rest already. Jack got in the way of a ball that was clearly being passed to you. Stuff happens. Let it go. You didn't even touch your ice cream."

Chris raised his head up and looked Billy right in his eyes.

"What are you talking about, Billy. That was all planned out. I did exactly what Lucas told me to do and now Jack is hurt. Really hurt. I did that to him. And then I lied about it to Coach Weber and the ref. It's not right. It's just not right."

Billy glanced around the ice cream parlor to make sure no one could hear what Chris had just said.

"Keep your voice down, Chris," he said in a low, disturbing tone. "Whatever happened to Jack he did to himself. How many times do I have to point that out to you? What you did tonight, you did for the good of the team. We don't need Jack to win. We won the last two games without him, basically. If anything, he stops us from working together. I don't know what is going on in your head right now, but you did us all a favor. Right, guys?"

The boys all grunted their approval.

Chris shook his head. "I don't know. I think I should talk with the Coach." He looked down into his lap as if to solidify his confusion.

Billy's eyes flashed orange for half a second and his arms and shoulders locked tight as he balled his hands into hard-clenched fists. He was about to lay into Chris verbally, but realized that there were still some customers in the ice cream parlor within earshot. He softened his posture and tried a different tactic.

"Chris, look at me, buddy. Do you want to damage your standing on the team by going to the Coach and telling him that you fouled your own teammate on purpose? Do you think Coach is going take that lightly? He'll kick you off the team before you can say 'I'm sorry.' Be smart about this. What happened tonight happened for the best. How many times do I have to convince you of that? But there's something else to consider here. I didn't want to say anything until the end of the month, but you're kind of forcing my hand right now. What you did tonight was kind of an initiation - a way to show us that you are really one of us, a star player. Can you keep a secret?" Billy didn't wait for an answer. "Ever since the start of this team, me and some of the other players have been going to a special place in the woods where we...well, we basically celebrate the sport of lacrosse on our terms. Only the best players can come, and guess what? After the way you proved your loyalty to the team tonight, we decided that you are ready for that next step. You are ready to come and be a part of the elite squad, the best of the best."

Chris stopped sulking for a moment and appeared interested. "Jack was MVP last year, did you invite him to join, too?"

Billy sighed. What he really wanted to say to Chris was "Jack, Jack, Jack...that's all that comes out of your stinkin' mouth!" but he stopped himself and continued with a measured tone.

"Jack...was invited but turned us down. He said we weren't good enough for him, if you can believe that. The nerve. But that's old news. You are the new news and we would love for you to be a part of our crew. But that all goes away if you are kicked off the team, buddy. Think about it. Ultimately the choice is yours, but just think about what you'd be missing after working so hard."

Billy turned away from Chris and started talking and laughing with the others. Chris looked around at all the boys chatting and joking with one another. If he told the Coach what happened, all his hard work to get where he was right now would be gone. Maybe Jack was wrong about Billy all this time. Maybe it was Jack who was causing all the problems. After all, Jack only moved to Barnaby Hills last year and Chris didn't ever remember problems like this happening between kids at school.

"Billy."

No response.

"Billy." Chris tapped him on the shoulder. Billy turned away from the rest of the team slowly, giving them all a sly eye as he did so.

"Yeah, buddy, what's up?"

"Okay, I won't tell Coach. And I want to be part of the elite team."

"Now you're talking. The end of the month can't come soon enough. We'll all have a howling good time. A howling good time."

Chapter 3

April 14, 2011

"What are we doing out here, full moon after full moon? Playing lacrosse? More like wasting time. We turn into monsters and play a never ending game with sticks and a ball. I've been doing it for nearly a year now and I still don't know why. And when I ask questions, you say, 'All will be revealed when the time is right.' What does that even mean? I say the right time is NOW!"

Jack had heard these words before. They were eerily familiar. In fact, he was pretty sure that he had said them, but they weren't coming out of his mouth right now. They were coming out of someone else's.

"Did you hear me, Jack? I say the time is right NOW!"

Jack looked up at the person talking to him. It wasn't a person. It was a wolf.

"Some friend you turned out to be. Look at what you let them do to me. Why? Just because I hurt your wrist? They made me do that. And then you left me and now look. I'm a wolf. Why did you let this happen, Jack?"

"Chris, I'm sorry, dude. I didn't want this to happen. I tried to stop it. You know I did."

"You didn't try hard enough, Jackie-boy, and now you have to pay."

It wasn't Chris anymore. It was Billy in human form. He reached out and grabbed Jack by the injured wrist and started twisting it. The pain was intense. Jack swung out with his right hand to hit Billy in the face but every time he did, Billy would dodge the punch to the left or right and would go back and forth morphing between human and wolf with each blow thrown. He laughed and laughed throughout the whole ordeal.

Out of the darkness, a voice commanded both boys to stop. "Switch sides," it said.

Now Billy stood before Jack. His arm in a brace, a pained expression on his face. A whistle was blown and Billy cowered at the sound. Jack looked around, confused at what was taking place.

"Grab his wrist and squeeze," the voice said.

Jack stared at Billy who had begun to whimper in anticipation. Jack reached out to grab Billy by the wrist and stopped.

"Grab his wrist and hurt him like he hurt you," the strange voice said.

Jack reached out again but drew his hand back and said, "No."

Billy let out a small laugh in relief. "I knew you couldn't do it."

All of a sudden, Billy transformed back into Chris. He had a lacrosse stick in his hand and he slammed it down on Jack's wrist. Jack's hand and arm exploded with pain.

"Take the stick and hit him back with it," the voice commanded.

Jack looked at Chris who was staring blankly at him - almost through him. Anger was welling up behind the pain and Jack was close to doing as the voice commanded, but again, Jack said, "No."

Chris looked relieved and said, "Thank you, Jack," and disappeared.

"Your will is strong, Jack, but your humanity makes you

weak." The voice seemed to be coming from everywhere around him. "This can be overcome. With training, you will achieve much. You will be ruthless, determined, a leader to be respected and feared."

"Who are you?" Jack asked. "Show yourself."

"All will be revealed when the time is right."

"Stop playing games, Billy. I know it's you. Come back and let's settle this."

The voice started to chuckle and slowly the laughter grew and grew until it reverberated painfully in Jack's ears. It stopped abruptly and everything became completely dark, and then directly in front of Jack's face, two piercing yellow eyes and gleaming white fangs appeared. The stench of rotten, fetid breath crept up Jack's nostrils. For a moment, it seemed as the partially revealed beast would just be content to stare silently but then it backed off by a foot as if retreating and abruptly came hurtling directly at Jack as if to bite his very face off.

Jack awoke, a scream lingering at the back of his throat, his chest heaving up and down like a frightened, panting dog. Immediately he felt pain in his arm. He was sleeping in his bed and had rolled over onto his wrist. He righted himself and turned on the light next to his bed. Another bad dream. They all felt so different but related, like clunky pieces to a difficult puzzle.

As with the other nightmares, Jack began to calm down as distance accumulated between him and the dream, but the pain in his arm persisted. He reached over and took some aspirin off the side table and swallowed them down with a swig of water as the doctor had suggested. Hopefully he would be able to get back to sleep, but right now, he was in puzzle-solving mode and began to think through everything that had been happening as of late, including the nightmares. *There might not be any more sleep tonight, he* thought to himself.

Chapter 4

April 17, 2011

Jack rested as much as he could on Saturday and Sunday as per his doctor's orders. His mom surprised him by making pancakes and bacon on both mornings, just the thing to boost to his spirits - and stomach.

News traveled fast and friends and neighbors called or came by to see how he was doing. Coach Weber even dropped by to apologize for not making it to the hospital. He explained how the game had to continue and by the time it was over and everyone had left the field, he called the hospital and Jack had already been discharged. Chris' mom also called to see how he was doing. She said that Chris was very silent but she could tell that he felt really bad about what happened, and that she was sure Chris would contact him soon and talk things through. Jack held back the urge to say, "Watch me as I hold my breath," but he knew that her sentiment was sincere. But the biggest thing that happened was Sarah coming over on Sunday afternoon to hang out for a little while. A little while turned into a long while and she wound up watching a movie with Jack and his mom and even staying for dinner. Jack wondered aloud that with all the special treatment, he should get hurt more often. Both Sarah and his mom laughed but basically told him to stop while he was ahead.

After having trouble sleeping on Friday night, the next two nights were dreamless and peaceful, and apart from the injury, it turned out to be a great weekend.

Jack got to school on Monday feeling relatively refreshed. Just like after the Centerville game, classmates gathered around him to find out how he was doing and to offer condolences. Two times within a week, Jack didn't finish a lacrosse game but was the talk of the town. He felt humbled by all the attention and good wishes from students and teachers as he walked down the hall before classes started.

"Jack, Jack...can I speak with you for a minute?"

Jack turned to see Coach Weber walking down the hall towards him.

"Hey, Coach."

"I know I spoke with you over the weekend but I just wanted to talk with you in school, too. I'm really sorry about the injury. It's not often that you see that kind of injury accidentally being doled out from a teammate. Chris is just devastated."

Jack raised an eyebrow. "Chris is devastated? I mean, yeah, I'm sure he is."

"It was one of those fluke kind of things. I know it could be easy to get mad about the whole thing, but I just wanted you to know that accidents do happen, even to the best of players. But we are really glad you are back at school and on the mend."

"Thanks. Um, Mr. Weber. What does this all mean for me and lacrosse?"

"Well, I spoke with the doctor and he said that you can't play for the rest of the season. I guess that is the current state of affairs."

"Yeah, I'm pretty bummed out about having to sit things out. Is there any way that I can be involved on the sidelines or anything?"

"I appreciate your enthusiasm, Jack, but I don't know what you can do. You have to watch that arm of yours. We wouldn't want anything to happen to you. Probably the best thing you can do for the team is just get better. You want to be able to try out for the high school team next year, don't you?"

"Oh, no doubt. But I'd sure like to stay close to the guys and all and help out where I can."

"Don't you worry about the guys. They'll be just fine. It looks like Billy has taken Chris under his wing as of late. He'll get his game where it needs to be. As for you, if you want to really help out, I'd say get your fan game on and root us on from the stands. What do you think?"

Jack pursed his lips a little and shook his head slowly. Billy taking Chris under his wing was exactly the reason he wanted to remain close to the action. Now was not the time to take a vacation. The full moon was coming in a couple of weeks and Jack was hoping to pry away Billy's claws from Chris' skin and psyche a little bit.

"Oh, I definitely plan on coming to the games, Coach. I may not be with the team on the field but I'll be there, you can put some money on that."

Coach Weber smiled. "Good, good. I know we can count on you for support. Who knows, maybe you'll get a whole new perspective on the game away from the sidelines and will be telling me how to run the team."

"Well, I don't know about that, but I'm always here if you need me."

"That's what I'm counting on. Thanks, Jack. I'll see you later in class. And don't think I'm going to go easy on your there just because you're hurt. No excuses for late homework. You got me."

"Yes, sir."

"Good man. See you later."

Mr. Weber turned around and made his way down the crowded hallway. Jack reached back into his locker for his Math textbook. He closed it and started walking to class. His mind was all over the place. Access to Billy and Chris would require more time and thought. The puzzle just got harder.

Chapter 5

April 21, 2011

The week went by at a snail's pace, for the most part. Jack did his best to get by with one arm. It wasn't too difficult, but his mom wouldn't let him skateboard to school. That was a complete bummer, but he sort of understood where she was coming from. And it was better for him to be careful. The next full moon was in less than two weeks and he knew that he would have to be ready for anything. He had no idea if his injury would carry over into when he changed into a wolf. The first time he thought about it, he actually laughed a little thinking about how he would look as a wolf with his arm in a sling.

He didn't really see Chris that much the whole week. His locker was right next to Jack's but it seemed that he was making sure that neither of them would be there at the same time. It was probably for the best. Jack honestly didn't know how he would react to him. Would he talk with him? Scream at him? Just ignore him? Any or all of the three? But it was definitely a big relief to not have to engage him. He didn't even see much of Billy or his boys, either. Tonight the lacrosse team had a big game against the Tompkinsville Tigers and during lunch, the Barnaby Hills team had been spending time out on the field throwing passes and working on plays. It was a nice reprieve from all of the angry faces and stares that would have taken place between him and Billy from across the cafeteria. For just about the whole week, Jack had lunch with Sarah. She'd start the period out eating with her friends and then say goodbye and join him for the rest of the period. It was almost like the way things would be if life were "normal" - whatever that meant.

Jack was just finishing his sandwich when she came over.

"So what did you have today?" Sarah said with a smile as she took the seat right next to him.

"Oh, mom has been going above and beyond. Sliced beef tenderloin with lettuce and pesto dressing. Yummy does not describe it."

"Tenderloin?"

"Yup, she said 'Nothing is too good for her little man." Her words, not mine."

"If I break my arm, will your mom take care of me, too?"

"Judging by how she likes you so much, I'd say the chances are good."

Sarah laughed. "Awesome."

"So you guys all ready for tonight's game? Any new cheers to look forward to?"

"Nothing new, but, yeah, we are ready. You're definitely coming, right?"

"Wouldn't miss it for the world. I'll probably be watching you guys more than the game."

"Awesome, again. But are you sure being at the game and not playing is going to be okay with you? I mean, just last week you were on the field and now you'll be in the stands. I don't think anyone would blame you if you didn't come. I want to see you, of course, but I'd totally get it if you didn't come."

Jack shook his head from side to side a little. "Nah, I'll be okay. Don't get me wrong; I love playing, but it's all good. Sometimes it's okay to step outside yourself to see what else is going on," he said with a wry little smile, knowing exactly how that sentiment felt on a month by month basis. He changed the subject. "Have you had a chance to see how lacrosse practice has been going this week?"

"A little. Coach Weber has definitely been keeping them

busy."

"What about Billy and Chris? Anything that you noticed?"

"They've been pretty close the whole week, but Chris just doesn't seem happy. No smiles. No nothing. I heard Billy yell at him a few times out on the field, but I couldn't really hear what he was saying. Do you think Billy is still up to something?"

Jack laughed a little at the question. "No doubt at all. This is far from over."

"But now that you're not playing because of your arm, won't that be enough to satisfy Billy? You're not a threat to him."

Jack looked right into Sara's eyes. How he wished he could just tell her EVERYTHING. It would make life so much easier - to just let it all fall off his shoulders. But things were going so well between them. If he tried to even hint at the fact that he and the others turned into Moonwalkers each month, that would be it. He was hoping to ask her to officially be his girlfriend. How does one go from that to 'Oh, by-the-way, I'm a werewolf.' One doesn't. He was about to tell her something along the lines of 'Billy doesn't know when to stop' when an idea shot through his brain like a bolt of electricity.

"Hey, Sarah. What are you doing on Saturday?"

"I don't think I'm doing anything. Why?"

"You want to go for a walk?"

"A walk? With you? Anyplace special?"

"Sort of, yeah."

"I'm in."

Jack smiled, but he wasn't sure if he was about to do the right thing - for him or Sarah.

Chapter 6

April 21, 2011

"I still can't believe that you're here. This is so unlike you," Jack said between bites of a steaming hot dog with all the trimmings.

"Well it's different. You're not playing. I don't have to worry about seeing you get hurt. Don't get me wrong; I don't want to see anybody get hurt, but when it's your own son in harm's way, it just makes things different."

Jack smiled at his Mom. "Well, I appreciate you tagging along tonight. I have someone to turn to if a case of the 'I-should-be-out-there-playing blues' hits me."

"What are mothers for? By the way, if those blues do come a knockin', might I suggest you focus your attention on that girl who can't take her eyes off you." Jack's mom raised her hand and waved to Sarah down on the sidelines. Sarah immediately waved back.

Jack waved, too. "She's great. Isn't she, Mom?"

"Well, great is a strong word. Don't you think?"

Jack immediately turned to his mother, ready to give her the most incredulous look he possibly could when he saw a slight smile on her otherwise serious face. He stared at her until she couldn't take it anymore. She broke out into audible laughter.

"For half a second, you had me," he said, nudging her with his shoulder.

"I have to work on being less obvious," she snickered. "I could have had you for much longer."

"Yeah, yeah, yeah. Sure you could. But I wouldn't have believed it if your expression was as still as the Mona Lisa's. You think Sarah's as awesome as I do."

"Ok, you got me. She is awesome. But I wouldn't expect anything less. She is dating MY son after all."

"Well, that's not official yet. I haven't asked her."

"Why is that?"

"Nervous, I guess. I mean, I think she likes me, but what if she says 'No." That would kind of stink."

"You know what I'm going to say?" his mother responded.

"You'll never know if you don't try," Jack replied, trying to sound just like his mom.

"Bingo."

An announcement came over the loudspeakers asking everyone to rise for the National Anthem. Everyone on and off the field got up. When it was over, Jack hugged his Mom.

"What was that for?" she asked as she hugged him back.

"Just for being the best mom in the world."

"I'll accept that," she smiled. "Oh, look, the players are running out. I guess the game is about to start."

"Yep, my fingers are crossed."

"For Barnaby Hills to win the game?"

Jack laughed. "Oh, yeah, that, too."

His mom smiled and nudged him with her shoulder."

Chapter 7

April 22, 2011

There it was again, that horrid, putrid smell of Howl House. Jack was back in the living room looking around. How did he get here? He didn't remember leaving his house or running through the woods. He wasn't even in the form of a Moonwalker.

"It's a dream, dude," he said aloud to himself. "Just another one of those dreams. No worries. Wake up and you'll be back at home in bed."

"Is it a dream, Jack?" a raspy voice boomed from all around him.

"Who's there? Who said that? Show yourself." Jack replied courageously while his insides felt as if they were melting from fear.

"I am the master of Howl House. A warrior imbued with the spirit of the ancient ones. You are right to fear me, Jack. I know what you think. I know what you feel. I smell the child hiding inside you, cowering in the corner, wishing that you would wake up from this horrible nightmare. Try as you may to wake up; you will only do so when I allow it to happen."

Jack took in and let out a deep breath. Like his other dreams, this one wasn't making much sense, but at least he knew that it was, indeed, a dream. Knowing that was enough to make him ease up a little.

"Adaptability, that's good, Jack. Very good. Your ability to reason and adapt to new situations is commendable, yet you fight the very gift you have been given. Why is that? Curiosity is

one of my failings, but it helps to pass the time. You have a rare opportunity to explain yourself. Take advantage, please."

Jack ignored the voice's question. "I'm tired of your games, Billy. Show yourself!"

A low guttural growl of a noise came from below Jack and grew to envelope him in a deafening howl of anger that reverberated throughout the house. Jack threw his hands up to his ears to help mute the pain.

"I AM NOT BILLY!" the gruff voice gushed afterwards. "YOU DISRESPECT ME WITH YOUR CLUMSY THOUGHTS! I OUGHT TO PUNISH YOU NOW FOR YOUR INSUBORDINATION!"

Taking his hands down from his ears, Jack looked around immediately for something to defend himself with. He saw the panel in the wall that held the lacrosse sticks. He ran to it, opened it and grabbed one out. He held it firmly in both hands in front of him.

Silence. No movement. The only thing Jack could hear and feel was the beating of his heart.

The raspy voice spoke again, calmly.

"You amuse me, Jack. You possess the capacity for greatness. You were one of my wiser selections, but even the best become tedious if they do not comply. Consider this dream a warning, Jack. A nightmare if you wish, but one with a lesson: no one is indispensable. You are a favorite, but my patience is running thin. There are others that will make do. They may not possess your innate skills but they will suffice, if necessary. Think before you act, for it may not only be you that gets hurt, but those that you love, as well."

Jack swung the lacrosse stick back and forth. "You leave everyone else alone," he yelled, looking around Howl House to

find the location of the voice. "If it's me you want, you deal with me and leave other people out of this. YOU HEAR ME?"

The voice chuckled. "Go back home now, Jack. Go back home to your bed. Wake up in the morning and kiss and hug your mother. Meet with Sarah and enjoy your walk together. Think about what was said tonight. Take your time. Take all the time you want, Jack. Take all the time you need...but your time is almost up."

Jack began screaming back at the voice, but it was to no avail as all he heard was loud laughter as he began to spiral around and around. Dizzy, he fell to the floor but landed in his bed at home. He sat up swinging his fists in the air, drenched in a cold sweat. Shaking, nerves rattled, Jack was completely aware of one thing: that was no dream.

Chapter 8

April 22, 2011

"And then he missed the pass. Missed it. I couldn't believe it."

"I know, right? The groan of disappointment from the stands was so loud. Me and the squad just knew we were going to have to work overtime to raise everyone's spirits at that point, but it was like cheering at a funeral."

"I know. I know. My mom and I could tell how hard you guys were working."

"7 - 0. I don't know when I have ever heard of Barnaby Hills losing by that much."

"Not during any game that I've ever played in - not that I'm saying I'm the reason they didn't win."

"Are you kidding me? You should be shouting that from the roof of the school. You not playing TOTALLY was the reason for the blow-out. The team can't do it without you, Jack. You will just have to swallow that fact."

Jack smiled, just a little. "Well, I don't know about that, but, man, I would have loved to have suited up and gotten into that game."

Sarah sped up a little and turned around to walk backwards so she could talk to Jack face to face. "And if that wasn't bad enough, Coach Weber went ballistic on all of them in the locker room. Anyone near the building could hear him. He was totally on fire. Billy tried to interrupt him a couple of times but the Coach wasn't having any of it. The last thing he said was, 'No excuses, Billy. Keep your lip zipped and listen up for a change!' Un-be-lie-va-ble."

"There's a part of me that wished I had heard that, but Mom was tuckered-out. That was the first time she stayed for a whole lacrosse game and she couldn't take it anymore. I give her credit for staying as long as she did. But she loved watching you guys."

"We were kind of awesome last night, if I say so myself."

"Good thing because everything else had gone to the dogs. Oh, watch out for that branch behind you!" Jack grabbed for Sarah's arm with his good hand, pulling her out of harm's way.

"Jack Wilson, if you wanted to hold my hand, all you had to do was ask."

"Well, then I wouldn't have had the chance to act like a hero. You know I planted that stick there just for that very reason."

"You don't have to save me from a branch to be my hero, Jack. Just be yourself."

Jack didn't know how to respond to that, so he didn't. They continued their walk through the woods hand-in-hand silently for the next few minutes.

"So," said Sarah, breaking the quiet, "where are we going?"

Jack had thought this through. Right after he woke up from last night's nightmare, he almost cancelled his plans to walk with Sarah today. The voice in the dream knew that he was going to be with her today. He tried to convince himself that there was no voice, that it was only a dream and that the voice knew where he was going because the voice was only part of Jack's subconscious, but he knew that wasn't true at all. It was then that he resolved to keep his plans with Sarah for the day - to take her to Howl House. Well, definitely not inside, but nearby, so he could tell her about Billy and his boys and the whacky lacrosse rituals they had - minus the werewolf part. It was as close to the truth as he was going to get. He couldn't let whatever that voice or wolf creature it was stop him from living his life and, more importantly, saving Chris.

Chris. He played as poorly or even worse than everyone else

at last night's game. Sarah and Jack had joked before about Billy missing a pass, but it was Chris who had thrown it and it wasn't the kind of pass that was going to go down in lacrosse history as one of the better ones. After the coach was done with his talk after the game, Billy must have handed Chris some heavy duty guilt for his role in the whole debacle. There's no way Billy would have passed up that chance. Last night was crazy in so many ways.

As for Howl House, they would keep a safe distance and Jack would tell Sarah what he could. He had to do something.

"It's a house out in the woods that Billy and all the guys call Howl House. It's a pretty creepy place."

"Do you take all of your girlfriends there?"

Jack was about to answer the question when he realized what Sarah had said.

"Girlfriend?" he managed to say.

"Well, that is what you planned on asking me today, isn't it?" Sarah stopped walking abruptly.

"Yeah, well, I was gon...going to ask ya...you...if that was something you would consider..."

"Hmm, let me think about it for a minute. Oh, look at that: minute's up. Yes, yes, I would like to be your girlfriend. Would you like to be my boyfriend?"

Jack smiled and shook his head up and down. He would have kept on shaking it but Sarah stopped him with a kiss. As she drew back, they both looked at each other and smiled.

"We'd better get going to Howl House," she said.

"Howl House? What's that?" Jack laughed.

"C'mon, Mr. Starry Eyes. The journey awaits."

They held each other's hands tighter and walked on.

Chapter 9

April 22, 2011

"Wake up, Mr. Sleepy, BAD PASS, Head."

Chris turned over from a deep but fitful sleep to see what was jabbing him so roughly in the leg.

"C'mon, Chris. Get up! There's work to do."

Billy was at the foot of the bed nudging Chris with his lacrosse stick.

"What, what are you doing here?"

"What am I doing here? I'll tell you what I'm doing here when you get up out of bed and grab your gear. Lucas and the other guys are outside on their dirt bikes waiting for you to get your butt out of bed. We've got things to do."

"How did you..."

Billy cut him off. "What is this - twenty questions? Your mom let me up. I can be very convincing with parents. Now get up."

"Geez, okay. Just give me a little bit of time to get ready. I have to get dressed and get a bite to eat."

"Ain't no time to eat breakfast. I've got candy bars in my backpack. GET UP!"

Chris sat up in bed and rubbed his eyes. "It's Saturday, Billy. What is so important that it can't wait until later?"

Billy leaned over and pointed the handle of his lacrosse stick right in Chris' face.

"There are things in life that you don't know yet, Mr. Stiles, but today, you may just get a peek at your future. Now get out of your bed and throw on some clothes. Time waits for no creature."

Chapter 10

April 22, 2011

Grey clouds blanketed the late April sky in every direction as Jack and Sarah walked through the woods to Howl House, but neither one of them noticed the weather. They were too busy laughing and enjoying each company. For a while, Jack even forgot about where they were going until Sarah slowed down and started looking around.

"This part of the woods seems different to me...not as open and airy. It's like the trees are so bunched up together that they are choking out the light."

Jack let out an audible breath. "Yeah, you've got that right. Howl House is just a little further ahead."

"Who would build a house out here in the middle of nowhere, and why would they name it Howl House? Seems weird. And you come out here with Billy and the gang? Why?"

Jack grabbed Sarah's hand a little tighter. "So many good questions. I'll answer what I can. I think this part of the woods was a sacred site to the Native American Indians for hundreds of years. There is something strangely mystical about it. You can almost feel it."

"Almost?" Sarah questioned, not waiting for a response. "I can definitely feel it...or something. I don't know what it is but it's there."

Jack shook his head in agreement. "I don't know who built Howl House or why. I don't even know how Billy found it, but they come here and get energized by it - like it is some primal source of power for the body."

"And is that how you feel when you come here?"

Jack looked into Sarah's eyes. She was so smart and so intuitive. How he ever thought she was taken in by Billy's personality and lies to begin with was one of the biggest blunders of his life to date.

"Just like you said you feel something being out here, I do, too. I've been wanting to find out more about it. But to answer your question, no, I don't feel the same way when I come out here like they do. I do believe there is something unexplainable around here, but I don't embrace it the way that Billy and the others do. They react to it like wild animals. I just want answers."

Sarah grabbed Jack's hand tighter this time. "Well, we're here. Let's go find some answers."

Jack looked at her with worry. "I'll show you the house, but we can't go inside."

"Why not? What's wrong?"

"It's, it's just not a place that we can go into. The house is old and the wood is rotting. I've been in before and it's not safe. Not safe at all. I can't bring you in there. You just have to believe me."

"I believe you. Okay, no going in. But can we go see it from the outside?"

Jack let out another audible breath. "Believe it or not, it's just right over there...behind those bushes and on the other side of that cluster of trees."

Sarah adjusted her stance and moved her head around to look for it.

"OMG, it's been almost in front of me all along and I didn't even see it. That is so freaky weird. C'mon. I have to see this thing a little closer."

She started walking towards the house and pulled on Jack's arm, but he didn't move.

"C'mon, Jack. Everything is alright. I'll protect you," she laughed.

Jack wanted to laugh, too, but nothing came out of his mouth. He let Sarah lead him over to the house.

Chapter 11

April 22, 2011

The line of dirt bikes cut through the forest, zigging and zagging left and right, avoiding fallen trees and branches. Billy was in front followed by the other boys and Chris. Lucas had taken up the rear position to make sure there were no stragglers. Billy had gathered everyone together and told them that they were going to practice lacrosse all day in the clearing by Howl House. After last night's horrific performance against Tompkinsville, he could have told them they were going to climb Mt. Everest to get ready for the next game and they would have done it. But lacrosse practice was not the main reason for this Saturday morning jaunt. When he woke up, Billy knew he had to go to Howl House - to stop Jack and Sarah. This was not the plan Billy had for his Saturday, but that's what it was now. And there was also the problem of Chris. He had never been to Howl House and Billy didn't want to even take him near it until the time was right, but once again, Jack Wilson had thrown a wrench into the works.

He turned the throttle and picked up speed, but his mind wasn't on the present; it was on the past. He always knew Jack would be a problem, right from the get-go. He had too much of an independent streak running through him to be a compliant member of the clan. And even though this annoyed Billy to no end, in some weird fashion he kind of respected Jack for it. To go against what everyone else was doing took a lot of guts - something that Billy felt he didn't have all that much of lately. It felt like all he did as of late was take orders. On one hand, he was the undisputed leader of the lacrosse team and was well aware that most of the kids at school either hated him or feared him which was fine with him, but on the other hand, he was feeling more like a pawn in a game that never ended. How would he ever gain the power that he craved if he was relegated to playing the game rather than making the rules? This got him thinking about the people he surrounded himself with; the ones he called friends? Were they really his friends or did they just get off on being around the money his family had? Did any of them really like him? And what about his teammates? Yeah, they were Moonwalker brothers and all, but what if they felt the same way Jack did and were just too scared to show it? There were lots of times when even he was unsure if being a Moonwalker was what he wanted.

"Shut up!" Billy yelled, the dirt bikes being too loud for anyone to hear that he was actually badgering himself.

"Just shut up already," he cautioned in a lower tone of voice. This time almost begging himself to stop the line of thought he was pursuing. If he didn't, HE would know, and HE wouldn't be pleased.

"Think of something else. Think of something else." His mind searched frantically for another topic. It found one: Sarah. With most of his attention taken up by Jack and Chris these days, Billy had almost forgotten about her. She was spending so much time with Jack now - both in school and out. This was troubling. Not because he was interested in her. He really wasn't. Lacrosse and the clan took up the bulk of his time and that was good enough for him. But Sarah was in his circle of friends. Friends that he liked to keep close. Friends that he could persuade to do things if needed. As far as manipulation went, he never really had to do too much of that with Sarah. It was more like if he was in the right place at the right time with Sarah nearby, he could make it look like she were part and parcel to whatever was going on. She never knew it, however. And that had worked out fine in the past, but now that she was hanging with Jack a lot, POSSIBLY DATING HIM, that could be problematic. And what made things worse now was that HE was aware of what was going on. HE told Billy last night about Jack and Sarah going to Howl House and that he was to do anything he needed to do to stop them from going in. Billy started to get internally angry again. How dare Jack get Sarah involved in all of this? If she were to get hurt somehow, if HE were to hurt her, it would all be Jack's fault.

"JACK WILSON!" Billy screamed into the wind as he sped the bike up. Jack Wilson was the cause for all of this. Why did he ever have to move here? Things would be so great without him around to mess it all up.

"JACKIE!" Billy yelled and then spit off to the side. "WE'RE COMING FOR YOU, JACKIE!"

Billy twisted the throttle all the way and zoomed off ahead of the pack of bikes. Just before the others did the same, they could just barely hear the sound of maniacal laughter drifting over the hum of their bikes as it sped off into the distance.

Chapter 12

April 22, 2011

"Oh, geez, this place is dripping with creepy all over it."

"*You should see what it's like inside,*" Jack thought to himself. But Sarah was right; there was nothing warm, welcoming or fuzzy-wuzzy about Howl House. If you could take all the haunted houses and horror shacks from the movies and smash them all together, this is what would be left standing. As scary as it was at night, it was somehow worse during the day because you could see all the little disturbing nuances of its construction - the cracks and holes in the wooden clapboard siding, the roof shingles hanging at precarious angles, the large splinters of wood that reached out from the stairs and porch as if to purposefully stick into a foot. The place just screamed "RUN AWAY!"

"I still don't get the attraction," Sarah said, shaking her head in disbelief. "What would possess you guys to come all the way out here and practice lacrosse?"

Jack didn't answer. He just shook his head in disbelief, too.

"Okay, let me take a stab at rationalizing all of this," Sarah said, trying to answer her own question. Billy is out of his mind and he's trying to take you and the rest of the lacrosse team with him. I mean, it's one thing to be obsessed with the sport. It's another thing to be THIS obsessed with the sport. To think that coming all the way out here and basking in some creepy, primal energy is going to make you better than everyone else like it is some dark-side spa for the soul is just plain nuts. We have to tell someone about this...the principal or Mr. Weber...maybe Billy's parents. This can't go on. People are getting hurt. I'm starting to get a bad feeling even now as we..."

Jack stopped Sarah mid-sentence and turned around and looked off into the woods.

"Do you hear that?"

Sarah looked around. "Hear what?"

"Dirt bikes. Billy and his boys are coming."

"I don't hear any..." Sarah stopped herself. "Yes, I do. I hear them."

Jack looked around for a branch or something to use as protection.

"Are they coming here to practice, Jack? Should we hide around the back of the place?"

"No, they are here for us. There's no place to hide."

"What about going inside the house? Let's just go in until they leave."

Jack turned to Sarah and looked directly into her eyes. "No, we can't. Under no circumstances can we go into that house. I don't care if a biker gang of ninjas with sharp swords tried to make us go in. Okay? You'll just have to trust me, please."

"I trust you, Jack. We don't have much time. What should we do?"

A nervous laugh came out of Jack's throat. "I was hoping you were going to have an idea."

Sarah smiled. "We make a great team, huh? The boy with a broken arm and the girl without a plan."

Jack laughed and then stopped abruptly when the conversation that he had with his mother a few weeks ago came rushing back to him...the one that they had about his father. His mother's voice rang out clearly in his head: *I guess you could say he had a calmness about him, a thoughtful kind of stillness. No matter what was going on, he could think his way through it. Nothing really rattled him too much. He wasn't the type that went looking for trouble, but he also wasn't the type to back down when trouble came around...*

Jack grabbed Sarah's hand. "I've got an idea. If things start to get bad, just follow my lead. Calm and cool is our mantra right now. It will work. We ARE a great team. We can do this!"

Sarah smiled. "I have no doubts." She squeezed his hand tighter.

The roar of bike engines was very close now and one bike emerged from behind the tree line before all the others. It was Billy. He turned off the bike and took off his helmet. A cheap smile appeared on his face. He got off the bike and stood next to it tapping his foot as if impatiently waiting for the others to arrive. He said absolutely nothing. He wasn't going to waste any words without an audience present.

The other bikes started arriving a few moments later and took positions in a semicircle around Billy. Chris and Lucas were the last to arrive.

Billy took a look around to make sure everyone was there and turned back to Jack and Sarah, his smile gleaming from ear to ear.

"Look at what we have here, boys. You just never know what you're gonna find in the woods - or who. Jack and Sarah. Imagine that. Looking for some property to buy when you get married?"

The group started chuckling, everyone except Chris. He was just completely confused, his mind swirling with questions. What was a house doing out here in the middle of nowhere? What were Jack and Sarah doing here? Was he still sleeping in his bed? Nothing made sense.

Billy continued. "So, whatcha doin' all the way out here, Jackie-boy? Come to join us for some lacrosse practice or maybe up to some mischief? My bet is on the latter. But, please, do tell."

"I was about to ask you the same thing, Billy. I don't remember us ever coming out here to practice lacrosse on a Saturday. Why the need for so much practice all of a sudden? Not having any problems on the field, are you?"

Billy's smile faded. "You know why I'm here, Jack. I'll tell you what. This is between you and us. There's no need to get Sarah involved. I'm gonna let Chris take her back to town on his bike so we can chat some more."

Sarah grabbed Jack's hand even tighter, but not in fear...in anger. "Whatever you have to say to Jack, Billy, I'm all ears. I'm not leaving with Chris or anyone else for that matter. The only person I leave here with is Jack."

"I've got no beef with you, Sarah. We've known each other way too long to let someone like Jackie here ruin our friendship." He turned towards Lucas. "Lucas would you please escort Miss Sarah away from Jack. She'll be leaving now."

Lucas grinned and started walking over to Jack and Sarah. Sarah dropped Jack's hand and spoke to Lucas in a calm but stern tone. "Lucas, you take one more step, and I can assure you that someone will be riding YOU back to town, draped over the seat in pain - if you get my meaning."

Lucas stopped and looked at Billy. Billy wasn't smiling anymore and nodded for him to return back to his bike. No one spoke. In the distance, a woodpecker could be heard drilling into the hard bark of a tree like the frantic ticking of a clock. Billy stared directly into Jack's eyes and then looked over at Howl House. He could tell they hadn't gone inside, and based on Sarah's words and demeanor, Jack hadn't told her what Howl House was all about...yet. HE had told Billy last night that Jack and Sarah were to be stopped from going into the house. HE didn't say that they had to be taught a lesson...yet.

Billy started smiling again. "You always let your girlfriends fight your battles, Jack?"

Jack didn't answer. He grabbed Sarah's hand and held it tight as if to say, "Yep."

"Well, I don't think anyone here wants to make Sarah any angrier than she already is. She might be inclined to beat us all up to protect her broken-armed man. We've got some practice to get to and you guys have a long walk home. Our job is done here, boys. Let's head over to the clearing and do what we came here to do."

Lucas piped up. "But Billy, we can't let..."

Billy interrupted Lucas. "Never mind what we can't do, Lucas. I'm calling the shots here. Jack and Sarah are leaving. We are gonna let them leave. Ain't that right, Skateboardin' Jack?"

Jack nodded his head in agreement. With Sarah's hand in his, they started walking away from Howl House and disappeared through the line of trees.

Jack laughed lightly to himself.

"What's so funny?" Sarah asked.

"Remember when I said for you to follow MY lead. From now on, I'm following yours."

"I like the way you think, Jack. I like the way you think."

They both laughed and quickly picked up their pace.

Chapter 13

April 24, 2011

The bell rang and Mr. Weber closed the door to the classroom.

"Okay, everybody. Settle down. Settle down. Thank you. We've got a new week ahead of us. We're all done with our poetry unit and will be moving on to something else. I know how upset this makes you."

Some students pretended to be upset by the news but then burst out into laughter and mild cheers. Mr. Weber laughed along with them. Truth was, that while many students liked to complain that they absolutely hated the poetry unit and couldn't wait for it to be over, most of them didn't mind it all that much, and some even liked it. It was kind of cool to work with language in different ways, but they would never admit it.

"Anyone want to take a guess our next unit is going to be about? Agnes...

"Fiction, like writing our own stories and stuff?"

As a whole, the class seemed to like that answer.

"No. You'll be covering fiction writing next year in high school...and stuff," smirked Mr. Weber. "Someone else?" He looked in the back of the class. "Alejandro? What do you think?"

"Non-fiction?"

"Very close Alejandro. It's a form of non-fiction. How about...Chen. What do you say?"

"Is it going to be autobiography?"

"Oh, close but no cigar. Almost there. Auto-biography is writing about yourself, but this unit will be concerned with you writing about someone else. The answer is..."

"Biography," answered about a third of the class.

"Yes! Biography. Not only will you be researching information about someone famous from history, but you will also be writing about someone you know in your own life and comparing and contrasting them together. The person you know could be family, a friend, or even me. Extra points if you pick me, of course - just kidding. So who are you going to pick?" Mr. Weber looked around the class again. "Jack, what about you? Who are you going to write about?"

Jack had been caught daydreaming again. He was physically in the room but mentally back at Howl House on Saturday. He had been thinking about Billy and all the guys coming to cut him and Sarah off at the pass, so to speak. Obviously, whoever the entity was that visited Jack while he was sleeping was also talking to Billy and telling him what to do. If he had been there alone, things might not have gone very well. Although he didn't want to put Sarah in danger, she was the one that saved them both. She was tough and Jack felt himself falling for her even more. Beyond his good feelings for Sarah, though, there were some bad feelings that came out of the whole encounter. For one, Chris was there. What had Billy told him about Howl House? There was no way that Chris knew about him and Billy and the rest being Moonwalkers. Billy was probably hoping to save that tidbit of information for the next full moon. From what Jack remembered, Chris looked a little too confused throughout the whole thing. He probably didn't know too much and was even thrown more into a state of confusion when Billy said that he would be driving Sarah home. That must have sent his thoughts and feelings into a tizzy. The next thing was how Billy basically let them go without putting up too much of a dramatic fuss. Even Lucas seemed a little perplexed by it. The whole thing smelled of strangeness.

"Jaaack!"

Realizing that his name was being called, Jack came back to the present.

"Yeah, Mr. Weber."

"You were off in La La Land again. Thinking of anything or ANYONE special?" The class started making oohing and ahhing sounds. Mr. Weber verbally shook them out of their childish reaction. "That's not what I meant. I mean is there anyone you are thinking about writing a biography about?"

"I...I guess I would write one about my Dad."

"Nice choice. Parents are always a good subject for a biography. Sometimes when we dig a little, we find out things about them and ourselves that we never knew."

"I hope so," Jack said under his breath.

"What was that, Jack?"

"Oh, nothing, I just said I agree."

"Great." He turned his attention to everyone in class. "Your biography assignment will be due next week and we'll talk about it more in a little bit. Right now, take out a piece of paper for a pop quiz on the elements of poetry."

The class moaned and groaned for real.

Mr. Weber laughed. "Like music to my ears."

Chapter 14

April 24, 2011

"Why didn't you gather us for practice on Sunday, Billy? Billy?"

The noise of the cafeteria had lulled Billy Jenkins into a welcome stupor of sorts, helping him to forget the calamity that was basically the weekend. Conversations were taking place all around him like they did during any typical lunch period, but he wasn't hearing any of them. He was mentally somewhere else. Even his friend grabbing and shaking his shoulder hardly had an effect on him.

"Billy, what's wrong, man? Are you okay?" Lucas asked, unsure of what to do next if there was no response to physical contact.

Billy turned and looked toward the person grabbing him but his eyes didn't immediately comprehend the situation. He didn't want to come back from his mental hiding place. Coming back meant dealing with problems and that was all he felt he was doing lately. Problems weren't cool; they were anything but. Just a little bit longer away from reality. Just a few more minutes...

Lucas shook him some more until it finally started to register that he was in the cafeteria and someone was trying to get his attention. Vacation was over.

"What?" he muttered with annoyance.

"Dude, are you okay? I was asking why you didn't gather us for practice on Sunday and you wouldn't answer. I thought you were having a brain aneurysm or something."

"I was thinking."

"Okay, but I still don't know why you didn't gather us for practice like you did on Saturday."

"Because..."

"Because why?"

"Because I was busy, Lucas. 'Nuff said," Billy growled.

Lucas put up his hands as if to say, "Okay, okay..." He knew Billy well enough to know when it was time to back off and let things be. With all that was going on, his brain must be overloaded. The loss of Friday's game and then finding Jack and Sarah at Howl House yesterday must have been driving Billy nuts. It would be best to just give him some space and not get up in his grill for an answer to his question.

Billy turned away from Lucas and started looking around the cafeteria. He couldn't see Jack and Sarah anywhere. His gaze finally came back to the table where he and his friends were sitting. Something was wrong.

"Where's Chris?"

Lucas looked around to see if Chris was just out of view, maybe behind someone.

"I don't see him. Maybe he had something to do in one of his classes...like making up a test."

"Did he tell you that specifically or are you just speculating?" Billy asked with a bothered expression on his face.

"I guess I was speculating," Lucas admitted guiltily.

"Ya think?" Billy cracked back sarcastically. "I want you to go and find him NOW. Take some of the boys with you. Full moon will be here in a little over a week and I don't want Chris away from my side. There are too many variables at play for us to take any chances."

Lucas shook his head.

"Last thing we need is for Chris to become friendly with Jack again. That will ruin everything. Go find him and get him back here. If your 'speculation' was actually correct, stay outside the room until he is done and then beeline it back here or follow him to his next class if the bell is about to ring."

"You got it, Billy. I'm on it."

"Good. That's what I like to hear. Get going."

Lucas grabbed two of the other boys and ran out of the cafeteria.

A student walking by Billy's table yelled out that Barnaby Hills would win the next lacrosse game. Billy stuck up his thumb and smiled. When they were gone, he put his head down, closed his eyes and ran his fingers through his hair and massaged his head as if to soothe a growing migraine. Reality was too much of a pain to deal with. He rubbed his temples hoping for his mind to escape once again and be far away. The white noise of the students laughing and talking in the cafeteria helped to take his mind off the present. He wanted to drift off to a better place, but he knew that wasn't going to happen any time soon.

Chapter 15

April 24, 2011

The school library was a good place to be during lunch. Most students were in the cafeteria and, as opposed to other periods during the day, only students who were serious about getting work done popped in to make the best use of their time.

Chris Stiles figured he would dip into the library before heading off for lunch to look for a biography of someone famous for Mr. Weber's class. If he didn't find one early, all the best books would be taken and he would have to settle for someone he didn't want to learn about. He wasn't all that psyched about doing the work in the first place, but it would be almost intolerable if he had to read a whole book about someone he didn't even know. He walked over to the biography section, a narrow section in the back between two tall bookshelves. Beyond the books, this section was best known to be the place where kids who were dating would try to sneak some making out into their day. Here among the great figures of history, students would literally kiss each other until the librarian would find them and chase them out. Luckily that wasn't the case right now. Chris could take his time and look for a book without being intruded upon.

He scanned the lower shelves looking for a name or title that would jump out at him and scream "READ ME!" Using the computer catalogue may have been a better way to start a search but this way had worked once or twice for him in the past, so he went for it. Crouching all the way down, he found a book about Nathanael Greene, one of George Washington's most trusted generals. He was really interested in the Revolutionary War, so he sat down on the floor and started flipping through the book to see if it would hold greater interest for him. A couple of minutes later, some students came into the library and sat down at the back table, not too far away from him, just on the other side of the biography bookshelf. They spoke softly and quietly and he would have barely realized or cared that they were there until he heard his name.

"What do you think was going through Chris' head when they all arrived at Howl House and saw us there?" a female voice said.

"I can only imagine. I cast a glance his way when we were in the midst of everything and his eyes were open wide with a strange look of paralyzed disbelief. Had I been in his shoes, I'm sure I would have looked the same way," replied a very familiar voice.

Chris got up to his knees and pushed some books to the side a little so he could get a sneak view of who was talking. It was Jack and Sarah, and they were talking about him.

Jack continued. "I'm not sure what caused him more confusion, though: the creepy house in the woods or the fact that we were hanging out in front of the creepy house in the woods. I don't think he was prepared for either, but Billy was definitely going to be taking him there sooner or later."

"How do you know?"

Chris watched silently as Jack considered his answer. His eyes looking upward as if searching for the right way to say whatever it was going to be.

"If Billy wants Chris to be in the inner circle of the team, he will take him there just like he took me. There's no doubt."

"I'm still intrigued by all of this, Jack. I asked you the other day why it is called Howl House. You didn't answer me. What importance does...no, not importance. What power does it have over all of you?"

Chris was right up against the shelf as if he were a book himself, straining to hear every word of the conversation. His knees were killing him but he didn't want to move or make a sound that might give away that he was listening to them.

Jack exhaled a slow, deep breath. "Billy calls it Howl House because he believes it has spiritual powers connected to nature, specifically wolves and the American Indians who lived in this area long ago."

Sarah chuckled. "The native Americans didn't live in houses, Jack. Billy knows that, right?"

"Yes, he knows that," Jack managed to say with a little smile. "Billy thinks the house was built there to protect or to commemorate the place in some fashion."

"Well, you've been in the house, right? What did you see?"

Chris knew Jack pretty well and he could tell that his former friend was trying his best to carefully formulate his words to describe what he saw. Jack was usually very straightforward about things, but this situation was calling for him to think things through before speaking. If Jack was acting like this, there was something he knew or saw that had freaked him out, or worse.

Jack finally opened his mouth to answer when the library doors swung open with a loud bang.

"Chris, you in here?" shouted a voice.

"And just what do you think you are doing, Lucas?" asked the librarian at her desk near the front door. "There is no shouting allowed in the library. If you are looking for someone, you may look quietly, but if you can't, I am going to ask you to leave."

Lucas looked around, saw that Jack and Sarah were sitting at a table in the back, laughed and then left. The interruption was enough to stop Jack from talking any further about Howl House.

"C'mon," he said to Sarah. "Let's get out of here. Now that Lucas knows we are here, you never know who else will show up."

Sarah shook her head. "Agreed. Lunch isn't over yet. How about we get a snack...sound good?"

"You got it."

Jack and Sarah left the library. Satisfied that no one else was around to notice that he had been listening to their conversation, Chris lifted himself to his feet. His legs felt dead after being in the position that they were for so long. He tried moving them around so some life would come back into them. Lucas sure had ruined things. Just when it seemed like Jack was going to say something about Howl House, too. All of a sudden it hit him who Lucas had been looking for. HIM. Billy must want him for something. *Geez, how often do I have to be at his beck and call?* As life started flowing back into his legs, Chris picked up the book he found and brought it over to the checkout desk.

"Oh, this is a wonderful biography about Nathanael Greene," the librarian said as she scanned the book into the computer. "General Greene was one of Washington's closest military advisors and friends."

Chris didn't say anything, but he smiled and shook his head. For a second, he wondered weirdly what Nathanael Greene would have to say about the battle that seemed to be growing between Jack and Billy. And more importantly, what would he say about Chris' part in the whole thing.

The librarian handed the book to Chris and he left the library. He reluctantly started walking to the cafeteria.

Chapter 16

April 24, 2011

"So, Lucas found you?" Billy asked as Chris took a seat at the lunch table.

"Uh, no. Was he looking for me?" Chris held up the book that he just borrowed from the library. "I was getting a biography for Mr. Weber's class and then stopped in the bathroom. What does Lucas want?"

Billy glanced at the book and nodded his head. "Nothing, I was just wondering where you were and asked Lucas to look for you. I just wanted to talk about the upcoming game Friday night."

"Oh, sure, sure. We're gonna win this time. I feel it."

"No doubt about it. But we can't take anything for granted. We have practice after school each day this week. I just want to make sure that you will be there."

Chris nodded his head this time. "Oh, I'll be there. I don't have anything else going on that would stop me from coming to practice."

Billy smiled. "That's good. Really good. Hey, listen, Chris. I've been meaning to talk with you. Things have been crazy lately, and I think I've been taking it out on you a little bit. You know, with what happened with you and Jack on the field and then coming to your house on Saturday for an early practice in the woods...only to find Jack and Sarah up to no good near our clubhouse. I can only imagine what you must be thinking right now." Billy looked at Chris strangely as if to gauge what was on his mind.

"Um, no, everything is cool, Billy. No thoughts or anything," Chris said nervously feeling a little uncomfortable from Billy's staring eyes.

"Oh, c'mon. You must be thinking something. You can tell me. Unless..."

"Unless what?"

"Unless you've already spoken with someone about everything."

The conversation was getting strange. Chris took a quick look around to see if anyone else was hearing it.

"Uh, no, Billy. Who would I speak to?"

"Did you tell your mom and dad where you were when you came back home on Saturday?"

"No, not at all."

"Okay. Good. Anybody else?"

"No, no one."

Billy leaned closer into the conversation. "Not even Jack?"

Chris was taken aback by the question. "Jack? I don't even talk to Jack anymore. What would I possibly talk to him about?"

"Well, I thought you may have some questions about Howl House and were afraid to ask me. When I didn't see you at lunch, I thought that maybe you were trying to get some answers from someone else, seeing how crazy Saturday was and all."

"No, no. I haven't talked to Jack in a long time. I haven't even seen him around." Chris started to sweat a little.

Billy eyed Chris carefully for a few seconds and then sat back in his chair and smiled. "Well, that is really good to hear, Chris. I wouldn't want anyone to spoil the surprise."

"The surprise?"

"Yeah, sometime next week, we are all going back to Howl House for your initiation into the elite team. You're going to become one of us. I wouldn't want anyone to spoil it and tell you anything beforehand. That's all."

Chris smiled back cautiously. "I want that to be a surprise, too, Billy. I can't wait."

"That's what I like to hear. Awesome. Hey, there isn't much time left for lunch. You should go eat something. After all, we have practice this afternoon and you want to make sure that you have enough energy."

"Oh, yeah. Thanks for reminding me. I'm gonna grab some right now. Thanks. Maybe you'll still be here when I get back and we can talk about practice some more."

Billy put his hands up to his temples to massage them. "I wouldn't have it any other way."

Chapter 17

April 25, 2011

"You almost slipped up, Jack," the gravelly voice said calmly. "That is a definite no-no."

Jack was standing in a dark room, the voice trailing off into the blackness. Another dream. As much as Jack was scared, he was also angry. Who was this person, this creature...this entity that invaded his sleep like a terrorist? Who were they to assume such power as to disrupt the very lives of others?

"Show yourself!" Jack yelled.

"In due time, my eager friend, but you slipped up."

"What do you mean?"

"You almost told your friend Sarah about Howl House, didn't you?"

"I didn't say anything to her."

"But you almost did. That has consequences. You know what consequences are, right Jack?" the voice chuckled in a foreboding fashion.

"Sarah isn't part of this. You leave her alone."

"You made her part of this, Jack. YOU. But there is a way to make things right all around. Are you interested, Jack?"

No amount of pinching his own skin was going to wake him up from this nightmare. They were dreams but they were also very, very real. Too real for Jack's liking. He felt powerless knowing that he had to see them through to the end before waking up.

"What do you want?"

"It's very simple, Jack. Come back to the fold. Take your

rightful place in the clan and stop fighting against us. If you do, both Sarah and Chris will be left alone. It's you that I want, Jack. I have big plans for you."

"Why me? You already have Billy. He is willing to do anything you ask him to. What is so important that you have to control a middle school lacrosse team?"

The voice broke out into deafening laughter. Jack thrust his hands against his ears to stop the pain. Even after the laughter stopped, it took a while for the echoes of it to dissipate.

"Barnaby Hill's lacrosse? Is that what you believe this is all about? Oh, I have so much to teach you, Jack. When I'm finished, you will look back on this night and laugh at your own naiveté. Do we have a deal?"

"And if I don't take the deal; what happens then?"

"Ah, well I think you know what happens to Chris, and as far as Sarah goes, let's just keep that an unpleasant mystery. The choice is yours, Jack. Do we have a deal?"

Jack stood silently mulling the situation over in his head, but something about the whole thing was bothering him: why this deal and why now? It didn't make sense. If the creature thought that it had the upper hand to begin with, it wouldn't be so eager to strike a deal. Things didn't add up.

"Do we have a deal?" the voice said with a small degree of annoyance.

Jack thought fast. "As I am looking to protect my friends, your deal interests me. But I also have to think of myself here. If I say 'no,' you will undoubtedly follow through on your threats, and, most likely, I will have to worry about my own life, too. But if I say 'yes,' my life will change in ways that I cannot even fully comprehend at the moment."

"You are correct on all counts, Jack. Such a thinker you are. Do we have a deal?"

"I need some more time. There are lives hanging in the balance, including my own. I need to think this through. Give me just a little more time."

"Self-preservation. I like that, Jack. I like that. Together we will do great things. I am not as unreasonable as you believe me to be. I will give you the time you ask for."

"And what about Billy?"

"What about him?"

"Will you tell him to back off while I think things through?"

"Of course, of course. And Jack, when you come back to the fold, YOU will be giving Billy the orders, my young protégé. Big plans, Jack. Big plans...big plans...big plans..."

Jack awoke in his bed. The voice's final words resounding in his head, but at least his heart wasn't beating frantically this time. He sat up and looked around his room. Even in the dark he could make everything out. His life lay scattered about him - lacrosse gear, some music posters on his walls, photos of family and one of him skating in downtown San Francisco...so many small but significant things. Down the hall, his mother slept in her bed. No worries to keep her awake. Jack thought about Chris and Sarah - his friend and his girlfriend. He cared about both of them deeply, more than they knew. A chill ran down his back as he thought about all of these things, all of these people going away. He was able to stall for time, but the choice still remained. His back was against the wall and he didn't like what he was staring at in front. He got up from his bed and grabbed a towel and went into the bathroom to take a hot shower. He needed to wash himself clean of the dream and the decision for the time being, but more so, he felt the need to clean his mind and soul from brushing up against what felt like the devil himself.

Chapter 18

April 25, 2011

The undeniable odor of hot, fresh pancakes roused Jack easily. Taking a shower and washing off last night's dream definitely helped him relax more, but getting back to sleep hadn't been easy and was hardly satisfying. He rolled over and slid out of bed. His arm was still in a sling, but he had gotten used to it pretty quickly and getting dressed didn't cause much of a problem. Before long, he was making his way downstairs to the source of the delightful smell.

"Look at that. Awake and downstairs before I even called out your name. Is it just the smell of my famous pancakes that got you up or something more sinister?"

Jack's eyes widened. "What do you mean by 'sinister,' Mom?"

"Oh, like the sleep fairy jabbing you with pins or something like that."

Jack smiled. "You are so weird."

"Guilty," his mom said smiling maniacally. "Seriously, did you have bad sleep?"

"I guess you could call it that. To be honest, I haven't been sleeping all that well for the last couple of weeks."

"My son has the weight of the world on his shoulders. Take a seat and let's see if we can lighten the load a little."

Jack took a seat and his mother brought over a small stack of pancakes on a plate followed by maple syrup and a glass of milk.

"You're too good to me, Mom," Jack said as he poured the syrup on his pancakes.

"Well, you're worth it. So what's troubling you?" she said, sitting down across from him with some pancakes of her own.

Jack didn't want to rehash everything in a sanitized form for his mother. It took so long to rethink and explain things in an alternate form, so he just started talking about the biography project for Mr. Weber's class. He told her that he wanted to write about "Dad" and she smiled - her eyes even welling up with some tears.

"I know you've told me a lot about Dad over the years, but is there anything that I don't know about him?" Jack asked as he reached for more syrup.

"Did you know that at one time, before you were born, your father and I were so poor that we couldn't afford the very kind of syrup you are using right now? We had to use butter and sugar."

"Well, that doesn't sound too bad. I like butter and sugar, but why didn't you guys have any money?"

Jack's Mom grabbed the syrup when she was done, looked at it with a smirk on her face, and began to pour some on her own pancakes.

"There was a time when your Dad was trying to be a professional musician."

Jack shook his head. "Yeah, you've told me that he was a bass player, right?"

"Yeah, but I don't think I told you that he quit his job to become a full-time bass player in a touring rock band."

"Quit his job? No, you never told me that. But he must have been making money in the band if he was traveling around and playing shows and stuff, right?"

"Nope. Not enough to speak of anyway. Those were some lean years, I gotta tell ya. There was one Christmas when all we could afford to give each other were candles."

"And you didn't tell him to stop, Mom?" Jack asked with surprise.

"Tell him to stop? I couldn't tell him to stop. I was too busy dancing to the music and sometimes joining him on the road when I could. Your Dad and I never told each other to stop something that we knew was important to the other. You can't stop someone's passion. When you care about someone, you have to let them be who they are and help them when you can. It's just the way things should be. Your Dad was my partner, and I was his partner. No bosses in a partnership. There are a couple of more pancakes. Do you want them?"

Jack didn't answer her question. He was still thinking about the last thing she said...*No bosses in a partnership.*

"Oh, Jack look at the time," his mother said as she was clearing dishes. "We both have to get out of here."

Jack's mind came back to the present and he got up and brought his dishes over to the sink. He was about to turn and run upstairs to get his stuff when he turned to his mother.

"Mom, can I have a hug?"

"Oh, definitely and always," she said as she gave him a one hundred percent pure mom hug. "I'll never stop giving those - even when you stop asking for them."

"Thanks, Mom." Jack held her for as long as he could and then broke away to get his things.

Chapter 19

April 28, 2011

It was Friday. It came quickly, way too quickly, but this had become Jack's reality - living a life of extremes that was now held in the ticking hands of the clock. He had to find a way to rectify the situation with the dream creature who wanted him to assume a greater role as a Moonwalker. If he came back to the clan, his friends and loved ones would be safe from harm. If he did not capitulate to the creature's demands, not only would he place the lives of others in danger, he himself would suffer the same fate. Time seemed to be the only thing holding everything at bay...for now.

Strangely enough, the biography project that Mr. Weber gave his classes was keeping his mind from melting down with worry. He had chosen his father as the person in his life that he wanted to write about, but he also had the idea to write about his mother. He asked Mr. Weber if he could do that, but Mr. Weber insisted that the second person had to be someone famous that influenced history in some way or form. Jack figured that if he couldn't write about his mom, the least he could do was balance things out by writing about a famous female figure. He started doing some investigating on the internet and came upon someone he never heard about before. Her name was Sophie Scholl and she lived in Germany during the time of the Nazis. She was part of a non-violent political action group called The White Rose Society and was killed by the government for circulating anti-Nazi leaflets on a college campus when she was only twenty-one, along with her brother and a friend. They didn't even have a fair trial. They were arrested on February 18, 1943 and were killed only four days later. There was something about her story that really touched Jack, especially her last words:

"How can we expect righteousness to prevail when there is hardly anyone willing to give himself up individually to a righteous cause? Such a fine, sunny day, and I have to go, but what does my death matter, if through us, thousands of people are awakened and stirred to action?"

He was amazed that he had never heard of her before. She was so brave and her words were so important. This young person who lived and died over seventy years ago was speaking to him across generations. Her words as important today as they were when she spoke them.

He knew right away that Sophie Scholl was the second person to write the biography about. He learned as much as he could and started writing about her. The biographies weren't due until next week, but here it was Friday and he had finished one of them. When he saw Sarah at lunch, he told her all about Sophie.

"Wow!" Sarah exclaimed. "She was amazing. It is such a sad story, but she was an incredible person."

"I know. I know. I have never been so interested in a writing assignment before."

"Well, pat yourself on the back for two reasons: first, for choosing such an incredible person to write about. I'm also proud that you chose a woman to research. I don't think any of the guys in this school would do something like that. Your mom and I are having a good influence on you," she said laughing. "And second, for getting half of your project done so early. I wish I had your motivation."

Jack smiled. "Thanks. And you're right; you and Mom are a good influence on me. And to show my appreciation, I'll buy you a cookie. How about that?"

Sarah leaned in and spoke quietly. "In lieu of a kiss, since we are in the school cafeteria, I'll accept that. But only if I can reciprocate tonight after the lacrosse game by buying you some ice cream."

"Deal," Jack said, then realizing that the lacrosse game against Centerville was tonight. "Is that tonight? I totally forgot."

"That's actually a good thing. Sorry for bringing it up."

"Nah, no big thing. I was going to remember one way or another."

"Are you sure you want to come to this one? It's not a home game. I can see you later at your house if you can't make it."

"And miss you cheering? No way. I used to think running around on the field was the greatest thing about lacrosse. Not anymore. Centerville's not that far away. I can skateboard on over."

"Even with the arm? I'm sure you could bum a ride from someone. Maybe your mom wants to go to another game?" Sarah said with a wry smile.

"Oh, yeah, that's what she wants to do, not. Actually, she would drive me but I'll be fine."

"My parents will be coming to the game. I'll be going by bus with the cheer squad but we can ride home with the folks. Perfect time to meet them and then get some ice cream."

"Parents then ice cream. Sounds like a good plan."

Sarah grinned but her attention was drawn to something

else in the cafeteria. "You know what's weird?" Sarah said leaning in again. "I haven't seen Billy or anybody at his table look over here once the entire week. What's up with that?"

Jack rubbed his hands together and brought them up to his face to ponder her question for a moment. He reached out and grabbed her hand.

"I say, don't look a gift horse in the mouth. C'mon; let's get you that cookie."

Chapter 20

April 28, 2011

"Okay, huddle up!"

Coach Weber called his players to the center of the locker room.

"Some of you may be worried about playing tonight because of our last game. I don't even want to talk about our last game. It's in the past. I've blocked it out of my mind. I'm only looking to the future now. I'm looking at us playing Centerville and winning. Is that what you see?"

"YES, COACH!" the team roared back.

He looked at all of his players. They were eager for this win. Last week's game was a shambles. They wanted to forget about it, too.

"This team can do great things. I've seen you do it before and I'll see you do it tonight. I see a bright future and that future includes winning this year's lacrosse championship and beyond. So what are we gonna do tonight?"

"WIN!"

"I don't think I heard you. WHAT ARE WE GONNA DO TONIGHT?"

"WIN!"

"That's right, boys. Now get out there, get on the bus and psyche yourselves up on the way over to Centerville for tonight's game."

The team all screamed loudly and ran out the door to the field. Before exiting himself, Coach Weber looked back and saw Chris Stiles bending down to get his gear from a bench but taking his time doing it.

"Chris, what's going on, buddy. The team is already gone. Get your gear and get out to the bus. We gotta leave."

Chris glanced over at the Coach. "Yeah, Coach Weber, I'll be right there. It's just that I wanted to talk to you about...nah, forget about it. Another time."

Coach Weber walked over to his player. "It's just that what? Are you feeling okay? Not sick, are you?"

"No, no, not sick, Coach. It's just that I've got some stuff on my mind."

The Coach looked at his watch. "Alright, Chris, spit it out as fast as you can. I don't want you going out and not having your focus entirely on the game. What's got you?"

Chris looked around the locker room to make sure no other players were still there.

"Um, it has to do with Billy and lacrosse. He's been acting really weird lately, and he's been putting a lot of pressure on all of us."

"Pressure? What do you mean by pressure?"

Chris let out a deep breath. "Well, last weekend, the day after we lost the...I mean the day after our last game, Billy got all crazy and had us follow him out into the woods to practice."

The Coach looked confused. "Okay...but I don't get the problem. What's so wrong about practicing after a bad game?"

"He made us take our dirt bikes really far into the woods and we ended up at this old, creepy house in the middle of nowhere. And Jack and Sarah were there, too. It was almost like Billy knew he would find them there."

"And what happened? Jack and Billy didn't get into a fight, did they?"

Chris shook his head. "No, no. I mean, at first it seemed like that might happen, but it didn't. Jack and Sarah wound up leaving but we stayed and practiced in a field near the house. The whole thing was weird because we could have just practiced here at school. And there was something really strange about that house. We didn't go in it, but Billy...I don't know...maybe he's gone in there before or something."

Mr. Weber shook his head as if confused. "This is nuts. What is Billy thinking? I'm going to have a talk with him. Thanks for letting me know, Chris. Strange behavior is one thing, but I want to make sure you guys are all safe. Practices shouldn't be held far off in the woods. What if one of you got hurt? I don't like this one bit."

"Coach Weber? Chris said as if asking a question. "That's not all."

"Something else? Can it wait until later on tonight, Chris? We really have to get on the bus. Give it to me quick."

"Well, it's about Jack and his arm."

"Chris, I've told you not to get down on yourself too much about that. Accidents happen. I'm sure Jack doesn't blame you. Lacrosse is a rough sport."

"No, that's not what I was gonna say." Chris started squirming in place. "The accident that Jack had and all...it wasn't an accident."

Coach Weber's eyes narrowed and he looked directly at Chris. "What do you mean it wasn't an accident?"

Chris continued, his eyes watering up. "It wasn't an accident, Coach. It was on purpose...and Billy told me to do it."

Coach Weber's jaw dropped and his face turned a little pale. "What?

Chris dropped his gaze downward. "Billy told me to hurt Jack."

Coach Weber stood silent for a moment and then said slowly, "We've got to get on that bus. Not a word of this to anybody."

Chapter 21

April 28, 2011

The sky was glowing as the sun set in the late afternoon. The beautiful blue was interlaced with streaks of yellow and orange. Reddish purple clouds stretched from east to west in wispy, soft strings. It was more like a painting than real life. Jack thought about stopping for a moment on his skateboard and taking a picture of it with his phone, but he knew it wouldn't compare to the memory of it. He decided to just enjoy the moment for what it was and how it made him feel. Simple things were often the best things.

It felt good to be on the skateboard again. Before he left for the game, his mother had gone back and forth about letting him take it because of his arm, but after he convinced her that he wasn't going to head to the nearest skate park and try out some tricks, she reluctantly agreed. Her last words as he left the house were still ringing in his ears: *If anything happens you call me immediately!* She could be such a mom sometimes, but it's probably one of the reasons he loved her so much (although he wouldn't admit that to anybody).

The route to Centerville was in pretty good shape considering that the winter had been harsh. He had traveled on this road before but only on a bus with the lacrosse team. He remembered from that vantage point that there was room enough on either side of the road for bikes or skateboards. Tonight was the perfect occasion to try it all out. He rode on, figuring that he would get to the lacrosse field in about 30 minutes or so. His mind started drifting away from the beauty of the sunset to the craziness that was weighing heavily on him, but he pushed back on the urge, convincing himself that a few more minutes of worry-free time would suit him well.

A minute or so later, he heard a vehicle coming up the road behind him. He looked back over his shoulder and saw that it was a school bus. It had to be the one from Barnaby Hills that had the lacrosse team on it. For a second, Jack thought about grabbing onto the back of the bus and hitching a wild ride to Centerville but then he remembered what he told his mother and laughed at the stupidity of the idea. The bus got closer and Jack stopped and kicked up his skateboard to watch as they passed. His eyes immediately fell on someone who was sitting near the front with their head leaning against the window. It was Chris but he didn't see Jack looking at him. He was too busy staring off into some far off distance, his face expressionless and pale. Jack continued watching him as the bus passed by but then he heard a voice that yelled, "Hey Jack, think fast!" He turned just in time to see Lucas throw an empty can of soda at him from one of the back windows. Jack ducked just in time to feel it sail closely over his head and land in the grass on the side of the road. He looked quickly towards the bus to see some of the boys laughing as they peered out the back window. He couldn't see Billy specifically, but he knew he was being watched. He could just feel it.

The bus went around a bend in the road and was gone. Jack shook his head and walked over to the get the can. He wasn't going to let a foolish act against him also ruin the environment. He'd throw out the can in a recycling bin when he got to Centerville. He reached down and picked it up.

"Jack."

The familiar gruff voice was all around him, echoing in the fading light of the afternoon. Jack turned in every direction to see if there was a body to accompany the sound. Nothing.

"Jack. That was close. You almost got hit. What a shame that would be, but an empty can isn't really dangerous in the

grand scheme of things. Don't you agree? So many other things to worry about. So many other things to fear."

Jack was taken aback - this was the first time the voice had ever spoken to him outside of a dream. He grabbed his skateboard tighter and pulled it up to his chest for defense...just in case.

"What's your decision, Jack?" the voice asked without waiting for Jack to respond to its first question.

"Decision?"

"Don't play games with me, Jack. You won't win," chided the voice.

"I told you I needed time."

"Time is precious, Jack, as are your friends; I'm sure."

"They've done nothing. Leave them out of this."

"Oh, if that were only true, Jack. It would seem your friend Chris has a big mouth. Not good. Not good at all. He'll have to be disciplined when the time comes. But, then again, that is entirely up to you."

Jack's fingers tightened around his board. Silence hung in the air except for soft, emerging sound of evening crickets.

The voice cut through the silence. "Since you are having difficulty, Jack, let me help you out. If a decision is not made by tonight, you, your friends AND your sweet mother, will feel the pain of your stupidity."

Jack erupted in anger.

"SHOW YOURSELF, YOU COWARD! FIGHT ME RIGHT HERE, RIGHT NOW!"

The voice chuckled. "Now you understand why I want you in the clan, Jack. You have passion. I need someone with passion and courage for my plans to come to fruition. You are that

someone, Jack. You don't see it now, but you will. You will. By tonight, Jack. Make the right choice...by tonight."

The voice faded away into the neighboring woods.

Jack's heart was beating fast and loud. His fingers were still gripping the skateboard tightly. He looked around to see if anyone had witnessed what had just happened. No cars, no people. He tried to slow his breathing and gain some control of the situation. A line had been drawn in the sand for him, and as mad as that made him, and as much as he willing to give his life to protect his friends and family, he now had a deadline for his decision - something that he was hoping to hold off on until he had a solution in hand.

The sound of crickets was louder now. Evening was approaching and Jack still had to get to Centerville. He put his board on the ground and kicked off. There was no pushing away any bad thoughts now. That's all he would be thinking about for the duration of his trip.

Chapter 22

April 28, 2011

"Are you okay? Was the ride here really difficult...because you look like you are out of it?"

Jack wanted to tell her everything. Just spill his guts and let it all free. Maybe she would freak out and back away like he was nuts, but at this point he felt like his brain was having trouble handling what was happening on its own.

"Yeah, the ride was rougher than I thought it was gonna be. Took a long time."

Sarah smiled and cupped his face with her hand. "Why don't you go find a seat in the bleachers and take a load off? Your legs must be killing you. The game will be starting really soon. I've got to get back to the squad. Remember, ice cream after the game on me. My parents will be coming to pick us up. Okay?"

Jack managed to smile back. "You mean I don't have to skateboard home alone? Sounds better than you know."

"Awesome. And don't forget to watch some of the game tonight. Just don't stare at me the whole time."

They both laughed. Sarah gave him a quick peck on the cheek and ran over to join the rest of the cheerleaders. Jack took a look around for a good place to sit. He didn't really feel like being social tonight so he figured he'd sit in the home team bleachers - maybe even sit right behind the Centerville lacrosse team and see what life was like from the other side.

By the time he made it over to the Centerville side, both teams had already been announced and were getting ready on the sidelines. The bleachers were packed with fans but as luck would have it, he was able to find a single spot just behind the team. He tipped his board up vertically, leaned forward and rested his chin on his hands and watched the Centerville team get ready.

"I couldn't believe it. He was screaming at them from the top of his lungs in the locker room."

A conversation between two of Centerville's players was taking place right in front of him. Normally he might not have even noticed with all the action around him, but the kid telling the story was loud and animated as he told his buddy about something that had just happened.

He continued. "I went to the bathroom and washing my hands when I heard some yelling through the vent. It sounded like the coach was tearing into his team about being sloppy on and off the field. Man, he was on fire."

His teammate seemed nonplussed. "What's the big deal? Coach Manning has yelled at all of us at one time or another. It's part of the job."

"That's not all. He started yelling that if he caught any players making any forms of illegal contact during the game, they would be kicked off the team."

"I wonder what he meant by that? I mean, that's a given. If our coach had to remind of that, that would mean someone was guilty of doing it."

"Ya think? But here's the weirdest thing of all. I was the last person to leave our locker room and as I was just about to leave, I heard two people talking near the door. It seems that two of the Barnaby Hills guys were also late leaving. It was that kid Billy and I think the other one was that newer guy, Christopher or Chris, I think. Billy was tearing into the new guy just like he was the coach or something."

"What did he say?"

"He told him that he better not screw up tonight and to keep his big, fat mouth shut; otherwise he wouldn't be going to the initiation ceremony on Wednesday. It was totally weird, man."

"What did he mean by 'initiation ceremony'? Did he say anything else?"

"Nah. He said they better get going, but reminded him he better not screw up."

"That Billy kid is a nasty punk from what my friend at Barnaby Hills says - a rich kid who thinks he's in charge of everything or something like that."

"Maybe he's pissed off because their best player is out of commission right now."

"I don't know, but if their coach is warning them about illegal contact, we need to watch out. With their guy out with a busted arm, that means that nutjob Lucas will be filling in the gaps. I bet their coach was referring to him. I don't trust him at all."

"Yeah, I hear that. Yo, put your mouth guard in. Games about to begin."

The players got up off the bench and trotted out to the field. Jack sat leaned back in his seat and rubbed his eyes. He felt a growing headache behind them. It sounded to him like Coach Weber was right: Billy and the gang were being sloppy, but not in the way the Coach meant. Things were starting to get out of control. Jack knew the next full moon was this coming Wednesday, but he wasn't sure if Chris was aware of what was planned that night. They probably told him that he was going to be a part of some special lacrosse brotherhood or something. Wednesday was going to come fast, but Jack's answer to the creature was going to have to come faster - tonight.

Jack would have stayed in his own world if all the fans around him in the Centerville bleachers hadn't jumped to their feet and screamed for joy when Centerville got possession of the ball after the face-off. He wanted to scream, too, but not for joy...definitely not for joy.

Chapter 23

April 28, 2011

Jack walked across the field to the visitor's side. Sarah was talking to some of her cheerleading buddies. Jack approached the group and waved hello.

"Hey, you guys all know Jack...my gorgeous boyfriend."

The girls started giggling and Jack's face turned redder than a ripe tomato.

"I'll see you guys at school on Monday," Sarah said giggling herself. She turned towards Jack. "Hope I didn't embarrass you too much. Just said what was on my mind."

"As soon as my face turns back to its regular color, I'll forgive you," he joked.

"That's good. So, I saw you sitting across the way. How did the game look to you from over there? Hopefully better than it did from this side. A total blowout. I can't believe Barnaby Hills couldn't score a point. Not one."

Jack had seen the whole thing. It was a massacre. 11 - 0. It was so bad that Jack actually felt bad for all of them, including Billy.

"This team is just not the same without you Jack Wilson. Facts are hard to deny."

"I don't know about that, but a part of me wanted to run out on the field and help out - even with my bad arm. It was crazy, and the Centerville crowd was eating it up by the bowlful. It was really hard to sit over there and see it all happening."

"I bet. Hey, my parents are probably in the parking lot. They're like your mom - not all that interested in watching sports. Are you ready to meet them?"

Jack took a deep, exaggerated swallow. "Yep."

"They're gonna love you, silly boy."

Jack and Sarah walked over to her parent's car. Jack wasn't really all that nervous about meeting them; it was more so the TIME that he was meeting them, right in the middle of incredible craziness. But he was down for anything that was going to stop him from thinking about it all.

Sarah's mom and dad opened up their car doors and got out to meet them.

"Mom, Dad, this is Jack. The boy I've been telling you about...over and over and over again."

Both her parents smiled. "The famous Jack," said Sarah's dad reaching out his hand. "Glad to finally meet you."

"And to meet you, too, sir," Jack replied.

"There's nothing "sir" about me."

"Yes, sir....I mean Mr. Bartley." They both laughed.

"Jack, this is my mom. She's not a sir, either," Sarah chuckled.

"So nice to meet you, Jack. You don't pay Sarah's father any mind. He's a big joker."

"Well, then we should get along pretty well. Clowning around is kind of a hobby."

"I hope eating ice cream is another one."

"Oh, definitely."

Sarah's father motioned for them all to get in the car. "Well then let's get going before other families eat it all up. On the way, you guys can fill us in on the game."

Sarah grabbed Jack's hand and pulled him towards the closest door. "Oh, we'll fill you in alright, but it may ruin your appetite."

"That bad?" asked her mom.

"Not just bad - dreadful."

Jack nodded his head in silent agreement.

"Oh, dear," replied Mrs. Bartley, gritting her teeth. "We may need an extra scoop of ice cream after hearing about this."

Jack nodded his head even more.

Chapter 24

April 28, 2011

Apart from the revving of the bus engine and the sound of the wheels on the blacktop, the ride back to Barnaby Hills was eerily silent. No one said a word. Coach Weber sat in the front of the bus and just looked out the front window. The rest of the team sat in their seats doing the same or staring off into some unknown space. Never had this team experienced a loss as great as they did tonight. 11 - 0. That wasn't just a number on the scoreboard; it was now a number that was emblazoned on the team itself. Something that would be hard to shake off for a long time. A collective feeling of disappointment hung thickly in the air.

Billy sat in the last row all by himself. No one on the team dared go near him right now. The angry frown on his face spoke volumes. He felt like he was losing his grip on reality and his teammates, even Lucas, knew not to bother him. He replayed the night's game in his head and everything leading up to it. Not only were his players letting him down, he was letting himself down. With Jack out of the lacrosse picture, this was Billy's chance to show HIM that he also possessed great skills. It should have been easy, but he was failing. All his best intentions and plans were falling apart. Maybe he wasn't worthy of leading the clan.

STOP! He screamed at the negative voice in his head. *You haven't changed. The game has changed. Who knew it wasn't a good idea to bring Jack into the fold last year? YOU DID! Who knew Chris wasn't up to taking Jack's place? YOU DID! You knew all these things but decisions were made for you.*

Billy shut his thoughts down abruptly. He knew that HE had

the ability to enter the mind and hear thoughts.

Good! Let him hear. He needs to hear. The team was good, really good, before Jack Wilson came along and would have been fine without him. But now look at everything. It's falling apart and it's not your fault. Even HE can see that. Or maybe HE is so wrapped up in his own...

"SHUT UP!" Billy said to himself aloud. His teammates turned around to see who Billy was talking to, most of them glad they weren't sitting next to him.

Billy glared back at them, forcing them to squirm and look away quickly. He knew he had to get away from himself right now. He couldn't be trusted with his own thoughts. He got up from his seat and started walking forward. He looked to the left and right as he slowly made his way down the aisle. When he found what he was looking for, he plopped himself down in an empty seat. Right next to Chris. He didn't plan on saying anything. He was just going to sit there and let Chris quiver in the uncomfortable silence.

Chapter 25

April 28, 2011

"It must be hard, Jack, seeing your team getting pummeled on the field but not being able to do anything about it," said Mr. Bartley, taking a big bite out of his ice cream cone.

"It is. I was telling Sarah before that I really felt like jumping on the field to help out. Although I don't know how much help I would have been with my arm the way it is."

"Sarah told us about your accident," chimed in Mrs. Bartley. "That must have hurt so much. Your mother must have been beside herself with worry. I know if I had a son, that would have been the end of his lacrosse career right then and there."

Mr. Bartley chuckled. "Would you say the same if Sarah hurt herself doing a backflip?"

Mrs. Bartley raised her eyebrow at her husband sternly but then smiled. "Okay, point taken, but you know what I mean."

"Oh, my Mom was plenty worried, but she is also realistic about these things. She knows that injuries are part of the game. She doesn't like to come to games just for that reason, though. Had she actually seen what happened, she may have wanted to stop me from playing any more. Lucky for me she didn't see it."

"How is your arm doing? Mr. Bartley asked.

Jack looked down at his arm resting in the sling. "I think it is doing pretty good. It's only been about two weeks since it got injured, but I'm pretty much able to do most things without a problem. If they had put it in a hard cast, I'd probably be miserable, but this isn't too bad. I have a follow up with the doctor in another week and he'll x-ray it and tell me how things are going inside, but it feels okay now.

Season will be over by the time the doctor says it's okay to play."

"Sorry to hear that."

"Thanks, Mrs. Bartley."

"It's not that bad, Mom." Sarah chimed in. "Just means more time to hang out with his girlfriend."

Jack began to turn red again.

"Oh, oh...I've made him blush for the second time tonight. One more time and he'll turn into a rose bush."

Everyone started to laugh, which made Jack blush even more. He slowly got up from the table.

"If you don't mind, I'm gonna flush myself down the toilet right now. Nah, I'm just gonna throw some cold water on my face before I start flowering. Be right back." As he turned to leave, he heard Sarah's mom tell her dad, "That's so cute." He started to feel his cheeks heat up again so he quickened his exit from the table

Sarah yelled after him. "Don't worry; I swear I won't do it again tonight, but I can't say the same for my folks."

Jack wanted to turn and smile but he knew that would just make his face even redder. He really didn't mind when Sarah made his cheeks light up like that. It was more that he didn't want to sit there and stand out literally like a sore thumb for everyone else to gawk at in the ice cream shop. He made it to the restroom and quickly locked it behind him. He went over to the sink and turned on the cold water. He looked at his reflection in the mirror above the sink and laughed aloud. His face looked like the side of a barn. He bent his head down and cupped the cold water in hands. He splashed himself gently a few times and then reached over to the paper towel dispenser. He wiped his face and hands clean and leaned back over to see if some of the red had gone. What he saw in the mirror almost assuredly turned him white. His blood ran cold and he dropped the paper towels into the sink. Staring back at him was his face as a full-fledged Moonwalker.

"Ready to go back out and have more ice cream, Jack?" the voice laughed.

Jack put his hands up to his face to rub his eyes and see if this was all a dream, but when he did, his hands were now large, clawed paws.

"This can't be real," he said more to himself than to the voice. "It's not a full moon. It can't be real."

"Oh, it's real, Jack. It is real because I make it real. Haven't you learned that by now? Imagine Sarah's surprise when her boyfriend comes out of the bathroom as a werewolf. Would she scream or calmly say, 'What exactly do they put in this chocolate ice cream?' The voice howled with laughter that reverberated back and forth against the tiles in the bathroom. After a few more seconds, the laughter stopped abruptly.

"What is your decision, Jack?"

Jack stared at himself in the mirror. He was in wolf form, but his eyes were still his. His light blue eyes. They were almost reaching out to him, calming him down, letting him know that everything was okay...that deep down he was still Jack, no matter what.

Jack pushed back away from the sink and looked around the small bathroom.

"You want my answer?"

"Yes."

"You want to know if I will join you?

"Yes."

"Well here's my answer." A small but confident smile came over his face. "Never," he said in a low, steady tone. "Never."

The voice replied in a similar tone. "Have it your way," and then abruptly screamed an unearthly sound that reverberated throughout the small room, knocking the mirror off the wall, the glass smashing loudly as it hit the floor.

Jack held his hands to his ears tightly to drown out the sound the best he could. He continued holding them there as the scream began to fade and the sound of knocking on the door became apparent.

"JACK! JACK! Are you okay?"

It was Sarah.

"Jack? We heard glass breaking. Is everything alright?"

Jack took his hands away from his ears. With the voice gone and reality sinking back in, he began to panic. The mirror lay on the floor in scattered shards. He looked for the biggest piece and was about to grab it, when he stopped himself.

Calm down, Jack. You'll cut your hand to shreds if you're not careful. Take it easy. Whatever the reflection says, you'll deal with it as it comes. Nice and easy.

He reached out and carefully picked up a piece of the mirror.

Okay. Here we go.

He slowly brought the mirror up to his face. In the reflection was Jack Wilson the human, not Jack Wilson the Moonwalker. He breathed a huge sigh of relief.

"Jack?" Sarah was banging against the door now.

He walked over and opened it up.

Sarah's worried face relaxed. "Oh, you had me so scared. Are you okay? We heard glass breaking and..." She looked down on the floor and saw the mirror smashed to pieces. "Jack, what happened in there?"

"To be honest," he said stepping out into the hallway, "I'm not exactly sure, but I think I'll know soon enough."

Overtime

*"Courage is not the absence of fear,
but rather the judgment that something else
is more important than fear."*

Ambrose Redmoon

Chapter 1

May 1, 2011

The Monday-morning rumor mill was at it again. Along with the news about the loss to Centerville on Friday night, gossip was flowing about Jack Wilson at the ice cream shop, too.

Jack was so pissed off about the team losing that he ripped the mirror right off the bathroom wall.

One of the Centerville players showed up shooting his mouth off at the ice cream shop and Jack gave him a beating in the bathroom!

Jack confronted Billy about why the team is doing so badly and they had it out.

Jack was surprised by an evil werewolf in the mirror, asking for Jack's loyalty, but Jack said "No!" and the werewolf promised revenge against Jack and all the people he cares about.

No one knew the last one, of course, just Jack. And it was on his mind the whole weekend. He spent Saturday and Sunday contemplating what happened, and, more so, what could happen. It was pretty depressing. Now sitting in the library, he had the whole period to contemplate it all again.

Jack knew the creature meant business - even though there had been no physical contact as of yet. That part was good, but he also knew that could change at any moment. It was one of the reasons he stayed by himself for most of the weekend. If the creature was going to attempt something, he didn't want anyone nearby to get hurt, too.

But after two days of thinking about it all, Jack started to believe that Wednesday would be the day that everything would hit the fan. Wednesday was the next full moon. If the creature truly wanted to hurt him, why didn't he do it right in the bathroom on Friday? There would have been nothing that Jack could have done to stop it or protect himself, and with Jack out of the picture, he could have hurt the others that he threatened. But that didn't happen. Why? It took a while, but Jack came to the realization that the creature's powers were most likely limited when there was no full moon. Without a full moon, the creature could only do very little (although still quite remarkable by human standards) and relied more on threats and intimidation more than anything else. This took a little weight off of Jack's mind and shoulders, but only for a little while. Wednesday's full moon was only two days away and it was supposed to be a crystal clear night - not a cloud, not even a wisp of one. EVERYTHING would happen on Wednesday.

Stop thinking about it!

He had to get his mind off the subject, as difficult as that was. He'd go insane if he didn't.

He opened up his English notebook and looked over the information that he had been jotting down about his father and Sophie Scholl for Mr. Weber's biography assignment. All his conversations with his mom had helped him to gain more info about his dad, but in many ways, this assignment was like writing about two people he didn't know very well. He had written more about Sophie than his father.

As he poured over his notes, he heard the door open and close. It was Chris. For a half second, their eyes locked on one another and then just as quickly, Chris looked away and started walking over to an empty table close to the computers. Jack watched as he sat down and took his books out of his backpack and laid them out. He sat down in a chair with his back to the rest of the room, opened a book and began shuffling through the pages. Jack continued to look, wondering if Chris was going to ignore his presence the whole period or maybe take a look back over his shoulder and show interest in the fact that he was in close proximity to his ex-best friend. After a couple of disappointing minutes, Jack decided to get back to his own work when he saw Chris slowly shift his in his chair a little and turn his head around. As soon as he saw Jack looking at him, he turned right back and put his head down directly into an open book. It was all so awkwardly performed that Jack actually chuckled a little. And that was enough to make him realize that sitting around in a state of doubt and fear wasn't helping him one bit. He needed to get up and do something bold.

Leaving his books behind, Jack walked quietly over to Chris and tapped him on the shoulder. Chris swung his head around quickly as if in a mental state for a zombie attack.

Jack smiled in response. "Do you mind if I sit down? I'd like to talk."

Chapter 2

May 1, 2011

He sat on the coarse asphalt roof, his back against the brick wall next to the access door. His legs were bent, elbows resting on the top of his knees, hands clenched together and pressed against his mouth. So much to think about. So much to do.

The door opened with a bang. "Billy! There you are. I've been looking all over for you."

Billy shook his head in disbelief. "Why don't you go over to the edge of the building and announce to the whole school that I'm up here, Lucas. Geez. Close that door and shut your mouth."

"Sorry. It's just that I wanted to tell you something. I was walking past the library and I saw Jack and Chris sitting in the library at the same time. I was gonna go in and get Chris out of there, but I figured I'd talk with you first. Should I go down and get him?"

Billy shook his head again. "Nah. It doesn't matter anymore. I've been told that Jack made his choice. He could tell Chris everything if he wanted and it wouldn't make a difference to the outcome. Wednesday is on."

Lucas smiled. "That's good. Really good, right? Jack will finally get what's been coming to him for a long time, and Chris will take his place." Lucas looked down and saw that Billy wasn't smiling, too. "What's wrong, dude? This is what we've been waiting for...to get Jack out of the way...for good."

"Do you know what 'for good' even means, Lucas? Do you?"

"Billy, what are you talking about? Just last month we were going to take him out - in Chris' backyard."

Billy sneered. "Yeah, yeah, yeah..."

"What? Am I missing something here?"

Billy looked at Lucas. Directly into his eyes. They were dark. Almost completely black. Lucas was the perfect right-hand. Not too bright, but strong and willing to do anything that was asked of him. A dangerous combination. It's true that last month, they were supposed to take out Jack and transform Chris, but Billy knew deep down inside that Jack would probably be okay. Who among the clan had the heart to actually rip out the throat of a rival? Lucas, sure, but anyone else? Billy figured last month that they'd threaten Jack and give him a beat down at best, and that would've been enough to stop Jack from fighting against the clan, especially if Chris was now one of them, too.

But that was all last month. Things had changed dramatically since then and maybe, just maybe, Billy had overplayed his role in the whole thing way too much. To the point of no return. He closed his eyes.

"Billy. Did you hear me? What am I missing?"

Billy took a deep breath, opened his eyes and got up off the ground, brushing bits of asphalt off his palms.

"Nothing. You're not missing a thing. There's a lot of planning to do before Wednesday."

Lucas grinned. "Yes! What do we have to do first?"

"Let's gather up the boys for a meeting in my basement tonight."

Lucas grabbed the handle of the roof door and eagerly held it open. Billy just shook his head.

Chapter 3

May 1, 2011

"So how are things?"

"Things have been good," Chris responded to Jack's question. "Really good."

"I'm glad to hear it. It's been so long since we talked and I was just wondering and all."

Quiet.

"Um, how about you? How's things with you?" Chris asked, his eyes glancing downward at Jack's arm in the wrist splint.

"To be honest, not so good."

"Uh, why not? What do you mean?"

"Well, for starters, I lost my best friend. So there's that..."

Chris continued gazing down, going back and forth between looking at the table and Jack's arm.

"Chris, look at me, man. I don't care about the arm. I care about you. I'm really worried. Billy... Billy's got you thinking up is down and down is up. It just ain't good."

Chris slowly raised his eyes up to meet Jack's.

"You know what I'm talking about. I've heard the stories around school. He's been treating you like dirt, like you're nothing. He gave you a dirt bike. So what? Does that make the way he talks to you okay? There's a part of Chris Stiles in you that knows the obvious answer to that."

"It's not what you think, Jack," Chris responded quietly.

"Well then tell me what it is. I'm more than happy to listen."

"You wouldn't get it."

"Try me."

"Just leave it be, Jack. I gotta go."

Chris started to get up from his chair.

"No, Chris, don't run away. I'm here. I'm listening to you. What is it?"

Chis' eyes watered up a little and he rubbed at them with the back of his hands. He sat back down and looked directly at Jack.

"For the first time in my life, I'm part of something, Jack. I'm part of a group. I've got friends. You don't know what it's like. You're so good at so many things. I'm not. You come waltzin' into town and become a lacrosse star. I've been living here my whole life and I'm nuthin'. You come along and get the girl. I've got nuthin'...NOTHIN'. You don't have any idea what that feels like. So, yeah, Billy isn't a nice guy, but at least he invited me to become part of something. I can't just give that up, Jack. I'm so sorry that I hurt your arm. I didn't want to do it. I swear. But I was so afraid of going back to being a nobody. I don't want to be that guy ever again."

Tears were coming down Chris' face now. Jack took off his sweatshirt and handed it to him to use and wipe his face. Chris took the shirt without saying anything and covered his face quickly so no one would see how upset he was. After a few minutes, he brought the shirt down to the table.

"I'm sorry, Chris. You're right. I probably wouldn't understand what you are feeling because I'm not you. Only you know what you're feeling, and I'm sorry you're hurting. I've always been an outsider in one way or another, but I've never felt like I needed to be an insider. I probably don't know what you're feeling. All I can say is that I'm sorry. But please know that anything that has happened has not been planned on my part. I was never trying to stop you from being a star on the team, or even thinking about getting involved with someone you really liked. That just happened. I did nothing to make it happen. One thing I've always said, though, is that you are a good guy. I know you didn't mean to hurt me, and I didn't mean to hurt you either. Just remember that I'm your friend and will always be your friend. Even if stuff gets really bad, please don't forget that."

Chris managed a tiny smile and tried to hand the sweatshirt back to Jack. Jack snickered.

"Why don't you hold onto that for a while. Give it back after your mom washes it."

"Okay."

Jack got up from the table and turned to walk away.

"Jack," Chris said before he left. "Thanks for talking with me."

Jack smiled. "What are friends for?" he said and walked back to the table with his books.

Chapter 4

May 1, 2011

"Jack, come downstairs and help set the table for dinner!"

"Be down in a minute. Just gonna finish talking with Sarah and then I'll be right there."

Jack laid back down on his bed and put the phone back to his ear.

"My mom needs some help downstairs, so I gotta run soon."

"No problem. You were just about to tell me how things went with Chris. I can call you later, if you want...after dinner."

"That would be great. I don't think I can rush through the conversation that I had with him. I'll just tell you that it went well...much better than I could have expected."

"Oh, that's really good to hear. Maybe this is the start of repairing your friendship. I'm so happy for the two of you."

"Thanks. Like I said, I had no idea what was going to happen but you'll never know if you don't try, right?"

"Exactly. Oh, before I forget, you made quite the impression on the folks Friday night."

"Yeah, I bet I did...with that mirror in the bathroom breaking and all. They must think I'm a psycho who goes around destroying things."

"No, not at all. My father's been in that bathroom enough times to know how rickety that old mirror was. He said, and I quote, 'I always judge a restaurant by the state of its bathroom, but I must have had ice cream clouding my thoughts for too long.' End quote. I swear."

"Well, I'm glad they don't think I'm a lunatic."

"Oh, I'm sure they think you're crazy - crazy about me."

"And on that point they would be correct."

"See? Lunacy isn't all that bad."

From downstairs. "Jack! Set the table."

"Okay, I gotta run. Mom's getting annoyed."

"I'll see you tomorrow at school."

"Yep, byeeee."

Jack hung up the phone and made a beeline downstairs.

"Sorry, Mom. Was talking with Sarah."

"Yeah, I know, but dinner can't wait forever. Plates and forks are clean in the dishwasher."

Jack took out what was needed and sat down.

His mom brought over a platter with chicken and rice and took a seat at the table.

"So..." she said.

"So what?"

"I didn't really see you much this past weekend. We never got a chance to talk about you meeting Sarah's parents. How did it go?"

"Well, I told you about the mirror in the bathroom falling off the wall, right?"

"Yes, that part you told me, but I don't know anything else."

"They were really nice. I had a good time talking with them."

"Okay...what did you guys talk about?

"They just asked me questions about school and lacrosse. Um, they also wanted to know about my arm and how it was healing."

"That was nice of them. Oh, I forgot the veggies." She got up from the table and was soon back with some sautéed peppers and onions.

Jack took a bit of everything.

"When I was just talking with Sarah upstairs, she told me that her parents really liked me."

"They have excellent taste. Speaking of taste, how do you like the chicken? New recipe."

Jack popped a piece into his mouth. "It's awesome, Mom," he said between bites.

"So if things went so well on Friday night, how come I barely saw you over the weekend?"

Jack took a big drink of water and swallowed.

"No real reason. Just had a lot of work to do. That biography project is due this Wednesday."

"Jack, I've never seen a school project keep you in the house for two days straight EVER. What's going on?"

Jack looked at his mom. Her intuition was incredible. If it were any stronger, he was sure she would just be able to read his mind. Once again, he found himself wanting to tell her everything but knowing he could not.

"Just the normal stuff. Nothing too big. School, lacrosse...usual things that wear on me."

"Is it the biography project? Thinking about your dad a lot?"

That wasn't the worst of it, but Jack knew she was right. He had been spending a great deal of time on the project and whether he wanted to believe it or not, there was a sadness about the whole thing that couldn't be avoided.

"Yeah, that's probably it, Mom. I've been thinking about Dad so much and it gets pretty heavy on my mind."

"I knew it. What can I do to help?"

"Nothing. Well, I mean just be there for me like you always are."

"I love you, honey. I'll always be here for you and to protect you as much as I can."

Protection. If she only knew who was really protecting who.

"I love you, too, Mom. Thanks for everything you do. As hard as my life gets sometimes, being a single mom can't be any picnic, either. How about we try and protect each other."

"I'll drink to that!"

Jack and his mom raised their glasses of water and clinked them together. It felt like a moment of loving calm before the storm.

Chapter 5

May 1, 2011

Billy was waiting for everyone in the basement. His mother had laid out bowls of chips and popcorn and they all started snacking. Billy didn't join in. He sat there looking at all of them as they chatted and chomped. He shook his head in disgust by the spectacle. After he couldn't take it anymore, he spoke up.

"Alright, enough eating. You're grossing me out. We've got business to discuss. I sent Lucas to Chris' house to make sure he shows up, but I didn't want him here yet so we could all talk. Actually, I'll talk; you guys listen." He took a deep breath. "As we all know, Wednesday is the big night. It's going to change everything. And I mean EVERYTHING."

The team had their eyes fixed on Billy and were nodding their heads in agreement.

"Now there may be some things planned that you didn't expect. Things that we've never done before. But the reality is that that's where we are headed. No more fun and games, if you get what I'm talking about. Yesterday it might have been all about lacrosse but now we're on the cliff of something different and the drop is pretty steep. Think about it. We have powers that no other human beings have. Amazing powers. It's time we use them...to our advantage."

Most of the boys continued to look at Billy and nod, but a couple of them looked around nervously at one another.

"Wednesday will be Chris' initiation to the clan. To be honest, I've gone back and forth on this but it's what we are expected to do, so it has to happen. But it's not going to be easy because we will have company. Jack will be coming to Howl House with everything he has to stop us. You all know how I feel about Jack, but I'm going to be honest right now. He's powerful. You may think you're one tough wolf, but when it comes down to it, Jack can take all of you one-on-one, even with his busted arm. But that's why we are a team, a clan. Brothers of fur and fury. We don't roll over like puppies for no one. But with Jack, we are going to have to weaken him before we can finish him. So we are going to have a guest with us."

The boys were surprised by this and they started talking with one another and asking Billy who was coming. Howl House was supposed to be off limits to anyone who wasn't part of the clan.

Billy shut down the chatter. "QUIET! I told you there were changes coming. You don't get to ask questions. You just follow orders. Don't forget your place. You know what can happen."

All the boys stopped talking immediately.

"Good. So Wednesday night, before the full moon, we are going to round up..."

At that moment, Billy was interrupted by his dad coming down the stairs followed by Lucas and Chris.

"I guess you have two late comers to your party. Did you get to cleaning your room like your mother asked you?"

"No, Dad," Billy said impatiently.

"Since you have the team all here, maybe they can help you clean up your room. How many times do you have to be asked before you get things done?"

Billy looked around at everyone and rolled his eyes a little bit.

"Hey, don't get wise with me," his father said getting louder. "Especially when you haven't done what you were asked to do. Do you get me?"

Billy nodded his head. His father raised his eyebrows disapprovingly and waited.

Billy bit down on his lips. "Yes, sir. I get you. Sorry."

"That's better. Sorry for the interruption, guys. You can go back to whatever it was you were doing. We'll talk more later, Billy."

His father walked up the stairs and Lucas and Chris walked down and sat down on the couch with the other boys.

Billy put both his hands behind his head and tilted his head back. He brought his arms and down and blew out his breath. He looked around at the group, all sitting around in uncomfortable silence. Billy tried to lighten the mood.

"Welcome to the Jenkins household on a Monday night, fellas. How about we get back to what we were talking about later. Right now, let's fill Chris in on his big night on Wednesday. You excited, Chris? We are super excited. Right, boys?"

Everyone in the basement agreed and let their focus eagerly shift to Chris.

Chapter 6

May 2, 2011

"Jack...Jack...wake up. It's time to get schooled!"

Jack was in the forest...in the clearing near Howl House. It was night but the moon was full and he could see everything before him. It was a dream. Another nightmare.

"You know, Jack. The funny thing about dreams is that they can seem awfully real. More real than reality itself. Have you ever died in one of your dreams, Jack? What do you think will happen? Nothing? Or just maybe you die, too...for real. Shall we find out?"

Jack looked all around and couldn't see where the voice was coming from. "Show yourself," he yelled out, his voice echoing across the field and through the woods.

The voice continued. "Not just yet, little puppy. You shall see your master soon enough. But tonight, let us deal with your misbehavior. A punishment before the punishment, if you will."

Jack heard a strangely loud cracking noise that seemed to be coming from nearby. He turned just in time to see a tall pine tree falling directly towards him. For a second, the surreal vision of it all rendered him motionless, but then self-preservation kicked in and he dove out of the way just as it landed where he had been standing.

"Bravo, Jack. Bravo. That was a close one. I caught a moment of indecision there. Are you sure you're okay? I mean, if you're not feeling up to this, we can do it another time. Oh, wait. No we can't." As if on cue the wind began to gust wildly. Leaves, twigs and bits of dirt and small rocks became airborne and started

to pelt Jack in the face. The force grew and Jack found himself being pushed backwards. He put his hands up to protect his eyes from the all the little projectiles. His cheeks and palms of his hands began to sting with pain as the objects began to slash at him with the growing speed and ferocity of the howling wind. His feet began to lose traction and he found himself being thrown backward as he tripped over the fallen pine. He landed in its branches and the sharp pine needles pushed into his skin through the clothing. He screamed in pain but the intensity of the wind was so great that he could not even hear himself.

And just as quickly as it started, it stopped. Jack tried to roll himself out of the thicket of pine branches and needles but found himself struggling to get out. The more he struggled, the more it seemed like the pine itself was preventing him from leaving. He looked over at one of his hands and was stunned to see a branch wrap itself around his wrist. He quickly tried to push himself out from the entanglement with his free arm when the branches wrapped themselves around his whole body, stopping his movement completely. He was imprisoned.

The voice began to laugh. "Jack, Jack, Jack...you seem to be a bit tied up at the moment. Such a shame. I really thought this was going to be more fun. I am so disappointed. But not just in you, Jack. I'm disappointed in myself - in the choices that I have made the last year or so. If there is one thing that I've learned, it's that you can't trust anybody except yourself. Right, Jack? Oh, but look at you now. You trusted yourself rather than placing your trust in me and look at the predicament you are in. So, let me revise my statement. I should have said that you can't trust anybody but ME. So, on your tombstone, I will suggest to your grieving mother that she inscribe: He should have trusted

HIM. What do you think about that, Jack? Fitting, right? Speak now or forever hold your peace." The creature started laughing uncontrollably, his voice almost as painful to hear as the branches digging into Jack's flesh.

"This is a dream. Nothing but a dream," Jack said to himself as the voice continued its maniacal laughter. Jack looked all around for something that would get him out of the mess he was in. Dream or no dream, he was trapped and hurt. There was nothing that he could reach out and grab to use. He tried struggling some more but the branches just grew tighter.

The creature's laughter finally died down. "Jack? You still with me? Good. I want to thank you for making my job easier this week. Wednesday night will be a hassle-free new beginning. And you know what, I'm doing you a big favor. You'll die in your sleep and won't feel a thing when you wake up. Why? Well, because you won't wake up. That's how this kind of works. But I'm not completely heartless, Jack. I'll even sing a song to entertain you as the branches slowly choke the life out of you. One of my personal favorites. Goodbye, Jack."

As Jack began to feel branches slither upwards towards his neck, the creature began to sing softly, "By the light of the silvery moon..."

Jack instinctively looked up upon hearing the lyrics. The moon. It was full and beaming down on him. A branched wrapped itself around Jack's neck and started to tighten. Jack closed his eyes and felt the moon's glow envelope his body.

Was it possible? Could he try? In a dream?

As if on cue, the muscles in his body began to contract and contort.

"I want to spoon..."

Jack's body spasmed wildly. The tree tightened its grip and Jack felt himself being flattened under the growing weight of thick limbs and bark. Oxygen was being forced out of his lungs. After a while, his body stopped moving. The branches of the tree stopped, too.

The singing ceased. The voice spoke softly. "No more moon dances for you, Jack."

But from the thicket came a sound...a deep, solitary breath.

An explosion of wood, pine needles and dirt came flying out in every direction as Jack jumped to his feet in full Moonwalker form. Arms reaching to the sky above, claws opening and closing, he howled angrily at the Moon.

The creature screamed in a voice that nearly matched the intensity of Jack's bellow. "NO!"

Jack stopped howling. His ears acted as his eyes. The creature's voice wasn't coming from an indistinct place in the forest this time. He twisted his body to find its exact location: Howl House.

Jack jumped clear of the fallen pine tree and sped directly to the House. The creature continued yelling, repeating the same word over and over again, "NO, NO, NO..."

Jack reached the front door, opened it and jumped inside. He found himself falling, falling faster and faster. He landed with a thump onto something soft. He pushed himself up from a face down position.

Jack Wilson looked down. His arms were thrust in front of him, beads of sweat dripping from his forehead, injured arm throbbing. He had fallen into bed.

Chapter 7

May 2, 2011

"He's afraid. Afraid of me. I just know it."

"Who's afraid, Jack?" Sarah asked, between bites of her snack.

"Um, Billy. Sorry, I was kind of talking to myself there for a minute."

"Chip?" she asked, pointing the open bag towards him.

"No, no thanks. I've gotta go, actually."

"Lunch isn't over yet. What's up?"

"I still have to finish my biography. I'm gonna go to the library and do a little more research."

"Do you want some company? I promise I won't crunch any potato chips while you're working."

Jack smiled. "You are always true to your word, but I'll probably get more work done on my own. Thanks, though."

"Alright, but it's your loss."

Jack got up from the table. "Don't I know it. I'll catch you later." Just as he was about to turn and run out of the cafeteria, he grabbed a chip from the bag and tossed it in his mouth. "One for the road," he said as chip crumbs fell off his lips."

Sarah laughed and blew him a kiss.

Jack made a beeline for the exit, hoping to get some research time in before the next period. Just as he was walking out the door, Billy came walking in.

Both boys stared at each other, almost nose to nose, but neither moved. Finally Billy spoke.

"Wednesday, Jack. Wednesday. Hope you're ready."

Jack leaned in a smidgen of an inch more until only a paper's thickness of a divide actually stopped their noses from touching. "Don't you worry about me, Billy. But maybe you should be worried about who or what you have sold your soul to. I think there are some chinks in the armor."

Billy took a nervous half step back. "What are you talking about?"

Jack smiled. "Oh, you didn't get an update? That's interesting. Why don't you go to the bathroom and try channeling him from a toilet and find out what happened."

Billy looked Jack's face over carefully. He didn't like what he saw, but he wasn't going to give Jack any satisfaction. He stepped off to the side and waved his arms dutifully as if to give Jack proper passage out of the cafeteria. "Ladies first."

A slight hint of a smile appeared in the corner of Jack's mouth. He proceeded slowly through the door and took a right turn towards the library.

Lucas came running over from the table. "Man, I thought it was on. I was just waiting for the first punch and then I was gonna be over here before the second one could be fired off. What just happened?"

Billy turned and looked at Lucas. He spoke quietly but assertively. "Things just became unexpectedly more difficult."

Chapter 8

May 2, 2011

As soon as Jack got to the library, he asked for some help.

"Looking for more information on Sophie Scholl, Jack?" the librarian asked. "I don't know if I have any more resources for you."

"No, no, Mrs. Talbot. I'm looking for something else. Where would I find information about land ownership in and around Barnaby Hills?"

"Oh, that's an easy one. You can get on the computer and look up real estate records through the County Clerk's office. They have a whole online database. And the best part is that it's free - public knowledge."

"Oh, that is great, Mrs. Talbot. You just made my day."

She smiled. "I don't hear that too often. Thank you, Jack."

"No, thank you."

Jack walked over to the computer section and sat down at a desktop computer that wasn't near anyone else. He logged on and started searching for the County Clerk's webpage. It came up quickly. Jack moved the cursor over the search bar on the page and was about to type when he realized that he didn't know what to type.

He started with the obvious entry: Howl House. No information was found. For some reason, Jack hadn't considered that finding information about a hidden place was going to be hard. *Don't blame yourself too much; you've had a lot on your mind as of late.*

Jack started searching the database in his head to see if he could come up with anything that would help this search. The only name he actually knew didn't bring up anything. He thought back to the first night when Billy and the boys took him into the woods. Was something said then? Jack had a pretty good memory but this was definitely causing a strain on the brain.

Billy said it was near something; didn't he? What did he say...what did he say...? Whoa, wait...he said that Howl House was only a couple of miles away from a...a...timber mill. No. Not a timber mill. A TIMBER DAM! That was it. But he said the name...he totally said the name, too. It was like someone's initials. What...what? That's it! W&W. The W&W Timber Dam.

Jack threw the name of the timber dam into the search engine. It brought up a number of hits. One of them was a map. Jack zoomed out away from the actual spot of the dam and started looking within a couple of miles. He had never seen what the area around Howl House had looked like from above but when the map widened out a bit, he saw a giant clearing that looked like it could be the field next to Howl House. He cross-referenced everything with nearby roads and streets that were familiar to him. Yes, that had to be it. He found it. But who owned the land?

Okay, if the timber dam was owned by W&W and they were logging the land, then there's a good chance that W&W owned it all.

Jack went back to the original page that had many links to W&W. Jack clicked on the first and then felt his stomach bottom out on itself.

W&W stood for Weber and Weber - as in Coach Weber.

Chapter 9

May 2, 2011

"What? Coach Weber? It doesn't make sense. Why would Coach Weber be putting Billy and the rest of the team up to all this weird cloak and dagger behavior out in the woods? And your arm...did he order them to do that, too? I don't know. It all seems just too weird."

Jack wondered if Sarah would still think it weird if he told her everything. Yes she would, but not in the way that Jack would like.

"I understand your disbelief. Believe me; I'm there with you, but it just seems so out there that it is possible. I can't explain it any more than that. It is just a gut feeling telling me something isn't right."

"You're right about it being weird...that house...in the middle of the woods on property owned by the Weber family...and Billy and the boys hanging out there...it's as weird as it gets. But I keep coming back to one, simple question: why? What would Mr. Weber get out of it all? He's already the lacrosse coach. Up until recently, he had the best lacrosse player in the school on his team. What good would it do for him to let Billy intentionally harm you? Since you have been on the sidelines, the team has been playing badly. So why?"

Jack basically had the answer to Sarah's question - give or take one or two reasons - but, again, he could only respond to a point and then retreat. He hated it.

"I'm not sure," he shrugged.

Both of them looked up. They were at Sarah's house. It felt like no time at all had gone by as they walked home from school.

"Do you want to come in and hang out for a little bit?"

Jack smiled. "More than anything in the world, but I can't."

Sarah grabbed his hand. "I knew what your answer was going to be. Was just hoping for a miracle of sorts."

"Don't stop hoping. If a miracle was ever needed, now is the perfect time. I wish I could just forget everything but I have to go home and finish up my project for tomorrow's class, and, surprise-surprise, try to figure out what my next move is now that I have new information."

"Jack Wilson, can I just tell you how incredible you are. I'm not even going to explain why. You just are. No explanations ever needed."

Jack started to turn red. "Oh, oh...call the fire department."

Sarah laughed and gave him a hug and a kiss. "You get your work done...all of it...and I'll see you tomorrow. Okay?"

"Yep. Will do." Jack paused for a moment and looked directly into Sarah's eyes. "Do you trust me?"

She didn't hesitate to answer. "With my life."

They held hands for another moment without saying anything and then Jack turned to head home.

It was one of the hardest things he ever had to do.

Chapter 10

May 3, 2011

The bell rang and some stragglers in the hallway rushed to get inside before Mr. Weber closed the door to his class. Today was the day that biography projects were due so the class chatter was a little louder than usual as students talked with their classmates about the people they chose to write about.

"Okay," Mr. Weber said loudly. "Settle down; settle down. Lots to do today. We are going to try and get as many presentations done as possible. But first, give me a show of hands. How many of you didn't finish the assignment?"

Two hands went up.

"Wendy. Why didn't you finish?"

"I'm sorry, Mr. Weber. I'm almost done. My cat got sick last night and we had to take him to the vet. He's like 15 years old and just isn't doing so well. I totally would have finished if it hadn't been for that. I swear. You can call my parents. I'll definitely have it tomorrow. Promise."

Mr. Weber ran his tongue back and forth against the inside of his bottom lip. "If it's not in tomorrow, you're gonna lose points. Do you understand?"

"Yes, Mr. Weber. I got you. Thank you."

"Jeremy, your hand was up, too. What's up with your project?"

"Well, half of it is done, Mr. Weber. I wrote a biography about my brother, Pete. He has the coolest car. It's an old 69 Mustang convertible. I'm sure you've all seen it cruising around the neighborhood." He looked around the class to see most of them smiling.

Mr. Weber looked annoyed. "The assignment wasn't to write a biography about a car, Jeremy."

The class laughed. "No, I know that, Mr. Weber. That is just part of the biography. The rest of it is about my brother. He's awesome."

"So why don't you have the assignment finished?" Mr. Weber said rubbing his forehead aggressively.

"Well, the one about my brother took so long and came out so well, I kind of forgot about writing about someone else. Sorry. I'll get it done, though."

"Indeed you will. You have one more day."

Jeremy swallowed almost audibly. "One more day? That's not enough time, Mr. Weber. Can I have a little more than that?"

"If your assignment is not handed into me tomorrow during this class, you will be losing points on it daily. Got me?"

Jeremy nodded his head up and down woefully in agreement and sat back down.

Mr. Weber moved around from the front of his desk to the side of the room. "Now that we got that out of the way. Let's listen to some biographies. Who wants to go first?"

Jack had been sitting in his seat quietly during this whole time. He had spent most of last night working on the biography project. He had made some changes. He slowly raised his hand.

"Jack! Volunteering to be the first, I hope?"

"Yes."

"Good. Good. Come on up."

Jack got up from his seat and walked to the front of the room. Mr. Weber moved to the back so he would be able to listen better. Jack looked around the room and then made eye contact with Mr. Weber who motioned for him to begin.

"Um, the two people I originally chose for the biography project were my father and Sophie Scholl - a young woman who was killed with her brother by the Nazis during World War II. She wanted people to know that they should rise up and resist the actions of an evil regime. My father died when I was very young, but the stories that I have been told about him paint a picture of a person very much like Sophie - someone who wasn't afraid to speak their mind or help others when they needed it. So with both my dad and Sophie in mind, I'd like to change the topic of my biography."

Students looked around at each other a little confused. Mr. Weber shifted his stance, not sure as to what Jack was doing.

"I want to tell you about two brothers from local history that had a big impact on Barnaby Hills. Two brothers that owned a timber mill. Two brothers that changed the literal landscape of this area and who did so by taking advantage of the native American Indian population and desecrating their land, traditions and even their burial grounds. Today I'm going to talk about W & W Timber and Logging owned by George and Harrison Weber. The ancestors of our own Mr. Weber. And what I have to say isn't pretty. So here it goes..."

Chapter 11

May 3, 2011

"Mrs. Wilson, thanks for coming down and meeting with us today. Maybe we can all get to the bottom of what happened."

"Thank you for calling me, Mr. Joyce." Jack's mother thanked the principal, but her eyes were staring directly at Jack sitting next to her. The principal and Mr. Weber were across from them on the other side of a conference table. "But if you don't mind, I'd like to hear what Jack has to say about what took place first."

"I think that is a good place to start. Jack, you want to tell us what's going on?"

Jack had been staring down at his hands in his lap since he first arrived. He knew people were waiting for him to speak, but he felt he had already spoken his peace in class."

"Jack," his mother said, "let's hear it."

He looked up from his hands and his eyes fell on Mr. Weber.

"Shouldn't we be asking him to speak first? I mean, he's the reason we are all here. Right, Mr. Weber?"

"Jack, I don't know what you're talking about. What did I...." Principal Joyce motioned for him to stop speaking.

"Jack, we want to hear from you first. Like your mother said. Could you please tell us what happened today?"

"Okay. What I did today was expose something that has been going on at Barnaby Hills for a while. Mr. Weber has created a lacrosse team within a lacrosse team. He has been training selected players at a place in the woods that he owns. A place that was handed down to him by his ancestors - the owners of W & W Timber and Logging."

"Jack. What are you talking about?" his mother asked

completely confused.

"This is what I'm talking about, Mom." Jack pointed at his arm in the brace. "He had members of the team conspire to hurt me...members of this secret lacrosse team he is creating."

The principal leaned forward. "And why is Coach Weber creating this secret team, Jack?"

Jack furrowed his brow and stared directly and angrily into the eyes of Mr. Weber. "I can't tell you."

"Why not?"

"I'm not fully sure and even if I could tell you, you wouldn't believe me."

"Jack," the principal said leaning backwards, "you realize how ridiculous this all sounds. I'm having trouble believing you right now."

Jack's mom interrupted. "Is this what you were researching all night on the internet? Information about Mr. Weber's family history to make a point about something you believe is happening today?"

"Yes."

She shook her head in confusion. "I feel like I've just entered the Twilight Zone. What exactly is going on here?" She turned to Mr. Weber. "Can you provide some answers?"

Mr. Weber stammered a little. "I...I...don't know what to say. I think I'm more in disbelief now than I was when he started railing against my ancestors in class. It was like he was possessed."

"POSSESSED? That's a good one!" Jack shouted. "You should know all about possession. The way you have taken control of Billy and the rest of them. The way you have tried to get control of me. If you're so big and powerful, why don't you tell everyone here about the house in the woods and about how my arm injury wasn't an accident? Go on; tell them!"

Mr. Weber crossed his arms and looked at the others in

disbelief.

The room was silent for a minute and then Jack's mother spoke. "Jack, you've been going through a lot lately - the injury, writing a report about your dad. Maybe you need a little time to relax and calm down.

"That sounds like a great idea, Mrs. Wilson," Principal Joyce added.

Jack turned to his mom. "No, Mom, I'm okay. Really. You have to believe me. He's behind all of this and I'm not gonna let him hurt you or anyone else. I'm not."

Mr. Weber was about to say something when the principal interrupted. "I'll tell you what, Mrs. Wilson. Why don't you go to the main desk and sign Jack out for the day. Let him get his mind off of these issues. Let him take as much time as he needs to feel better. Sound good?"

"Yes, that sounds like a plan."

"But Mom...."

"That's what we're doing for today, Jack. Tomorrow is a different day and we'll take things one day at a time. But this is not the time to argue. Grab your things. Mr. Joyce, Mr. Weber, thank you for your time."

Mr. Weber spoke. "Jack, I hope you feel better. No hard feelings here. Everything will be alright."

Jack got up from his chair. Before he turned to walk out, he gave Mr. Weber one last look.

"I'm not afraid of you. I'm not."

Jack's mother grabbed him by the wrist and rushed him out the door.

Chapter 12

May 3, 2011

Signed out from school for the day, Jack and his mother made their way to the exit. Students were in their classes and the main hallway was empty. Just before reaching the doors, Jack stopped abruptly.

"Jack, what are you stopping for? I want to get you home and we can try and figure out what is going on."

Jack took a deep breath. "Mom, I know this all sounds crazy, and I know that it looks like I've flipped out and all, but there is something going on here."

"Honey, you know I'm your biggest supporter and I'll fight to the death for you, but the story that you just told about Mr. Weber is out there. Really out there. Are you angry with him because he wouldn't let you finish out the season? I just don't get why you would tell such a wild story..."

"It's not a story, Mom. Mr. Weber's family owned a timber mill and hundreds of acres of forest land outside of Barnaby Hills. There's a house out there deep in the woods that Mr. Weber has the students going to and participating in weird lacrosse rituals. I know; I've been there."

"You've been there? Why haven't you told me about this before? Mr. Weber has taken you and the rest of the boys out into the woods to this house? I'm going to call the police."

"No, Mr. Weber hasn't taken us out there. Billy has taken us there."

"And he told you that Mr. Weber owns the house and the land?"

"No, not exactly."

"Jack, so you have been to a house out in the woods with Billy and some other boys and you think Mr. Weber has something to do with this because his great, great grandfather or something owned the forest land where the house is?"

"There are other things, too."

"Like what?"

"I can't say."

"This is where things got really weird before, Jack. Why can't you say what you know?"

"Because it is so unbelievable, I almost don't believe it myself."

Jack's mom grabbed his chin and looked at him with great concern. "Jack, you have never lied to me. For years now, it's been you and me against the world. Why aren't you telling me everything about this situation?"

"I would if I could, Mom. You have to believe me. And the worst part is that things could get worse."

"Worse than this? I just had to leave me my job to come and meet with your principal and your teacher about something that sounds like it came out of a comic book. And you're saying things could get worse? I think we both need to get home and get some rest. This has been a day for the record books."

Jack grabbed her hand. "I'm sorry, Mom. This isn't what I wanted to happen. I really didn't want to get you involved. I can take care of this myself - like Dad would."

A tear ran down her cheek. "Jack, your father was the love of my life and a great man, but he didn't go out and take on the world by himself. When trouble arose, he had me...he had his friends. He never took the world on his shoulders by himself. And you don't have to either."

Jack knew she was right.

"Let's go home and have some food and get some rest, okay?"

"Okay, Mom."

They exited the doors of the school and headed down the steps towards the parking lot. As they got closer, Jack could see a flyer on the passenger side windshield.

"Jack, would you do me a favor and see what that is?" his mom asked fumbling for the car keys.

Jack pulled the paper out from under the wiper blade. It said one thing:

By the light of the silvery...

Jack's mom opened the car doors. "What does it say, honey?"

Jack crumpled the paper up and put it in his pocket. "Just a flyer for a school craft fair. That's all, Mom."

Chapter 13

May 3, 2011

"Aren't you going to eat your dinner?"

"Not very hungry."

Jack had been pushing his food around on his plate from side to side for a good ten minutes or so. It was a reflection of how he was pushing ideas around in his head - giving each thought a little contemplation and then brushing them aside to make room for the next. There seemed to be no end in sight for new ideas to be obsessively contemplated.

"It reminds me of what you used to do when you were little."

"What? Sorry, Mom. I guess I'm not the best dinner companion tonight. A lot on my mind. What did I used to do when I was little?"

"Move your food around your plate. But you had a reason for doing it."

"What was the reason?"

"You used to try and hide the food that you didn't want to eat around the plate."

Jack chuckled slightly. "Oh yeah. I remember. I hated broccoli..."

"Still do," his mother interjected with a smile.

"Yep, still do, but I figured in my young mind that if I moved the broccoli around the plate instead of it staying in one large lump, it would look like I had eaten some of it."

"You were always thinking, even back then."

Jack smiled for a moment and then other thoughts came rushing back into his head. He started moving food around his plate.

His mom grabbed his hand. "Talk to me, Jack...about anything. How about what happened today. What happened leading up to today? You can talk to me about candy bars if you want to. Just talk to me."

He put his fork down on his plate and grabbed his mother's hand.

"If Dad were alive, would he like me?"

His mother's eyes widened in shock. "What kind of question is that? Like you? He'd love you more than I could possibly describe in words. Why are you even asking that?"

"I don't know. I just think that I've made some decisions that haven't worked out for the best over the last year. I guess I don't like myself very much right now and I'm just trying to find more ways to hate me."

"Oh, Jack. What are you doing? This isn't like you. Bad decisions? What bad decisions could you have possibly made? You didn't decide to break your arm. You didn't decide to have problems with Billy and his friends. You've got to take it easy on yourself. You are a great kid. You're not even a kid anymore. You're a great young man. I see it. Sarah sees it. And your Dad definitely would have seen it."

Jack tried to smile. "Thanks, Mom. I guess I don't see it right now."

"Well, then you are going to have to tell your brain to take a back seat for the moment and let the opinions of others doing the driving in that head of yours. Okay?"

"I'll try, Mom. Things did get a little crazy today, though. You must have been pretty embarrassed getting called into the office and all. I must have seemed like some crazed lunatic. I'm really sorry."

"No apologies necessary. And to tell you the truth, Jack, I do believe you when you say something is going on. I know my son better than anybody, and you're not crazy. Something really strange has gotten you to this point and I'm going to get to the bottom of it."

Jack looked at his mother with some concern. "What do you mean?"

"I'm going to make a phone call over to Billy's house and talk with his parents."

Jack panicked a little. "Wha...why?"

"Because this is all going on much too long for my liking. I want to tell them about what you have been experiencing and straighten all of this out."

"Mom, you don't have to do that. I can take care of this."

"I know you can, but sometimes a little help from Mom is needed in situations like this. You've got the weight of the world on your shoulders and I want to take some of it away."

This time Jack grabbed his mother's hand.

"Mom, listen to me. I've got this. You have raised me to be independent and strong. I may be forgetting some of it right now, but it is going to come back. Just talking with you has made me feel better. I don't need you to fight my battles for me."

"I don't know, Jack. I don't like seeing you like this. It breaks my heart and I want to protect you."

"I appreciate that, but you can't protect me this time. I've got to do the protecting. You have to trust me."

She looked directly into her son's eyes and could see he was determined.

"Okay, I'll let you do this. But if you need my help, I'm here for you. You're not alone."

Jack wasn't so sure about that last sentence. Even if he wasn't alone, it sure felt like he was. And what would he feel like later on tonight - when the full moon arose over Barnaby Hills.

"Hey, I have a great idea," his mother said smiling. "It's still early. Why don't you head over to Sarah's house and hang out with her for a bit. I bet that would perk up your spirits a little. What do you think?"

Jack smiled back. "Now that is a good idea. Thanks, Mom, you always know what's needed just at the right time."

"It's a gift," she laughed.

Jack walked around the table and gave his mother a huge hug. For the first time all day, he felt like life wasn't so impossible.

Chapter 14

May 3, 2011

The walk over to Sarah's house gave Jack time to think things through some more. He had spent so much time last night preparing for Mr. Weber's class that he neglected his real homework: getting ready for tonight at Howl House.

There was no doubt that Billy and the gang would be laying a trap for him. And Mr. Weber? Now that Jack knew about who the creature was, there was no need to hide himself any longer. Based upon all the dreams that Jack had experienced, the Coach would be a formidable opponent in wolf form. The real question was how they were going to surprise him. Would it be like what they attempted at Chris' house - a whole group effort? Would they come at him one-on-one to wear him down? Or would Coach Weber just come at him right from the get-go? AND WHAT ABOUT CHRIS DURING ALL OF THIS? Would they be using him as a pawn to break Jack's will? Would he be standing on the sidelines watching all of this go down as Moonwalkers fought viciously against one another? Or was the plan to transform Chris as everything else happened - maybe even coerce him against his will to take part in the mayhem in some fashion? Probably not, but the biggest question for Jack right now was how to protect both Chris and Sarah. How could he convince her (without telling her everything) that she needed to be watchful throughout the night, to make sure that all the windows and the doors of her home were locked and that she was to be ready for "anything."

Jack! What about your arm?

Throughout all of this, he had totally forgotten about his injury. He had no idea how that might impact what took place. It had only been mending for a couple of weeks. It felt better, but the fact was, it was still tender and Jack wasn't sure what shape it would be in after he transformed into a wolf.

Are you ready for this? Are you really ready for this?

It didn't matter if he was ready; it was going to happen ready or not. At the very least, he might be able to put up a good enough fight to scare all of them, even Coach Weber and maybe that would put a stop to all the madness for a while - maybe not forever, but at least for the foreseeable future. If he had more time, even another month, he might be able to come up with a plan that would ensure no one he loved got hurt - including himself.

He was so involved in his own world of thought that he almost walked past Sarah's house. He walked up to the front door and rang the bell. A couple of seconds later, it opened.

"Hi Jack," said Mrs. Bartley. "It's good to see you."

"Hi, Mrs. Bartley. Good to see you, too. Is Sarah home?

"I'm afraid not, Jack. She went out with some friends about half an hour ago."

"Oh, do you know where she went?"

"Can't say that I do. It's funny; I actually thought it was you that came to the door earlier."

Jack's eyes widened. "What do you mean?"

"Well, you have been the only boy coming to the house, but then I saw it wasn't you. It was Billy."

Jack's heart dropped to his knees. "And Sarah left with him?"

Mrs. Bartley smiled. "Oh, don't worry, Jack. Have no fear. Sarah only has eyes for you. Billy must have needed her help or something. Do you want to come in and wait for a bit? It probably won't take too long whatever it is."

Jack didn't even respond. He turned and ran away from

Sarah's house as fast as he could. He was headed home.

Chapter 15

May 3, 2011

"MOM! MOM!"

No answer. Jack had just ran the entire distance from Sarah's house to his own, bursting through the front door with only one thought on his mind: his mother.

"MOM, ARE YOU UPSTAIRS?

He didn't wait for an answer. He zoomed over to the staircase and ran up the steps, taking them three at a time.

"MOM?"

Again no answer. He ran to her bedroom. Nothing. He looked down the hall to the bathroom. The door was wide open and she wasn't in there.

OMG! They got her, too!

Jack's brain was like a pinball machine, lighting up all over the place. He ran to his room to get his backpack with the items he thought he would need tonight: a change of clothes, flashlight, rope, pocket knife, a bottle of water, and a picture of him and Chris. He wasn't sure how the last item was going to help, but it seemed to help him now. He slung the bag over his shoulder and made a beeline for the stairs. Just as he was about to speed down, he heard the back door open and close.

"Jack? Were you calling me? It was hard to tell. I was in the backyard trying to get some of the soil turned over before night fell. Is everything okay?"

Jack had to stop his momentum mid-stride and almost tripped over his own feet down the stairs.

She's okay. She's okay.

"Yeah, Mom. It was me. I...I just got home from Sarah's and didn't see you. I thought something happened to you."

"Something happened to me? That's a strange thought. Come down, I want to show you how the garden is going to look."

Jack took a deep breath to calm himself and was about to walk down the stairs when he realized he had his backpack on. He tossed it into his room and went down to join his mom. Before she said anything, he gave her a big hug.

"Okay, wow," she laughed. "Two hugs in one night. Is it my birthday?"

Jack stopped hugging her and backed away. "I'm just really glad that you're my mom, Mom," his eyes glistening with tears that he willed not to fall.

"Was everything okay at Sarah's? Oh, no, did you guys break up?"

"No, no, nothing like that. Um, Sarah wasn't home, so that's why I'm back so early."

"Well, then you're just in time to see what I have planned for the garden. C'mon; take a look with me."

Jack feigned a yawn. "Okay, Mom. I'll check it out but then afterwards I'm gonna hit the sack early. Today has been crazy and I think a good night's sleep will really help me get my head screwed on the right way for school tomorrow."

"I like your thinking. Today was a long day. A good night's sleep is exactly what is needed - for both of us. Come. The backyard is waiting. This is going to be the year that I get my green thumb on. We'll be eating veggies and fruits galore. It's going to be awesome."

Jack followed his mother outside to check out the situation. She pointed out where everything would be - *lettuce over there, tomatoes over here, and next to that, a space just meant for herbs.*

Jack pretended to listen but his mind wasn't anywhere near the garden. He was already mentally at Howl House - searching for Sarah.

Chapter 16

May 3, 2011

Fading light filtered through the trees. Soon it would be dark and the forest would come alive with nocturnal creatures waiting for their chance to roam. Billy and Sarah walked along at a quick pace.

"Are we almost there?" Sarah asked, her breathing somewhat heavily from exertion and annoyance.

"Yes, it's only a little farther."

"Just what were you guys thinking going out to that...that house by yourselves? That place looks like it is old and rotting. You couldn't talk things over at school or on the field? You had to come all the way out here?"

"I'm sorry. It was my idea. I went over to his house for us to have it out once and for all."

"What?"

Billy shook his head. "No, no, nothing like that. I told Jack that the bad blood we have between us has been going on way too long."

"You think?"

"I know. I know. I take the blame. All of it. I just felt threatened by him. Here comes this new kid to town who has never played lacrosse before and he is really good. And everyone else in the school likes him - including you. It was just too much for me to take. So I turned the lacrosse team against him. To make things worse, I turned his best friend against him. I guess my conscience finally caught up to me and I just wanted to say I was sorry and make amends."

They both hopped over a fallen tree. "But why didn't you guys just shake hands and make up in town? Why did you come out here?"

Sarah said panting from the quick pace.

"Well, the conversation turned to Howl House and what's inside. Jack had never seen the upstairs because that's where we found...." Billy stopped talking.

"That's where you found what?"

"The reason for why we go there. All us guys on the lacrosse team took a secret oath to never reveal what we found. I've never seen anything like it before. It must be super valuable."

Sarah turned her head to look at him while still trying to be careful walking on the uneven ground of the forest. "What is it?"

Billy smiled a little. "I'd like to tell you but I can't. You're not on the lacrosse team."

"I swear; boys are such idiots."

"I know. I know," he smiled sheepishly.

Sarah continued. "Okay, so you guys are talking about Howl House and you mention this "item" to Jack and what happened next?"

"He asked if he could see it."

"That doesn't sound like Jack."

"I know, right? But he was so interested and we were getting along really well, so we decided to go."

"And now Jack is stuck in the house?"

"Well, yeah, kind of. We went up to the second floor and we were almost at the room that has "it" and one of the rotting floorboards gave way and Jack's leg went down and wedged itself up to his thigh."

"This is the nuttiest thing I have ever heard," Sarah said, her eyes turning back to the ground in front of her.

"Yeah, for sure. The thing was, I didn't have the strength to pull him out. His leg is totally stuck. Jack tried to help but he couldn't get any leverage with his bad arm. There's no cell phone service out here and when I told him I was gonna go back and get some help, he said *NO. It's too embarrassing.* The only way he would allow it is if you came back with me."

Sarah let out a sigh. "Unbelievable."

Billy nodded. "I know. I know."

"And why are we walking there instead of taking your dirt bike?"

"You see the light fading. I don't have a headlight on that thing."

"But won't it be too dark to walk back - especially with us holding Jack up and him limping probably?"

"That's not a problem. I know these woods like the back of my hand. We'll get him out of there and be able to get home before you know it."

"Next time you guys decide to do something stupid, please make sure you do it within the city limits. Is that too much to ask?"

Billy let out a strange high-pitched laugh. "Sarah, you are too funny. No wonder Jack likes you so much. I can see why you guys are meant for each other."

"That's all well and good, but how about we pick up the pace?"

"You got it. You got it."

Sarah didn't see Billy's eyes flash orange and the disturbing grin that briefly spread across his face.

Chapter 17

May 3, 2011

As Billy and Sarah made their way to Howl House, Chris had a visitor show up to his front door.

"Oh, hey Lucas. What's going on?"

"What's going on? Tonight is your initiation into the elite team. C'mon; let's get going."

Chris feigned ignorance. "Oh, is that tonight? I totally forgot about it. Problem is that I told my mom and dad I would help them around the house with...cleaning. We've all been so busy lately and the house has gotten really messy."

Lucas said nothing in response.

"So...um...I can't make it tonight, but I'm sure I can make it another night. Maybe after the season is over. We'll all have more time then. Thanks, though, Lucas."

Chris tried to close the screen door and Lucas grabbed it the handle and held it open.

"Okay, this is the deal, Chris. The team is waiting for you at the house in the woods for your initiation. Billy sent me here to get you. There is no other night. There is only tonight. It's gonna be a little chilly so you might want to bring a sweatshirt or something."

Chris was going to protest some more but saw that Lucas' eyes were not going to have any of it. He could tell Lucas to hold on one minute and then ask his parents to get him out of the situation, but he could only imagine what Lucas would say to all the guys about what happened. It was better to just get the whole thing over with.

"Um, yeah, okay, Lucas. I get what you're saying. No problem. I'll go get a jacket or something and I'll be right down.

Lucas said nothing in response.

"Uh, be right down and then we can go. Initiation here we come."

Lucas only smirked.

Chapter 18

May 3, 2011

By the time Jack was able to sneak out of the house, it was already dark, but that wasn't a bad thing. The full moon wasn't supposed to appear for a couple of more hours and getting to Howl House under the cover of darkness was preferred. It wasn't like Jack's arrival would be unexpected, but it would be better to make his way through the woods with as much stealth as possible.

Like Billy and the rest of the boys, Jack knew how to get to Howl House like the back of his hand. He didn't need Moonwalker senses in order to do it, and he was relying on everyone not being able to see or smell so well in order to get inside the house without being detected. It was a long shot, but he was going to try. For their plan to work, Jack surmised that Sarah would have to be watched by at least one member of the team - maybe even Coach Weber himself. And Jack was doubtful that Chris and Sarah would even be within close proximity to each other. Chris would be following the others down the hall to the cave, but Sarah would probably be kept somewhere else in the house. Where that would be was the question of the night and Jack didn't have time for guessing games. He needed the answer immediately.

If Billy has hurt Sarah in any way...

Jack tried to push the thought away from his mind. He had to keep a clear, calm focus or he wouldn't be able to do what was needed. In fact, he might get in his own way if he let emotion get the best of him. This was something he had tried in lacrosse games as well. To outsmart your opponent, you had to use logic and cunning.

Lose your cool, lose the game.

He hated repeating Coach Weber's lacrosse mantra in his head, but Jack knew it was correct. Jack also knew that Coach was not above losing his cool. That could be very beneficial. It showed he was vulnerable which could lead to mistakes and indecision - the very things that could tilt the balance of power in Jack's favor.

He was very close now.

Jack backed up against a nearby tree and took off his backpack. He reached inside and took out the bottle of water. He unscrewed the cap and took a mouthful. He closed it up and put the water bottle back inside the backpack and slung it around his shoulder. He was about to continue when he heard noises coming from behind him to the right. He crouched down low and made his way around to the tree for greater cover. He could now make out the noise as footsteps, plodding through the dark of the woods, without a doubt, going to the same destination as Jack. As best as he could tell, there was more than one person but it wasn't a large group by any means. He poked his head around the tree and could just barely make out two approaching shadows. Based on the path they were taking, it didn't seem that they would get any closer to Jack than twenty to thirty feet at the most. All of a sudden, one of the shadows stopped moving.

"Lucas, I don't remember it taking so long to get here."

The other shadow stopped moving and turned to the first.

"That's because we took dirt bikes the last time, Chris. Geez. If you stopped complaining, we would be there already."

"Sorry. This is just taking a lot longer than I thought it would. I told my mom that I wouldn't be long. And tomorrow's a school day. I'm gonna head back home. Just tell Billy that I couldn't make it this time."

Jack watched as the shadow that was Lucas got even closer to Chris.

"I've had enough out of you. All your whimpering and weakness. I can't believe that you are being chosen tonight. Here's what's going to happen. You are either going to follow me and SHUT YOUR MOUTH right now, or I am going to knock you out and drag you the rest of the way to Howl House. Your choice."

The shadow that was Chris rocked back and forth in uncomfortable silence, crunching leaves and sticks under its weight. Jack readied himself. He wasn't going to wait to see if Lucas took a shot at Chris. Meeting up with both of them here in the woods might be an unexpected stroke of luck. He would tackle Lucas and pin him down and tie his hands. He would tell Chris to get out of there and then he could use Lucas as a bargaining chip to get Sarah.

He grabbed the bark of the tree with his left hand was about to run at Lucas when he heard another sound. A voice. It was coming from the direction of Howl House and it was getting closer quickly.

"Lucas! Is that you?

Lucas didn't turn away from Chris but he responded. "Yeah, it's me."

"You got Chris with you?"

"Yeah, I got him."

"Great. You guys need to get to the house now. Billy sent me out to look for you. Everyone's waiting."

Lucas yelled to the voice. "Be right there." He then addressed Chris in a lower tone. "You were about to say something, Chris."

The rocking shadow stopped. "Um, I didn't realize we were so close. Okay. Let's get this done so I can get home. I don't want to get into any trouble."

"Trouble?" Lucas laughed. "Getting into trouble with mommy and daddy is the least of your worries."

The two shadows walked away until they dissolved completely

into the darkness. Jack knew that his chance was gone, but he at least took heart that Chris did not want to be there. He would have to use that to his advantage. More opportunities were sure to present themselves. Jack had to keep his wits about him and be ready to act as each opportunity arose. His life and the lives of others depended on it.

Chapter 19

May 3, 2011

"Oh, this place is disgusting and it reeks like a pig sty. Why would you ever want to hang out in here?"

"Maybe because it's a place to call our own, a place to get away to and have fun with friends. After a while, you don't smell anything bad. The place grows on you."

Sarah shook her head in agreement. "Oh, I think there is something growing on me right now. I don't want to spend any more time in this place than I have to. Where's Jack?"

Billy pointed to the staircase. "He's up there and down the hall a bit in one of the rooms."

"I don't think those stairs will hold either one of us. What could possibly be up there that is so special that it would make you take your lives into your hands?"

"I told you I can't tell you. Okay, how about this? Since you've come all this way to help out our pal, Jackie-boy, why don't I let you get a sneak peek? Just don't tell the team. They would be so mad at me for letting the secret out of the bag."

"I don't care about your secret. I just want to help Jack."

"Suit yourself, but this place is magical. Don't you feel it, Sarah? The electricity in the air? It's like the whole place is wired with magic."

"What are you talking about? I'm done. Let's get Jack."

"Anything the lady asks for," Billy replied with a smile and a fake British accent.

Sarah turned away from Billy in palpable disgust and started to make her way carefully up the staircase. Billy followed closely behind, delighted that his plan was working so well.

"The nerve to tell me that I don't have the skills..." he muttered to himself.

Chapter 20

May 3, 2011

Jack waited until he couldn't hear Lucas and Chris make their way to Howl House. If he couldn't hear them when they were tromping through the forest, they definitely wouldn't be able to hear him sneaking around. There was always the possibility that Billy had stationed some of the boys in various places in the woods around the house, but Jack figured that separating them would dilute their overall strength. Billy would have come to the same conclusion. No, they were all inside waiting to pounce. Going through the front door would have been suicide. He was going to have to find another way in. He decided to circle all the way around to approach the house from the other side, not the usual way that he and the others would get there. Maybe there was something in the back of the house - a window, or one of those old fashioned basement doors that opened up on an angle from the floor - that would allow him to gain entry.

He tried to keep a fair amount of distance between himself and the house as he deftly made his way through the brush. When he reached the back, he cautiously moved forward to get closer. He would take a step or two and then stop to listen. Nothing. He didn't detect any other movement than his own. He crouched down low to the ground and stepped out of the woods into an open, grassy section between the house and forest. He continued walking with each footstep barely making any sound. Within a short amount of time, he was leaning against the house, his back up against it so he could see to the left, right and center out to the forest. Again, all was clear.

He waited a few moments and then took a few steps out to survey what his options were to get inside. There was a tool shed that butted up against the house with a large, old pile of firewood logs right next to it, but no back or basement door. There were also no bottom floor windows, just three second floor ones.

Eenie, meenie, miney, mo, Jack.

Jack carefully began climbing the woodpile to get to the shed's roof. This got him closer to all of the 2nd floor windows, but two of them were still well out of reach. He could make a jump for one of them, but with his arm being in the condition it was, he wasn't sure if he could hold his own weight and pull himself up and into a room. And if the windows were locked, he would have to drop down to the ground, possibly hurting himself even more while making lots of noise in the process. The middle window that was only a foot or so above him was the safest bet, but probably not the best one. If Billy was expecting Jack to sneak into the house, this window was a likely entry point. There might be someone waiting just inside that room, but what other choice did he have?

Jack reached up and was able to get his fingertips on the window ledge. As he pulled himself up, he could feel his injured arm tighten and throb with pain. When his eyes became level with the lower part of the window, he tried to peer inside but it was too dark to see anything at all. He pulled himself up a little more and pushed at the window with his hurt arm while the good one held him up. It took a bit of effort, but the window began to move upward. He was able to open it enough to narrowly climb through, but he knew he didn't have the strength to do it. He lowered himself back down to the roof of the shed and rested his back against the house. He would have to rest a few minutes and regain some strength in his arms - especially the injured one. He turned his head upwards to see if he could see anything - or anybody - at the window, almost hoping that Sarah was going to be there and he could get her out safely and then help Chris.

But there was no motion to be seen or heard. In some strange fashion, that was a good thing, too. He didn't know what he was going to find when he entered that room. He had never been on the second floor of Howl House. There might be nothing or there could be a whole host of bad. He had to be ready for whatever he found.

Feeling a little more rested, Jack grabbed the window ledge and pulled himself back up.

Chapter 21

May 3, 2011

"So? Where is he?"

"Just inside that door. Go ahead; open it," Billy said shining his flashlight on the door knob.

Sarah reached her hand out to grasp it. She and Billy had just made their way up the treacherous staircase to the second floor and down the hallway to what seemed to be the last of three doors. The air was thick with mildew and smelled like a zoo. She couldn't understand why ANYONE would want to spend one second of their time hanging out here - least of all Jack.

When Billy told her that Jack was stuck and possibly hurt in Howl House, her instinct to help him kicked in immediately. Nothing else mattered. But now as she stood here in the house, she realized something was wrong. There is no way that Jack would have come here with Billy. When they were here almost two weeks ago before Billy and his gang showed up on their dirt bikes, she could tell by Jack's reactions that he did not like being around this place. If someone offered him a million dollars to come here, he would probably turn them down. Something was very wrong. A weird tingling sensation ran up and down her spine. She pulled her hand back from the knob and turned to face Billy.

"Jack's not in there. Is he?"

Billy brought the flashlight under his chin to illuminate his smiling face. "I have to say Sarah, you must really like Jack because I didn't think I had a shot in hell of getting you to come here without physically forcing you. Love makes people do stupid things. You are correct. Jack is not in there. Although I do believe he will be showing up pretty soon. The only thing inside that room will be you. Open the door."

"I don't know what this game is all about, but I'm so done."

Sarah made a motion to walk back down the hall and Billy grabbed her wrist.

"You can't leave now, Sarah. Things are just about to get good. You can't deny Jackie-boy the chance to save his girlfriend, can you?"

Sarah looked down at Billy's hand holding her wrist.

"The first thing you are going to do is take your hand off of me. The second thing is I'm leaving this house of stink and heading back to town to get the police. I don't know what you and your friends or even Mr. Weber have been doing here, but it is going to stop. So, the question is when the cops come, do you want to explain yourself with your hand okay, as it is right now, or broken if you don't let go of me. Your choice."

Billy let go of Sarah, but he didn't let go of his smile. "So predictable. Just like we thought. It didn't have to be like this, Sarah, but, like I said, love makes people do stupid things. Maybe some time in the room will change your mind."

No sooner had Billy finished his sentence when the door behind Sarah opened up and two arms reached out and pulled her into the room. The door slammed shut and then there was silence.

Billy mused aloud, "Oh, I forgot to tell you that door is very thick and no one will hear you screaming for help. Not that it matters. You can't even hear me." He laughed at the irony and then started walking down the hall to the main staircase humming a happy little tune of his own creation.

Chapter 22

May 3, 2011

"What is this place? What are we doing here? Where's Billy?"

"SHUT UP! JUST SHUT UP! I can't take it anymore. All the way here, all the way down the hall and the tunnel - whine, question, whine, question, whine. I literally can't listen to your voice one more minute. Just shut up and wait and only speak when spoken to."

Chris was about to ask why but thought better of it and closed his mouth. Lucas had been getting more and more aggressive as the night wore on. He wouldn't answer any questions and kept threatening violence.

If there is one thing that Chris had learned being on the lacrosse team it was that Lucas, when pushed (which could be at a moment's notice) could act quite crazy and back it up with strength. The other boys on the team were friendly with him, but they knew not to get on his bad side. And even though all of that was true, it didn't stop Chris from talking and asking questions because he knew it wasn't Lucas who was in charge tonight. Billy was pulling all the strings. If Lucas was acting of his own accord, he would have hurt him earlier in the woods. Billy wanted Chris to be here tonight in one piece. But it was obvious that Lucas was fast reaching a point where he was going to explode in a rage that few people would be able to get him to calm down from. The way he kept tugging on Chris' arm as they walked down that dark, smelly hallway hurt like hell but he wasn't going to give Lucas the satisfaction of knowing it. Instead, he asked questions about the horrible smell and the creaky floors. It drove Lucas nuts but it helped Chris to take his mind off the pain.

Finally, they reached this place with the weird glowing liquid and Lucas let go of him, but none of his questions were ever answered and he was just as nervous and unknowing as ever. Apart from knowing that he was in the basement of Howl House for the most part, he knew nothing else.

Lucas began to pace back and forth like a caged tiger, almost forgetting that Chris was standing near him. He stopped abruptly when he heard the creak of the door that led into this cave-like part of the house.

"Billy, is that you?" Lucas asked straining to see down into the darkness.

"Yeah, it's me," Billy answered back, making his way forward.

Lucas cast a glance at Chris. "It's almost time," he sneered.

Billy came into the glowing light with a smile on his face. "Two down, one to go."

"Awesome," Lucas said. "I'll go upstairs with the rest of the gang and wait for the guest of honor."

"No, I want you to stay here with me and Chris. We will usher him into the brotherhood while the others take care of the problem."

Lucas shook his head. "That's not fair. Why do they get to have all the fun? I've been stuck watching Mr. Personality here for most of the night. I can't stand another minute being near him and his stupid questions. I want to go where the action is." He started walking towards the door.

The smile on Billy's face turned quickly to a look of anger. He reached out and grabbed Lucas' wrist. "You will go nowhere. Do you understand? A plan has been put into action and we will follow the plan. You are needed here for the initiation and as insurance in case something unforeseen happens."

"Is this you talking or HIM?" Lucas questioned.

Billy's grasp on Lucas' wrist tightened as he spoke behind

gritted teeth. "As far as you're concerned, it doesn't matter. Now go stand next to Chris and do what you have been told."

Lucas stared at Billy and then shook his arm free. He turned and walked slowly back to Chris, bumping into him with his shoulder before he spun back around to wait for the next order.

Billy took a moment to calm himself and then turned his attention to Chris.

"You must be wondering what-in-the-world is going on, huh? Don't worry; all your questions will be answered very soon. Tonight is the first night of your life, Chris. The first night of your life."

Chapter 23

May 3, 2011

The room was pitch black but the person who grabbed her seemed to know their way around every square inch of it. Before she could even muster a scream, a hand had covered her mouth and closed the door leading to the hallway. She was pulled and pushed harshly in the dark and then thrown down onto the floor. Behind her a squeaky, metal door was closed quickly and locked. She instinctively kicked out with her feet in case the person was still near but she only connected with metal bars of some sort. She got up on her hands and knees and reached out blindly to grab what she just kicked. Her hands fell on it and she pulled herself up to her feet, stretching her hands out to the left and right. . She was in a cage or a prison cell of some sort.

"So sorry if I hurt you, Ms. Bartley," said a man's voice, "but things like this do happen from time to time. Regrettable but definitely for the best."

"WHO ARE YOU?" Sarah shouted. "WHAT HAVE YOU DONE WITH JACK?"

"Oh, how incredibly thoughtful of you - caring more about your boyfriend instead of your own dire situation. How touching. Neither of your questions is relevant at this point and the answers even less so. I will tell you this: if you and your boyfriend would like to see each other again, you will do exactly as I tell you. If not, well, let's just say that not seeing each other will seem like small potatoes compared to what else awaits."

"Mr. Weber? Why are you doing this?"

The voice laughed. "Do we have a deal, Ms. Bartley?"

Sarah assessed the situation. Physically she had been pushed around a bit, but she was okay. However, she was in a dark room in a cage in a creepy house in the middle of the woods and an unseen voice was threatening her life and the life of her boyfriend if she did not do what was asked. She needed to stall for more time and even in an anxious state, she knew there was only one way to do it.

"Yes, we have a deal."

The voice snorted confidently. "Smart choice. Here is what is going to happen and what you are going to do when it does..."

Chapter 24

May 3, 2011

Jack pulled himself through the window head first into the dark space. His hands, arms and upper torso hung down off window sill as he tried to wriggle his waist and legs through the narrow opening. But just as his body cleared the window and fell to the floor in tiring success, he found himself being grabbed and held from all sides. His hands and wrists were quickly and tautly pulled behind him and he heard the sound of handcuffs locking on them. His legs were also held and then shackled. He was pulled quickly to his feet and a sack was placed over his head. He was led brusquely across the floor of the room, chained legs barely able to keep up with the pace that was set for him. A door was opened ahead of him and he could feel himself being led through the doorway into another space. His body was forcibly turned to the right and he was again led a number of feet and heard yet another door open. He was pushed and pulled through this doorway, too, and then pushed to his knees. The hood was pulled off his head and a blinding light was directed at his face.

"Welcome, Jack!" a voice said, enveloping him from almost every direction.

Chapter 25

May 3, 2011

"Billy, I thought you said this was an initiation for the elite squad."

"It is, Chris. It is."

"Then where are all the other guys and what is this place?"

Lucas turned towards Chris with his fists raised.

"Lucas!" Billy snapped. Lucas looked over at Billy, shook his head and lowered his hands.

Chris persisted with his questions. "I'm really confused. What are we doing here?

"You are entitled to your questions, and I hope to answer all of them. But at the same time, I ask that you trust me and keep an open mind about all that you will see and experience here tonight. Can you do that?"

Chris shifted his feet uncomfortably. "I don't know. To be honest, I feel like every time I've trusted you, um, things happen."

Billy laughed. "Yep, things do happen. You are right about that, but up until now, you never knew why. Tonight all your questions and concerns will be answered and you will have more knowledge than you ever thought possible, Chris. But you have to trust me one more time for it all to happen. I ask you again; can you do that?"

Chris looked closely at Billy's face as the glow of the shimmering liquid created warm ripples of light upon it. Chris rubbed his hand across his face. "I'll try. That's all I can promise."

Billy smiled. "I'll take that as a yes."

Chapter 26

May 3, 2011

"So much for meeting face to face. Come out and show yourself. Or would that be what you called "anticlimactic" in English class, isn't that right Mr. Weber?"

A booming laugh reverberated through the room. "You have learned much in school, Jack, but there is so much more to learn. Why do you fight my desire to teach you?"

Although Jack couldn't see them right now, he knew the voice was coming out of speakers that must have been mounted in various places in the room. Mr. Weber probably wasn't even in this room right now. The light shining brightly in his eyes didn't allow for him to see much else other than the silhouettes of the boys from the lacrosse team as they stood around him.

"Teach me? If the last year has taught me anything, it is not to trust you or Billy or anyone else associated with this cult."

"Cult? That's an interesting way to describe a superhuman life."

"What kind of superhuman brings middle school students out in the woods to change their very existence to suit his own needs?"

"That's the very question that I have been trying to answer all along, Jack. And I've been trying to answer it for you specifically."

"I don't want to know your answers. I don't want to know you. I don't want to any of it. Just leave my friends out of it. You and Billy can do whatever you want. Just leave us all alone." Jack struggled to rise to his feet and free his hands free from the handcuffs.

"I can't do that, Jack. But maybe you will change your mind and take your rightful place among us."

"NEVER!"

"Ah, I thought you'd say that."

A second bright light appeared in the room and it lit up a corner revealing a metal cage or prison. Inside the cage Sarah sat tied to a chair, her mouth taped shut. Her eyes immediately closed in response to the bright light but she tried to squint so she could see Jack. Around her neck hung a small crystal vial with a glowing liquid.

"SARAH! NO! LEAVE HER ALONE!"

The voice laughed. "I always said I would, Jack. I'm a man of my word. Join us and I will let her go. If not, Chris won't be the only newbie howling at the Moon tonight."

Sarah's eyes grew more accustomed to the light and she was able to look at Jack almost fully. He was relieved to see from her gaze that she was scared but okay.

"Well, Jack?" This is your last chance and hers."

Jack struggled a bit more but realized he couldn't break free, not in his current form anyway.

"Let Chris go, too."

"Chris, Chris, Chris...what is it with you and Chris? He gave up on your friendship but still you persist." The voice chuckled. "That's almost poetic, isn't it? Ah, but Billy is not going to be happy about this. He could never control you, but he can control Chris. Well, since I'm the Papa Wolf around here, I'm going to make an executive decision. One of you boys head down to the cave and tell Billy there's been a change of plans. Bring Chris up here."

The door opened and someone left the room.

"See, Jack. A man of my word. Now you be a man of yours. Tell me that you are joining us."

Jack looked over to Sarah. How could he let them change her into one of them? He couldn't. He knew what he had to do. Jack looked at Sarah and tried to let her know through his eyes that everything would be okay, but he wasn't sure himself if that was true. He turned back to the light shining on him.

"I...I..." and at that moment Jack's eyes rolled to the back of his head and he slumped forward upon the floor.

Chapter 27

May 3, 2011

One of Billy's boys ran into the cave and looked sheepishly at Billy. "Lucas is to take Chris and come with me."

"WHAT?" Billy screamed.

"I'm sorry; it's what HE wants," said the boy.

Lucas grabbed Chris by the arm.

"Take your hand off of him, Lucas. He's not going anywhere," Billy commanded.

"Are you crazy?" Lucas replied tightening his grip. "You can't say no. We've been told what to do."

"And now I'm telling you what to do. Let go of him...NOW."

"I'm gonna follow orders, Billy - HIS orders."

Chris looked back and forth from Billy to Lucas and Lucas to Billy. He didn't have a clue what was going on, but he knew it was bad - really bad.

Billy turned towards the boy. "Go upstairs and tell HIM that Chris and Lucas are staying down here with me."

"NO," yelled Lucas. "Tell HIM that we will be coming upstairs very soon - with or without Billy."

The boy didn't know what to do and Chris felt sorry for him. This is exactly how he had been feeling for quite some time - caught between Jack and Billy. It was a horrible place to be.

Billy and Lucas slowly walked towards each other, both of their fists clenched and ready.

Not wanting to come back too late upstairs and definitely not wanting to be around what was about to happen in the cave, the boy turned and ran for the door. Neither Billy nor Lucas ran after him.

They just kept advancing forward.

For the first time all night, Chris was absolutely speechless. The light of the liquid in the ground was now flickering around the whole cave as if flashbulbs from paparazzi cameras were going off one right after the other, capturing photographs of the battle royale to come. Chris really didn't want to be where he was, but his feet were riveted to the floor at this point as his curiosity prevented him from trying to leave. He managed to back up a few feet until his body was pressing against one of the cave walls. This was going to be absolutely insane.

Chapter 28

May 3, 2011

"See what's wrong with him, but be careful. This may be a trick," the voice said with some trepidation.

As the boys in the room bent down to see what was wrong with Jack, the door flew open and the boy from the cave came running in, almost falling over the others.

"Billy and Lucas are about to have a fight in the cave!"

"WHAT?" yelled the voice, feedback and distortion from the microphone creating a loud crackling over the speakers.

The boy was scared but continued. "Billy didn't want to bring Chris up but Lucas did. They got into an argument. I ran as fast as I could to tell you."

"Where is Chris?"

"He's still downstairs."

"YOU DIDN'T THINK TO BRING HIM WITH YOU?" screamed the voice.

The boy put his hands up in front of him protectively as if expecting something to happen. "I'm sorry. I'm sorry. I thought it best if I came up here to tell you first."

The voice started screaming in rage, the speakers in the room crackling like crazy, unable to contain the volume of the outburst. Most of the boys tried to cover their ears and Sarah could only wince in pain being tied to a chair.

Something else began to happen, too, as wails of anger from the creature filled the room: the full Moon appeared.

Chapter 29

May 3, 2011

What started out as chest bumping turned into pushing, and then throwing punches, and then both boys flailing at each other on the ground as they rolled about vying for bodily control of one another. Chris looked on in disbelief. Billy fighting Jack. Sure. Lucas fighting Jack. Yep. Billy fighting Lucas? It was completely surreal.

And then it stopped.

Both boys abandoned each other and started rolling around as if fighting themselves, contorting their bodies in what had to be painful positions. They both curled into tight balls as if on cue.

Is this part of the initiation? Like some crazy college hazing ritual? Chris wondered.

It wasn't long before both boys stopped moving again. The hazy glow of the liquid made it difficult to see what had happened, but whatever was going on, Chris couldn't just stand there silently anymore. He slowly started walking over to them.

"Billy, Lucas...are you guys okay? You can stop fooling around now. You have officially freaked me out. Guys? Seriously. Is everything alright?"

Chris was about to reach out and shake one of them, when both boys jumped up with their backs to him and shrieked deeply at the top of their lungs with their hands in the air as if they were wounded animals. They stopped and stood with their bodies heaving up and down as they breathed.

"Guys?"

Billy and Lucas turned towards each other, their faces no longer human. Instead of noses, long snouts were now almost

touching one another, and hair bulged out from underneath clothing that was stretched to the near-point of ripping. Billy and Lucas were no longer Billy and Lucas. They were wolves.

Chris screamed and stumbled backwards, falling on his butt and back. Lucas turned towards him and snarled viciously. He sprang quickly at Chris but was stopped by Billy reaching out and holding him by the belt of his pants. Lucas turned back towards Billy and swiped at him with a spread of sharp claws.

Chris screamed again and in a wild frenzy kicked and pushed himself as far back as he could go. His head banged into the cave wall, but he did not feel it. He looked at the creatures before him and felt reality slipping away.

Billy ducked under Lucas' clawed fingers. He grabbed at the belt he was holding with both hands now and jerked it with such force that Lucas was lifted off his feet and thrown backwards into the cave wall opposite Chris. The whole cave shook with the force. As Lucas slid down to the ground, Billy pounced on top of him and delivered a series of blows to his chest.

Lucas brought his leg up and around Billy's body and kicked him in the side of the head. He fell off to the side, but took no time in jumping up to face his opponent who was now on his feet, too. They flung themselves at each other and became locked in a mangled grip of fur and fangs.

Chris rubbed at his eyes furiously. He couldn't be seeing what he was seeing. He opened his eyes again. Two wolf-like creatures were wrestling, snarling and snapping at each other with long threads of spit dripping from their thrashing muzzles.

Chris started screaming again.

Chapter 30

May 3, 2011

One light was still fixed firmly on Sarah in the cage. The other was still pointed in the area that Jack had been kneeling, but all that could be seen was a hazy tangle of bodies writhing and moaning around in pain. The voice over the speakers was still screaming but this now it seemed as if it were timed in some fashion to what was happening to the boys.

Sarah was firmly tied to the chair in the cell, her mouth taped closed. She wanted to help Jack desperately but she couldn't do anything. She could only look on and hope that Jack had a plan.

All of sudden, everything went quiet in the room. Even in the voice coming over the speakers fell dead silent. This lasted a few seconds and then the screaming started all over again with a flurry of movement, but this time it was different. Everyone in the room and even the voice over the speakers was screaming and whooping like rabid dogs. For the first time of the night, she was glad she was in the cage and not outside of it.

In all of the howling craziness, one voice rose above all the others, as if the person it was emanating from was groaning and struggling to lift an incredible weight. These screams reached a fever pitch and then she heard metal falling to the floor and an ear-piercing guttural cry. Only one thought shot through her mind: Jack is free.

The room turned into a free-for-all of fighting. The light shining in her eyes and the position of the other light prevented her from seeing anything clearly but she could tell bodies were being thrown about. One of them was thrown against the cell with such force that Sarah thought the bars would come crashing down on her in the dark. The body slumped to the floor and she clearly heard a whimper come from whoever it was.

The sound of monstrous growls rebounded against all the walls as more bodies hit the floor. Sarah could hear deep scratches being carved out in the old wooden floorboards as people tried to get up or away from whatever was throwing them about like human-sized rag dolls. The ferocity of it all was mind-blowing. Another body was thrown against the cell and then another. Sarah could make out shadows slipping down against the bars - some getting back up, others not.

The violence did not abate for some time but it finally came to a halt.

Sarah could hear someone breathing heavily, drawing in and expelling huge amounts of air. She wanted to hear Jack's voice. She wanted to yell and find out if it was him, but she remained imprisoned inside the cell.

The speakers crackled to life. A voice came out of them, but it was unlike the voice she had heard coming out before. This one was thick and raspy like it was being filtered through a wood chipper. All of the bedlam in the room must have broken the speakers.

"Very impressive, Jack," the gravelly voice conceded. "You are everything I believed you would be...and more. We can do great things together."

Silence.

"Nothing to say," continued the voice. "The unstoppable Jack Wilson is now shy. Oh, I get it. You don't want to speak in front of Sarah. Afraid that she won't like the new you? Understandable, but weak. Do not run from who you are, Jack. Embrace it. Do you really think that you will make it out of this room without Sarah getting to know the 'real you?' How eagerly

we hold fast to the past, like a good luck charm. But change is good, too - especially when it makes you better than you were before. But, I have to be honest. You were pretty good from the get-go. A fabulous mix of nature and nurture. Your parents did a great job raising you. Oh, hold on; let me revise that. Your MOTHER did a great job raising you. No father to speak of. Pity.

"SHUT UP!"

Sarah instantly pushed her back against the chair she was tied to. The harsh, roaring voice came from only a half a dozen feet away from her. In the darkness of the room, she could not even distinguish that anyone was there, let alone someone with the presence that could release such throaty fury.

"Ah, that's it. I think I touched a nerve. You want to get Jack's dander up, just mention dear old dad. Wouldn't he be shocked to see you now - don't you think?"

Whoever or whatever was standing near the prison cell let out a shriek of incredible intensity.

The voice over the speakers laughed. "I could watch you lose your cool all night, Jack, but there are things that need to be done. Judging by all the unconscious puppies I see sprawled out on the floor, I would think they are no longer of any use to me tonight. I could come out and face you myself, but that's not where I want to be right now." The voice paused for a second. "I know what to do. Time to let Sarah in on your little secret. That should keep you both busy while I figure out what to do next."

No sooner had those words come out of the speakers when another light turned on in the room directly onto Jack from the wall opposite the prison cell. Also on the wall was a large mirror that spanned from one end of the room to the other. Standing in the middle of it all was a reflection of Jack - Jack as a

Moonwalker.

Sarah's eyes grew wide. Jack's back was to her, but she could see him totally in the reflection. She yelled his name but only a lengthy grunt came from behind her taped mouth.

Jack wanted to smash the lights in the room but he knew it was useless. Sarah could see him. There was no hiding what he was. He could see her staring at him from the cell behind him in the mirror's reflection. Their eyes locked together. His heart felt heavy.

"Oh I wish I had some music playing in the background," the voice said. "Something sad yet sweet would do nicely at this moment."

Jack said nothing in response. He continued to look at Sarah and she at him.

"So touching. I think whoever came up with the phrase "puppy love" didn't have this quite in mind, though. But I digress. Take a last look at each other. I've decided what I want to do and it doesn't bode well for Sarah. Your reflection is the last thing she will ever see."

Jack may have been looking at Sarah but he was listening to everything that was being said, and he was having none of it. He crouched down low and sprang into a backflip. He landed right next to the cell. A part of him wanted to take another look at Sarah but he knew that every second counted. He grabbed a hold of one of the prison bars and pulled it with all his might. At first it didn't seem like the bar was going to budge but then the squeal of metal on metal could be heard at both the top and bottom points where it was anchored into steel cross beams. Jack twisted and pulled at the bar with all his might and heard it pop from the bottom and then the top. He turned towards the mirror.

"What do you think you're doing, Jack?" the voice asked with confused concern.

Jack said nothing. He picked up the heavy bar like a spear. He cocked his arm back and then thrust the bar forward directly at the mirror.

"NOOO!" screamed the voice as if knowing what was going to happen next.

The bar smashed the mirror but didn't stop upon impact. IT WENT THROUGH THE MIRROR!

The voice let out an impassioned yelp that could be heard through the speakers but also through the broken mirror itself. Jack ran to the remnants that was once the mirror and looked inside. It was a control booth with computers and other scientific gadgetry. Jack looked in further. On the ground lay a large Moonwalker with the metal prison bar protruding from its chest. Its eyes were open and fixed on the ceiling and its tongue was hanging from its mouth. Blood covered the entry point of the bar. There was no movement whatsoever. Jack pulled his head back from inside the booth and turned around to face Sarah. Her eyes were still wide open. Her arms were tied down by her sides and they were shaking uncontrollably. Jack ran over to the cell and grabbed the two bars that were on either side of the one he wrenched out. He pulled them both to either side of his chest. They began to stretch and bulge away from their rigid vertical positions. Jack pulled them more and more until he could fit through the bars. He climbed in and crouched down in front of Sarah and began to speak.

"Now is not the time to explain any of this. Chris is in trouble and we have to save him. I wish I could just let you go and do it myself, but we are not out of danger yet. In fact, I

believe the danger is even greater." As he spoke he undid the ropes that bound her to the chair. "I am going to take the tape off your mouth, but you have to just trust me and not ask me any questions. There's no time for answers. The hallway and the stairs are dangerous, so I am going to carry you to where we have to go. Do you understand?"

Sarah was still shaking but she nodded her head yes.

Jack pulled the tape carefully away from her mouth. A rush of air went through her mouth and filled her lungs and she immediately exhaled it. He put his hand gently to her face to try and comfort her the best he could. He thought she was going to bristle at his touch, but she didn't. Taking her hand, he beckoned her to come through the bars of the cell. When they were both out, he picked her up and lay her across his shoulder. He kept her still with one hand and with the other opened the door and ran out. He made a beeline for the cave.

Chapter 31

May 3, 2011

Chris was out like a light. The combination of fright and a lack of oxygen from breathing too quickly and shallowly knocked him out cold, but the battle raged on.

As they wrestled for bodily control over one another, Billy tried to convince Lucas to his way of thinking, his voice even more hoarse than usual from all the physical exhaustion.

"Lucas, you have never disobeyed me before. Stop all of this now. Listen to reason."

"No, it is you who must listen to reason. HIS reason. We are all greater than we were because of HIM. You have changed, Billy. I listened to you before because you spoke what HE spoke, but you don't anymore. If Chris is not to become one of us because HE says so, then we must obey."

Billy pushed upwards on the underside of Lucas' muzzle and pinned him against a wall of the cave.

"None of us is closer to HIM than me, Lucas. But he was wrong about bringing Jack into the fold. You know that to be true. HE is wrong about Chris now. HE makes mistakes Lucas."

"You are just jealous because you are not his favorite anymore. You don't have what it takes to lead us, Billy. Neither does Chris. He is weak and you only want him to be a part of the clan so you have someone else to control. That makes you weak, too."

Lucas clasped claws together and brought them down on Billy's head. This knocked him to his knees but opened another area for Billy to attack. Billy bit down hard into Lucas' abdomen, drawing some blood. Lucas screamed in pain and brought his claws down again upon Billy's head, forcing him to slump down further away from his stomach. Billy wrapped his arms around Lucas' legs and lifted, knocking him off balance and forcing both combatants to the ground yet once again.

Billy managed to continue talking. "I am the rightful leader of the clan and will be the clan master one day. HE is not infallible and has compromised our collective with an outsider who will only destroy us all."

"Maybe he will destroy you, but he will not destroy me. I am too strong - even for you. One day the master will recognize my true potential and I, too, will be made a clan leader. I am done with you, Billy."

Lucas rolled on top of Billy and pinned his head and neck down with one of his claws. With the other, he spread his fingers and his long nails almost sparkled in the glow of the liquid. Billy fought against the hold but couldn't get up. He was too exhausted. Lucas was indeed stronger than him, but nowhere near as clever - or devious. Billy reached out with one of his free hands and grabbed a fistful of dirt and gravel from the cave floor and flung it into Lucas' eyes. Lucas, howling in pain, released his grip on Billy to clear his eyes. Billy acted quickly and pushed Lucas off of him. He then grabbed Lucas by the back of his neck and forced his head down into the dirt and pushed it towards the hole filled with liquid. Lucas was able to open one of his eyes a little and could see what was happening. At the same moment, Billy grabbed one of his arms and twisted it behind his back and pushed with greater intensity.

Lucas screamed, "Billy! No! Don't do this! I'll stop! We can go up to HIM together and work this out! Please!"

"I'm sorry, Lucas. I never wanted this to happen. Believe me. Goodbye, my one-time friend."

Billy forced Lucas' head into the glowing liquid, holding onto his arm and the back of his neck to make sure that he could not escape.

Lucas thrashed about wildly, trying to reach back with his free arm to grab hold of any part of Billy that he could grab. There was nothing but air. He then used the same arm to push against the rim of the hole, hoping to force his head out of the liquid, but his strength was starting to leave him. Lucas began to struggle less and less, but Billy continued his hold. Just as Lucas was about to cease all movement, Billy heard a noise behind him. He turned his head. It was Jack and Sarah.

"Killing a member of your own clan, huh, Billy? So much for honoring the spirit of the ancestors."

Chapter 32

May 3, 2011

Billy let go of Lucas and rose to his feet. He kept his eyes on Jack and Sarah but he also looked at the narrow space between them and the hallway that led to the door out. There was no way he would be able to bum rush them and slip past and escape. He began looking nervously all around for anything that he could use as a weapon.

His eyes fell on Chris, still passed out against the opposite wall from the exit. He ran over and grabbed him roughly by the hair and brought his other hand to his neck with his claws extended.

Jack rushed over to the hole and pulled Lucas' head out of the glowing ooze. He moved him over to the side. At first, Lucas was completely limp and unmoving, but soon started to sputter and cough. He was alive.

Billy didn't look at Lucas at all. He kept his gaze fixated on Jack with his claws pushing into Chris' exposed neck.

The cave was silent except for Jack attending to Lucas as he lay on the ground in a semi-conscious state trying to expel any remaining liquid. Sarah just stood where she was, trying to take in anything and everything that was going on. The expression on her face was one of intense curiosity more than fear as her mind tried to process all that had taken place up to and including now. It was a tremendous learning curve.

Billy broke the silence.

"Skateboardin' Jack to the rescue. Always the man of the hour, huh? I'm sure Sarah is very impressed with her werewolf

boyfriend. Sarah, give your pup a kiss why don't you."

Jack got up from helping Lucas.

"It's over, Billy. All of it. Over. Your master is dead. Your boys strewn all over the room upstairs, injured and in need of help. Get away from Chris."

Billy shook his head and laughed. "Nothing is over until I say it is over, Jack. This has always been about you and me and we're still here, dancin' by the light of the silvery Moon."

"We were both duped, Billy. Let's end this right now, peacefully. I never wanted to be a Moonwalker, let alone the leader of the clan. And I'm sure you didn't want to be placed in the middle of it all. Lucas is alive. The boys are alive. We are alive. That is something. Don't stay a pawn in the game."

"I WAS NEVER A PAWN!" Billy roared. "I'm me - Billy Jenkins. I'm smart. I'm strong. I can be the leader of all of it. I don't need you. I don't need HIM. I don't need anybody. This is over when I say it's over."

Jack took a step closer and Billy pushed his claws a little deeper into the skin of Chris' neck."

"One more step, Jack, and say goodbye to your friend. Got me?"

Sarah spoke.

"Billy, look at me."

Billy cast a glance over at Sarah and then quickly brought his eyes back to Jack.

"This has nothing to do with you, Sarah. I never wanted you to get involved this far, but you had to start liking him, didn't you? Do you still like him? Look at him! Look at what he is! This is what he will be forever. Can you continue to love...that?"

"I know what is in Jack's heart and I will always love him

for that. There is good in you, too, Billy. Please leave Chris alone. This is all done. Don't change him for absolutely no reason."

Billy turned to look at Sarah. "You might as well start liking Chris over here because I can't change him. The liquid has been polluted. Its properties contaminated. Billy Jenkins the great leader shoved his friend's head into the elixir and in a fit of rage corrupted it. I couldn't change him if I wanted to know that..." Billy's voice trailed away as he glanced down from Sarah's face and noticed something glimmering around her neck.

The crystal vial.

A wide smile broke out on his face.

"Oh, the Moon must love me tonight."

Jack looked where Billy was staring.

"Forget it, Billy. It's not going to happen."

"You're not the leader here, Jack. You said you killed the leader. Doesn't that leave me in charge? And if you want to see your friend Chris alive tomorrow, Sarah is going to give me that vial hanging around her neck and we are going to call this a night - once Chris is transformed, that is."

Sarah instinctively reached up with her hand and grabbed the vial, ready to dash it to the ground.

"I don't think the present predicament has sunk into your brain, Sarah. Give me the vial or Chris dies. And if you doubt my sincerity, you need only look down and see how close Lucas came to being a dead werewolf. Give me the vial."

"Jack?" Sarah said nervously.

Jack looked at the claws that were now pushing into Chris' neck. He knew Billy was capable of what he said. Without HIM being around anymore, Billy felt empowered beyond even his own dreams.

"Do what he says, Sarah."

Sarah took her hand away from the vial and carefully reached behind her neck to unclasp the necklace it was attached to. She slowly started to walk over to Billy. She paused when she was a foot or so away from him.

"Give it to me!" Billy demanded.

Sarah took another step and held the vial out for Billy. He took his claws away from Chris' neck and reached out to grab it. Just as he did this, Chris opened his eyes, grabbed a fistful of dirt and rocks from the cave floor and threw them into Billy's face and rolled away from his captor.

Billy screamed and swung wildly with his arms and claws. Chris' face almost caught a razor-sharp blow but he was able to scramble away. He got to his feet, grabbed Sarah's hand and quickly pulled her over near Jack.

Billy howled and rubbed at his eyes to clear them of debris. He blindly got to his feet.

"YOU ARE ALL DEAD! I WILL RIP THE THROATS OUT OF YOUR PRECIOUS FRIENDS AND YOU CAN WATCH THEM DIE, JACK! THEN I WILL KILL YOU!"

Jack said nothing. He pushed his friends behind him and held out his arms to protect them.

Billy rubbed his eyes with one hand while swinging with the other, hoping to make contact with something. He came closer, nearing where Lucas was on the floor still dazed and barely conscious. Billy's foot snagged on Lucas and he tripped. He tried to stop himself from falling by throwing his other leg out in front of him, but he stepped into the hole with the shimmering liquid. His leg went down into the hole but the speed of the fall brought all his weight to bear where his thigh met the rim and a loud snap of thick bone reverberated throughout the cave. Billy bellowed an unearthly sound as the pain raged throughout his mind and body. He swung wildly again, but not to grab or hit anybody, but because his body didn't know what else to do.

Sarah and Chris closed their eyes and raised their hands to their ears to block out the incredible screams. Jack didn't waste any time. He scooped them both up and draped them over his shoulders. He turned away from the grotesque spectacle before him and ran for the door that led out of the cave and into the hallway. He wasn't going to stay one more minute in Howl House.

Once in a Blue Moon

"Three things cannot be long hidden: the sun, the moon, and the truth."

Buddha

Chapter 1

May 4, 2011

It was just past midnight when Jack, Sarah and Chris arrived in the woods bordering Chris' house. Once Jack had picked up his friends in Howl House, he left and didn't look back. He ran non-stop with them on his shoulders until he got to a point that he felt was safe and far away from what they had all experienced. He was out of breath when they arrived. He put them down and tried to regain some energy by walking a slight distance away. Chris and Sarah said nothing. They were still stunned by all that had happened. The light of the Moon filtered down through the new leaves on the trees and everything was quiet and peaceful. It was picture perfect in many ways, except for the fact that one of them was a wolf.

When he was ready, Jack came back over, ready to answer their questions, but all Chris and Sarah could do was continue to stare at him.

"Heard any good jokes? Jack asked trying to break the ice.

Caught off guard, Sarah started to laugh.

Chris, not ready to react in the same fashion, shook his head in disbelief.

"Am I dreaming? What the hell happened tonight? Why am I

standing in the woods at night talking to a werewolf? I'm not sure what is going on."

"I'll explain everything the best I can," Jack said, taking a deep breath. ***"What happened is...."***

Sarah interrupted him. "What happened is...Jack saved our lives. That's what happened."

Chris nodded. "You're right. Even in my insane brain right now, I know that we would be dead if it wasn't for you. But I'm just not sure what is going on. I know I haven't been listening to you for a while, but I'm all ears now, Jack. I promise."

"Thanks, Chris. Get ready for the tale to beat all tales."

Jack told them everything as best he could. From the first day he set foot in Barnaby Hills to them standing where they were right now. When he finally finished. Sarah and Chris seemed even more stunned than they were before.

"Jack, all I can say is that I'm really sorry for how I treated you. You are my best friend and I tried to end our friendship because I believed what Billy was telling me.

"Hey, don't even go there. You didn't try to drown me in a golden liquid. But I appreciate you understanding how hard it was to see Billy manipulate you and drive a wedge between our friendship. Never again."

"Never again," Chris repeated wiping away wetness from his eyes.

"Jack, what about the other Moonwalkers...Billy and his boys. What's gonna happen now?" Sarah asked with some hesitation.

"That's a really good question. I don't know the answer. All I know is that they were hurt tonight, and not just physically. With Mr. Weber out of the picture, I don't know what they will do. Billy tried to kill Lucas. They won't accept him as clan leader

anymore. Lucas may try to rise to the occasion, but I just don't know. The bigger question is what is going to happen in school tomorrow in terms of the Coach."

"School tomorrow? You're going to school? AFTER TONIGHT?" Chris spat out. "There's no way I'm going to school. I'm coming home after midnight. I wouldn't be surprised if my parents don't have the Barnaby Hills' police looking for me right now. I'm up the creek without a paddle. I'm gonna have to fake an illness - maybe amnesia - to get out of this one. You won't see me in school tomorrow. Maybe not until next week."

Sarah laughed. "You know what, Chris. I do like you. How can I not like the best friend of my boyfriend?"

Sarah couldn't see it, but Jack could tell that Chris was blushing.

She turned to Jack and smiled. "Do you think that you could give me a 'lift' home?"

All three of them started to laugh.

Chris said goodnight and took one last look at Jack before turning to leave for his house. He shook his head again in disbelief and then ran away.

"You ready?" Jack said to Sarah.

"Does a wolf howl at the Moon?" she said smiling.

Jack picked her up and placed her gently on his shoulder. He ran through the forest and then through the park. It was difficult to get through parts of Barnaby Hills carrying a person, but he was able to do it. He brought Sarah into her backyard.

Jack sighed.

"What's wrong?"

"I can't believe that I got you mixed up in all of this. Now it's my turn to say I'm sorry."

"Are you kidding me? No sorries. Just promises that you'll never hold back on me again. You can tell me anything - even if your next incarnation is a vampire."

Jack smiled.

Sarah reached up and touched the side of his face. "I guess I won't see this side of my boyfriend for another month, huh? Pity. I was kind of getting used to dating an 8th grader with a full beard. Anyway, see you tomorrow at school?"

"You sure you want to go?"

"And not be by your side? I'll see you there, bright and early."

"Bright and early it is."

She turned to leave and then turned right back again and gave him a big hug.

"I love you, Jack Wilson - no matter what." She grabbed his hand and placed something in it.

"I love you, too. Sarah."

Sarah left to go into her house. Jack watched as she entered. He looked down at his hand and opened it to see what she had given him. It was the crystal vial of glowing liquid.

Chapter 2

May 4, 2011

"Jack! Get up! It's time for school!"

Jack woke with a start, his mother's voice waking him from a surprising deep sleep. He rubbed his eyes and then took a look at his hands. Regular human hands. It was a groggy but welcome sight.

He washed up, put on clothes and came downstairs relatively quickly.

"Wow," his mother said very surprised. "I usually have to wake you up a dozen times before you actually come down. What's the occasion?"

"No occasion, just thought I'd actually do what you say for once," he said smiling.

She walked over and roughed up his hair. "Wise guy."

"Do we have any milk left for cereal?"

"Check the fridge."

He went over and opened the door, scanning the shelves.

"Hey," his mother said with a tone that made him immediately nervous. "Where is your brace for your left arm? Doctor didn't say that you were good-to-go without it yet."

Jack looked at his arm. He thought for a second and then realized that his brace was in a second floor room in Howl House laying on the floor completely destroyed from his transformation.

"Oh, um, I must have left it upstairs when I was getting ready. My arm feels much better, though."

"Don't even. Go upstairs and get it. Give me a kiss goodbye right now. I've got to jump in the shower. Got a call about an important meeting at work. There's a possibility that I might be a little late to make dinner. Is that okay?"

"Yeah, no problem. I have to integrate myself back into school after everything that happened yesterday, so I may be late, too." He walked over and gave her a kiss on the cheek. "I love you, Mom."

"I love you, too. Everything is going to be fine at school today. No worries. We all get a little nutty from time to time. Okay? Oh, now go up and get that brace."

Jack laughed. "Okay, okay. See you later."

"Remember, everything is going to be fine."

Jack ran upstairs and pretended to get his brace. He wasn't as confident as his mother that everything would be okay, but he was willing to entertain the thought until reality maybe showed him otherwise.

Chapter 3

May 4, 2011

There she was, as promised, waiting on the top step of the school entrance as he skateboarded into the parking lot. He kicked up his board and started bounding up the steps. Without saying a word, they both embraced like they hadn't seen each other in ages.

"You know," she whispered in his ear, "I thought Jack the wolf was pretty cute, but he just doesn't hold a candle to Jack the human."

"Those are exactly the words I needed to hear," he said happily.

He grabbed her hand and they walked into the school together.

"When do you have Mr. Weber?"

"I have him first. It's a flipped schedule today."

"Do you think the school will make an announcement at some point today when they haven't heard from him?"

"I doubt it. But I have a feeling that I'm gonna be called to the office."

"Why?"

"I had that altercation in his class and in the principal's office yesterday. They are going to be asking anyone and everyone who might have an answer if they know his whereabouts."

"What are you going to say?"

"I'm going to say that I don't know. I mean, it is the truth. I don't know where Mr. Weber 'the human' is.

"I guess you're right."

"What else do I have to say?"

Sarah shrugged her shoulders.

The first bell rang.

Jack squeezed Sarah's hand more tightly. "Okay, here it goes. I'll meet you at lunch."

"Okay. Do you think any of Billy's boys will be there?"

"Not a clue. We'll deal with that problem if and when it comes."

"Okay." Sarah squeezed his hand, too. "See you later. Love you."

"Love you, too."

Jack started walking to English class.

Chapter 4

May 4, 2011

Last bell for first period. No Mr. Weber. The class looked around at each other. This was strange. Mr. Weber was never late. He had little tolerance for when students were late and even less for himself.

The kids in class started talking to one another wondering what was going on. Jack didn't ask any questions but a couple of students asked him if he knew anything, seeing what had taken place in class yesterday when he gave his presentation to the class.

"Did you embarrass him into not showing, Jack?

"Did he quit?"

"Was he fired?"

The rumor mill had a life of its own.

Finally after being asked so many times what was going on, Jack opened his mouth to say that he didn't have a clue when the classroom door closed abruptly behind someone.

It was Mr. Weber.

"I'm so sorry everyone. Flat tire. I hate being late but it couldn't be helped. Did you miss me?"

The class groaned with laughter.

Jack stared at Mr. Weber, eyes and mouth wide open.

"Close your mouth back there, Jack. You tryin' to catch flies? Hey, today's a new day. We can talk later after class but I hold no animosity about yesterday, okay?" He then turned to the rest of the class and said, "Let that be a lesson to the rest of you. Holding onto grudges in your life only takes precious time away from living it. You can quote me on that - a Weber original. So, who is on deck to give their report today?" Mr. Weber scanned his grade book. "Danny, Monika and Louis, today is your day. Let's get going.

Jack watched as Mr. Weber walked to the back of the class. He passed by Jack and gave him a friendly little smile.

Jack sank into his chair as his classmate began to give his presentation.

Jack didn't know if anything at all was real anymore.

Chapter 5

May 4, 2011

"I saw him in the hallway. He said 'hello' to me! Jack, what is going on?"

Jack looked over at Sarah and almost wondered if she were truly there in the lunchroom with him.

"Sarah, I'm in shock. Total shock. I saw him there last night, laying in the control booth with a wrought iron prison bar sticking through his chest. He wasn't moving. He wasn't breathing. I have no words."

"This is crazy. How could he be here now then, and why didn't he kills us as soon as he saw us this morning? I mean, it would have been super difficult to do that and get away with it, but he wasn't even mad. He was downright nice."

"Tell me about it. He basically forgave me for yesterday and turned it into a life-lesson for the rest of the class. It was classic Mr. Weber. I don't think I can eat lunch today. My stomach hurts."

They both sat in silence for a few minutes as the rest of the kids in the lunchroom went about their daily business of eating, talking and occasionally throwing things.

Sarah grabbed Jack's hand. "Jack, I just had a really horrible thought. What if the creature...."

Jack finished her sentence. "...wasn't Mr. Weber after all."

The hair on both their necks stood up.

"That's impossible. How could I be that wrong? Every puzzle piece fit together and pointed to him."

"I understand, but what if it wasn't him?"

"Then who was it? Who did I kill last night?"

Jack's mind was off and running. He couldn't hear the noise of the cafeteria. He forgot that Sarah was sitting next to him. He forgot that he was in school altogether. And although he said he wasn't hungry, Jack picked up his sandwich and started mindlessly eating it.

Sarah looked at him doing so with curiosity.

"Jack, where's the brace for your arm? Jack. I'm talking to you."

Jack came back to the present. "What did you say?"

"Your arm brace. Where is it?"

"Did you get a phone call from my mother this morning? She asked the exact same thing."

"No, I didn't get a phone call. Where's your brace?"

"During last night's transformation, it must have been destroyed when I changed into a Moonwalker."

"How does your arm feel?"

Jack took a look at his left forearm. "It actually feels really good. Doesn't hurt at all. I guess I healed-up faster than the doc thought I would."

"Or it healed in the process of changing to or from a Moonwalker."

Jack slowly swallowed what was in his mouth and put his sandwich down.

"Did I kill anyone last night?"

They both grew silent again.

Chapter 6

May 4, 2011

The day went by at a snail's pace. Apart from shuffling from class to class, Jack didn't even realize what class he was in most of the time. He promised to meet up with Sarah on the front steps of the school right after ninth period.

Just like the morning, she was there waiting for him. He told her that he wouldn't feel comfortable unless he walked her home and knew that she was safe. She told him the exact same thing - but about walking him home. It took a while, but he convinced her he would go straight home and everything would be okay.

"One thing has been going through my head all day long," she said as they walked. "If you experience injuries before or while you are a Moonwalker and then they are healed when you return to human form, why aren't any of the other guys in school today?"

"I'm not sure about that, but I can tell you this: when you physically exert yourself in Moonwalker form, you are definitely tired the next day. I know I have always been after a full moon. I can't see how any of those guys - healed or not - wouldn't be completely exhausted today. If I didn't have the motivation to find out about Mr. Weber today, I probably would have stayed home, too."

"Do you think HE is alive? And is Billy's leg all better?"

"Good questions. But the greater question is who HE is? I've been stumped all day long."

"Well, what's the plan? Where do we go from here?"

"We? There's no 'we' right now, Sarah. I don't even know if there's a 'me' in all of this."

"But you can't fight this all on your own. You are going to

need help."

"Probably, but we've got some time - another month. We will work out something before then. For now, let's just be vigilant and see if we can figure this riddle out."

"Okay. But remember, no more hiding things. Alright?"

"Me? I've learned my lesson. Nothing but honesty from now on."

"Is that a lie?" she asked with a humorous smirk.

"I don't know. We may have to see what happens later to know if it was a lie or not," Jack chuckled.

"Well, it's a good thing we can find something to laugh about today. I didn't think there was a funny bone left in my body."

"I'm with ya. Hey, we're at your house already. I'm gonna head home and wrap my brain around this some more. Maybe surprise my mom and make dinner for once."

"Stay safe. We'll figure this out together."

"Yep."

Jack gave Sarah a kiss and then left to go home. All the way there he heard Sarah's voice saying the same thing over and over again. *Stay safe.*

Chapter 7

May 4, 2011

Jack got home without a problem. He walked into the house and carefully looked all around before heading to the kitchen and pouring himself a big glass of orange juice. He sat down at the table and took a long swig. There was so much to think about, he didn't know where to begin.

When he arrived home last night, he was still in Moonwalker form. It was weird to go to bed in wolf form, but it wasn't the first time it had happened over the course of the year. He was just glad his mother had never walked in and saw him like that. Sneaking in and out of the house late at night as an 8th grader and possibly getting caught wasn't ideal, but getting caught as a werewolf? Totally different story...and he didn't want to know about the ending. Before he fell asleep, though, he contemplated what had taken place earlier at Howl House. He had felt a sense of triumph. He had protected his friends and vanquished his enemy (or so he thought). And right after thinking this, he thought about his father. And in some strange fashion, he thought his father would be proud of him. Jack had been so upset with himself when he allowed Billy to manipulate him into becoming a Moonwalker. Not knowing his father, he could only assume how disappointed he would have been. Jack's Mom had always told him what a stand up guy his father was. The notion that he would be disappointed in him had been a recurring thought throughout the year. Beating the creature and Billy seemed like a way to make things right - especially in regard to his feelings and thoughts about his Dad.

All of that had changed today. He was feeling less triumphant and more defeated and starting to worry to the point of shutting down.

If you just sit here and think all afternoon, nothing will get done and Mom will come home after a long day and have to cook dinner. Is that what you want? You can think while you work.

Jack shook himself from his stupor and got up and started checking the cabinets and the fridge. His mother had gone shopping a few days ago, so there definitely had to be something he could make. And maybe, just maybe, it wouldn't taste too bad, either.

He found some chicken and peppers in the fridge and sweet potatoes on the counter. He looked up a recipe on the internet - stir fried chicken and baked sweet potatoes - and got to business. It wound up that keeping busy with dinner turned out to be just the thing to even his thoughts out. The simple acts of cutting the chicken and peppers into smaller pieces calmed him down and kept him from going crazy with worry. Within ninety-minutes, everything was done.

Jack set the table and got some drinks ready. He checked the time. 6:30. His mother usually got home around 5:30. She said she would be a little late.

I thought she'd come walking through the door just as I took the sweet potatoes out of the oven. I guess I can cover everything up to keep it warm. Better a warm surprise than no surprise.

He went back into the kitchen and made sure everything was taken care of and then went into the living room and turned on some TV to pass the time until his mom got home. He started watching a game show, but soon his eyes grew tired and he started falling asleep.

"Jaaaack. Jaaaack. Wake up, Jack. Time to go to school," a soft voice whispered to him.

Jack turned over on the couch. He didn't want to go anywhere. He was so tired.

"Not today, Mom. I just wanna sleep."

"But it's time to go to school."

"Just a little more sleep, Mom. Please."

"No, Jack. You have to get up. And I'm not your mother. Your mother is gone."

Jack's eyes sprang open. He sat bolt upright and put out his hands in defense.

"Got your attention now," said the voice that Jack had grown to know all too well over the last month. ***"Aren't you a little old to be losing your mommy, Jack?"***

"Where is she?" Jack yelled, wiping the sleepiness away from his face.

"Really? That's your first question? Not 'Who are you?' or better yet 'How are you doing?' You're worried more about your mom than what you did to your MASTER LAST NIGHT!" the voice bellowed back.

Jack ignored the voice's banter. "If you do anything to her..."

"Or what? You'll kill me? That didn't work the first time, now did it? This time you're going to shut up and do what I say or you'll never see your mommy again. Do you understand me?"

Jack stopped himself from going over the edge or into a fit of rage. "Yes."

"Good. You are to come to Howl House tonight. Arrive at 9 pm, no sooner, no later. When you enter the house, go to the second floor and enter the first room on the right. Do you understand?"

"Yes."

"And Jack, come alone. No girlfriend. No best friend. Just you. DO YOU UNDERSTAND?"

"Don't worry. I'll be alone. How do I know my mother will be safe?"

"You won't. That's why you'll do exactly as I say. Oh, I almost forgot. Silly me. Bring the vial of elixir with you. You didn't think I forgot about that, right? See you later, Jack."

The voice dissipated and Jack bent over and put both his hand through his hair. HE had taken his mother. His mother. How did this happen? And to make it worse, Jack still didn't know who HE was. Jack looked at the clock. It was 7 pm. Two more hours to go.

Two agonizing hours.

Chapter 8

May 4, 2011

Jack walked quickly through the forest. He pretty much knew exactly how long it would take to get to Howl House. Before leaving, he ate some of the food that he had cooked for him and his mom. The last thing he wanted to do was eat, but he knew that he was going to need some energy. He brought nothing with him this time - only the vial. He had killed the creature last night and he came back to life today. What could he possibly bring that was going to make a difference this time?

But you have knowledge, Jack.

Last night was crazy but he did learn a lot. Billy said that the liquid in the hole was no longer viable. He shoved Lucas head into it and that must have poisoned the well, so to speak, contaminating it to the point of stopping its effectiveness. That is why HE told Jack to bring the crystal vial with him tonight. It must be the only pure elixir left. Having possession of it was the only bargaining chip that Jack had.

And what about Howl House itself? Why did the second floor have cages and equipment - a large mirror concealing a control room? It just didn't make sense.

The biggest question still revolved around the identity of the creature. Jack had been so sure it was Mr. Weber. Remorse was now kicking in and Jack felt really bad about accusing him. He had embarrassed both of them at school - in front of the principal even.

But what if it was Mr. Weber?

After seeing the Coach in school, he totally fell off Jack's radar. But if a healing process can take place during transformation, wouldn't that just mean that Mr. Weber had gotten better? And that by showing up at school as if nothing had happened, he would throw Jack completely off the trail. It could still be Mr. Weber!

Not so fast, Jack. Be cool and calm. You don't know anything right now. You are back at square one. No more jumping to reckless conclusions. You're really upset and you're not thinking straight. Calm down and be ready for whatever reality you are presented with tonight. You owe it to your mother to be focused and in control.

Jack took a deep breath and exhaled. He had to stay in control.

Howl House loomed ahead of him. He stopped and looked at his watch. 8:50 pm.

He slowly continued on the path.

Stay in control.

Chapter 9

May 4, 2011

He arrived.

As Jack approached Howl House, he could see a group of people on the front steps. It was Lucas and the other boys. Some of them started to grumble and began to walk down the stairs to meet Jack head on.

"Leave him alone."

It was Lucas.

"HE doesn't want us to touch him. Move out of the way and let him enter."

One of the boys couldn't control his frustration. "But what about last night, Lucas? You know what he did. HE may not want us to do anything, but I don't think he'll be upset if we rough him up a little bit."

"NO ONE TOUCHES HIM!" Lucas yelled.

All the boys stiffened up a little bit from the harshness of Lucas' voice. They knew he meant business. If anyone touched Jack, they would have to contend with Lucas first and then HIM. They all moved back and allowed Jack to walk up the stairs to the front door. Lucas even opened it for him.

"First door on the right upstairs. HE's waiting for you."

Jack hesitated a moment before walking in, looking Lucas directly in the eyes. For the first time in a year, Jack could not detect any feelings of contempt when Lucas looked at him. Maybe it was as close to a thank you for saving his life that he would ever get. Whatever was said or wasn't said in the silence of the gaze, Jack was just grateful he didn't have to fight his way into the house and that

Lucas wasn't seething with hatred at the sight of him.

Jack walked in and the door closed behind him. It was hard to see but Jack knew where to go. He carefully made his way up the dangerous staircase and stopped at the top landing. He looked down the hallway. First door. He reached his hand into his pocket. The vial was there.

This is it, Jack. You're on your own now. Whatever or whoever is behind that door, you have to keep your wits about you. Don't let them intimidate you. Don't let them manipulate you. Your mom's safety is the priority. Whatever you have to do to ensure that, you will do. Just remember who you are and what you believe in. You can do this.

Jack walked over to the first door and turned the knob. He pushed it open and entered.

He wasn't prepared for what he saw.

Chapter 10

May 4, 2011

"Welcome, Jack. Glad you could make it. Can I get you something to drink? Maybe a soda or juice? Just give me a second to adjust this strap. It's so much easier when a subject is awake, you know? They just hop up on the table and can even help out buckling their legs in. Not that your mother isn't helpful. She is a wonderful person. There. Got it! All buckled and strapped in. How about that drink?"

Jack stood dumbfounded as Billy's father calmly spoke to him as he strapped his mother down onto a lab table.

"Oh, and I wouldn't try anything stupid if I were you, Jack. Those wires connected to her body will shock her with a lethal dose of electricity at the push of a button from the remote I'm holding in my hand. Understood? So what will it be - cola, root beer?"

Jack walked a few feet forward. "What have you done to her?"

Billy's dad chuckled. "Oh, nothing...yet. She was given a sedative of my own creation. Unconscious and unharmed, for now. And if things go according to plan, she won't even remember a single thing about how she got here. Who says science isn't fun? But you know, I was worried that I wouldn't be able to get her to come to Howl House, but she really is such a good employee. When I contacted her office for help in scouting out a new property, she was more than happy to join me."

Jack's brain was spinning. "She works for you?"

"Yep, although she doesn't know who I am. She thought I was some corporate peon from the west coast office. Little did she know that your Dad and I go way back and I was responsible for you and your Mom coming to Barnaby Hills."

Jack almost fell against the table.

"Oh, wow. Overwhelming, huh? Let me get you that drink. You'll feel better."

Billy's dad walked over to a refrigerator, opened it and pulled out a can of soda. He walked over and handed it to Jack.

"I'm sorry; all that's left is orange. I hope that is okay?"

Jack looked down at the cold can in his hand.

"Ah, I know what you're thinking: *Is it poisoned?* I can assure you that it isn't. Athletes aren't the only people who work up a thirst. Researchers do, too. Go ahead. Drink up."

Jack just held the can in his hand.

"Maybe you'll want it later," mused Billy's dad.

"How do you know my father?" Jack demanded.

"Not one to waste any time. That's what I like about you, Jack. Your father was like that, too. Basically, your father and I were lab rats - participants in an experiment."

"What are you talking about?" Jack asked, truly confused.

"The story is a long one, but I guess you should know. I'll have to give you the quick version, though, so I hope you don't mind if I leave out some unimportant details. Sure you don't want to crack that soda open?"

Jack said nothing. He just stared at Billy's dad.

"It all started in San Francisco. I was a research assistant for a bio-engineering firm that had contracts with private industry and the government. We were working on creating chemicals that would enhance the abilities of soldiers in the military. I won't bore you with details but countries and governments have been trying for centuries to make their soldiers the strongest and best fighters on the planet. Just in the last century you had the Germans, Russians and Americans working on performance enhancing drugs. Crazy stuff. Are you still with me, Jack?"

"What does this have to do with my father?"

"I'll speed things up a bit. I can see that you are losing your patience. And we don't want Jack to lose his patience. Right?"

Jack did not react at all.

"So the bio-engineering firm I worked for had developed a serum. But it wasn't like anything that had been produced before. Most of the other 20th Century experiments revolved around creating chemical compounds that either sped up human metabolism or tried to control how subjects would think and perceive reality under certain situations, trying to inhibit fear responses and such. But our serum was developed using DNA from animals - lions, tigers and bears, oh my! We figured that a biological cross-connection between animals of great strength and endurance and humans would usher in an unstoppable fighting force - humans with animal strength. But, none of the pairings proved promising. Somewhere along the line the biochemical signatures would fail. All except for one: wolf DNA. Wolf DNA retained its chemical composition when crossed with human samples in all the preliminary tests.

"Theoretically we believed it would work, but we needed to do experiments first. We needed volunteers and were willing to pay good money for them. I don't know how, but your father showed up at our door. Initial physical and mental tests proved him an excellent candidate. That's how we got to know each other." Billy's father smiled. "Am I boring you or do you want to know more?"

Jack stared silently but nodded his head affirmatively.

"Good, good, Jack. I want you to know everything. So much to learn, so little time."

Chapter 11

May 4, 2011

"Why my father? Why not volunteers from the military?"

"That's a good question, Jack. Let's just say that although we were contracted for military projects, we weren't beholden to OUR military alone. There were quite a few people interested in our research and we were interested in the highest bidder. If we conducted experiments on soldiers, then our project would solely be a government project. Not very lucrative given what the competitors were supplying."

"But that still doesn't answer how my father got involved. Other than money, what would be the motivation to be part of an experiment that was creating hybrid animal/human warriors?"

"So inquisitive. I love it," chuckled Billy dad. "You don't really think that we advertised the experiment in the local paper like THAT, do you? None of the final participants were told the truth. We put together some booklet about increasing stamina for sports and whatnot. Pure lies. Your dad was a musician, Jack. That translates into NO MONEY. This seemed like a legit way to make some good cash while taking vitamin supplements. We had volunteers lining up at the door. But we only took the best of the best. Your dad was chosen. So was I."

"Hold on," Jack said incredulously. "I thought you said that you were one of the researchers."

"I was, but I was also a participant. You see, we couldn't just rely on getting feedback from people who didn't know anything about the project. We needed someone who knew everything about it to take an active role so we could understand exactly what was happening. I was part of the project from its inception, so I volunteered willingly...eagerly."

"So my father was a Moonwalker?"

"I never said that, Jack. Don't put words in my mouth. It ruins the story. I said your father was a participant in the experiment. He never actually transformed into a Moonwalker. It was quite disappointing. Out of all the participants, only one actually became a Moonwalker. Me."

"Why? If it worked on you, why not the others? Why not my dad?"

"Another great question. And that wasn't answered until relatively recently. Want to know the answer? Nature and nurture. Nature and nurture, Jack."

Chapter 12

May 4, 2011

"What do you mean you can't get in touch with him?" Chris asked, bringing the phone into his bedroom closet.

Sarah continued. "I've been calling his house and there's no answer. I'm really worried."

"Maybe he and his mom went out for some ice cream."

"I can barely hear you, Chris. Where are you?"

"I'm in my closet. Do you know how much trouble I got into? My parents think I'm totally psycho for coming home so late and claiming I didn't know where I was. If they hear me talking to a friend on the phone, I'm so dead."

"You're dead? I just told you everything that happened in school and how the creature wasn't Mr. Weber after all and how there's a really good possibility that IT is still alive and now Jack is missing and you are worried about you being dead?"

"Well, when you put it that way..." Chis trailed off. He jumped right back into the conversation. "But you still haven't convinced me that something has happened to him."

"I don't know how else to describe it, but I just feel there's a problem. You gotta help me, Chris. We gotta do something."

"Like what?"

There was a long pause and then Sarah spoke. "We have to go to Howl House."

"WHAT?" Chris yelled, quickly putting his hand over his own mouth after doing so.

"It's the only place he would be."

"Sarah, we just escaped that place by the width of a hair. We can't go back there. If we do, that will be the end of us. Totally."

"If we don't go back there, it will be the end of Jack. TOTALLY."

Chris was quiet for a moment. "Okay, you're right. I'll get dressed and meet you in the park by the swings in fifteen minutes. Man, I don't know how I'm going to sneak out of here. If my parents catch me, they are going to kill me - no funeral, no nothing. They are just going to bury me in the backyard and pretend like I never existed."

Sarah sighed. "Are you done?"

"Yeah. I'll see you in the park in a little bit."

"Great."

Chapter 13

May 4, 2011

"What do you mean - nature and nurture?"

"Do you know what a placebo is, Jack?"

"Yeah, it's a fake pill or something like that."

"Correct, but it is a little more than that. When someone takes a placebo they are getting a pill that basically has zero medicinal value - a sugar pill, so to speak. But the person taking it is told that they are receiving something that will make them feel better or that might even cure what ails them. They believe that what they are taking is real. Their belief is so psychologically powerful that they actually feel or get better - without any real medicine. It's called the 'placebo effect.' Really interesting stuff."

Jack looked at Billy's dad in confusion. "So what does this have to do with nature and nurture?"

"Think about it Jack. The nature part is biochemical. The nurture part is what takes place psychologically up here." He pointed to his head and smiled.

"So what you're saying is that my father didn't believe he would turn into a wolf, so he didn't."

"Exactly. We didn't realize the interaction between psychology and chemistry when we did the experiments. Remember, none of the participants except for me were told what was really going on. I transformed because I alone truly believed in what I was doing and what the serum could do."

"But how does moonlight figure into all of this? If the combination of liquid and belief are present, why can't we transform at will? Why does it only happen in the presence of a full moon?"

"You see, Jack. This is why I said you were the product of good genes. You've got a keen intellect. Smart, strong...you, like your father, perfect for the program. At first, after taking the serum, nothing happened to any of us. We actually thought the project was a complete and utter failure. But then something happened a week later when the Moon was full. I changed."

"Why?"

"Phototrophic effects. You probably haven't covered that in science yet, huh? Phototrophic relates to organisms receiving energy from a light source - like plants do. For some reason, the organic properties of the wolf serum, when integrated into human cellular structures, are fully activated phototrophically in low levels of light - specifically the exact levels found during a full moon. Once a month, the conditions are perfect for the organic compounds in my body to feed, basically, and react on a cellular level. When this all comes together, BAM, Moonwalker."

"And you didn't learn about all of this until recently?"

"Relatively so, within the last few years."

Jack looked down at his mom. She was still asleep. "But what does all this have to do with my family? My mother and I had nothing to do with any of this. You said that my father was unaffected by the serum and that this all took place in San Francisco. What is going on?"

"Confession is good for the soul, Jack. And I have had something weighing on my brain for a long, long time. I'm going to reveal it to you tonight, right now, even. I hope you're ready. It's going to make me feel a whole lot better. You? Not so much."

Chapter 14

May 4, 2011

"How do you remember where you're going?" Chris asked, trying to keep up with Sarah's pace.

"To be honest, I'm not sure. I guess I'm just following my instincts, but this is the third time I'm going to Howl House. Third time's the charm, right?

"I hope so...for a number of reasons. So, what's the plan when we get there? I don't think we can just waltz in through the front door."

"I would imagine not."

"So?"

"Well, Jack told me that he snuck into the house from the back through a window last night."

"Yeah, but weren't they waiting for him?"

"They were but they were also expecting him."

"And they won't be waiting for us, too?" Chris smirked.

"That is the million dollar question. If Jack is at Howl House, he is there for a specific reason. He was coerced somehow and was probably told specifically not to bring or tell anyone about it."

"I can see you have given this a lot of thought."

"Desperate times call for desperate thoughts."

Chris nodded his head in agreement.

"Let's say you're right about this and we sneak in without anybody seeing us. What then?"

"We look around and try to find Jack."

"And when we find him?"

Sarah turned to Chris. "You ask a lot of questions."

"I'm sorry. I don't mean to..."

"No, it's okay," Sarah interrupted. "I like that."

"Lucas didn't like it too much last night."

"Lucas? Who's he? I'm talking to Chris right now - Jack's best friend. And one of two people who are going to save him tonight."

A large smile broke out on Chris' face. "You know what, Sarah?"

"What?"

"You and Jack make an awesome couple. I'm lucky to have such good friends."

"And we're lucky, too, Chris. Let's go get Jack."

They picked up their pace.

Chapter 15

May 4, 2011

"Confession time. So the project had some bugs to be worked out, and we tried to get right to it. After all, it worked on me; we just didn't know why. So we went back to the drawing board. All the participants were paid and dismissed from the project. A couple of years go by and we learned more. Not everything, but more. We learned that the changes made to the DNA of the test subjects were permanent. They would forever be Moonwalkers in waiting, essentially."

Billy's father paused.

"And?" Jack pressed.

"And the powers that be didn't like that. They worried that word of the experiment would leak out and that the participants could be used against the project by interested parties."

Jack's face tightened. "What did you do?"

"I'll be honest, Jack. It wasn't my idea, but I could see the future and it made sense."

"WHAT DID YOU DO?"

"We had all the participants killed to protect the project. There was nothing else we could do. All their deaths were fast and looked 'accidental.' It was a shame and dark blemish on the project as a whole, but you know what they say about the path of progress being undeterred."

Jack cradled his head with his hands to stem the incredible pain that exploded within his brain. He was screaming inside, but no sound emanated from him. He finally raised his head and fixed a deadly gaze on Billy's dad. "I'm going to kill you." He made a slight motion with his body as if he were ready to attack.

Billy's dad put his finger on the remote control. "I wouldn't if I were you. I understand your anger, Jack. I really do. And you're right. Someone is actually going to die tonight, but it won't be me. Who it is remains to be seen, but I digress. Take a moment for yourself. I'll wait. You deserve to hear the end of the story before the sequel starts. But I warn you; if you make any attempt to attack me, I'll press the button."

Chapter 16

May 4, 2011

Lucas and the other boys were sitting on the front steps of Howl House.

"Are they all there?" Sarah asked in a hushed tone as she and Chris watched from a set of bushes about fifty yards away.

"It's hard to say for sure since only one of them has a flashlight, but it looks like only one of them is missing."

"Who?"

"Looks like Billy isn't with them."

"I'd rather they all be there, but we'll take what we can. Let's head around to the back and see if we can get in through a window."

"Okay. Let's backtrack a little so there's less of a chance that they hear us. Then we can circle around."

"I like your thinking, Chris. I'll follow you."

"Are you sure...I mean, are you sure you want to follow me? You've done a pretty good job getting us this far."

"I'm totally sure. This is a team effort."

"Team, right. I've never been on a team that actually listened to what I have to say."

"I'm listening. Go on. Take the lead. I'll be right behind you."

Chris smiled. "You got it."

They backed away from the view of the boys and made their way to the back of Howl House.

Chapter 17

May 4, 2011

"So your next question - before I told you that your father was killed - would probably have been about San Francisco and Barnaby Hills. Light years away from each other, huh? Well, after the project ran into trouble, some of our investors decided to back out. I knew what we were doing was a success. I just needed time and money to work out the kinks. So I began talking to people on the side. People that were interested in MY way of redoing things. Money was exchanged. Lots of money. I started investing that money and buying all the shares in the project company. I also diversified and bought shares in up and coming companies, too. Seems I had a talent for it. When I had acquired enough money and resources to completely fund the project on my own, I bought all the rights and patents and decided to leave the west coast...for safety and secrecy, of course. I couldn't just pick up and move to another large city, so I investigated an area that would allow me to have utter privacy to do whatever I wanted. Thank you Barnaby Hills. I even opened up a branch office of one of my companies in the area."

Still reeling from the news about his father, Jack kept close attention to what was being said. There might be something revealed that would help him and his mother survive the night.

"And Howl House?"

"Wonderful, isn't it? I bought this and all the land around here from the Weber family trust. They didn't have a clue what to do with it all. As far as Howl House, it seems that back in the day, someone had discovered some gold and began some crude form of tunneling to get more. They were afraid that others would find out, so they had this house built around above and around the whole operation to keep them off the scent. I couldn't have asked for a more perfect place to set up shop."

"And the liquid in the cave? The Native American lore?"

"Pure theater, Jack. Now, the liquid is real, but remember what I said about belief before. As I did more and more research, I realized that I needed to get prospective participants on board believing in something that had some truth in its history. Yes, the Native Americans played incredible games of lacrosse but they did not transform into werewolves. But if you tell the right people the right lie, anything can happen."

"And the right people were kids."

"Bingo, Jack. Kids don't have the hang ups that adults do. They are born believers."

"So you concocted a fairy tale to lure kids into doing what, playing lacrosse in the moonlight?"

Billy's father laughed. "Good one, Jack. Let's put it this way: today lacrosse, tomorrow the world. Starting with young men, I figured I could create my own race of super strong fighters. Why let governments have all the fun? My fighting force would be dedicated to me and whatever cause I deemed worthy, and lucrative."

"And you sacrificed your son and his friends to your desires."

"You call this a sacrifice? I call it a gift."

"So why am I at the receiving end of such a gift?"

"You and Billy were part of this whether you wanted to be or not. Remember what I said before about the serum making permanent changes to DNA. Guess what got passed down to our kiddies? When I realized this was the case, I had a detective agency delve into the lives of the original participants. It would seem that you and Billy were the only children conceived before everyone was killed. You guys were born to become Moonwalkers. So I kept tabs on you and your mom over the years. I even bought the company she worked for in San Fran - you know, thinking ahead and all. Meanwhile, I perfected the formula, worked out all the kinks and started experimenting again. As you know, it all came together nicely. But what I was missing was a leader for my young clan of Moonwalkers. That's why you're here. I had your mother transferred to the nearby affiliate company and then, long story short, here you are. Quite the story, huh, Jack? So much to take in, but I figured you could do it. You are quite the specimen."

"I'm not joining you. You know that."

"I know you BELIEVE that, Jack. I actually have a left over scar from last night as evidence," Billy's father said rubbing his chest. "But if I have demonstrated anything to you, it is that I do not give up easily." He looked down at his watch. "Oh, look. It is almost time."

"Almost time for what?"

"For the full moon, silly. Don't tell me you didn't realize tonight was a blue moon - an extra full moon this month? Well, I won't fault you. You have been very busy as of late - fighting me. You probably didn't get a chance to check the calendar. Oh, well. We are going to be leaving this room soon and going out to the field."

Jack gave Billy's father a puzzled look. "Is that where you and I are going to fight?"

"Me and you? Oh, heavens no. You are going to play Billy in my kind of a one-on-one game of lacrosse - to the death."

Chapter 18

May 4, 2011

Sarah and Chris had made it to the back of the house without being seen. They climbed onto the shed and pulled themselves into the same room that Jack had the night before. No one was there to ambush them.

Chris whispered. "So while I was down in the creepy cave last night, you were up here on the second floor?"

"Yes, in the room at the far end of the hallway."

"If the cave is where they turn people into wolves, what goes on up here?"

"I'm not entirely sure, although the room I was in had a cage and fake wall with a mirror for observation purposes, most likely. Having been in both places, I'd choose the cave any day."

"I know I ask this question a lot, but what do we do next?"

Sarah thought for a moment. "I'm betting that the room on the right is pretty much out of commission based on what took place last night. When we leave this room, we should head to the left. That will put us outside the first room - the one closest to the staircase. I have a feeling that is where all the action is taking place tonight."

"But all the guys are downstairs on the front steps."

"That means Jack must be in the room with the creature."

"Is now a good time to say I'm scared?"

Sarah smiled. "If it makes you feel any better, so am I."

"I don't think it makes me feel any better, but I appreciate the companionship."

"Let's get out of this room. From now on, we are as quiet as mice. Got it?"

"I just don't want to be as quiet as a dead mouse."

"You have a pretty dark sense of humor, Chris. Don't lose it. We're gonna need it. We are definitely going to need it."

Chapter 19

May 4, 2011

"Billy?"

"Let's just say that Billy hasn't been such a 'good puppy' as of late, to use his terminology. To be honest, I think I failed him as a father, but that is because he, to be blunt, has been such a failure as a son. Last night was the worst he's been in quite some time - almost killing Lucas and all. If it weren't for your heroics, Jack, the clan would have lost one of its most valuable members."

"How come we didn't lose you?" Jack asked, his subconscious mind curling his fingers into a fist.

"Simply put, you never killed me. Looks can be deceiving, Jack. Next time check for a pulse when you throw a metal rod through someone's chest. As Reagan once said, 'Trust but verify.' A newbie's mistake. Don't let it bother you too much. I'm actually grateful," chuckled Billy's dad.

Jack changed the subject. "What about Chris?"

"Come on, Jack. Chris? He was only being used as a bargaining chip to get you down with the program. I never wanted Chris in the clan. But Billy sees himself as a player in all this and wanted to recruit Chris against my best inclinations. You see, it's almost like you and Billy are polar opposite siblings. He is so jealous of your abilities. I guess it comes down to wanting to impress me. Like I said, I think I failed him as a father. Call me a softy, but I'm giving both him and you one more chance to impress me. You will play a game of lacrosse against one another - to the death. The winner will be the one who survives and will go onto leading the clan as we move on to bigger and better things.

"You are sick. Billy is your son. How could you do this to your own son?"

"Grow up, Jack. The world is a dangerous place - family or not."

"If I win, you know that I'll never join you."

"That's why we have dear old mom on the table. If you refuse, she dies. Actually, if Billy wins, you die and she dies. Yikes. And at some point down the road, your friends will die, too. So much death. It's a shame. You had better try really hard to win, Jack."

Jack put his hand in his pocket and grabbed the vial of elixir. "But I have the vial of liquid."

"Oh, yeah, that. You are going to hand that over to me, but it's not the bargaining chip you believe it to be."

"You sure? Billy let it out of the bag that the supply down in the cave has been corrupted. It's just a hole of unusable liquid."

"For once, Billy is right. The bad news is when the formula comes into contact with other organic matter, it loses its efficacy. The good news is being comprised of a hybrid formula of stem cells, it replicates on its own when given time, room and the right conditions. The batch in the cave once started from a small amount of serum - about the same amount as you have in your pocket right now. But you don't hold the winning hand, Jack. I can make more. It will take some time, but believe me, there will be more. You giving me the sample in the vial just speeds up the process a whole lot faster. So let's not prolong the inevitable. Hand it over to me now."

Jack took the vial out of his pocket and held it up in the air. "I'll crush it right now."

"For a smart guy, I'm kind of surprised at your foolishness right now. Hand over the vial or I push the button and mom dies. It's that simple and I really don't have any emotions one way or the other."

Jack had no more leverage. He reluctantly put the vial down on the table next to his mom.

"That was the right decision. I knew you had it in you. So, what do you say about letting mom rest here a bit more and we'll go take a walk out to the clearing. Lacrosse is a great game, isn't?"

Jack looked shook his head slowly. "It was."

Billy's dad chuckled. "I just love your sarcasm. Don't tell anyone this, especially not Billy, but my money is riding on you tonight, Jack. Great things in your future. Great things."

Chapter 20

May 4, 2011

Chris and Sarah were just about to leave the middle room when they heard a door open in the hallway. They quickly closed their door but left it open a crack to see and hear what was going on.

"So how do I know my mother will be safe in this room while we are in the clearing?" they heard Jack ask.

"Please, you hurt my feelings by asking such a question," they heard another voice say. "I'm a man of my word, Jack. Your mother will be as she is now. You have my promise that nothing will happen to her while you and Billy go at it - unless, of course, something happens to you."

"You better not be lying to me."

"I'm not. And I can tell somewhat through our mental connection as Moonwalkers that you have not alerted your friends to come and surprise us. That's very good. When you fully join the clan, I will teach you how to have greater mental telepathy, too, Jack. It is one of the added benefits for true believers. It allows the brotherhood to keep in constant contact. I know how much you relished our dream state get-togethers, ha-ha."

Jack didn't respond. He began to walk down the stairs with Billy's dad following him.

Sarah and Chris heard the voice trailing off, "Great things, Jack. Great things..."

When they were definitely alone, Sarah whispered to Chris. "Did you get a look at who the other person with Jack was?"

"I did and I feel like I'm going to get sick to my stomach."

"Who was it?"

"It was Mr. Jenkins. Billy's dad,"

Neither of them said anything for a moment or two. Sarah finally broke the silence.

"Okay, so here's the bad news. Jack is going to be surrounded by all of them right now. I don't know what's going on in the clearing, but there is no way we can approach them and do anything."

"Agreed."

"The good thing is that they're not expecting us. Don't tell Jack I said this, but I'm glad he didn't say anything to me this time."

"I'm not gonna say a word. I think we both know that Jack is quite capable of taking care of himself. I also think we know what we have to do now."

"Yes, we do. We are going to save Jack's mom."

Chapter 21

May 4, 2011

Lucas and the rest of the boys followed closely behind Jack and Mr. Jenkins. As they got closer to the open field, a single solitary figure could be seen standing in the center. It was Billy. Lying on the ground next to him were two lacrosse sticks - the old kind that were hidden in the panel of the Howl House.

Billy's head was tilted down to the ground. As Jack got closer, he could see that his eyes were glowing orange in the darkness surrounding his face and his breathing was labored and chaotic. He constantly shifted his weight back and forth between his feet as if uncomfortable. It was almost as if he were a frightened animal backed into a corner.

"Let's just get down to business. Okay, gentlemen?" Billy's dad said. "We are all bonafide Moonwalkers, after all. No need for us to make any speeches about the ancient ancestors or any of that gobbledygook. The clouds will be dissipating soon and the Moon will be shining brightly upon us. Let me lay down the ground rules for tonight's match. Basically, there are none. When you transform, pick up your sticks immediately and fight to the death. It's that simple. If either of you tries to escape or do anything other than fight each other, the rest of the clan is here to make sure it never happens again."

Mr. Jenkins looked over at Lucas. He nodded his head. The other boys looked around at each other in uncomfortable silence.

"There is much at stake, so battle wisely. The winner will be the official leader of the Moonwalkers and will join with me in shaping the clan in its new and lucrative direction as a fighting force for hire to be reckoned with on a global scale. So without any more fanfare, I wish you good luck. May the best wolf win!"

Mr. Jenkins and all the boys moved away from the middle of the field and formed a large circle around Billy and Jack. All eyes were on the sky as it began to clear and the light from the second full moon of the month began to push against the thinning clouds.

Jack and Billy were facing towards each other about four feet apart. Billy continued to move about anxiously, his eyes glowing. Jack stood his ground. It was all he could do as the wait for the full moon seemed to take forever. He bent down and rubbed his hands on the ground. The grass was dry and brittle. He wiped his hands slowly against one another and then cleared his throat.

"You know, Billy. We don't have to do this. We never had to do any of it. He manipulated us. We are just a means to a self-serving end for him."

Silence from Billy.

"You know he had my father killed. Did he tell you that? My father was killed to protect the Moonwalker project and now he wants us to kill each other. He doesn't care who wins. What kind of father does that?

Billy shifted his legs and his breathing spiked harshly.

"I don't want to hurt you, and I don't think you want to hurt me. Your father will never trust either one of us. And Lucas? Lucas will never be the same after last night got so out of control."

Billy raised his head and looked directly at Jack.

"What do you say we end this right now, Billy? All of this can stop right now if we join together to do it. No one has to suffer anymore. What do you say?"

Billy shrugged his shoulders and bent his head to either side and cracked his neck.

"Say hello and goodbye to the last Moon you will ever see,

Jack Wilson."

At that moment, both boys were instantaneously bathed in moonlight.

Chapter 22

May 4, 2011

Although it appeared no one was guarding Jack's mom, Chris and Sarah snuck into the first room as quietly as possible. Unlike the room that they had just come from, this room was lit up by a number of light fixtures hanging from the ceiling. There was scientific equipment against every wall, and, in the middle of it all, was a laboratory table with Mrs. Wilson strapped to it unconscious. There were wires attached to her that led away to some of the equipment. It looked like someone was trying to recreate the Bride of Frankenstein.

"Any guess what those wires are for?" Sarah asked nervously.

"You're asking me?" Chris shot back.

"I just thought you'd surprise me with some deep understanding of electronics. Don't hate me for trying."

"I can tell you this: they don't look like they are there to make her feel good."

"They sure don't. Why don't you take a look where they lead to and I'll look more closely around the table to see if there are any other things we should be concerned about."

Chris shook his head affirmatively and walked off to follow the wires. Sarah got down on her hands and knees and started check underneath the table. Apart from what appeared to be a means to raise and lower the table, everything appeared to be harmless. She got up and walked around the table looking more closely at the straps that held Jack's mom down. It seemed like they could be easily undone. The wires concerned her the most. As she started to walk around to the other side of the table, her eye caught something reflecting light on the table itself. She made her way around and saw that it was the crystal vial from last night. It was just sitting there right next to Jack's mom. A shiver immediately ran down her spine when she thought about the liquid being used to transform Ms. Wilson. She picked it up and put it into her pocket quickly. She saw Chris fussing around with something in one of the corners and joined him.

"Well, what did you find?"

"Seems like an electric generator. My father has one in the garage just in case there is an emergency and we lose power. This one is way more modern, though. You can barely tell that it is running."

"Is it powering things in the room?"

"It doesn't look like it. Seems to just be connected to the wires that go to Jack's mom."

They both looked at each other with a mix of surprise and distress.

"We've got to unhook her from that right away. Please do it, Chris. Please," Sarah pleaded.

"I really want to. I just have to check that there isn't a way that we trigger something to go off if we start removing wires from her."

"Okay, whatever you have to do..."

"Even if we unhook everything and take off those straps, we are going to still have to get her out of here. It looks like they gave her some kind of drug to knock her out. Maybe you can see if you can wake her up. That will give me a chance to figure this all out."

"How should I wake her up?"

"Look who's asking questions now," Chris smiled. "I don't know. Why don't you start by saying her name and moving on from there?"

"I'll try anything to get us out of here in one piece. Okay, you keep doing what you're doing and I'll do what I have to do. And let's hope we meet in the middle and nothing stops us from getting out."

"I'm on it." Chris began looking at the wires more closely.

Sarah walked over to the table. She looked down at Jack's mom and took a deep breath. "Mrs. Wilson. Mrs. Wilson. Can you hear me? Please wake up. We need to get out of here. We really need to get out of here RIGHT NOW."

Chapter 23

May 4, 2011

The field was full of transformations as the boys and Mr. Jenkins changed from humans to Moonwalkers. They all writhed on the ground in unison like worms desperately trying wriggle themselves off of hot concrete. The forest reverberated with grunts and groans. The cacophony of it all was almost enough to wake the dead. And then, shortly after it began, all grew quiet as the first breaths to be drawn waited patiently to erupt. ***As if on cue, full-fledged Moonwalkers sprang from the ground into full form, taking in large quantities of air and howling in frustration at the Moon.***

In the center of all of this, Jack and Billy scurried to grab the lacrosse sticks that lay near them. Billy happened upon his first and thrashed his body around viciously to be the first to land a blow. Jack was still bent over grabbing his stick but sensed danger as he heard something behind him cutting quickly through the air. Instead of trying to turn and block what he could with his arm, he dove forward into a shoulder roll, managing to grab his stick at the same time. He could feel Billy's swing just miss him as he rose into a crouched position. Billy had put so much of his weight and energy into the swing that he couldn't stop his motion and he careened to the side off balance.

Mr. Jenkins erupted into throaty laughter. "What was that, Billy? You start off a fight to the death with a weak miss? Get back in there and stop embarrassing all of us."

Billy's eyes flamed orange and he went on the attack again. He ran directly at Jack and poked the stick directly at his face. Jack ducked down and swung his stick in a short arc to catch

Billy behind the knee, knocking him into a kneeling position. Jack then pitched himself forward and pushed Billy backwards onto the ground, holding him to the grass by his shoulders.

"We don't have to do this, Billy. Please listen to reason," Jack implored while trying to stay on top.

Billy squirmed underneath him. "You don't understand, Jackie. There can only be one winner, and it has to be me."

Billy gained control of his stick and pressed it up sharply in to Jack's rib cage. Jack let out a gasp and his weight shifted to protect the area. That was enough for Billy to slide out from underneath and scamper backwards to get out of Jack's reach.

"Is this a fight to the death or the circus? Let's see some pain, gentlemen!" Mr. Jenkins yelled out. "Better to give some pain now rather than get some later," he said followed by raspy laughter.

Jack got up into a standing position. Billy did the same. They began circling each other. Jack's ribs still hurt but Billy's blow wasn't hard enough to cause any dangerous internal injuries. It was the same for Billy's knee. They eyed each other for any other weaknesses they could find, but also used the break to catch their breaths.

"Grab your partner dosey doe..." sang Mr. Jenkins. "What is this - a square dance? You're Moonwalkers, not dance buddies. Need some more motivation? Remember what will happen to your mother, Jack. The very same fate as your father. And Billy, if you do not beat this west coast skateboarder in five minutes time, I will kill you both and Lucas will become the clan leader. You wanted some motivation, well there it is! Now show me some fangs and claws..."

Billy let out a horrible scream and sprinted directly at Jack

with the lacrosse stick raised. Jack looked directly into is eyes. Billy was coming in for the kill.

Chapter 24

May 4, 2011

"She just said something. She moved her head a little bit and then mumbled something. I think she is coming out of it," Sarah said excitedly.

"That is great. If we can get her mobile, then we can get out of here before they come back," Chris responded, working feverishly in the corner with a group of wires coming off the table.

"I'll keep talking to her. How are things going over there?"

"Actually, things are going pretty well. I think we can unhook her from all the electricity without anything happening."

"Okay, come over and let's do it."

"I just need a little more time. It seems that the juice that flows through these wires is linked to a remote control of sorts. I think I can bypass how it's networked and get it ready to work again, but in a different way."

"Why do you want to do that?"

"I think we can leave them with a little surprise," Chris chuckled.

Mrs. Wilson started moving again. Sarah turned her attention back to her fully.

"Mrs. Wilson, it's Sarah. Can you hear me? You have to wake up."

More mumbling.

"Hey Chris, I'm going to take these wires and straps off her now. I think if I shake her a bit, it'll help."

"Alright, go for it."

Sarah began to remove everything connected to Jack's mom.

Whatever Billy's dad had planned for her, it was definitely not good. She breathed a sigh of relief when she removed the last electrode. Next she started working on the straps around her legs.

"Where am I?" a weak voice said.

Sarah looked up to the head of the table. Jack's mom was looking slowly from side to side, her eyes squinting from the light shining down on her.

"Mrs. Wilson!" Sarah cried out. "You're awake. I'll have you out of these straps in a minute."

"Straps? What straps? Where am I? Who are you?"

"It's Sarah Bartley, Mrs. Wilson. We are gonna get you out of here."

"Sarah? Where's Jack?"

Getting the strap off her legs, Sarah moved up to the one that held Mrs. Wilson down at the waist.

"Tell me what you remember last."

Jack's mother yawned. "I remember coming out into the forest to look at something with someone..." She closed her eyes.

"No, Mrs. Wilson. You have to wake up. You can't go back to sleep." Sarah shook her shoulder and started working on the strap holding her upper body down.

Jack's mom opened her eyes and looked at the person working frantically next to her.

"Oh, Sarah. What are you doing here? I don't know where I am. Why am I lying down like this?" She closed her eyes again.

"Chris, I don't think she knows what happened to her."

Chris bounded over to the table with a great big smile on his face.

"I'm done. I'm not saying I'm an electrical genius or anything, but let's put it this way: I think my future career in electronics starts tonight."

"That's all well and good, but did you hear what I said? I don't think she remembers anything about where she is or how she got here. What do we do?"

Chris pursed his lips and thought for a moment.

"If she doesn't remember anything, I'm not gonna be the one to tell her that her son is a werewolf. Let's tell her that she was abducted by someone and we found out about it and came to get her."

"That sounds a little weird."

"Really? What's the alternative - telling her the whole truth and nothing but the truth?"

"Good point. Help me wake her up."

Chris started to pat her gently on the cheek.

"Mrs. Wilson. Time to get up."

"Is that you, Jack?" she asked with a grin. "I love you."

"No, Mrs. Wilson, it's Chris. Jack's friend. Can you get up off this table? We have to leave."

"Oh, Chris. Do you know where Jack is?"

"Yes, I do. He's helping us all out right now. Can you come with us now? We want to get you home, too. Can we help you sit up?"

"I think so," she responded, trying to use her arms to push herself up.

"It's working!" Sarah cried out.

Chris waved his hand to get Sarah's attention. She stepped a little closer.

"What's up?"

"We can't just waltz out the front door."

Sarah brought her hand to her eyes and rubbed them. Then she looked seriously at Chris.

"She's going to have to leave the way we came in - out the window. We have no other options."

"Out the window," Mrs. Wilson responded as she finally got into a sitting position. "That sounds like fun."

Chapter 25

May 4, 2011

The attack was swift. Billy lashed out with his lacrosse stick and caught Jack on the right side of the face. He then spun around and brought the stick down and around low, catching Jack ankles and knocking him off balance. As Jack put his arms out to break his fall, Billy slashed downward with his stick and hit Jack in between his shoulder blades, forcing him to the ground hard and fast. Jack howled in pain. His face on the ground, he pushed himself upwards to get on his knees but Billy threw his whole weight on his back and forced him back to the ground. Throwing his own stick to the side, Billy grabbed Jack's stick as it lay underneath him and wrenched it up to this throat. Jack pushed back but could not get any leverage to stop the stick from choking him. Billy dug his knee deep into Jack back as he pulled harder and harder upward.

"Kill him!" Billy's father yelled running towards both boys.

Jack could feel it getting more difficult to get any air.

"Billy, you don't have to do this," Jack managed to say as he struggled to get free.

"Kill him now, Billy! I order you to kill him!" He father yelled standing only a few feet away.

Billy continued pulling up and applying pressure.

Jack gasped for more air and tried again. "Billy, please stop. I...was...never...the...enemy."

Billy didn't let go, but he eased up on the pressure a little bit. He looked down at the back of Jack's head, his arms below him struggling to pull the lacrosse stick away from his neck.

"If you don't kill him now, Billy, I will kill you. I'm sick of having a disappointment for a son. Show me that you are like me and KILL HIM NOW, YOU PATHETIC WEAKLING!"

Everything stopped for Billy. For a moment, it was almost like he wasn't a Moonwalker in the field fighting against Jack. He was just Billy - tired and alone, wondering how he got here, wondering who he really was. A voice in his head started giving him answers, but he didn't like the voice. The voice wasn't his; it was his father's.

Billy stopped pulling the stick against Jack's throat. He pulled it out from under him and Jack's head dropped to the ground. He got up and turned around, facing his father. His eyes were bright orange and sweat dripped down from his snout. A low growl began to emanate from his chest.

Mr. Jenkins smiled a wide, toothy grin, his fangs shining in the moonlight.

"I figured as much, Billy. I knew it was only a matter of time before you made the biggest and most foolish decision of your life. You don't know how to win. You only know how to lose. That's what you've done all your life. And, Jack...he's almost as bad. I have had it with both of you. I've been so thick-headed and short-sighted. You have both wasted my precious time and I don't have the patience or desire to shoulder either of your bullcrap any longer. Lucas!" he called over his shoulder. Lucas ran over quickly and stood next to Billy's dad. "I am going to kill Jack. You are going to kill Billy. Problem solved. No more speeches. Game time is over, boys."

Chapter 26

May 4, 2011

Jack's mom was groggy but she was moving. Sarah and Chris had put their arms around her and were able to help her off the table. They walked her into the hallway carefully and then into the middle room.

"Tell me again why we are climbing out a window?" she asked as she gained some more strength and clarity. "Can't we use the stairs in this place...where are we again?"

"We can't use the stairs because there are some bad people just outside the front door of this house, Mrs. Wilson. We have to sneak out the window," Chris explained patiently but anxiously.

"Oh yeah, and my Jack is taking care of the bad people. Right?"

"Yes, he is," Sarah chimed in. "Most definitely."

"I love him so much," Mrs. Wilson said warmly.

The three of them made it over to the window.

"Sarah, you go out first and then I'll lower her down to you the best I can. Then I'm gonna run back into that room and put that surprise into effect," Chris said. "You guys go ahead and put some space and time between you and this house. I'll catch up to you later in the forest."

"No, Chris. We get out of here together."

"We will. We will. I promise. But I want to make sure you guys are far away when the surprise comes. Don't stop, no matter what you hear happening behind you."

"What exactly is the surprise?" Sarah asked with some trepidation.

"Oh, don't you worry. It's the mother of all surprises."

"I trust you, but the mother of all surprises may be the surprise of actually getting this mother out the window and out of this house."

"Oh, there is no comparison. We can do this. Let's get her out and then you guys head back to town. Promise?"

"We promise," said Jack's mom smiling.

Chapter 27

May 4, 2011

Lucas and Mr. Jenkins began to circle around Jack and Billy. Their claws bared and fangs protruding to intimidate their prey. They taunted both boys back and forth in low, guttural growls.

"You tried to kill me last night, Billy. Now it's your turn to die..."

"I had high hopes for you, Jack, but you are weak and stupid, just like my son..."

"Your father is going to make me the clan leader. ME! That will be your last dying thought..."

"After I'm done with you, your mother is next and then your friends. And it is all your fault..."

Jack and Billy backed up against each other and formed an inner circle, moving slowly with their attackers, watching their every move. The rest of the boys stood nearby almost dumbfounded. Nothing like this had been talked about beforehand and they had no idea how to react. This wasn't playing lacrosse in the moonlight anymore. This was a battle for life and death. Their crazy world had now been turned upside down and sideways as Billy and Jack now faced off against Lucas and Billy's father. This was way beyond the surreality of being a Moonwalker. This was murder.

Jack kept his eyes on Mr. Jenkins but turned his face slightly to talk to Billy.

"Are you ready for this?"

"I was about to ask you the same question."

"Seems like we both lost our fathers, huh?"

Billy took a second to reply. "I wish you could have met your father, Jack, and I wish I had never met mine. How messed up is that?"

"Not messed up. Just our own slice of reality. We may not be friends, but at least we have something in common to build on."

Again, Billy took a moment to respond. "Sorry that this all happened, Jack. You're a good guy. I don't think I can say the same for myself, but I'm ready for whatever comes. Let's do this."

Before Jack could say anything back, Billy's dad screamed and jumped forward with his arms wide open. He swung with both arms directly at Jack's head. Jack ducked just in time to hear two pairs of clawed hands slap together just above him. He dropped immediately with his back against the floor and launched both of his legs straight up into Mr. Jenkin's abdomen. The force of the kick lifted Billy's dad off the ground and threw him backwards about ten feet. He landed with a loud thud and growled in discomfort.

Seeing Billy's dad flying through the air, Lucas made a beeline straight for Billy with his arms and claws flailing lethally in a non-stop letter X configuration. It was like a razor-sharp, slashing wave of wildness. Billy watched as Lucas came at him, but he hesitated for a moment, contemplating letting Lucas get him - some comeuppance for the night before when he tried to drown him in the elixir. Just as Lucas was about to cut into him, Jack came leaping over Billy's head and kicked down hard onto Lucas' head. He fell backwards, completely dazed and confused.

"Are you okay?" Jack asked grabbing Billy's face so he was looking directly at him.

Billy shook his head back and forth. "Yeah, yeah...I'm okay. I got lost in my own mind."

"Today's a new day. Don't worry about what happe...." In less than the blink of an eye, Jack yanked quickly and harshly on Billy's shirt, tossing him to one side as his father dove right at him. Mr. Jenkins landed on top of Lucas, both of them grunting and rushing to get away from one another.

"I guess all bets are off. You don't care who you kill, even your own son," Jack said, reaching down to give Billy a hand up on his feet.

Billy's dad got up at the same time, winded and wincing from the kick he had just received. Lucas put out his hand for help but was ignored.

"That's the beauty of being a Moonwalker, Jack. You can do what you want, when you want, and not care about anybody else." He caught sight of the boys looking on from a number of feet away. "Right boys?" he yelled. "Let's show these two traitors what a real clan can do. KILL THEM!"

The gang didn't know what to do. They looked at each other nervously.

"WHAT ARE YOU STANDING THERE FOR? GET THEM NOW!"

None of the boys moved.

"KILL THEM RIGHT NOW OR I WILL KILL EACH AND EVERY ONE OF YOU, TOO!"

Nothing.

Suddenly there was a voice that cut through all the tension.

"Look!" Lucas said with some haste in his voice, pointing towards Howl House.

Everyone turned. Smoke and flames were pouring out of the roof and the wooden slats of the house.

Mr. Jenkins' jaw dropped open at first and then he screamed, "NOOOO!" He started running frantically to the burning structure. Lucas picked himself up and ran directly after him.

"MY MOM!" Jack yelled, and he started to run, too.

Chapter 28

May 4, 2011

"Do you smell smoke?"

"Yes, I do, Mrs. Wilson. We had better keep going," Sarah said hesitantly, almost wanting to disregard her own words.

The pair picked up some speed as much as they could. Mrs. Wilson was getting stronger but could not walk on her own. Sarah held her up as best she could as they made their way through the forest. The light of the full moon was filtering through the leaves and it landed on the ground in soft, glowing clumps as if to form a path for their escape.

"Was Jack right about Mr. Weber?" his mother asked. "Is that what this is all about?"

Of all the things Sarah had been able to figure out tonight, telling Jack's mom about everything was not one of them.

"Yes and no," she said, hoping the short response would do.

"Can you expand on that thought a little bit more, Sarah?"

Mrs. Wilson was definitely feeling better. Even in a semi-groggy state, she was still quick-witted.

"Yes, there were bad things happening at Howl House but, no, it wasn't Mr. Weber. It was Billy's dad."

"Billy's dad? My brain is still fuzzy but was that who took me out here?"

"Most likely."

"This is all so crazy. What was he trying to do?

"I'm not sure exactly. Whatever it was, it wasn't good."

"And Jack was trying to stop him?"

"Yes."

"That smoke...is Jack in trouble...is he in danger? He's all alone."

A slight smile appeared on Sarah's face. "He's not alone, Mrs. Wilson. He's with Chris."

Chapter 29

May 4, 2011

Just as Jack started towards Howl House, he was knocked to the ground from something that came down and hit him hard on the back of the head. He almost blacked out from the force of it. Dizzy and in pain, he looked up to see what had hit him. It was Billy holding one of the lacrosse sticks.

"Sorry, Jackie. It's not your time to die." He turned to the boys who were no longer looking at the fire, but directly at him and Jack - totally shocked and dumbfounded.

"You guys keep Jack here. I'm going in to get his mom. Whatever you do, DON'T LET HIM IN THAT HOUSE! Do you understand me?"

Unable to speak, they shook their heads affirmatively and ran over to Jack. Billy took off after his father and Lucas. One after the other, they entered the growing inferno.

Jack got up on his feet, dazed but still aware that his mother's life was in jeopardy.

"I've got to save my Mom!" he yelled, but the boys would not let him pass.

"LET ME GO! MY MOTHER IS IN DANGER!"

He pushed against them to get by but he was physically drained and could not break through the line.

"Please let me help. My mother..."

BOOM! BOOM! BOOM!

Jack's pleas were violently interrupted by a series of huge explosions. The concussion of the blasts knocked Jack and the boys to the ground. Hot ash and fragments of wood and metal rained down upon the forest. Everyone instinctively covered their heads and curled up on the ground to avoid getting hit by falling debris.

Jack pushed himself up on his hands and knees and then slowly got to his feet. It was hard to see everything at first through the smoke, but then it all became readily apparent what had happened.

Howl House was gone.

A giant flaming hole surrounded by scattered, burning rubble was all that remained.

Jack ran as close as he could to the devastation. His throat burned from breathing in all the soot and vapors, but he screamed as loud as he could.

"MOM! MOM! CAN YOU HEAR ME?"

He tried to wade farther into the charred mess, but the heat was too intense. The other boys came up behind him and started looking for life among the ruins, too. They yelled out Billy and Lucas' names, but there was no response. They all worked together, sifting through the rubble that they could. The blast was so intense that almost nothing remained other than smoldering shingles and pieces of metal that were too thick to disintegrate. Jack looked down and saw some of the bars that had once been part of the cage that had imprisoned Sarah. Near to that he saw remnants of the straps that had been used to restrain his mom.

"NO!" Jack screamed and howled. "MOM! NO!"

He fell forward onto the ground. His body heaved up and down with the incredible sobbing that came from deep within him. His mother was gone. No mother. No father.

Some of the boys came and stood by Jack. A few began to

cry silently themselves.

"Jack!"

A voice could be heard from the other side of the debris field in the woods.

"Hey! Over here!"

Jack lifted his head slowly to see which of the boys was calling him.

Out of the haze of smoke, a figure was running towards them. Jack couldn't make out who it was at first, but then he recognized who it was.

Chris.

"Your mother's alive, Jack! She's alive!" he yelled and laughed with joy as he got closer.

Jack sprang to his feet and bounded towards his friend. "Chris! What? What are you saying?"

They reached each other and Jack grabbed his friend by the shoulders.

"Ow, dude. You're hurting me!" was all Chris could say at first. "Your claws..."

"What are you saying? How do you know my mother is alive?"

"I know she's alive because Sarah and I saved her. We got her out of the house and I went back in and, well, you know..."

"Where is she?"

"She's with Sarah and they're heading back to Barnaby Hills. She doesn't remember anything. All she knows is that she was taken and you are saving her."

Jack threw his head back and howled with delight at the Moon. He lifted and tossed Chris into the air, catching him as gently as he could.

"I love you, too," Chris managed to spit out as he composed himself from the abrupt toss, "but please don't do that again."

"I won't! I won't! You saved my Mom, Chris! You and Sarah saved my Mom!"

Jack turned to the other boys, wanting to share the good news and then he saw their faces. Reality came rushing back.

"We have to continue looking for Billy and Lucas!" he bellowed. "They could still be alive."

"I don't think so," Chris said silently, putting his hand on Jack's shoulder. "I don't think anyone could have survived that. I really didn't mean for them to die. I didn't figure that anyone would go running back into the house. I guess...I guess that I...."

"You didn't kill them, Chris," Jack anticipated. They made their own choice to go back into Howl House."

"I know, but I didn't want that to happen."

"Billy saved my life by stopping me from going into Howl House, Chris. It was almost like he knew what was going to happen. On some level, Billy is a hero, too. Don't come down on yourself. You did nothing wrong."

"And I guess Billy and Lucas were victims. Just like all of us," Chris said softly, almost to himself.

Jack took a deep breath and took a good look at all the Moonwalkers. "Listen, everybody," he said, taking charge of the moment. "We are no longer victims of this. Billy's dad is to blame for all that we have been through. He is responsible for the deaths of our teammates. He is responsible for the death of my father. I now know the truth but it doesn't make anything easier. Just the opposite.

Chris put his hand on Jack's shoulder.

"As for the future, we have to move past all of this - all the

hate and anger. ALL OF IT. We are Moonwalkers, and, who knows...that may never change. But we can't use what we are for bad purposes. We just can't. I wouldn't be able to live with myself if I did and I don't think any of you could, either. Are we together about this?"

The rest of the boys slowly shook their heads in agreement and then one of the boys spoke up.

"Are you the new master of the clan, Jack?

Jack's mind immediately took him back to the dream in which Billy "Welcome, Master. We've done what you asked of us." He shook his head as if to chase the nightmare away. "No. There is no master. There is no clan. We are individuals. Individuals with special powers. We must listen to ourselves and not go against what our conscience tells us is right and true. We are not a clan, but we have to have a group responsibility not to hurt others. I can only imagine how many questions will be asked about what has taken place tonight and everything that led up to it. Not just by the police, but also by our neighbors and friends - our families. We will come up with answers but we will never let ANYONE know who we are. If others were to find out, word would spread and there are those out there who would desire our help for evil purposes. We are Moonwalkers, but we are not evil. We must keep who we are to ourselves. Is this understood?"

Everyone agreed.

"Alright, before we talk and come up with an excuse about EVERYTHING, join me as we say goodbye to Lucas and Billy in our own way. A Moonwalker way. TO LUCAS AND BILLY!"

All of the boys, including Chris, raised their heads high to the full Moon and howled, their voices trailing off into every direction of the forest.

Epilogue

"Always reach for the moon, because if you miss, you'll land amongst the stars."

Unknown

June 22, 2011

The middle school auditorium was packed with parents and family members. It was the afternoon of the 8th grade promotion ceremony and there was a lot of excitement in the air.

Jack walked in with his mother and tried to take it all in.

"Incredible."

He turned towards his mom. "What's incredible?"

"That I have a son who is going into high school in September. It just boggles my mind."

"Because you think you look too young to be the mother of a teenager?" Jack laughed.

"No, smarty. Because my baby is growing up. It's crazy."

Jack smiled. "I know. Sometimes I can't believe it myself. I wish Dad were here today."

"He is, Jack. He's right here," she said pointing to his chest. "He's always with you."

"Thanks, Mom." He gave her a big hug. She took out a tissue and began wiping away tears from her eyes.

"I haven't even graduated yet."

"You know me. Why don't you go and find Sarah and get to your seats. The ceremony should be starting soon."

"Okay, I'll see you later. Don't get too emotional. I don't want to see a river of tears flowing down the aisle."

His mother chuckled. "I make no promises. Get going."

Jack started to make his way down to the chairs in front of the stage. He high-fived a bunch of kids as he passed them by. All of a sudden, two hands covered his eyes from behind."

"Guess who?" a very pleasant voice said.

"Hmm, Brittany? Give me a kiss quick before my girlfriend sees you."

"Ha, ha, ha...very funny," said the voice as she took her hands away and spun him around. "Don't you look spiffy today."

A wide smile broke out on Jack's face as he took a good look at Sarah.

"Me? You are absolutely stunning."

"Did you say that to Brittany, too?" she laughed.

"Never."

A voice came over the loudspeaker.

"Would students and family members please take your seats? We are about to begin."

Jack and Sarah joined the rest of the student body as they all began to sit down.

Principal Joyce walked up to the podium on the stage. Everyone grew quiet.

"Good morning. This has always been one of my favorite duties as principal of Barnaby Hills: the 8th grade promotion ceremony. As we all know, this has been a year of great successes but also tragic losses."

Sarah grabbed Jack's hand.

"We lost two members of the Barnaby Hills Middle School family and a parent, and so many others were deeply and negatively affected by what took place without most of us being aware. It is something that I still find very difficult to talk about. But I would like to for a minute, if you don't mind. After everything our community has been through, I would like to offer my condolences to those directly impacted by the horrific events, but also my apologies...to all of you. As principal, I should have been able to protect the students of our town more. I should have listened more," he said looking over to Jack. "I should have been talking with staff more and acting on any and all concerns. I should have been there for families more....I...I just wish I had done more. Would things have turned out different? I don't know, but there is a part of me that feels I have failed all of you, especially Billy and Lucas.

Principal Joyce stopped and cleared his throat. "Mr. Jenkins had an illness. A mental illness. Police reports called it "delusions of grandeur related to schizophrenia." I call it a cry for help. But if no one is listening, a cry will never get answered. I should have been listening more. I want to listen more. Throughout my life as a teacher and principal, I have always lived by the maxim that mistakes are the steps to success. So many mistakes have been made, but so much has been learned. I thought deeply about stepping down as principal but I, too, have learned a lot. I don't want this to be my last graduation at Barnaby Hills. I want to continue here at the school, if you will have me. And I promise all of you that I will do my very best to make sure that our kids are safe, our families feel supported and that I am always listening."

It didn't take the attendees long to decide. They began clapping and ultimately gave the principal a standing ovation. Jack and Sarah let out a few good-natured whoops and whistles to signal their support.

Mr. Joyce smiled and waited for everything to quiet down. "I thank you all, truly. And now, it is time to turn the microphone over to Coach Weber who will be announcing special, end of the year awards."

The audience clapped again as Mr. Weber came forward.

"Hello, Barnaby Hills!" he said. "Before I begin, I would just like to reiterate some of the sentiments that Principal Joyce offered. It is never easy to witness horrible things happen. But good things happen that sometimes balance out the bad. Now is that time. I have the pleasure of announcing the sports awards and if it is okay with you, I'd like to get right into it."

Someone in the audience yelled, "You got it, Coach!" which made everyone laugh.

"Thank you, kind sir," Mr. Weber smiled. "I usually save this award for last as to build up everyone's excitement, but I'm going to break my own protocol and make this announcement first. I just can't wait to do so. This student showed me what courage is all about. In the face of utter craziness, he took a stand and showed the rest of us what it means to be a teammate, an outstanding student in this school, and, more importantly, a good friend. It is with great pride that I give the lacrosse MVP award to this year's recipient - Chris Stiles!"

The auditorium erupted into great applause as Chris came out from behind a curtain on the side of the stage and walked towards the podium. All the students sitting down in front got up on their feet and cheered.

Mr. Weber handed the MVP trophy to Chris and then gave him a pat on the back. Chris walked to the front of the stage and held the trophy in one hand and pointed down at Jack with the other. All the students looked over at Jack. He smiled and pointed back at Chris. The students began to cheer even harder - including Mr. Weber.

Sarah gave Jack a kiss on his cheek and he began to blush and smile. Jack could only think one thing.

Oh, Jack, what have you gotten yourself into now?

The End?

Made in the USA
Middletown, DE
16 April 2023

28884789R10276